HOLODOMOR

OTHER BOOKS BY JAROSLAV (JERRY) PETRYSHYN

Fiction

The Fenian Season: A Historical Thriller

The Man with the Notable Face

Alberta North Mystery Series

A Death Most Cold

Burdens to Bury

Nonfiction

Peasants in the Promised Land: Canada and the Ukrainians, 1891–1914

"Made Up to a Standard": Thomas Alexander Russell and the Russell Motor Car Company

Butterfly Farmer (poetry)

HOLODOMOR
A CRIME NOVEL

Jaroslav (Jerry) Petryshyn

IGUANA

Copyright © 2025 Jaroslav (Jerry) Petryshyn
Published by Iguana Books
720 Bathurst Street
Toronto, ON M5S 2R4

This is a work of fiction with the characters, names, places, and incidents a
product of the author's imagination. It is set, in part, against historical
events. In marrying fictional characters with actual personages, the author
has tried to be as accurate as possible to the latter.

Publisher: Cheryl Hawley
Editor: Allister Thompson
Front cover illustration: Melissa Novak
Front cover design: Jonathan Relph

ISBN 978-1-77180-748-7 (paperback)
ISBN 978-1-77180-747-0 (epub)

This is an original print edition of *Holodomor: A Crime Novel.*

For AnneMarie and Paul:
dear friends and dedicated bookworms

FOREWORD

This is a work of fiction with the storyline(s) and concomitant characters a product of my imagination. However, the historical context in which this crime novel takes place is not; the main protagonists and antagonists bear witness to a truly inhumane and tragic period in Ukrainian history known as the "Holodomor."

Beginning in 1929, the Bolsheviks under Joseph Stalin launched a "revolution from above" designed to in one brutal swoop crush the implacable resistance of the peasantry — particularly the Ukrainian peasantry — to the communist regime. Stalin ordered the collectivization of all Ukrainian lands. At the same time, a campaign was initiated against the *kulaks*, so called rich farmers (defined loosely as those with ten to twenty acres and one or more cows) resulting in large-scale killings and the wholesale deportation of millions to Siberian labour camps. Private property was now to be abolished and the agrarian population "collectivized" into huge state farms under Soviet state control. From 1929 to 1933, the individual holdings of some 25 million farmers were transformed into approximately 250 thousand collective and state farms.

During this process of "collectivization" and "dekulakization," the death toll, at a conservative estimate, reached a staggering 6.5 million. Indeed, the census of 1937 revealed such unbelievable carnage that Stalin had the leading census takers shot!

But the collectivization/dekulakization campaign was only a preview of what was to come. In 1932–33, those households already collectivized in Ukraine and its neighbouring areas — the Don, Volga, and Kuban — were now to be executed by starvation. All grain was seized with impossible delivery quotas imposed, the livestock confiscated, and the borders sealed, leaving 40 million human beings with no sustenance. It was the first time in recorded history that a government premeditatively planned and used such a horrible weapon to kill its population. As one eyewitness wrote: "On the battlefield men die quickly, they fight back, they are sustained by fellowship and a sense of duty. Here I saw people dying in solitude by slow degrees, dying hideously, without the excuse of sacrifice for a cause. They had been trapped and left to starve, each in his home, by a political decision made in a far-off capital around conference and banquet tables..." (Victor Kravchenko, quoted in Robert Conquest, *The Harvest of Sorrow*, [Edmonton: University of Alberta Press, 1986] 245).

The genocidal famine of 1932–33 in Ukraine is one of this century's most horrendous, yet least known, mass murders. In his seminal book, the aforementioned *The Harvest of Sorrow*, Robert Conquest calls it Stalin's "terror-famine." Today, more generally, it has become known as the "Holodomor" (based on the Ukrainian word *holod*, which means hunger). The term refers to an act of genocide and the campaign of deliberate starvation conducted by Stalin and the Soviet state in 1932–33. It seemed an appropriate title for this crime novel.

In the course of my research, many secondary as well as primary sources were consulted. Besides Professor Conquest's comprehensive tome, I add Miron Dolot's autobiographical novel, *Execution by Hunger: The Hidden Holocaust* (New York: W. W. Norton, 1985) and Anne Applebaum's *Red Famine: Stalin's War on Ukraine* (New York: Penguin Random House, 2017) as most helpful.

MAJOR CHARACTERS AND ACRONYMS

Kyiv

Katya Karina Kharsova (a.k.a. **Oxana Gerkil**), secretary to Kyiv Commissar of Commerce and Industry

Oleksander Pylyp, agronomist, Kyiv Agricultural Institute

Kreil Gromeko, commissar of Commerce and Industry

Vasar Sholtz, commissar of Procurement and Labour

Emil Krypniuk, captain, Kyiv Police Criminal Investigation Department

Nickolay Nickolayevich Lubick, sergeant, Kyiv Police Criminal Investigation Department

Boris Pavlick, commissar, Kyiv Office of Special Investigations, Unified State Political Administration (**OGPU**)

Anton Rubiniuk, retired city resident

Bila Sich

Lev Devchenko, landowner, farmer, resident

Vlas Chorney, landowner, farmer, resident

Tomash Chozh, landowner, farmer, resident

Makar Belynski, chairman, Bila Sich Soviet Council

Ivan Prasha, secretary and administrative assistant to **Belynski**

Dimitri Tolstoy, chairman, Bila Sich Soviet Council

Anton Fedryk, commissar, Oblast Party Regional Council

Glossary

dedushka – grandfather, elderly man

kolkhosp – collective farm court

kolkhoz – collective farm

kulak/kurkul – derogatory terms for rich peasant farmers who exploit the poor ones

muziks – literally translated as men

sekrehita – secretary and mistress

shapka – cap, hat

vozhd – exalted one, all power, akin to the almighty

zhlob – literally translated as a stupid and ill-mannered man

CHAPTER ONE

Bila Sich
November 1929

"I'd hoped that it was all stupid rumours," Lev Devchenko said, shaking his head and stroking his grizzled beard. "No such luck!"

"Inevitable, I suppose," replied Vlas Chorney, Lev's neighbour and friend. They worked adjoining fields, with Lev the elder spokesman in the village as far as Vlas, ten years younger, was concerned. "I heard those rumours as well... Looks like they're true. Little we can do..." He trailed off. "If they want to collectivize us..."

"They tried before," said Lev, shifting in his seat to better observe the procession of party commissars and their entourage entering the village, two large sleighs filled with bundled men, some in white sheepskin and others in cavalry coats with dark patches on their shoulders (CHEKISTS, no doubt). Their brown, pointy-top *budyonovka* caps were pulled down; the breeze was strong with the large red flag stiff at the back of the first sleigh, pulled by two snorting black horses. There was no mistake. Lev, Vlas, and several other villagers in Dnipro Tavern knew these men. "Bolshevik devils," someone muttered loudly.

"I'd raise a glass to that," remarked Vlas, taking in hand his tankard of dark ale, lifting it to his lips.

"Well, they did try before," Lev repeated, "and failed." He remembered the world conflict not that long ago, followed by the brutal civil war that raged through their land. It was Lenin who attempted to "dekulakize" the peasantry and "collectivize" their farms, seizing them for the socialist state during the so-called war communism period. The result was a fierce resistance that had party officials, CHEKA, and Red Army commanders shitting their pants. Lenin had barely survived. "Here's to Nestor Makhno, his warriors, and the Kronstadt sailors who prevented Lenin from destroying the countryside." Lev raised his tankard, wondering if there was anyone who could stop this new threat now.

There were murmurs of agreement. The backlash in the rural areas had been vehement, wild, savage, almost bringing the Bolsheviks to their knees. Farmers already had their agricultural cooperatives and self-help associations for obtaining credit and buying seed. They didn't accept the state grabbing their land under the guise of some alien, altruistic ideology that would destroy their birthright. And they most certainly had no use for the food requisition detachments sent into the villages during the civil war to steal their grain, leaving millions to starve. In the end, with his regime in peril, the last thing Lenin could afford was an all-out peasant war. Prudently, he had backed off by the end of '21. And yet, eight years later, they were back. Could Stalin, the new *vozhd* and Lenin's successor, be made to back off as well?

"Yes," Lev announced to no one in particular, "they're here again … commissars and comrade pencil-pushers. They will set up local village committees, make us attend special meetings, tell us what to do, and how we should do it. Pretty soon, you won't be able to go to the outhouse without a commissar's signature on a piece of paper. They've come to organize, mobilize. By the looks of it, we warrant a local commissar, maybe two, a CHEKIST escort, and some scribes with Komsomol bands to follow, judging from who arrived today."

"Organize for what, exactly?" a rough voice queried from the back of the smokey, dimly lit tavern.

"Our glorious joining of their collective farms," Lev replied sarcastically.

***

As a senior administrative commissar of one of the largest cities in the region, Makar Belynski thought he had power and stature. However, his career had taken an unexpected and nasty turn when he was relieved of his position and reappointed to Bila Sich, a strung-out, inconsequential village that he had trouble finding on the oblast map. He had one explicit order: *persuade* the local population to join the *kolkhoz* and weed out the *kulaks*, which he interpreted as those who resisted joining the state collective farm.

Belynski didn't know precisely whom he had offended (although he had a couple of strong suspicions), but obviously his upward party trajectory was interrupted — temporarily, he hoped — by this assignment. He had ruffled someone's mighty feathers, got noticed, and a clear message was sent: *You're dispensable.*

Achievement breeds resentment, invites bad bother and collateral fallout, he surmised bitterly. He was fortunate that it had only resulted in a demotion. No matter, he'd accomplish his task and move back to … civilization. Still, the circumstances he found himself in allowed for little leeway. Nonfulfillment of quotas would have dire consequences for his stalled career, if not his life.

In truth, Belynski couldn't have imagined himself in such a backward village. It was in the middle of nothing, with two main roads that went to nowhere. *Well, not quite,* he thought; to the west, the road led to the Korsun Railway Station and on to Kanev, a small provincial town. But that was about it. The eastern extension ran through fields and a forest until it reached another village that was even smaller than Bila Sich. The north-south route too meandered into the hinterland, bush, and swamps, eventually joining other roads connecting numerous villages and agricultural fields.

Bila Sich sat where these two roads crossed. Little lanes sprouted on either side with low, diminutive, whitewashed houses, most with plaited willow fences in front, forming a crooked but vaguely linear pattern. *Uninteresting cottages,* thought Belynski as his party glided by toward their temporary location, a large two-storey structure on the northern edge of the village. Identified as the local barracks, it would have to do until he could find and expropriate more suitable accommodations for himself and his officials.

***

The next day, Comrade Makar Belynski took a brisk, officious walk down the length of Bila Sich. His strides were purposeful, energetic; he needed to project resolve. Of course, the belt and holster with a Nagant revolver around his waist ensured that his authority would not wear too thin. Villagers were naturally suspicious; he was sure that many eyes were upon him, sizing him up. After all, he was their newly appointed chairman of the Bila Sich Soviet Council, and he would not disappoint them.

Ivan Prasha, his judiciously efficient secretary, was at his side, making notes in a little black book whenever they paused. Belynski's thoughts once again returned to the question of why he had found himself in this predicament in this bleak settlement. It may have had less to do with party politics and ambitions and be more the result of his other pursuits, he realized. He was irresistible to a number of ladies, a particular one being the wife of a high-ranking commissar. She may have blabbed or had been forced to blab. Or, perhaps, unintended eyes had seen or ears had overheard them. It was impossible to know and unwise to investigate further.

That may well have been it, he thought; his curse, in a way. To be sure, he was approaching forty and had the beginnings of a soft middle and a slight wattle under his chin, not to mention the hair suddenly sitting higher on his forehead. Nevertheless, he made an impression on women in various social circles whose husbands regressed toward middle age much quicker than he ... or the bottle, which, alas, was becoming his mistress as well. *Enough!* He broke away from his wandering thoughts. It was cold, the air starching his shallow cheeks, and his slightly bent, vaguely sinister, nose was starting to drip. Time to identify suitable personal accommodations as well as a party/administration headquarters and a place large enough for villagers to gather. Prasha had a list of potential kulaks and anti-party revolutionaries/hooligans who might be dispossessed.

"Let's have a look at where the mayor, the merchant of the co-op stores, and the head schoolmaster live. After that we'll visit the church," Belynski instructed Prasha, who nodded and seemed to take copious notes.

***

A week later, the village council head (the mayor), the co-op store merchant, and the schoolmaster were summarily arrested and along with their families were tightly packed in sleighs and whisked away. Without ceremony or trial, they were declared "enemies of the people." Their homes and usable chattels were confiscated, with the merchant's two-storey dwelling becoming Belynski's residence. Although the mayor's abode was more modest and smaller in size, it was designated the party's administrative headquarters. The schoolmaster's home remained unassigned.

"Comrade Fedryk, Commissar of the Oblast Party Regional Council, is coming in a few days, and we'll need to accommodate him for as long as he stays. Also, we need to secure a large gathering area," Belynski informed Prasha as they sat in his office at the newly installed party headquarters. "We must keep Comrade Fedryk happy."

"There aren't many places available to fit hordes of *muziks*," noted Prasha, peering intently at Belynski through his thin-rimmed spectacles. *The fellow takes his work very seriously*, thought Belynski. He had come attached with the demotion, although Belynski didn't exactly know his origin.

"The church should be able to accommodate, don't you think, Comrade Prasha?" In all of the activity, they hadn't gotten around to inspecting the church property or dealing with the local priest. It was now time.

CHAPTER TWO

December 1929

Truth be told, Makar Belynski knew of Anton Fedryk; in fact, they had briefly met at a district party committee meeting some months ago and had taken an instant dislike to each other. Part of it, Belynski was sure, involved the physical contrast between them. Belynski filled his suit well and attracted attention; Fedryk did not and tended to repel. A short man, five foot four inches at most, Belynski judged, Fedryk had a narrow face, as if squeezed too tight at childbirth, dominated by impenetrable black orbs for eyes and a thin-lipped mouth that, when opened, emitted reedy, nasal sounds. Fedryk's voice was not only an octave too high but also immediately grating. The tacked-on goatee made him look like a puppet on stage rather than a leading comrade.

Jealousy, Belynski figured. *How could he not but envy those who are more naturally endowed than himself? Aside from being diminutive and deeply resenting it, he probably has other unsavoury and/or debilitating traits, health problems perhaps, maybe physical infirmities... Who knew? But one thing's for certain,* Belynski reminded himself, *Fedryk has a chip on his shoulder and therefore is dangerous!*

Belynski's apprehension and fear were heightened by other, less abstract, considerations. Fedryk was higher on the ranking scale, reason enough to be wary; but above that, it was rumoured that he had a close connection to Pavel Postyshev, a member of Stalin's inner circle in charge of propaganda and organization. Postyshev was also in charge of "persuading" peasants onto the collective farms in Ukraine and other parts of the Soviet Union. Belynski would have to be deferential and on his best diplomatic behaviour when the *dwarf* arrived.

As it happened, Fedryk and his party of three — two bodyguards and a personal secretary/valet — came to the Bila Sich local party headquarters two days early, before Belynski could properly attend to all of the oblast commissar's requirements. Much to his chagrin, Fedryk and his entourage stayed in Belynski's newly acquired home, reducing him to a manservant.

Then there was the issue of finding a large space in "order to instruct" the villagers on the necessary procedures for joining the kolkhoz. "It's an urgent matter," Fedryk informed Belynski in a squeaky but strangely flat voice.

Belynski indicated that the most suitable place was the church across from the village square, but that matter hadn't been dealt with yet, for which he profusely apologized. "I'll take care of it right away."

"And I'll come along with you," said Fedryk, nodding to Slivka, a solemn, silent wisp of a man hovering in the shadows. Belynski wasn't sure if Slivka was a first or last name or what his job was exactly — secretary, valet or … other? In any case, Prasha would have some time to himself.

***

Father Parayma wasn't sure what to do. The wiry and wizened priest had endured similar times a decade or so ago, and now, it appeared, he must do so again. Belynski and this newcomer named Fedryk — short, gaunt with coal-black feral eyes — Belynski's superior, he presumed, stood before him. Behind them were two mute militiamen and an unidentified third person. *Well, they certainly come prepared,* he thought.

"Mr. Belynski—" the priest began.

"It's Comrade Belynski and Comrade Fedryk, commissar of the Oblast Party Regional Council," Belynski interrupted sternly. They had marched into Parayma's modest lodgings behind the church while the two militiamen and Slivka remained at the door. It was

Saturday evening, and he was getting ready for bed when he heard the loud banging on the door. *Inevitable*, he supposed, and not the first time. It was in '20 or '21, he couldn't remember which, when these "comrades" came, dragged him from his church, beat him, and sent him off to prison. Now, they were back with the same message and tactics, no doubt. No matter, he would do what he did the last time: defiantly stand his ground and trust in God.

Belynski glanced about the room at the icons that hung on the whitewashed walls, the bench seat, and the small wooden table in the centre. The oven hearth radiated heat, quite cozy, really. He focused on the shrivelling priest with the unevenly buttoned nightshirt. He had taken off his collar. "I hear you are hindering our work," he stated simply.

From whom? the priest wondered but kept his own counsel.

"You are not preaching the good news to your flock," Belynski continued. "On the contrary, your jibber is seditious in nature — treasonous, in fact!"

Ah... Parayma realized that there was an informant, possibly a few, in his congregation, who reported to these new, invading authorities his sermons — or at least their essence.

"Collectivization is good for the farmers here; it should be joyously embraced and shouted out from the pulpit. Instead, you denounce it; you mock it." Fedryk took over the accusatory conversation, staring at the priest, eyebrows arched.

Fedryk finally found someone he can look directly in the eyes, Belynski couldn't help silently musing. "I do what I believe God and my conscience dictate, and I pray it is the right thing," he replied, unfazed.

"You are a foolish, deluded old man," sneered Fedryk, voice rising, his yellowed teeth bared, accentuating the dark hollows deep within his eyes. "Tomorrow you will give a sermon imploring your parishioners to join the county kolkhoz without delay and maybe, just maybe, you can continue with your delusions here."

"You think God's work is delusional and that you can come here with impunity and—"

"Save your holy outrage for someone else," Fedryk cut in, thrusting himself forward into the priest's face. "All I need to know tonight is that tomorrow you will tell the villagers it is their duty as Soviet citizens to join the kolkhoz."

"I cannot do this," Parayma said, shaking his head.

"Well, that's unfortunate," Fedryk said, smiling.

Meanwhile, Belynski stepped away quietly and seemed to study a hanging icon. The man truly in charge was holding court. *So be it...*

"But, as you wish," Fedryk continued. "I have a much better use for your church." He turned to the militiamen. "Take him away."

***

Next morning, an unfamiliar crowd gathered in front of the church; the regular parishioners were held off on the perimeter by a line of militiamen. They were allowed to watch but not get too close. Suddenly, as if on cue, a group of mostly young men and a number of women, dressed in more fashionable winter attire than found in the village, surged forward. They started to shout in unison: "Down with the church; long live the collective farms; long live the Communist Party."

It took but a few moments for the locals to realize that these were intruders, activists, party members who were there on a mission. The heavy wooden door of the church suddenly swung open, and they rushed in. Father Parayma was nowhere to be seen. That something had happened to him was apparent. No doubt, he had been arrested and, many feared, would simply disappear like many other notable villagers of late.

The rushing rabble knew what their objective was: strip the church of its religious artefacts, not necessarily destroying the contents, although from the clanging and breaking of fragile relics, not too fine a point was put on it. Most of the icons, paintings, and statues were hauled away onto waiting wagons. A clear case of looting to the dismayed villagers. Stones were thrown and windows broken, possibly overexuberance that would result in severe reprimands for destruction of socialist property.

Much to the mounting horror of the restrained flock, while the hooligans were carrying out their trophies, six men lumbered forward holding a long ladder, two at the front, two in the middle, and two at the rear. They raised and set it against the wall with the end firmly planted in the hardened snow. Two carriers acted as anchors, one on either side, while one of the men in a floppy fur *shapka* and heavy coat with a loop of rope over his shoulders made his way up. The stunned members of the community realized that this was an orchestrated attack on their church.

The man was agile, despite the bulkiness of his clothing; he quickly made his way up the roof's steep and slippery slope — no easy feat — reaching the structure's cupola with the orthodox cross atop. He tied the rope firmly around the base of the cross and made his way back down, one end of the rope in hand. The cross swung back and forth as men at the bottom pulled ferociously until with a sharp crack it tumbled over and slid down the snowy roof. Over the edge it went, hitting the snow-crusted earth with a dull poof.

People gasped in revulsion at the sacrilegious act. No doubt, the cupola and bell were on the agenda as well but were spared for the moment. Bells were valuable and once brought down would be broken into more manageable chunks and melted for state use. There was no resistance. A few shouts and wailed protestations, but the militiamen, mostly from the OGPU, were armed with rifles and were more than a match for the clubs, scythes and pitchforks, the only readily available potential weapons to the villagers. They stood stupefied; old women prayed while the men, sullen and angry, stared helplessly, not knowing what to do.

Two days later, the church was proclaimed Bila Sich's community hall, where compulsory public meetings would be held on a regular basis. Important party officials would inform the villagers about saboteurs, the dreaded *kurkuls* (if the speaker was Ukrainian) or *kulaks* (if Russian was used) in their midst that they were obliged to expose; of dangerous collaborators; of grain delivery quotas; and of the need to *voluntarily* join the glorious collective farms. No mention was made of the raid on the church and what had happened to the icons, altar, and other heavenly chattel. The interior had been hollowed out, and a large red flag was draped on the front wall with a portrait of Stalin as the new high priest. That a smaller picture of Lenin hung on the other side of the flag seemed an afterthought.

No one ever discovered what had happened to Father Parayma. Surprisingly, though, a replacement arrived a couple of weeks after the assault on the church. He presented himself as Comrade Gorpski, a young man with sallow cheeks, narrow eyes, and straw-blond hair. "I am the new deacon," he announced at one of these community meetings. There would be no religious services per se, since religion was a bourgeois concept to distract the people, but he was available for social advice/discussion and would be happy to hear confessions. Nobody came to confess, and the confessional booth, curiously having survived the looting, remained dark and lonely. Effectively, the village was now godless. Instead, there was a new deity to satisfy: the Communist Party and State. Spring would come soon enough, and there were fields to sow and required grain quotas to fill. Propaganda brigades appeared in the new year, extolling the virtues of joining the collectives.

The village remained silent and sullen, even as they attended these compulsory meetings. There was no choice, really, not with the OGPU militiamen setting up shop in and around the church. The exclamation point came when a heavy machine gun mounted on a wagon pulled by a Fordson tractor arrived. It was carefully positioned on the church premises, pointing out into the village square.

***

In reality, the church could not hold all the people compelled to attend; thus, a loudspeaker was installed above the front door so that speeches could be broadcast to the overflow crowd in the yard. Lev and Vlas, along with their neighbour, Tomash Chozh, stood together a few metres from the front steps. It was a cold but bright day with the midmorning sun shining and barely a breeze, which would have made standing attentively in the snow for a prolonged period increasingly unpleasant. Lev, a big man with a thick torso and tree stumps for arms, did not seem to notice. The only sign of the brisk weather was his cherubic face reddening as if he had been drinking. On the other hand, Vlas, a much smaller man with a thin frame, exhibited more frenetic movements, shifting his feet and thumping his arms to his sides, all the while expelling his breath in rapid, agitated puffs. Chozh, like Lev, was large but taller, the weight more evenly distributed. His olive complexion hinted at more than a touch of Tatar heritage. He appeared oblivious to the cold. He simply stood, a head above the others, his dark, penetrating eyes staring at the open church door. Chozh was known for his occasional streak of uncommon volatility if circumstances warranted it. To Lev, it seemed that he was getting close, on the verge, barely restraining himself.

There were a number of speakers, some of whom they saw marching about the village like they were personages of importance, including Belynski, who now formally introduced Anton Fedryk, the Oblast Party Regional Council Commissar.

"I hope he isn't too long-winded. My feet are starting to get cold," complained Vlas. Along with the thirty or so other souls in the yard, he would have quietly slipped away long ago if not for the militiamen with menacing rifles stationed on the perimeter of the property and the village square across the road.

Alas, it was a long speech about the village suffering at the hands of the rich kurkul. The message was clear: the kurkuls had exploited the good people of Bila Sich, and they should be gotten rid of. Meanwhile, they all needed to join the kolkhoz as soon as possible!

"I don't rightly know who these kurkuls among us are who have done such nasty things to us," Chozh muttered loudly before lighting up a stubby cigarette and expelling a rush of coiling smoke. "And why should we join their collective? I heard all of this before, how life would be wonderful if we joined up. What a bunch of pig shit!"

"Not too loud, Tomash," whispered Vlas. "I heard there are informers about." He looked around nervously at the bundled men and women, restless, uneasy, and sullen. Instinctively, they all knew that the men inside the church did not bode well for the community;

they could not be trusted. They wished these men would just go away and let them be.

The speeches finally ended with Belynski rising once more and pronouncing that he hoped the villagers appreciated Commissar Fedryk's words and would take them to heart and that there inevitably would be dire consequences if they didn't.

These required gatherings and haranguing speeches continued on a weekly basis, as it turned out, along with the distribution of pamphlets and youth brigades banging on household doors and exhorting the value of joining the local kolkhoz in the process of being established. To most, they were little more than misguided nuisance mongers. Then, one day, Vlas saw what looked like dragoons marching down the main road, complete with a tractor pulling a wagon full of what? *Probably munitions under the tarp.* They passed the head schoolteacher's home, now occupied by a party member, and continued on by the doctor's office and militia barracks, only to stop at the main square across from the church.

"Hell's teeth!" Vlas exclaimed, hurrying across the snow-packed road to a small lane that led him to Lev and Nina's home. He found Lev around the side of the little house in the animal shed feeding gruel to a handful of pigs. He informed Lev of the procession he had witnessed. "What's this all about?" he asked as they watched the wagon roll down the road, accompanied by about a dozen or so troops.

"To intimidate us, I suspect," replied Lev. "To tell us they aren't joking. They mean business. Comrades Fedryk and Belynski perhaps believe they haven't made their point sufficiently about voluntarily joining the kolkhoz. This may be a new form of persuasion. For sure, they are not here to shoot rabbits!"

"So, what are they going to do? Shoot us?" asked Vlas.

"Ah, now that's the question, isn't it?" said Lev.

"We should do something. Our village is being invaded!" exclaimed Vlas with a sharp intake of air, his voice crackly.

Lev scratched his beard. "We are not talking about benevolent or even civilized people here, so we can't present a petition and pleasantly tell them to get the fuck out, can we? We could try contacting former members of the village council, but the good ones have disappeared, and the ones left have joined Belynski and the Bolsheviks. It would probably be unproductive and possibly fatal to contact them."

"I wish Father Parayma was around; he always knew what to do," said Vlas.

"Under normal circumstances. But these are not normal times and, of course, given what happened recently... Well, we no longer have a church or our man of God."

"I wonder what happened to him."

"Nothing good, that's for sure," Lev replied grimly. "Not with the likes of Makar Belynski and Anton Fedryk around... By the way, speaking of doing something, I've written to Oleksander, my brother-in-law, in Kyiv, informing him of the situation here. He should be aware, since a portion of the land I farm is legally his, and he needs to know of this collectivization danger we are about to face."

"Can he do anything?"

Lev shrugged. "He is a learned man but not a politically powerful one, as far as I know. Still, he may have some suggestions, possibly a course of action, although I'm out of clues as to what." He shrugged and added, "If we let them, these Bolshevik bureaucrats will swallow up the whole countryside, and we'll truly become their serfs."

CHAPTER THREE

Kyiv
January 1930

Katya Karina Kharsova sighed. Kreil Gromeko was a horrible man, and she was trapped. She needed a way to leave, get out, free herself from this relationship. But times were hard, and where was she to go and what was she to do?

Going back to her village was not an option. There was nothing there; that was why she left in the first place. By the grace of God, who gave her not only beauty but also brains, she found herself in Kyiv employed by the biggest employer in the country: the Communist Party, or rather, one of the many commissariats of the socialist government that had sprouted throughout the land. It seemed that commissars were appointed and commissariats established at random to deal with everything from housing and garbage collection to city finances. She was satisfied to do clerical work with a small salary that enabled a tiny apartment and total unanimity. However, she got noticed. Kreil Gromeko, city commissar of Commerce and Industry, one of the loftier departments, took a liking to his *sekrehita*, recently arrived from one of those countless towns/villages a couple hundred kilometres as the Dnipro River flows.

It wasn't a complicated relationship. From the moment he laid eyes on her, he identified what he liked: her thick black hair, the obsidian eyes, high cheekbones and full lips, and he told her so. That she was a good notetaker and efficient was admittedly a plus, but as he bluntly told her, "...not the top criteria, I have two other secretaries to do those things…" Katya's main role was cast the second day when she entered the office. "Come talk to me at the end of the day," he ordered. She quickly graduated through a rather direct process (which included not-so-subtle hints, veiled threats, and inducements) to becoming his mistress.

The fringe benefits were enticing. She moved to an upgraded apartment near the Bessarabska Square in the heart of Kyiv and received a generous increase in pay. Moreover, there was a clothing allowance because Gromeko wished her to dress fashionably. She acquired a wardrobe that included a stylish fox-fur hat, a flowing evening gown, and a nicely cut coat and fancy footwear. He was particularly partial to a tightly fitting bodice and full skirt that to him "possessed elements of class haute couture." As it turned out, she had little opportunity to wear her fancy apparel, since they rarely went out.

It didn't take long for the fringe benefits to diminish. Gromeko was prone to drink — nothing unusual there — except in his case it let out the darker, more sadistic nature of his personality. Although Gromeko never mentioned a wife, Katya knew that she existed from a source who herself inhabited the same apartment before she was "demoted." *What does Gromekovna think of all this — if she even knows?* wondered Katya as she climbed the four floors to her apartment. Slightly out of breath, she pulled out the key from her handbag. Gromeko said he'd meet her later, after he took care of some business. He'd visit on average about twice a week when the urge hit him, letting himself in whenever he felt like it. She was supposed to be ready, *on duty*, he joked, sometimes in the afternoon. Usually, he'd slip her a note.

Today, he hadn't, and she came home early tired and hoping just to sleep. He hadn't shown at his commissariat office, so he must have been off to some meeting elsewhere, she figured. *Good, hopefully he'll stay away the whole night.* However, as she was about to insert her key into the door lock, she heard voices inside — angry voices that rose to a crescendo through the thin walls. Katya couldn't quite make out all the words, but she recognized her boss's tenor tones and the deeper, raspy voice of Vasar Sholtz, the commissar in charge of Procurement and Labour. "We had a deal," he shouted. "You screwed me."

The calm, arrogant voice of Gromeko elevated into a half laugh, half snort: "So, report me, Comrade…"

Katya hesitated; it was best not to enter. She did not wish to advertise that she was Gromeko's mistress, although he was hardly discreet; moreover, this was obviously a tense, in all probability clandestine meeting, with Gromeko anticipating that the apartment would be unoccupied. He would not appreciate her showing up. She knew that Gromeko was far from aboveboard with the *people's money*. Corruption was rampant in most of the commissariats, and Gromeko practised it with aplomb. In her time, she had witnessed the fudging of financial figures and the under-the-table payoffs. Of course, in the new socialist state, it was best to know nothing, hear nothing, see nothing, and above all, attract no attention. As she considered her next options, Katya heard scraping of furniture and some strained grunts, followed by the report of a shot fired, which made her jump back from the door, almost dropping her key.

This was not good. She had to get out of there. As she turned away, a door swung open from across the hall, and an elderly man stuck his head out, eyes wide and alert. He gave her a quizzical look and promptly closed the door, with Katya hearing the rattle of a chain hastily sliding into place. She didn't know who shot whom, or if indeed it was a gunshot she had heard, but it would not bode well for her to remain. She needed to be elsewhere. With any luck, no one would have missed her at the commissariat, and the old man would instinctively keep his mouth shut. Seeing no one, hearing nothing was by now a national pastime. Her mind raced as she fled down the four flights of stairs and out onto the street.

***

Vasar Sholtz was not a forgiving man, and he most certainly could not tolerate being cheated out of receiving his fair share of the proceeds liberated from the enemies of the state! Still, he had not intended to shoot his "mentor" comrade and senior party official now lying on the floor in a pool of blood with a hole in his chest. Judging from the vacant stare of the eyes, Gromeko was, indeed, quite dead.

After the initial shock and inertia with the smoking Nagant limp in his hand, Sholtz recovered, carefully stepped over the body, and peered out the window. No doubt the shot was heard in the building and possibly outside. *Will anyone come? Probably not,* he concluded. He was safe then; no one had seen him in the building or enter the apartment, as far as he could tell, so he could quietly exit, return to his commissariat office, and continue with business as usual. Comrade Commissar Gromeko was shot by an enemy of the state in his own apartment. Who could say otherwise?

Just as Sholtz was about to turn away from the window, he saw a woman running from the building across the street toward a tram stop. She looked up directly at the window, their eyes locking as he stepped back away into the shadows. "Fuck!" he spat. He recognized her: Katya Kharsova, Gromeko's personal secretary.

Panic rising, he was about to give chase, track her down, make sure she saw nothing — least of all him. However, he remained rooted, forcing himself to think. In all probability, he wouldn't be able to catch up to her at that moment; she'd be dealt with later. At this point, he needed to understand. *What was she doing here?* A quick look into the closet, the dresser drawers, and toilet revealed woman's clothing, boots, hats, odd bits of cosmetics, jewellery, and other feminine apparel. *Of course, Gromeko chose to meet at his mistress's apartment, which, no doubt, he maintains. Well,* he thought, *how fortuitous for me.* It wasn't a hooligan or an enemy of the state bent on some sort of revenge but a lover's quarrel that did Gromeko in. Proof? All of Kharsova's chattels were in the apartment. She was a kept woman who rebelled! He would make sure that suspicion and blame fell on her. *Of course,* the inner voice spoke again, *it would be best to make sure she doesn't get to talk at all.*

Cold logic prevailed as Sholtz thought about the unfolding situation he found himself in. In all likelihood, Kharsova would attempt to disappear. Certainly, she couldn't come back to her apartment to pack; so, the departure would be hasty, perhaps a short stop by the commissariat to pick up any personal belongs she had and run ... where? Who were her friends? Did she have any? Sholtz really didn't know. But there was really only one obvious route out of Kyiv: the train. If he remembered correctly, she had mentioned in passing that she had come originally from a village southeast of Kyiv. The name escaped him for the moment, but she'd probably want to be aboard a southbound train sooner rather than later. His best bet was to be on that train as well. At the very least he needed to talk to her; perhaps she can be threatened/bought off, if only for a while until he sorted out how to solve the problem permanently. He decided to loiter around the Pasazhyrskyi Railway Station. Although it was still under construction and quite chaotic, chances were reasonable that he could spot her on the only platform available for southbound trains. It was worth a try for a day or two. Getting on that train without her seeing him would be even better. He'd attempt to negotiate, reach an understanding, but a quick final fate for her would be a much more preferable solution to arresting or detaining her and having her spread wild accusations about a high-level city commissar. There was time, Sholtz decided, since it was doubtful that Commissar Gromeko's corpse would be discovered soon.

CHAPTER FOUR

Kyiv

Oleksander Pylyp was hesitant to leave Kyiv, where he was happy enough in his position as an agronomist researcher at the Kyiv Agricultural Institute. He had just begun experiments on a proposed new theory by fellow agronomist, Trofim Lysenko, who rejected natural selection and, indeed, Mendelian genetics, for his own theories, a combination of prolonged cold dormancy and grafting to greatly stimulate seeds and increase crop yields. Oleksander was skeptical but excited to see if Lysenko's hypothesis was correct and if winter wheat could be converted into spring wheat. Certainly, the Communist Party was lavishing praise on Lysenko, with *Pravda* going so far as to predict that soon barren, inhospitable fields would yield grass for cattle or rich crops without the use of fertilizers!

Yet the troubling note from his brother-in-law, Lev, regarding recent developments in Bila Sich could not be ignored, especially since he could be directly affected. Oleksander was a landowner who for a nominal fee gave access and allowed Lev to farm it. A win-win arrangement as far as Oleksander was concerned, given that he was more interested in seed pollination and nutrients in the soil than in actually growing crops. And since his immediate family was dispersed (except for his sister, Nina, who had married Lev), his two brothers emigrating to Canada, he ended up ipso facto landowner and proprietor.

According to Lev, everyone's property was under threat in the village and beyond, including his. Bolsheviks had arrived with OGPU muscle, and local officials had disappeared, their homes confiscated for the new arrivals; even old Father Parayma, whom Oleksander had known as a kid growing up in the village, had been taken away. Meanwhile, the villagers were being harangued almost on a daily basis to "voluntarily" join the kolkhoz. *I hope you can visit soon,* Lev's letter admonished. *They want to take away our land, and I don't know what we can do about it. I write so that you should know and as a learned man, you may have some suggestions on how to prevent this from happening. We probably don't have much time before the seizures begin — and involuntarily, I fear.*

Lev's letter confirmed what Oleksander had read in the *Ukrainska Pravda* and other government newspapers. Since May of '29, the Council of People's Commissars, mouthpiece for the politburo, had been calling for a war on the kulaks, those wealthy peasants/landowners who were exploiting the peasants. The Communist Party had begun to "purge" those "opportunists" who wished to peacefully coexist with the kulaks. By the end of the year there were carefully staged "spontaneous" demonstrations for collectivization, and just a few days ago he had read in *Izvestiya* that Stalin himself announced the need to "liquidate" the kulaks as a class.

Oleksander's deepening unease over Lev's letter took on a new height of apprehension while waiting for the train that would take him on the roughly five-hour journey from Kyiv to Korsun and on to Bila Sich. His attention was diverted by what he could only presume were two state officials of some rank sitting on a wooden bench seat across from him, quite oblivious to his presence. They had been drinking, that was obvious, probably in a nearby bar, business as usual, even during the ongoing construction of the railway station. Nevertheless, their conversation immediately piqued his interest.

"We need to define what a kulak is before we can eradicate them, right?" announced the stouter of the two as he shifted in his seat toward his smaller colleague/comrade. Oleksander wasn't sure what they were. "We have some discretion but can't be too indiscriminate about this, right?" There was a momentary pause, during which Oleksander took out and again opened the newspaper he had tucked in his coat. He pretended to read. "The term *kulak*," the larger man continued in a distasteful voice, "where did it come from? An odd name for a group of miscreants, if our directives are true."

"Oh, it's real, Henrik, and comes from the highest sources… But to your question, it was none other than Lenin. He came up with the name for prerevolutionary exploiters of poor farmers."

"I would have thought that they would have been largely extinct with the fall of the tsar, the prolonged war, and the Bolshevik takeover. Isn't everyone poor in the countryside?" Henrik scratched his chin and gave a lopsided smile. An attempt at a joke? Oleksander couldn't be sure.

"Apparently not," the other said with little mirth. He lowered his voice, and Oleksander strained to hear. "At least not according to Stalin and the politburo. A directive is a directive, and the directive is kulaks exist in great numbers, and they are a *class enemy*." The latter was emphasized as if to leave no doubt. "That is why we are being sent to this decrepit village to establish a Committee of Unwealthy Peasants… But you're right, Pytro, the question remains: who is a kulak, or as they're called here, a kurkul? This needs an answer, since we cannot establish a committee of poor peasants to denounce kulaks if we don't know the difference between a rich peasant and a poor peasant. After all, we don't want to put kulaks on the Unwealthy Peasant Committee, do we? It'd be like putting a fox in charge of the hen house." They both laughed.

Oleksander sat stoically and let Henrik and Pytro continue their discussion, although under normal circumstances he would have interrupted just to question their assumptions, if not their judgement. However, these were increasingly unusual times.

"To be honest, I haven't seen a wealthy peasant for quite some time, not around here," Pytro pointed out.

"And unless I've been drinking too much rowanberry vodka, that's exactly the crux of the problem," replied Henrik. "Without a definition, everyone in the countryside is either a kulak or a poor exploited agricultural worker. To do our job, we must know who is who."

Pytro nodded his head in understanding of the task before them. Oleksander wondered where they were going, exactly. Hopefully not to Bila Sich. "So, there is no official definition of who is a kulak and what constitutes kulakism is what you're saying," Pytro clarified.

"*Da*, Pytro, *da*. There is no precise classification or definition given. I think it's up to us — at least to some degree."

"Okay, then, is a kulak a capitalist? You know … does he own the means of production?"

"Well, no, not in the Marxist sense. Out here in the countryside, there are no industrialists like that," responded Henrik.

"But he can own an estate, be a bourgeois?" persisted Pytro. "That would constitute wealth?"

Henrik shrugged. "Again, it goes back to definitions. What constitutes an estate, and how many farmers own estates? What is an estate? Perhaps a dwelling larger than the usual cottage with a tin roof? That might qualify."

"What if he employs a number of poorer farmers?" Pytro asked helpfully. What a bizarre discussion, thought Oleksander, yet it was deadly serious, not just vodka talking.

"Could be part of it," agreed Henrik, "but we have to broaden that out, or we will not find our quota of kulaks, I fear. So…" he thought for a moment, "rather than just limiting it to the number of workers hired, we should also consider how much land he has at his disposal and the number of horses, cows, pigs, chickens, and the like he owns."

"You mean come up with figures?"

"Probably, at least some range of figures for official reports. Also, I've been told in confidence to consider the political and psychological disposition toward the party when assessing potential kulaks. Are they cooperative? Or are they sullen and obstructionist? It makes all the difference."

"And we measure that how?" asked Pytro.

"That's easy; we call general meetings with compulsory attendance, outline the collectivization plans, and see who resists joining the kolkhoz."

"And those are the kulaks?" Pytro raised an eyebrow.

"Not necessarily, but we can make them so, if necessary. The problem is that we have a quota of those identified as kulaks to fulfill, and even if the majority joined the kolkhoz, that quota would still need to be filled."

"Suppose they don't exist or we can't find any?" asked Pytro.

"That can't be a possibility, not if we don't want to be in the same boat as the kulaks. We better find them. Kulaks exist. This is not an option. It is essential to the Party's program for peasant villages and the countryside. No kulaks mean no threat, and without a threat it will be difficult to control the peasants."

"So, we figure out who they are, how many there are, and how to deal with them?" Pytro counted his points on his thumb and two fingers.

"*Tak*, that would be good. One thing's for sure; we start with a workable assumption."

"Which is?"

"They are rich exploiters of poor peasants in the countryside. That's all anyone needs to know, and we decide what this means. If we don't do this, then why would we need to have a Committee of Unwealthy Peasants?"

"Okay, define rich?" Pytro asked.

If nothing else, Pytro was persistent, thought Oleksander. *Perhaps a bit dense but ... persistent.* The agronomist was both aghast and amused by this conversation that seemed to be going in circles.

"It has to go back to the land and animals. There are no former counts, dukes, or aristocrats with estates that can be confiscated, so we narrow it down. Say someone who owns twenty hectares of land, maybe has three horses, a cow, and hires day labourers — that's a kulak. Would you agree? As opposed to some *khlop* who doesn't own any land or animals but does work for someone who does. One is wealthy; the other is not... Does that make sense? Of course, we can be a little flexible depending on the circumstances about the amount of land and animals — even the number of hires."

"This stuff drives me to drink!" Pytro said, glancing around as if a kiosk bar would suddenly appear. "Most of the peasants that I have seen have a tiny plot of land to scratch and a cow, maybe a horse and wagon..."

"True," agreed Henrik. "Most would certainly have a nag."

"No, I mean real working horses, not the wife!" They both laughed and fell silent.

Oleksander checked the large hanging clock; it was almost time for him to get to the platform, since the train would be arriving soon — if it was on time… His attention, however, was drawn back to the two men.

"How about we look at it the other way around," Pytro said after a brief reprise into silence.

"How's that?"

"Who's poor?"

Henrik waved an arm as if shooing away a fly. "We covered that. Besides, we're not hunting for the poor."

"No, I mean in relationship to each other … you know — the kulak and the unkulak."

"I don't follow, Pytro."

"How about instead of a horse as a measure of wealth, let's say you're poor if you can't make your own borscht."

"What?"

"We point to those who have the means to make borscht as the exploiters and say they stole all the beets. And we are forming this Committee of Unwealthy Peasants because we want to do something about this, play a positive role in their lives."

"Which is?" Henrik asked.

"Stop those who are stealing the beets. Help the poor sons of bitches!"

There was a momentary pause, then both men burst out laughing. "Let's go find a bar," Henrik said decisively. "We have time."

With that, Oleksander folded his newspaper and made his way to the platform. What these comrades were contemplating was no laughing matter, but what they said was, Oleksander decided, and worthy of a grim chuckle as he grabbed his satchel and suitcase and made his way around odd bits of construction materials and groups of congregating people to the southbound platform.

CHAPTER FIVE

Kyiv to Bila Sich

Sholtz was on the train! Katya had spotted him getting on from her window seat as it was pulling away. This did not bode well. *What to do?* Panic gripped her momentarily, until she took a couple of deep breaths and settled herself down. It most certainly was not a coincidence that he was on this exact southbound train — it just couldn't be. He was on to her, verifying (not that there was much doubt) that he'd seen her from the apartment window. He had then followed her, first to the bank, where she withdrew most of her savings account, and thereafter to the railway station. That logic didn't seem quite right, though, since he could have intercepted her before she got to the station. Maybe it was a case of presumption and reasonable deduction. She was getting out of the city; where would she head except the train station? In any case, she had to assume the worst. He was in pursuit!

None of her questions mattered now. He was on board, and she had to find a way to deal with him. She rose from her seat, politely excusing herself as she brushed by an elderly man in the aisle seat clutching a battered suitcase to his chest. Instinctively, she knew that she had to keep moving forward in the carriage as far as she possibly could to buy some time. She needed to work out a plan, a strategy for her survival — something she had been doing for most of her life.

***

Katya saw him sitting alone in the second-class compartment, reading a newspaper. He appeared absorbed, the lips pursed, the eyebrows furrowed. A lanky fellow, although it was hard to tell given his slouched sitting position. As she approached, her thoughts swirling, she made note of his Nordic heritage: a linear aquiline nose and blondish strands of hair sticking out from beneath his reindeer cap, resting haphazardly on the collar of his coat. Clear blue eyes, a neatly trimmed moustache and a square, cleanly shaven chin tilted upward, sensing her presence. *He could definitely pass as a gentleman of means*, she surmised, who, hopefully, was susceptible to helping an attractive woman in her hour of peril. At this point, she could think of no other option.

She stopped beside his open compartment. "Excuse me sir, may I sit?"

His mouth brightened into a smile. "Please." He gestured, setting his newspaper aside. She sat directly opposite to him on the bench seat.

"Oleksander Pylyp."

"Katya Karina Kharsova."

"Pleased to meet you."

She gave a quick furtive glance over her right shoulder into the aisle and down the long carriage corridor. There wasn't much time… "Forgive my directness," she said. "I need your help."

"Ah… So, it wasn't my particularly handsome face." His smile widened and then wavered, seeing no immediate response. "Sorry … I couldn't resist … How can I be of service?" He moved the newspaper farther down the seat and leaned toward her.

"There's a man who has followed me from Kyiv and intends to do me harm. No time to explain; he will be here soon. He's going from carriage to carriage searching for me." Again, she glanced down the corridor.

Oleksander followed her widening eyes down into an indeterminate haze of slightly juggling passengers in their seats. The corridor was empty. "I see…" He hesitated. "And I should do what?"

"I-I don't know. I'm desperate. Rest assured he is not my husband or a scorned lover. Nothing like that. I saw him commit a crime … and he saw me!" She stopped abruptly, running out of words as she was running out of time, her pulse quickening. Indeed, what could he do? They were captive in a carriage on a moving train. There were other passengers, but who would interfere? Besides, Sholtz had a pistol and wasn't afraid to use it.

Oleksander was silent for a moment, studying her intensely, again pursing his lips. "Yes, here's what we'll do. First, give me a good description of your pursuer so that I can quickly identify him."

***

Vasar Sholtz methodically made his way through each carriage and connecting gangway to the next, moving forward with the train. Although he caught only a fleeting glance of her, he was quite sure that Katya had boarded. Why else would she be on the platform? He had returned to the commissariat after the unfortunate incident with Kreil Gromeko — truly, he was sorry that it ended the way it did — on the off chance that Katya would show up. She didn't, so he requested her employment file and confirmed that she was indeed from Shervobne, a village about a six hours' train ride south of Kyiv. With dispatch, his driver took him down Kominterna Street to the railway station, and he was out of the black sedan almost before it came to a full stop. She had to be here catching the southbound train to bring her closer to where she was born and where she would find support.

It took some time, but he had to be thorough, and now he entered the last coach. Taking in a sea of juggling hats and colourful shawls, no doubt carefully knitted by babkas, he saw that the carriage was relatively sparsely filled, only about three quarters, with second-class passengers. *Good, no crush of humanity to sift through!* Slowly, he made his way along the corridor, swaying to the movement and the steady click-clacking that seemed to give harmony to the motions of the car pulled by a powerful steam engine. Midway through, he saw a fellow a few seats up rise from his seat and make his way to the toilet at the far end. *One less place to look,* he thought as he continued the down the corridor.

At the end, he was puzzled. He could've sworn she was on the train. How could she not be? And there was no way that she could hide or get off. He seethed, disappointed. *I'll make one more sweep down*, he decided, *just in case — and get off at the next stop*. There was a brief stop, he knew, before Korsun Station. It appeared that he'd have to resort to a less direct method of neutralizing Katya Kharsova.

***

"Rather crowded in here," remarked Oleksander as he squeezed into the cubicle beside her.

"Good thing you're tall instead of fat," she said, flattening herself against the toilet wall.

They waited a few long minutes before he opened the door a crack, made a survey of the carriage, and decided it was safe to emerge. "The carriage is clear," he informed her as she surreptitiously slipped out of the toilet and made her way to their seats behind him.

"So... I do believe I need an explanation. Who was that man, and how did you come to witness what you witnessed? However," he held up a hand as she started to respond, "we'll put that into abeyance for now. Your friend may come back to look again. You've got to get off this train..." He thought for a moment. "Where are you planning to go?"

"Shervobne, my home village."

"Shervobne... That's well south of Kanev, isn't it?"

She nodded. "Yes."

"Would this fellow..."

"I prefer not to name him — yet," she interjected.

"Right, okay..." Oleksander paused, thinking. "How would he know that you're from Shervobne?"

Katya shrugged. "I suppose it isn't a secret. It's in my file at work."

Oleksander raised an eyebrow. "So, you work with your pursuer — this man of no name?"

"Not for him, but in the same building. He is a city commissar."

"I see… Lots of those around." Oleksander frowned. "Well, never mind… We will unravel this later. Right now, it is best that you not go to Shervobne."

"But where would I go?"

"We'll decide once we figure out how to get off at the next stop without being seen."

"You will help me?"

"To safety, yes, but thereafter you're on your own."

Fortunately, no further deception on how to elude Comrade Sholtz was necessary. At the next stop, just as Oleksander and Katya rose to depart and Oleksander reached for his small suitcase and satchel stuck below the seat, Katya touched his shoulder. "Wait."

He let go of the handle on the lid he was about to pull.

"It's him!" she exclaimed, peering out the frost-edged window. "He's gotten off and he's coming this way!"

"Get down on the seat, out of sight," Oleksander ordered as a tall, well-dressed man in a fur-collar coat and stylish four-flap fox-fur cap (which made him easy to identify) walked down the platform, peering into the windows. "If we're lucky, we may have gotten rid of him."

"I hope so."

"We'll know soon; it's a brief stop." Oleksander continued to observe the moving fur hat as it passed his window at a leisurely pace.

"Is he … is he getting back on the train?" Katya asked anxiously, her head almost touching the seat cushion.

"Doesn't appear so… In fact, he's making his way into the station."

Five minutes later, both Katya and Oleksander breathed a sigh of relief. Sholtz did not come out from the station. Most certainly, he would await the next train north to Kyiv.

"I still wouldn't advise you to go to your hometown. If he knows where you live, you might have an unwelcome reception party waiting for you. This is particularly true if he is an *important*," Oleksander pronounced the word with emphasis, "commissar, as you imply, and has committed a serious crime."

"But where would I go?"

"Hmmm… That is the question, isn't it?"

"I literally had to flee with the clothes on my back! I don't have the money to go elsewhere and disappear."

"Yes, I see."

Again, she noticed, those pursed lips.

"Well, I do have a temporary solution. You can come with me. I can put you up for a little while — till your situation gets sorted out."

"Where are you going?"

"To Bila Sich, a village slightly larger than Shervobne, I think. In another two hours or so we'll be there, or at least Korsun Station. It's maybe another hour by sleigh. My brother-in-law will be waiting for me at the Korsun Station, and I'm sure he won't mind an additional guest. Now, my house is very modest, and I haven't been there for some time, but it's intact and livable, or so Lev — that's my brother-in-law — assures me. I'm sure that Nina — my sister — can supply you with any clothing that you may need."

"Won't your wife object to having a stranger in the home?" *Especially an attractive female*, she didn't bother to voice.

"No, not at all. There is no wife. I now live in Kyiv, just on my way to visit Lev, who is the overseer of my farm and house."

"You're a landowner?"

"Hardly… Well, yes, I inherited the property, but it's modest, about four point five hectares, and I let Lev work it, part of the extended family, since my two brothers have long since emigrated to Canada."

"What do you do in Kyiv?" she asked, suddenly alert. "You a party or state official of some sort?" There seemed to be hundreds in the city, she knew.

"No, no, I don't belong to the party. I work as an agronomist at the Kyiv Agricultural Institute." *Although I won't much longer*, he thought, if he couldn't resolve the ominous situation Lev outlined in Bila Sich.

"A what?"

"It's someone who studies and deals with seeds and the soil. Went away to study and never came back!" He smiled. "So, I guess I do work for the state — indirectly. When my brothers left for Canada, now about four or five years ago, Lev agreed to farm the land, along with his own; so far, the arrangement has worked out. While the family house and farm remain, the Pylyp clan has left, except for me and Nina. But Lev is in charge," he emphasized as if this absolved him of such a responsibility.

"And you are going there to visit?"

"That's right, to say hello. It has been some time. Also, he invited me. As you may have heard, there's talk of collectivization in the countryside. Lev thinks the Party is dead serious in proceeding and is worried. Farmers are being increasingly scrutinized and the village council pressured to join the kolkhoz. But I digress… The point is you can come for a few days, hide, rest … plan your future." He shrugged.

Katya remained silent for a few moments, weighing her options, or lack thereof, before answering. "I accept. Thank you."

Oleksander nodded. "Probably should get some sleep. There's still a couple of hours before our stop."

CHAPTER SIX

Kyiv

Captain Emil Krypniuk of the Kyiv Police Criminal Investigation Department stood in the middle of the room, slowly taking in the contents before focusing on the corpse on the floor. It was a tidy living quarters: an overstuffed sofa and chair in one corner, a free-standing lamp with a yellowed shade placed between them, a small bookcase in the other with a few volumes of poetry huddled together and some stacked magazines at opposite ends. The only item that seemed to be askew was a small table in the centre. It had been moved sideways and the flower vase toppled over (there apparently had been no flowers — *not in season*, he guessed). The body was face-up to the left, the cold sun through a partially drawn curtain illuminating a narrow band from the head to the fine leather boots.

"Not much of a struggle, it would appear, before the fellow was shot," he said, as much to himself as to his partner, Sergeant Nickolay Nickolayevich Lubick, turning a slow 180 degrees. They had yet to thoroughly check the rest of the apartment — the bathroom and bedroom across the hall to the right and the tiny kitchen straight down the corridor — but it seemed at a glance that nothing had been disturbed. Certainly, not a burglary gone violently wrong.

"Good thing a water pipe burst the floor above, sabotaging the heating system, otherwise he would have been quite ripe before being discovered," noted Lubick in his usual stoic matter-of-fact manner.

"Do we know who he is?" Krypniuk asked, observing more closely the stiff human form on the brown woven fabric rug now stained in dark, rust-red frozen blood. With the water radiator system out of commission, the apartment had become frigid, their breath visibly exhausting as they spoke.

"Identity card says he's Kreil Gromeko, commissar of Commerce and Industry."

"Hmm..." Krypniuk frowned. A high-ranking commissar and party member — not good, he thought, particularly since it was not a self-homicide. He looked at his partner of five years, who nodded as if to confirm his thought.

"Right!" said Lubick, turning to the uniforms who had initially been called when the building manager discovered the body. "This is a crime scene," he announced in an elevated, officious voice. "No one is to pass without authorization." They nodded and went out to the hallway, stationing themselves on both sides of the apartment door, grateful to have a function other than staring at a dead man.

"Okay then... We'll let the pathologist and the rest of the forensic unit do their job. We need to know when he died before the trail gets any colder — literally..." Krypniuk shivered. "We'll also need a couple of our guys to interview the inhabitants in this building, beginning with this floor. For now, while we wait for the pathologist, forensic, and removal teams, let's have a good look around. I'll take the bedroom, you the toilet and kitchen."

Thirty minutes later, they came to an obvious conclusion. "We need to verify to be sure that this isn't Commissar Gromeko's apartment — at least he doesn't live here," said Krypniuk.

"More like his mistress, perhaps," agreed Lubick.

"Or perhaps his wife, if he has one." But that didn't feel right. "But then there's not enough of his belongings to constitute a proper domicile," Krypniuk amended, adjusting his glasses that had slid down his nose. He and Lubick had methodically gone through the bureau drawers and various cupboards and arrived at an inescapable conclusion.

"So, who is she? And where is she?" Lubick asked rhetorically.

"Apparently disappeared," suggested Krypniuk.

"For sure she hasn't been here for a while, a few days at least, depending on what the pathologist says."

"Well... We can't jump to conclusions. For now, her name is paramount. First, let's see if she or the commissar signed the lease... We'll get to her relationship with the deceased later."

***

The next day at the Kyiv Central Police Station, Krypniuk sat in his office reading the pathologist's preliminary report. Lubick knocked on the door, rattling the glass. Krypniuk waved him in, taking off his glasses and rubbing the bridge of his nose. It had been a long night, which now promised to stretch into a long day. Lubick dropped his short, heavy-set frame into one of the two wooden chairs set against a bare wall of the small, unassuming office.

"Two things... First, the apartment was rented by Taras Shevchenko — obviously an assumed name — and secondly, nobody saw or heard anything in the building," he said grimly, then shrugged fatalistically, "as expected."

"Hmm... I would be surprised if it was otherwise. Still, had to canvass," said Krypniuk, placing the wire-rim glasses back on his narrow nose. He glanced at what he had been reading. "Commissar Gromeko was shot with a seven-to-eight-millimetre calibre weapon."

"Like a Nagant?"

"Perhaps... And he's been dead for almost a week. If not for the water and heat problem, he probably wouldn't have been discovered until the smell got too bad, and even then..." Krypniuk trailed off. Soviet citizens were loath to draw attention of the authorities, especially if they found something, or in this case someone, in a disagreeable condition.

"Good thing the water pipe broke then," observed Lubick.

"And the building manager checked," added Krypniuk, "otherwise the commissar may have lain there for another few weeks."

"So, what's next?" Lubick slapped his hands on the knees.

"Downtown — the Commissariat Office. It's near the post office on Khreshchatyk Street... Apparently that's where Commissar Kreil

Gromeko," Krypniuk let the name roll off his tongue, weighing its importance, "carried out his duties to the state."

"Right."

"We need to proceed carefully here, Nickolay. This may involve politics, in which case we'll have the OGPU sniffing up our arse."

Lubick shrugged. "Not much we can do."

Krypniuk sighed. The Unified State Political Administration — the OGPU to everyone who encountered the agency — had been in the process of taking over the operational and bureaucratic leadership of the regular police forces in the Soviet republic for a number of years. That had been mandated by the politburo in Moscow. The party and state wanted full control of all police activities, not just those involving state and political implications. Although certainly criminal in nature, this case reeked of political intrigue and possible corruption (almost as a given), which would undoubtedly attract the attention of the higher powers.

***

Commissar Gromeko's office was at the end of a long corridor on the third floor of a large five-storey stone edifice complete with pediments over the corners, a central loggia, and multiple cornices with an impressive façade. Walking through an archway followed by a door, they found themselves in a reception room with three official-looking desks, one of which was unoccupied. Two females, constituting the sekrehita, sat at their stations like vigilant gatekeepers outside the commissar's dark and foreboding office door. One was quite young, with a pale complexion, almost milky, thought Krypniuk. The other, closer to the door, was older, more severe in posture, with chestnut-brown hair and pellucid grey eyes that grew instantly wary as he and Lubick approached. Krypniuk showed his credentials to the younger one, the first gatekeeper, as it were.

"We would like to ask you some questions," said Krypniuk, putting his card away. She looked quickly over to her older coworker behind a plain metal desk with an intricate-looking black typewriter with the word *OLYMPIA* across the front, which occupied a significant proportion of the desktop. She stopped typing, her hands suspended midair, her face inscrutable. "You are part of Commissar Gromeko's staff, correct?"

They nodded.

"And the empty desk?" Krypniuk had been drawn to it instinctively. Whose was it, and why was there no occupant?

"There are normally three of us," said the pale young woman after a pause, and not getting any meaningful support from her older colleague, she continued, "but she hasn't come in for the last several days."

"Oh?" Krypniuk raised an eyebrow. "What's her name?"

"Katya, Katya Kharsova."

As she spoke, Lubick pulled out from his coat a well-worn black notebook and stubby pencil, and flipping to the appropriate page, began to write.

"Is there any particular reason that she's not at work, sitting at her desk?" asked Krypniuk.

"Not that I'm aware of..." The reply was a little nervous, and again, Krypniuk noted the frazzled look at the senior secretary.

"Did she say why she would be gone for — a few days, you mentioned?"

"N–no." Clearly, she was becoming a little unravelled talking to a captain of police, unconsciously twisting a wayward strand of her hair. She glanced for the third time to her coworker and said, "It is assumed that on occasion when the commissar is away on business, he takes Katya along." This was said, Krypniuk noticed, with a small, knowing smile. "He may be on business and took her — for her dictation skills."

"Anna," the other secretary said with an edge to her voice — a warning, perhaps, not to say too much.

"Was there such a business trip scheduled?"

"Not that we are aware of," Anna's colleague answered. "Has something happened?"

Krypniuk reflected for a brief moment. No point withholding the truth of the matter. "Yes, Commissar Gromeko has been found deceased."

There was an audible gasp from both women, but their overall reaction remained remarkably composed — or at least mute. He continued, "We need to interview those who knew him, including, of course, yourselves and Katya. You won't know her address?"

Both shook their heads.

"Thank you. For the record, Sergeant Lubick will take your full names... We may need to talk at further length later on... Oh! I also need access to commissar's office." Krypniuk glanced at the dark glass door beyond them.

"We can't do that," said the older secretary. "Only Commissar Gromeko has ... had the key. He was very particular that way."

That gave Krypniuk pause. He recalled finding only one key among the commissar's belongings, and that was to the apartment. "Since Commissar Gromeko is unfortunately not with us any longer, who else would have a key?"

Each secretary looked at the other for a moment. Finally, the older one said: "No one ... maybe Katya." She shrugged.

"Oh, wait!" Anna blurted out. "Commissar Sholtz has a key. I saw him enter the office just the other day."

"Commissar Sholtz?"

"Yes, head of the Procurement and Labour Department," replied Anna.

"You saw him... Commissar Sholtz?" Krypniuk's eyes seemed to sharpen under his glasses.

"Yes. I'm–I'm pretty sure."

"And where is Commissar Sholtz located?"

"Room 312," Anna answered nervously as if suddenly regretting mentioning it.

"And where is that?" Lubick asked, scribbling in his notebook.

"He's back down the corridor from where you came. Turn left. That will take you to reception." It was the older secretary who responded, contributing to the conversation in a more officious way.

"Thank you," said Krypniuk. "As I say, we may need to speak to you again — perhaps after we've talked to Commissar Sholtz."

They both nodded.

**

Vasar Sholtz, commissar of Procurement and Labour, sat behind an enormous dark oak desk. He wore a grey military tunic with the turned-down collar and epaulets of certain high-profile Soviet leaders. He liked that it was simple but still signified authority. He uncapped his pen and was about to sign one of a number of documents when there was a timid knock on the door. He was an imposing figure with a high forehead, accented by a receding hairline. Now, his brows arched at the intrusion, stretching the crow's feet at the corner of his eyes in annoyance. It was more than the occasional irritation lately, he realized, but the increasing anxiety he felt living what now seemed like on the edge ever since the unfortunate meeting and incident with Gromeko. They had a good thing going. No one would be the wiser, if only Kreil had not tried to cheat him... Consciously, with great deliberation, he steadied himself both physically (a slight tremor in his hand suddenly developed, he noticed, when he lifted a glass or when putting ink to paper) and mentally, focusing his thoughts. "Yes," he said sharply.

His petite secretary opened the door, took a couple of steps in, and gently closed it. Staring more at the pale green wall beyond than the man seated at the desk where the ever-vigilant portraits of Lenin and Stalin glared accusatorially at anyone who entered, she announced, "There are two policemen from the Kyiv Crime Investigation Department asking if you are free to speak to them."

Sholtz capped his pen and slid his chair backward, literally taken aback. *What the hell... Be calm,* he counselled himself. "Have they stated the nature of their business with me?"

"No, Commissar."

There was a momentary silence that could have been an eternity. "Very well, then ... show them in."

A tall, rather gaunt-looking fellow appeared, followed by a much shorter and stouter individual behind him. There was nothing in their rather drab winter clothing or manner to suggest that they indeed were police from the criminal division, although he really had no idea what they were supposed to look like or wear. The secretary discreetly eased herself out, closing the door softly.

Sholtz mustered a smile, stood, and walked around his desk, hand extended. They shook, once considered a bourgeois habit that spread germs but now deemed acceptable.

"I'm Captain Emil Krypniuk of the Kyiv Police Criminal Investigations Department, and this is Sergeant Nickolay Lubick." They presented their credentials. "Thank you for seeing us."

"Yes, of course." Sholtz gestured to a couple of soft-seated chairs in front of his desk, complete with armrests, which Krypniuk appreciated, and Sholtz retraced his steps to his seat. He didn't feel as vulnerable there. "What brings you to the commissariat?" he asked cheerfully. "And how can I help?"

Krypniuk cleared his throat, crossed his legs, and laid his hands across his lap. Lubick leaned forward with his notebook out. "I'm afraid I've got some bad news. I understand you know Commissar Gromeko well?"

Sholtz looked from one policeman to the other, feigning concern (he hoped). "Not well," he answered carefully, "but Comrade Gromeko was a valued colleague."

"Was?" questioned Krypniuk, raising an eyebrow, his eyes seemingly growing larger through the spectrum of his lenses.

Damn, Sholtz cursed silently. That was a careless slip of the tongue. "You said bad news. I presume you're here because something has happened... He hasn't been at his office for a few days."

"You are correct. I regret to inform you that Commissar Kreil Gromeko was found dead in an apartment on Tarasov Street. Would you know if he lives there?" Krypniuk looked at Sholtz expectantly, with increased intensity that made the commissar uncomfortable.

"No, no... I don't... This is terrible news. What happened?"

"The investigation is ongoing, but it is a criminal inquiry."

"I see…" Sholtz sank back into his chair. "Criminal?"

"Yes, criminal in nature. So, I take it you've never been to Commissar Gromeko's home?" Krypniuk persisted.

"No, I don't know where he lives." Sholtz was having trouble getting a read on these comrade-detectives. The senior one with the prominent Adam's apple, was tricky, and he had to be handled with care.

As if on cue, the other stunted one flipped a couple of pages in his notebook and said, "Do you know Katya Kharsova?"

"Yes, of course… Commissar Gromeko's executive secretary."

"When was the last time you saw her?" Lubick asked.

Again, Sholtz feigned deliberation and surprise. "Come to think of it, I've not seen her in the last little while. Why?"

"We'll need her employment file, complete with a recent photo," Krypniuk broke in.

"I'm sure that won't be a problem. It would be with personnel records in Commissar Gromeko's office. Has something happened to her as well?"

"Too early to speculate," Krypniuk said briskly, then changed the subject. "I understand you have a key to Commissar Gromeko's office?"

"Who told you that?" Sholtz reined in his surprise and escalating unease. *How could they possibly know that?*

"You were seen entering Commissar Gromeko's office a few days ago."

Fuck! Mistake number two. There was a witness. It must have been one or both of Gromeko's secretaries. Who else would have told them? Sholtz fumed silently. *Damn nosy, talkative bitches.* He thought he had been careful coming by when there was no one in the reception area. The secretaries were gone. He had waited until they left before entering. And yet…

In the heat of the moment, he had the foresight to liberate the office key from Gromeko's body before leaving the apartment. The office had to be sanitized of any incriminating evidence. Indeed, despite the anxiety of being discovered, exposed, he methodically went through all the files and removed any materials related to their clandestine and highly illegal activities, particularly those pertaining to certain contracts and illicit agreements. Gromeko once mentioned that he kept a second ledger of recorded transactions, but Sholtz hadn't found it. Certainly, it wasn't in the office, and if it did exist — as *my insurance*, Gromeko once boasted while in a drunken state — it was probably in a deposit box somewhere that nobody would find — he hoped! Now, he had to admit to having a key. There was no point in denying it.

"Yes, yes, I do. Our ministries overlap," he continued by way of explanation, "and sometimes we need access to documents when one of us is away... It's a reciprocal arrangement. Kreil and I trust ... trusted each other. He has ... had," Sholtz again corrected himself, "keys to my office as well."

Krypniuk nodded, digesting but not accepting at face value that these men would readily exchange access to each other's offices and files. "Would you be so kind as to provide us access to Commissar Gromeko's office? We need to look around; perhaps he left an itinerary, calendar, diary of his activities, with whom he met, about what and the time and place... That sort of thing."

Sholtz didn't know whether they had the authority to snoop in Gromeko's office, but it seemed prudent not to argue and let them search. Besides, it didn't matter, since he had thoroughly vetted the place. They would find nothing. He made a point of searching through his desk's upper drawer before pulling out a large silver key. "Ah, here it is!"

***

Krypniuk and Lubick went through the motions of examining Gromeko's desk, which seemed exceptionally clean and devoid of any files, papers, and documents, never mind a notebook or calendar. A quick perusal of a small door filing cabinet yielded nothing useful, nor did they find any sort of locked deposit box or wall safe. But then, if Gromeko had some compromising materials about himself or others at the commissariat, he wouldn't have kept them around in the office, particularly if others (Sholtz?) had an extra key. On the other hand, Sholtz was in a position to have removed materials that he perhaps didn't want to see the light of day.

Afterward, Krypniuk and Lubick revisited Gromeko's secretaries about his meetings and schedule. They affirmed that he indeed kept a daily calendar on his desk and that Katya, his "personal" secretary, was in charge of his comings and goings. There were veiled hints about the commissar's "not so secret" relationship with Katya. Both shrugged noncommittally when asked if he kept an apartment for her. Otherwise, no new information came to light.

As they turned to go, Krypniuk paused. Gromeko's missing key, and the fact that Sholtz had an identical one (apparently), bothered him. "Just to confirm," he said, directly facing Anna, "you saw Commissar Sholtz use a key to enter Commissar Gromeko's office?"

"Y–yes."

"What day was that?"

"A few days ago — Friday, I think. It was late, everyone had left — me too — but as I was about to go outside, I realized that I had forgotten my scarf and mittens, so I came back."

"Did Commissar Sholtz see you?"

"N–no… I don't think so. It was fairly dark; the lights were off. I was coming in and about to switch them on when I saw him just as he was closing the door to Commissar Gromeko's office."

Krypniuk nodded. "And what did you do then?"

"Nothing. I quickly went to my desk, grabbed my things, and left."

CHAPTER SEVEN

Kyiv

Krypniuk came home totally exhausted. It had been a long, endless day, and it was a good thing his wife, Ivanka, and their fifteen-year-old son, Yuri, were off visiting her side of the family in Horodmya, near the Belarus Soviet Republic border. He wouldn't have been very amiable company now that he was engaged in an investigation. He needed solitude to think, roll the case over in his mind, contemplate where it was going, and how he would be able to navigate what shook out. And he was certain that there was something nasty to shake out.

First, though, he was hungry, and since Ivanka was not around to provide her usual exceptional fare, he would have to improvise. By the time he took off his coat and winter footwear, his dinner decision had been made. It wasn't exactly a "proper" meal compared with his wife's, but he was satisfied with his selection: a thick hunk of dark rye bread — not exactly a Borodinsky loaf that his Russian friends invoke as the best, but close enough — topped with pickled herring and whatever accompanying condiments he could find. True, it wasn't borscht with *smetana*, a fine cut of meat with vegetables and a side salad, but it was simple and as good as it got. Normally, he'd have a hot cup of tea, but he was too lazy to get the samovar going. A herring sandwich and beer would more than suffice.

Setting the food on a small side table beside his well-worn chair, which he had acquired when he and his new bride moved in over eighteen years ago, he sighed and shook his head. Not much had changed. Then, a two-bedroom apartment was considered a luxury. On further reflection, the passage of time had not altered that conclusion. Very much like the apartment where Commissar Gromeko was found, it still represented a step up from the usual drab newer flats found in Kyiv. He took off his glasses and rubbed his eyes. He had been on the job almost twenty years, and it showed if he looked hard in the mirror. Haunted, near-sighted eyes that had seen almost every form of criminal depravity; sallow, gravely creased cheeks; a pale, ghostly face, indicative, he presumed, of spending too much time in a smokey, airless room with little sun coming in; all topped off by receding brownish hair speckled with grey. He sighed; at forty-five he already felt past his best. *And today, I feel every bit my age*, he thought as he rubbed the stubble on his chin that seemed to reappear about as fast as it was scraped off.

He actually contemplated retirement, of perhaps doing something else — what, he really didn't know. This was a period of uncertainty, especially since the city constabulary, in line with a trend in all Soviet republics, was being subsumed by the OGPU — really the political arm of the state. Maybe he should get out. If he didn't, he'd soon have to answer to some apparatchik who in all likelihood knew little or nothing about police work and who'd always be looking over his shoulder for approval at best, or at worst trying to survive playing Soviet chess games of who was doing what to whom and protecting himself from any fallout. Political cases would take a decided higher priority over such mundane matters as murder, assault, robbery, extortion, and any number of other "ordinary" crimes.

As a result, Krypniuk found this case unsettling — personal motive, perhaps, but undoubtedly with an overlap of politics that he intuitively felt had its roots within the walls of the commissariat. His instincts were usually close to the mark. He needed to track down Gromeko's executive secretary, this Katya Kharsova; she was the key. Also, there was something about Sholtz that did not sit well. He couldn't put his finger on it, but the feeling sat there in the shadows; he couldn't shake it.

His thoughts were sent violently ajar by the discordant ring of the telephone, one of the few conveniences afforded to him because of his position. "May a duck kick my ass," he muttered, rising from his chair, walking over to the tiny ledge in the hall where the phone rested. He picked up the receiver on the third ring. "*Dobre vechure.*"

"Emil Krypniuk?" inquired a voice at the other end in a clear, crisp tone. *Too clear for ten o'clock at night*, he thought.

"Yes."

"You have an appointment with Commissar Pavlick, nine o'clock tomorrow morning. A car will pick you up."

"I—"

Before Krypniuk could respond, the voice said, "Good evening," and the line went dead.

Who was Commissar Pavlick, and did he have to take a suitcase with some personal things in case he wasn't coming back?

***

The next morning, after a fifteen-minute ride in an imposing black sedan, a young officer escorted Krypniuk to an OGPU operational site on Volodymyrska Street, not far from the city centre. He followed the officious young man through the side door of a five-storey nondescript building, down a long dark corridor to a door with the words *Boris Pavlick, Commissar, Office of Special Investigations* printed in large letters on full display. Left out, but no doubt implicit in the title, were the letters OGPU. Krypniuk was entering the sinister world of the state's security services, and Pavlick was probably just a step or two below the commissar of State Security.

Krypniuk was shown into the office, after which the young militiaman smartly made an about-face and marched out of the room, closing the door behind him. Pavlick was sitting behind his desk. The image of a Buddha came to Krypniuk's mind: overlapping circles, head, torso, and what remained. He had a cherubic face topped by a hairless dome. Without looking up from what he was writing, Pavlick pointed to a single chair strategically placed in front of his desk.

Krypniuk sat and waited, apparently for the commissar to finish his paperwork. "Krypniuk," he was moved to finally say.

"Yes, I was summoned."

"That you were," agreed Pavlick, straightening in his chair, leaning forward and looking directly at him. Till then, Krypniuk was distracted by a large portrait of Felix Dzerzhinsky, the founder and first commissar of State Security of the new Bolshevik state, hanging on the wall behind Pavlick. "You are in charge of the Gromeko case." It was more a statement than a question.

"Yes, Comrade Commissar." Not sure of the protocol regarding titles, Krypniuk used what the bureaucrats might use when addressing themselves formally. It didn't sound right, but Pavlick showed no desire to correct him.

"What have you found?"

"It's very early—"

"A quick assessment to date," Pavlick clarified.

"At the moment, it's all preliminary, but without question Commissar Gromeko was shot by a person or persons unknown."

"Suspects?"

"No one yet, only an individual of interest. Of course, further interviews will be conducted among the employees of the commissariat, his colleagues, friends, and we will be speaking with his wife—"

"About this individual of interest," Pavlick cut in, "what is known about him?"

"It's a her," amended Krypniuk, shifting in the uncomfortable wooden chair. "His personal secretary in whose apartment apparently he was found." They still had to verify that, but the assumption was sound.

"Have you interrogated her?"

"No Comrade Commissar. She's gone missing."

"I see…" Pavlick said nothing for a moment, as if this fact revealed everything. "You know, Captain Krypniuk," Emil noted that it was the first time his title was used, "I reviewed your record … to see if you were up to the task. You have an acceptable rate of cases solved… And this is a homicide? No question?"

"No question, Comrade Commissar. If it were an accident or Commissar Gromeko shot himself, the weapon would have been found."

"Suicide ruled out." Pavlick muttered it aloud, more to himself than to Krypniuk in particular. "For now," he added cryptically.

Krypniuk couldn't tell if Pavlick had sent him a coded message. He could only wait until the reason for this meeting was made clear. He didn't have a long wait. Pavlick shifted his substantial weight to one side and leaned well forward, his eyes focused intensely on the Kyivan policeman, the only sound a squeak of protest from the commissar's chair. "This case is somewhat delicate. Not only because nobody should be going around shooting one of the city's highly ranked commissars, but also it involves money — more to the point, a great deal of missing rubles from the state's purse that may be in some way connected. It was collected by the commissar's office and has disappeared. We can't have that, can we?"

"How much constitutes a great deal?" Krypniuk asked, his investigative instincts coming to the fore.

"Very," Pavlick replied dryly, his eyes narrowing into the folds of his pasty face.

Krypniuk nodded in understanding. The question was out of bounds. Not his concern.

"As a consequence," Pavlick continued, "this has become a confidential investigation. You will report to me. Understood?"

"Yes, Comrade Commissar." *Loud and clear.*

"You're not a party member?" The question came out of nowhere, taking Krypniuk by surprise with its bluntness.

"No," he answered curtly.

After a momentary pause, Pavlick laid his hands on the desk, his short, stubby fingers drumming on the felt top as if finally making a decision. "Right... You will continue with this case. It is yours, and you will solve it."

"Yes, Comrade Commissar."

"Good. Do what you need to do to find who killed Commissar Gromeko — and why."

The message couldn't be clearer now, and it was not lost on Krypniuk. There was more at stake than a simple homicide. He was to follow the money trail. Who took it? And where did it go?

"And remember," Pavlick warned, "all vital information must be reported directly to me."

CHAPTER EIGHT

Bila Sich

Lev Devchenko arrived as scheduled at the Korsun Railway Station in a horse and sleigh. Oleksander introduced Katya with a brief explanation that she was being pursued by someone who would do her harm and needed a place to hide for a short while. To Lev's skeptical look, he said he'd explain later. Lev simply nodded. "Okay, then … it'll be a tight ride but," he smiled, "so, a warm one… At least you're travelling light." He eyed the small suitcase in Oleksander's one hand and the satchel in the other. Katya had no baggage at all. Oleksander placed his luggage in the space under the sleigh's curved front dash, and they climbed in. *Tight indeed*, thought Oleksander.

"*Davyi!*" commanded Lev, giving a little flick of the reins. The little grey mare gave a snort and started to move hesitantly as if in protest. "Svetlana here," he nodded toward his animal, "notices the extra weight, but she's a good old girl… I'm glad you came when you did," he continued in a change of topic. "I was fortunate to leave the village — of course I went across the back fields onto the road. Still, rumours are spreading that soon there will be heavy restrictions. At this point, I suspect that they don't have enough OGPU militiamen to seal us in…"

It took about an hour to get to Lev's place. With Bila Sich still in the distance, he veered off across a field and followed a tree line. "Like to avoid hostiles," he commented as they glided through snow that thankfully wasn't too deep.

"What if they see us?" asked Oleksander, leaning over and across Katya, who sat sandwiched in the middle between the two.

"Chances are they won't, but in case they did, I'm counting on them being too lazy to chase us!"

It was getting quite dark by the time Svetlana and her cargo reached their destination, arriving through a back lane to Lev's home. "Go in and say hello to Nina and Misha. Nina is looking forward to seeing her fancy brother. I'll take care of Svetlana and the sleigh. I've visited your house, by the way, just before going out to pick you up. The stove is lit and should be crackling … give the place some warmth. I've brought wood in, a bit of food, blankets, a full paraffin lamp, and other odds and ends are on the table. I didn't know that you would have a guest though… Of course, you're having dinner with us tonight!"

"Thank you, Lev. I appreciate this."

"Well, you may find that this is not the village you once knew."

"Oh, I don't doubt that. I've haven't been here for a while."

"Beyond that," Lev waved off the comment. "Dark forces are upon us. I am not sure we can endure and survive what is to come."

"Tonight, at least," Oleksander exclaimed with all the cheer he could muster, "let's celebrate meeting once more. After, we'll face what awaits us tomorrow…"

"*Slava Jesu Christu*," ("Glory to Jesus Christ"), Oleksander announced the traditional greeting as he and Katya entered the home. He had long not been particularly religious, but old habits die hard.

"*Slava naviki*," ("Glory forever"), came the reply from Nina, who rushed over and gave him a hug. She was thin, with her brown hair pulled back behind the ears and tied in a red scarf with straying strands of grey popping through. Like her brother, she had blue eyes and an aquiline nose. Her cheekbones, quite non-Slavic in that they were not high (or low, for that matter), supported a pleasant elfin face with a round chin that opened into a warm smile, which hinted at a slight overbite. "Misha! Come here! Say hello to your uncle," she shouted to a door at the far end of the entrance, "and his guest…" She seemed delighted to see Katya, raising an eyebrow at Oleksander as if to ask: *Who is this, and is it serious?*

Misha emerged from a small room, coming out of the shadows of a dimly lit paraffin lamp.

Introductions were made, and Oleksander and Katya shed their outer garments and handed them to Misha, who placed them across one of the benches against the wall. Misha, a shy, reserved twelve-year-old, had the same delicate features as his mother, particularly the colour and shape of his eyes and nose. Undoubtedly, thought Oleksander, he would continue to grow tall and fill out like his father. He hadn't seen the lad for over a year.

"Let's sit." Nina gestured them to a wooden table with a bench on either side near the centre of the room. Oleksander cast his gaze over the entire living space. Nothing had changed, nor had he expected it to. As with other village houses, this one too was essentially one large floor area, although Misha had a room of his own that had a back door into the shed and barn. There were two windows on the north and south walls. Two simple icons hung alongside, with some shelves along the east and west walls. On the north wall, a bed consisting of pine planks with a mattress and thick embroidered blanket on top was built near a fireplace made of wood and earth plastered over and whitewashed, appearing as stone brick. It made for an inviting hearth. At the moment, an earthen pot hung from an iron bar over the fireplace. Along the other side was a long bench.

The table was set with bowls, a jug of milk, a dish with hardboiled eggs, dark bread, and a sheep cheese loaf. "Just freshly baked," she said, catching Oleksander's roaming eyes. "The *kolesha* is almost ready."

Lev came in from the back, through Misha's room, boots in hand. He placed them inside the front door, took off his coat and hat, hanging them on a hook above the boots, and rubbed his hands. "Before we begin," he announced, "let me propose a toast," whereupon he retrieved from one of the shelves a nearly full bottle of what could only be vodka. "From our finest potatoes for special occasions," he continued, pouring a generous splash into everyone's glass on the table, including Misha's.

"Lev!" Nina chided.

"It's not going to hurt him," he said. "Right, Misha? It's not every day that we get a visit from your esteemed brother, all the way from Kyiv…"

The main meal, maize-based porridge, bread, and thickly sliced sheep cheese, was filling and infused them with satisfaction. Lev turned foreboding after another healthy splash of vodka, noting that more and more pressure was being put on the village households to ante up what they owed the state. "The taxes," he averred, "in rubles and grain quotas demanded have more than tripled since you were here last. It's an obvious form of pressure to make us join their new kolkhoz, which, to be honest, has barely taken shape so far. If these tax hikes continue, they'll not only take away all the seed for spring planting but also our stores of goods."

Oleksander only nodded; he needed to think and assess the government policy and actions.

"Enough of economic woes and politics!" exclaimed Nina. "Tell us about your work and how you met Katya."

Oleksander gave Katya a quick glance and proceeded to mention his ongoing research at the agricultural college and Lysenko's theories on increasing crop yields.

"And Katya?" she asked before he could prattle on for too long.

"Actually, we met on the train coming here," Katya interjected. She went on to explain that she was employed in one of Kyiv's commissariat offices and that she witnessed what she believed was a shooting. The perpetrator saw her, knew her from work, and followed her onto the train. She feared for her life, but with the help of Oleksander had eluded the pursuer. She left out the sordid details of her job, who was shot, and that he was shot in her apartment.

"So, aren't you the dashing fellow," Nina said, turning to her brother.

"He was," affirmed Katya with a smile.

"And you escaped with just what you brought with you!" exclaimed Nina, wide-eyed.

"Literally the clothes on my back."

"*Bozhe, bozhe*," declared Nina, "how horrible!"

"That's why Katya is staying at the cottage … until we can sort this out," added Oleksander. "Right now, it isn't safe for her to go to her village."

Nina sprang into action, pulling from a large wooden chest beside the entrance to Misha's room a heavy blanket, a couple of linen blouses, and a blue skirt. "These should fit," she announced. "I'll get some more food prepared as well, and we have an extra lamp — the place hasn't been lived in for some time. It'll be cold, and..."

"It's being warmed as we speak," said Lev, holding up his hand as if to slow her down. "I've made sure there's a supply of firewood on hand for the stove. You should be good for a few days... Also, there are some basic provisions."

"Thank you so much, both of you," Katya said. "Very kind ... but I don't want to be a burden."

"Nonsense!" declared Nina. "We're happy to help."

Later, with Nina and Katya chatting about city and country living and life in general while clearing the table and washing the utensils, Lev took Oleksander aside to the bench beside the hearth. Misha too took a seat near the fireplace but remained quiet, content to listen to the conversation. Lev proceeded to take a tin of tobacco, along with a wad of tobacco paper from a small ledge, licked his fingers, and rolled a cigarette, offering it to Oleksander. He declined, one of a minority, it seemed, who hadn't taken up the nicotine habit.

"I really don't know how to fight this," Lev said without preamble as he stuck a splinter of wood into the fireplace and raised the burning tip to light the cigarette declined by Oleksander. "Most of the village leaders have disappeared, and those with us on the old village council have remained silent or joined Belynski and his Soviet council. We're becoming some sort of unrecognizable Soviet village run by aliens — strangers not from this land. However," he instinctively lowered his voice, "there is a core group of us left who meet when we can to discuss what to do."

"And what has this group concluded, in terms of what should be done?"

Lev shrugged. "Organize, fight. The problem is fight with what and organize how? We are increasingly watched and have to be careful getting together and speaking out. You'll see how bad it's getting, though, soon enough. There's a big compulsory village meeting at the church —

or what used to be the church. It's now a Soviet community meeting facility. They posted the notices around the village. Our new masters will be out in force at this one. You'll understand what we're against firsthand. But I wanted you to know that before this meeting, there'll be a men's 'work bee' out near the grist mill. We'd like your input…"

***

Oleksander's house was only about a kilometre away as the crow flies from Devchenko's dwelling, accessible but not on the main north-south road. Rather than have Lev take Svetlana and the sleigh out for another trot and glide, Oleksander insisted on walking. Tired as they were, it was a cold but not intolerable night with a bright moon to mark the way. They thanked Nina and Lev, and with a sack of food, clothing, blankets, and other sundry items, they made their way down the path, crunchy with snow, to the dark cottage.

The interior of Oleksander's family home was a smaller version of the one they had had just departed. True to his word, Lev had lit the stove, and while it was almost out now, there was residual heat and even smothering embers to easily reignite the fire. Oleksander added kindling to the glowing embers and rubbed his hands. "That should get the temperature up again," he said, familiarizing himself with the place where he'd grown up. Strangely enough, there were no haunting ghosts floating about, and the grip of nostalgia simply did not materialize. But then, he had never been overly sentimental. "It's not exactly like the apartments in Kyiv with running water and a toilet…" he smiled, "it's out back, by the way. Still, it's where we lived." He lit the paraffin lamp on the table and pointed to a partitioned area across the room. "I'll sleep over there; you sleep here on this bed." He pointed to a bench near the stove.

"I couldn't—" she began but was cut off.

"No arguments. Tomorrow we'll discuss the state of affairs we find ourselves in. For now, get some sleep. You must be exhausted."

"Are you sure?" she asked. "It's your home."

He waved her concerns away.

The next morning, Oleksander got up early, did his business outdoors, and set about boiling a pot of water for tea. In the small cache of supplies Nina had given them were some tea leaves, thick slices of bread, a soft chunk of sheep cheese, and some boiled eggs. This would constitute a reasonable breakfast.

Katya rose shortly thereafter, her hair ruffled and clothes wrinkled but none the worse for wear, to his eyes at least. "Good morning," she said. "You're up early, and you've been busy, I see."

He smiled. "Not exactly the Grand Hotel in Kyiv, but it's warm, and there's food — even if you need to put your boots on and go out to do your toiletries."

"This is great, thank you... And remember, I grew up in a similar place to this, which had about the same amenities."

"And enduring childhood memories, I hope..."

Over breakfast, they discussed their situation. "We need to get our stories straight in terms of our relationship," Oleksander explained. "It's a small community; people will talk and speculate, even if you try to keep a low profile."

"Okay ... and what story do we spin?'

"Ah... I propose the most plausible one, which, if I may be so bold, is that you are my bride-to-be from Kyiv. You came with me to see where I grew up, given that you lived in the city all your life." He shrugged. "Villagers will be curious and ask questions... Probably should give you a fictitious name as well. What do you think?"

"Hmm... I suppose that is as good a story as any," she said, taking a piece of bread and spreading some sort of berry jam over top from a jar Nina had shoved into the sack along with all the other items.

"What's your middle name?" he asked.

"Karina. Why?"

"Too close. Need to pick another name for your alias."

"How about Oxana — Oxana Gerkil."

"Sounds good. Where did these names come from?"

"Oxana is the name of my best friend growing up. Gerkil is the surname of a neighbour in our village."

Oleksander nodded. "Works for me."

***

Over the next few days, Oleksander ventured out about the village with Lev, meeting his friends, including Vlas Chorney and Tomash Chozh. They'd get together as inconspicuously as possible, sometimes a quick word and drink at the pub with select others, but most often in their respective barns away from prying eyes. Word was passed on a fuller meeting to be held in an annex building close to the grist mill. "Listen," Lev suggested to Oleksander, "and maybe offer us some advice in advance of that general meeting called by Belynski."

Oleksander had no idea what advice he could possibly give or why his brother-in-law had such faith in him.

At the appointed date and time, almost a dozen men found their way to a small structure barely larger than a shed. It was unremittingly dark inside except for rays of pale light through a small, dirty window high on the east wall. This was what they were being reduced to for any unofficial (which meant unsanctioned) meetings. Bundled in warm clothing and huddled together, anyone who wished to could offer their thoughts, say their peace.

"They have heavy weapons — two machine guns and a barrack with militiamen, presumably OGPU," explained Lev. "There's no way we can just kick them out of the village. In fact, if we don't give up our land and animals and join the kolkhoz, we'll be the ones kicked out and given a long train ride to Siberia."

"Or we could die rebelling, which might be preferable," offered a muffled voice behind a scarf and bushy beard.

"There's that, Ivan," agreed Lev.

"An impossible situation, then," came a comment from somewhere behind Ivan.

"Difficult — very difficult, but not impossible," said Lev. "Isn't that right, Oleksander?"

Way to put me on the spot, thought Oleksander. It *was* an impossible situation and one that was undoubtedly happening to countless towns and villages throughout the countryside. Still, they had to protest, to fight, show defiance. Otherwise, they'd be herded like sheep and led to their unwelcome fate. The trick was to fight smartly without being totally overwhelmed and destroyed. He considered for a moment. "Obviously, we cannot kick these Bolsheviks out of Bila Sich physically. Even if we somehow succeeded, it would be temporary; reinforcements would be sent in to deal with us."

"Sabotage?" suggested another belligerent voice from the darkness.

Oleksander shook his head. "I think not. We would surely be rounded up and the whole village punished." Even as he was making these comments, he realized that he was way out of his depth; he knew no better than anyone else what to do. Lev had, Oleksander suspected, brought him to this meeting and presented him as one with education and perhaps some savvy in the ways of power and influence — *is that what urban life gives you?* — to advise them on a suitable, most effective course of action, if not lead them. He knew of no suitable action and was in no position to advise, let alone lead. Accepting that, he resorted to the one thing that kept individuals, indeed, whole nations, moving forward. He offered hope. "Given our precarious situation, our best option is to resist, but wisely."

"How's that?" asked a small man in a woollen cap pulled down almost to his eyes.

"Play for time — that's our best chance," said Oleksander, actually surprising himself. He *did* have something to say after all. "As I understand it, they are going to great lengths — correct me if I'm wrong, Lev — to persuade us to join the collective farm they created. But they want, or perhaps need, to do it legally. So, they attempt to beseech you and coerce you into voluntarily signing over your land, livestock, and equipment to the kolkhoz."

"I'd sooner slaughter my cow and goats than let these Bolshevik bastards take them," thundered Tomash Chozh, looming large over the others.

"Let's hope," there was that word again, "it won't come to that," said Oleksander. "No, I'm suggesting enduring as best we can while playing out their game, which means not signing any of their documents but not totally rejecting them either."

"How's that to work?" asked Vlas.

"Finding ways of delaying their process and schedules, of saying 'I'm still thinking about it' or 'I need time to think about it.'"

"What good will that do us?" asked Tomash, frowning.

"Exactly that — buying us and the village some time. As I see it, at this moment we can hold out, even if for a short while. It's winter; they're just beginning to establish their collectivization system, which needs managers, cadres to be in place operating everything from grist mills to tractor stations. If they push us too far, the system will fail, along with their plans. They know that, and they cannot afford to fail — at least at the local level. You have the knowledge, the expertise, and, moreover, the seeds and equipment to make sure next year's crops are planted."

"They're starting to confiscate our seeds, I'm hearing," Vlas noted ominously.

"What I'm saying is that as an agronomist," Oleksander wasn't sure many knew what the term meant but continued, "they can't afford to ignore you, that if they confiscate everything, make households join the kolkhoz, there will be full-scale chaos. They are for the most part imported bureaucrats who don't know the first thing about farming. Without you, they cannot succeed, nor can this experiment of theirs."

"So, we resist!" exclaimed Tomash.

"Yes, but not physically, not bearing arms. We resist mentally. We wait them out until spring planting. These local party officials need the grain to be seeded and growing to fulfill their quotas. It's their heads as well if they don't. They will not initiate full collectivization until after the spring crop is planted — too disruptive. This gives us a little time for reason to prevail, for circumstances to change. This is really our only leverage. And we can only hope for the best."

Oleksander expressed this more confidently than he had a right to, since he had no idea what the politburo in Moscow had in mind, what directives were given to the oblast commissars, and under what pressures or what lengths local officials were willing to go to reach the targets set out for them. He was basing his remarks on hope and a prayer — the latter, in case there was a God. "We simply cannot give up hope," he concluded with as much bravado as he could muster.

It was getting colder, and the dozen or so men Lev managed to convince to meet clandestinely heard what Oleksander, the new arrival from Kyiv (but still remembered in the village), had to say. No one was convinced that the strategy, such as it was, would work or even that such passive delaying tactics were plausible. After all, the threats were getting louder, harsher, more persistent, and new higher taxes were being imposed, making them almost impossible to pay. Still, they listened before stiffly trudging off to their homes.

"Good speech," said Lev as they walked toward their houses.

"But?" Oleksander noted the skepticism in his voice.

Lev sighed. "I fear that the die is cast. We're about to be swallowed up and those who survive regurgitated onto that damn collective farm."

"We have no alternative but to resist as peacefully as we can and wait for this stupidity to straighten itself out."

"But that's the essence of stupidity." Lev gave a sad smile. "It's not in its nature to straighten itself out."

"You're most certainly right, but we have no alternative but to keep the faith — and hope."

"The first test is coming soon," said Lev as they parted ways. "As I mentioned, the compulsory meeting at church is not only with our imposed local Soviet council chairman but also with a gaggle of commissars who may even be worse than Belynski and Fedryk. That's what the notice — advertisement tells me anyway."

CHAPTER NINE

Bila Sich

"There you are," said Lev to Vlas as he came alongside him and Oleksander, Tomash, and others gathering on the steps of the former church turned Communist Party local community hall. It was a crisp late January morning, thankfully not too cold.

"No other place to go." Vlas smirked. "They made sure of that!"

Indeed, where would one go? pondered Oleksander as he surveyed the scene. The authorities were definitely tightening their grip on Bila Sich. Sentries guarded the main road in and out of the village, and those travelling were stopped and questioned. According to one resident he'd talked to, they demanded the reasons for leaving and the destination. "And if they didn't believe you or the questioner was in a foul mood," the man related, "you'd be marched to a more intense interrogation with a nastier interrogator in a more secluded place. Wise to avoid that…"

Oleksander worried that he would now be stuck in Bila Sich for a long time, until events resolved one way or another. This meant that he'd be away from his work, his apartment, and life in Kyiv. Fortunately, he had taken a couple months' leave, and the apartment was paid for until the end of March. Also, he had brought enough rubles with him to purchase necessary supplies — such as they were. Food, personal wares from boots to underwear and bedding, along with goods like tobacco and tea, household items like oil, washtub, even matches were dwindling in what used to be the co-op store now run by the state. Nevertheless, it seemed that if one flashed hard currency, the items requested would magically appear for purchase.

However, Oleksander would run out of funds soon enough, and he had no contingency plans to get back to Kyiv and obtain additional resources stashed in his apartment for emergencies or his meagre savings in the bank. It was just a matter of time before he too would feel the pinch. Moreover, as each day passed, he had a growing anxiety that his job at the institute would no longer exist and that he'd be rooted to the village to fight for his own as well as the village's survival. His *hope* speech to the fellows at the meeting was truly more a fervent prayer than an unshakable conviction.

And, of course, Katya was stuck as well. Making the best of it, from what he could gather. He toyed with the idea of somehow getting her on a train back to Kyiv and his apartment. She would be safe and much more comfortable, he presumed, but, putting the trust issue aside (although he was sure he could), the whole idea was becoming moot. One couldn't just walk or drive out of the village without going through check points, although he was confident that Lev would have escape routes through fields and along tree lines if absolutely necessary.

If the truth be told, he and Katya had settled into an amicable routine under very basic but manageable conditions. Any lingering reservations about a relationship were answered quite unexpectedly one night. It was a particularly cold evening, and she suggested that perhaps he'd be warmer sleeping nearer to the stove. Any hesitancy was peeled away layer by layer, and he happily succumbed to Katya's invitation. He hadn't enjoyed that kind of raw intimacy since his dalliance with a colleague at the institute. Unfortunately, she suddenly disappeared, becoming *persona non grata*. He had heard about such occurrences whispered around academic circles, but this was direct and quite shocking. No information had been forthcoming for her sudden removal, and he was out of clues. His tepid inquiries were dismissed with a warning: don't ask any more questions or you too may disappear. This was over nine months ago.

He didn't fool himself into believing that Katya (a.k.a. Oxana, he had to remember, along with Lev, Nina, and Misha) had any deep feelings for him, but perhaps in time, if there was a future... For now, this was an arrangement of necessity and a union of convenience. For her part, Katya proved quite adept and independent. She visited Nina and ventured out with some of Nina's friends, and, in fact, did most of the household shopping in the state store. There was little danger that she'd be recognized, he figured, and besides, she wasn't the type to sit contentedly like an old babushka in the small house day in and day out while he went about his clandestine business.

Oleksander came out of his thoughts when Lev nudged him forward and to his left. A small crowd had formed at the bottom of the church stairs — the inevitable overflow standing at a preferred spot, awaiting the start of the dreaded meeting. Whether they wanted to be there didn't matter, nor if they heard what was said or not. They were summoned, and refusing was not an option — at least not without consequences if informed on. And as Oleksander was coming to realize, there were many potential informers, quite possibly even someone in Lev's inner circle for all he knew. Still, coming when ordered was part of the passive survival strategy he had advocated. An integral part of buying time.

Inside the church, a raised platform had replaced the altar. Makar Belynski, chairman of the Bila Sich Soviet Council, made his way up the three squeaking steps to the podium and tinny loudspeaker. It screeched when he got close before adjustments were made. He proceeded to introduce Commissar Fedryk and two other commissars no one had seen before. The tightly packed crowd was informed that they all had important announcements. They were reminded that Fedryk was the party's oblast organizer, responsible for the smooth operations and success of the propaganda brigades whose job it was to persuade the farmers to collectivize. The second guest on the stage was the commissar of the local OGPU in charge of security. The third was the commissar of the Machine Tractor Station (MTS), whose task was to ensure that the kolkhoz was sufficiently mechanized and worked efficiently.

After he made the introductions, Belynski rambled on about the glories of the revolution and the strides made to date under the guiding hand of Comrade Stalin.

"Poor fellow," Lev said mockingly. A small group of men were now standing in their usual spots off to the side of the church steps (in fact, it was intrinsically understood that since every villager had to come, women and any attached children as well as old men stood inside where it was warmer and away from the wind and snow).

"Why would you say that?" asked Vlas, missing Lev's sarcastic tone.

"He's a pawn — probably has no choice. They made him the village council chairman, which is akin to being the goat for anything that goes wrong."

"He certainly defers to Fedryk… Seems tethered to him like … a goat!" Vlas laughed.

"What do you think, Oleksander?" asked Lev.

"Don't know anything about him or the others, but he's more than the party's useful village goat and the one we need to watch, I think."

"I suppose," said Vlas. "He does have that gun stuck in his belt."

"An interesting assessment," said Lev, "based on?"

"Nothing in particular, but he's the key person we'll be dealing with, I think, since the others have more remote duties and will come and go," observed Oleksander.

"Well, I heard that he's a nasty piece of work. Used to be a high apparatchik in Kyiv or some other big city before he was demoted," said Vlas.

"Where'd you hear that?" asked Tomash, who had sidled over and joined the conversation.

"Overheard some militiamen talking in the pub. They heard rumours."

"What kind of rumours?" pressed Tomash.

"For one thing, that he's a lady's man apparently, and not too particular about whose husband the lady may be attached to."

"Ouch."

"Yeah. Had to leave wherever he was last or have his nuts rung. Ends up being in charge here — go figure," said Vlas.

"Well, that might explain why he's not as high up the ladder in authority as he would like or been accustomed to then, I would venture," said Lev.

"Should have kept it in his pants then," snorted Vlas.

"Regardless, he's the one we have to deal with and buy time from," said Oleksander. "For now, we remain silent, listen or pretend to, nod when appropriate or when watched, and praise as much as our stomachs can stand. It's a question of how far he'll let us play the game…"

***

Lev, Vlas, Tomash, and others of their group had heard variations of the same speeches before. Fedryk quoted Lenin and described how miserable the farmers were, how they had been ruthlessly exploited but now happy days were coming — their miserable existence about to end thanks to the party. "You are privileged." His nasal voice rose harshly through the loudspeaker. "Your yoke of oppression is about to be thrown off! You are in the frontline to join the collective farm and throw off the capitalistic kurkuls."

"I didn't know we were being oppressed," Tomash announced. "And who exactly are these kurkuls again?"

"I believe he may be referring to some of us. We've become objects of some debate," Oleksander said, thinking of the bizarre conversation he had overheard at the train station.

"They are our enemies," Fedryk droned on. "They must be destroyed as a class — eradicated along with their families and supporters. We cannot allow vermin to flourish…"

"Last time I checked, I didn't see any kurkuls around here," someone muttered from a group huddled around, smoking.

"Be careful not to become one. It's a long, cold train ride to 'kurkul land' in Siberia," someone responded.

"Seriously," Lev turned to Oleksander, "what I am worried about is where all this is going to take us if we don't join their stupid collective farm, what will happen to us and our families?" And that was the rub. How long could they keep talking and simply ignoring what these blockheads said before they would all become the "enemies of the people"?

To that, Oleksander had no answer.

Amid forced and scattered applause, Fedryk took his seat, immediately to be followed by the local OGPU commissar, a short man with a large head, small, squinting eyes and a pointed chin accented by a nicely trimmed goatee. Not the sort of figure to head the security services, but he did have an erect posture as behooves a military man.

His message was thankfully brief and blunt: resistance would not be tolerated, nor would being sympathetic to the kulaks (he used the Russian designation) and their families. Disobedience of any kind to party directives, he took great pains to underline, would not be allowed, and those who did were doomed to suffer the same fate as the kulaks.

"More long trains rides to Siberia, I imagine." Tomash chuckled humourlessly.

"Or worse," Vlas amended.

Finally, after standing for over an hour, getting progressively colder with no opportunity to wander off thanks to the patrolling militiamen, the last speaker, Comrade Molot, rose. He was commissar of the local MTS. A thin, undernourished fellow, even in his grey Napoleon coat, he repeated the same message with more vulgarity than the speakers before him, railing against the kurkuls (back to the Ukrainian again) and imploring the assemblage to join the kolkhoz, where they would be well taken care of. Thankfully, lengthy verbosity was not his strong suit. "Success," he shouted in an inspired moment, it seemed, "is measured in grain and can only be delivered in sufficient amounts from farmers who collectivize. You will be well looked after," he repeated, "and receive what is owed you."

"Each according to his need," muttered Lev disgustedly, "which means an insecure and miserable life!"

Inside, the proceedings were suddenly interrupted by the shriek of a woman who rushed toward the platform. "Oh no, we won't!" she yelled. "Your stupid kolkhoz has stolen our cow! How can I feed my children without milk?"

Commissar Molot stepped back from the loudspeaker, surprised and chagrined. Recovering, he nodded to a couple of militiamen, who moved toward her, ready to take harsh measures, no doubt, against what clearly was a bourgeois humanitarian outburst that had no place in the socialist lexicon.

***

Contrary, perhaps, to what Fedryk and so many others thought of him, Makar Belynski was a fairly astute observer of human nature, and here was a situation that could escalate to a violent, uncontrollable confrontation if the militiamen decided to take it too far against a distraught mother. He did not want the spectacle of these party brutes manhandling the woman — not that it was unacceptable in principle, but to do so at this particular meeting would not only be bad form but counterproductive to his whole plan to convince the majority of these peasants to join the collective farm and dealing with the agitators/resistors as kurkuls. Besides, he had just read an alarming report from another village farther south of a *babski bunty*, a women's rebellion. There was nothing more potentially disruptive to plans for the village and surrounding countryside than to have women taking up knives, farm tools, household chattels of all kinds, and attack as a mob. No one would benefit from a massacre, not to mention that it would stiffen the spines of the men, who could inflict much greater damage and chaos if fully infuriated. Getting quickly to his feet, he made his way down the platform steps, stopping in front of the militiamen. "Give me a moment," he said quietly.

The distressed woman was still letting everyone know of her anger. "I'll slaughter the rest of the animals and burn the house down before I let you pigs take away all that we own…" For a brief moment, Belynski wondered where her husband was and if he was privy to this display of defiance … but to the immediate matter at hand.

Time to be diplomatic. Taking a glance at Fedryk and the other commissars, who now stood riveted in a state between stupor and outrage, Belynski approached the agitated hag. *She is ugly*, he thought, *from her distorted face and mouth spewing out spittle to her rail-thin form over which hangs a shabby coat like a drab drape.* However, he didn't address her; instead, in amongst the crowd of mostly women and their fidgeting children, his eyes spotted and focused on a particularly arresting woman who, by her demeanour and bearing, was not a typical village female waiting to become a babushka. Moreover, he had a vague sense that he had met or at least had seen her before, somewhere grander than this rustic village. He made an impulsive decision.

"Comrade madame," he addressed her thus because no better greeting came to mind, "this woman is distraught; I would appreciate it if you and the other ladies here could help calm her before harm becomes her. I will look into her ... missing cow." He added this as an afterthought.

Katya noted in surprise that he was speaking to her. Before she could formulate a response, he turned and faced the taut, agitated woman. "You are distressed, I understand, but this only aggravates the situation." He nodded to Katya, who had no choice but to come forward and console the protester. Fortunately, Nina, who had accompanied her to the meeting, was by her side, along with a couple of others. Nina took matters in hand, quietly steering the woman away from the podium: "Panyi Markovna, please come with us. We'll help you. Let's go and find Stephan, he's outside..."

With the impact of a suddenly deflated balloon, the woman's fury collapsed, replaced by abject despair as she was led away.

The meeting was over. Fedryk, with a scowl on his face, confronted Belynski on his way out. "What a farce!" he hissed. "You let rotten liberal sentimentality get in the way of socialist resolve. She should have been hauled away, made an example of." *And yet you didn't intervene*, Belynski thought, wondering why as he watched the back of Fedryk's narrow head receding out the church door with the other two commissars and militiamen escorts. *Snivelling little coward!* Although God was no longer in vogue, Belynski thanked Him, relieved that Fedryk would soon be leaving Bila Sich to attend to his other regional duties. For almost a month he had put up with the man. *With any luck, his duties will take him to the far end of the oblast, where he will fall into a swamp and be adopted by a family of lizards!*

Belynski lingered while people dispersed; he wanted to know who that striking woman was. There was a visceral physicality about her that had immediately drawn his attention. Certainly, she had a familiar face he had seen before. Exiting the church, he let his eyes cast over receding groups of people and spied her in the distance. He picked up his pace toward her and some individuals milling about in the vicinity. They quickly dispersed, except for a lanky fellow who also appeared a village misfit, with a city air about him, Belynski decided, like those young (for the most part) activists the party brought in from the cities to convince the village people of the socialist paradise that awaited them after they joined the kolkhoz. He wondered how many of these were true socialist cadres, as opposed to those who were there for the 120-ruble stipend per month that was promised to them. On the other hand, he concluded that it hardly mattered. He took a quick glance behind him to see the ever-present Prasha and a militiaman closing the distance. *For my welfare to keep track of me?*

He smiled at Katya. "I wish to thank you for your help," he said with a slight bow. "It would have turned out badly for that unfortunate woman otherwise."

Katya gave a feeble smile in return. "Glad to have helped."

When no further words came from her or the man beside her, Belynski pushed on. "You have the advantage of me. Undoubtedly, you know my name, but I don't know yours?" He looked from Katya to Oleksander, his face blank, his smile frozen.

"Oxana — Oxana Gerkil."

"I'm most pleased to formally meet you … and yours, Comrade?" he turned to Oleksander.

"Pylyp … Oleksander Pylyp,"

Prasha and the militiaman now stood directly behind the chairman of the Bila Sich Soviet Council, awaiting instructions, it seemed.

"Pleased as well… I haven't seen either of you here before. Why is that?"

"We're fairly new arrivals, my fiancée and I," Oleksander explained, knowing that they had just aroused unwelcomed interest and that it was time to be pleasant but obtuse and hope that Belynski went away satisfied with any suspicions placated, if not totally alleviated.

"Oh? Where from?"

"Kyiv."

"Ah ... and your business here?" Belynski was starting to sound like an interrogator. There was no point in fabricating a web of lies to entangle themselves.

"I'm originally from here."

"Pylyp... Yes, I recall seeing the name on the land registry."

"Yes, I lease to my brother-in-law."

"And you're here for a visit?"

"Yes, that is correct."

"What do you do in Kyiv, if I may ask?"

"I'm an agronomist at the Kyiv Agricultural Institute."

"How interesting... Just the kind of expertise we need around here," Belynski said, his smile lingering like a bad odour. He turned to Katya, appraising her from head to foot. "Have we met before? I feel as if we did."

"No, I don't believe so."

This was said a little too quickly from his perspective. "Are you from Kyiv as well?"

"Yes."

"Forgive me, Comrade Belynski," Oleksander interceded. "If you don't mind, it is a cold day, and Oxana and I need to go home, warm up, and do a number of chores."

There was a palatable pause, and for a moment Oleksander thought that Belynski would, with the help of his armed minions, insist that they answer his questions and/or be accompanied elsewhere for a more thorough chat. However, Belynski relented. "Yes, of course," he said, "I totally understand. It's getting colder, and these meetings, while important, do tend to be lengthy."

As Oleksander and Katya walked away, Belynski turned to Prasha and gave instructions. "See how much the Pylyp family have in landholdings. And contact the Kyiv Agricultural Institute ... agronomist, eh? See what you can find out about him... Oh, and see what information can be found on Oxana Gerkil, also from Kyiv."

CHAPTER TEN

Kyiv

Emil Krypniuk was sitting at his desk, brow furrowed in troubled thoughts, when Lubick knocked on his door, rattling the pane of glass before entering.

"Let's go for a walk," Krypniuk suggested before his sergeant could open his mouth. "I could use some fresh air."

Without a word, Lubick turned and marched out. It was a cold day, but the sun was out as they strolled down Khreschatyk Street at a moderate pace, huddled in their heavy coats. Few pedestrians were about, but those who were, moved with reluctant deliberation; they had somewhere they had to go but weren't particularly keen to actually get there.

"You think our office has listening devices?" Lubick asked without preamble.

"Don't know, but I wouldn't rule it out. I've had suspicions since my encounter with Commissar Pavlick a few days ago. And as of yesterday, Colonel Ezhovin has shown a decided disinterest in knowing about the progress we're making to date in the case. I'm pretty sure our esteemed chief of police has been warned off. Meanwhile, our new boss wants results and is becoming impatient..." Krypniuk trailed off as an old woman shuffled by them on the snowy sidewalk, followed by a young couple, their pace brisk against the slight breeze that occasionally picked up between the buildings.

"I'm surprised that the OGPU is letting us handle the investigation at all with a dead commissar and missing state funds involved," Lubick said.

"Pavlick could just be going through the motions, but having our chief disassociate himself from an active criminal case gives me a bad feeling. Something is at play that I can't quite get a handle on."

"Anytime the OGPU is involved is not good news," agreed Lubick, his reindeer cap now pulled over the ears, his hands buried deep in his coat pockets.

"Certainly, we're not getting the full picture. The OGPU is not in the habit of relinquishing control over city corruption and murder involving a senior apparatchik."

"So, what is their game?"

"A most intriguing question, Nickolay..." Krypniuk thought for a moment. "Perhaps, make us do the work; if we succeed, Pavlick takes the credit. If we fail...," Krypniuk shrugged, "it's another nail in our coffin. We'll become the scapegoats, and the OGPU will have another example of why they need to take over all the police functions in the city. That's why Ezhovin wants nothing to do with us or this case. Covering his bases ... just in case. Of course, it may go deeper than that. I can't believe that Pavlick doesn't know or at least doesn't have a pretty good idea of who took the money, where it went, and even who murdered Gromeko. He wants us to do the legwork and extract a confession, although the OGPU could do that as well in much shorter, more efficient time, given the methods they use."

"Could be part of the problem in itself. Under duress, who knows if the suspect's confession is true?" Lubick suggested, grimacing.

"A point taken... Regardless, Pavlick has an eye on us. It would be a serious breach of standard OGPU practice if he didn't."

"So, what do we do?"

"Don't have much choice at the moment but to complete our investigation."

"You mean solve the case." Lubick gave his captain a sideways glance.

"If it is solvable."

And therein lay the rub. Thus far, they had done their due diligence. The key appeared to be the missing sekrehita. However, while photographs of Katya Kharsova had been reproduced from her file and posted strategically throughout the city, there was no sign of her. The search was then expanded thanks to an observant clerk at the railway station who recognized the photo. It was ascertained that Katya had bought a ticket for Shervobne. Local authorities were notified, but it seemed that she never arrived in her hometown. Photographs were sent to all the railway stations along the line. Local Soviet council chairmen in towns and villages within fifty kilometres of the railway stations also received dispatches. The communiqué was brief: Kharsova was a person of interest in the death of a senior government official in Kyiv. Any information on her whereabouts was to be sent to Captain Emil Krypniuk, Police, Criminal Investigation Department, Kyiv. Someone must have seen her, must know where she was hiding. And yet she had not been found.

"So, how do we proceed?" asked Lubick.

"First, we go back inside. Get out of this fucking cold. Then, we pay another visit to Commissar Sholtz," replied Krypniuk, turning around and pulling up his collar against a funnel of wind. "As I see it, he's the other person of interest in this whole affair. I want to make him nervous."

"How?"

"Drop a few hints; see if he reacts."

***

"Our homicide investigation has expanded to include bribery and corruption involving large sums of state funds as a possible motive," Krypniuk informed Sholtz as he and Lubick settled into the chairs they had occupied during their previous visit. He was extrapolating from what little real information Pavlick had provided him, but it was a thread that might entangle Sholtz, make him tip his hand. However, the commissar of Procurement and Labour maintained an implacably stoic face, sitting rigidly behind his desk as he took in Krypniuk's narrative. Still, was it his imagination, or did Sholtz seem to shrink into his seat as he talked?

"I–I don't quite understand, Captain Krypniuk. Bribery? Corruption?"

"Evidently, there were … significant accounting irregularities and misplaced or missing money in the Commerce and Industry Department, and since you previously stated that *you and your department*, Krypniuk emphasized, "worked glove in hand on projects … well, you can see where we're coming from, how it all looks, and the kind of conclusions it leads to from our perspective. So," Krypniuk put his hands on the arms of the chair and raised his voice, "what do you know about Commissar Gromeko's side activities, shall we say, and alleged crimes?"

"Nothing. I mean, this is news to me!" Sholtz declared in alarm, his eyes darting from Krypniuk to Lubick and back again. "I thought you were looking at a suspect — Katya Kharsova — the one who disappeared!"

"True," Krypniuk acknowledged, "but what would be the motive?"

"I… From what I heard around the commissariat offices, she was his mistress, and since he was found dead in her apartment — lovers falling out?"

"We'll ask her when she becomes available."

"So, you haven't found her?"

"No … not yet, but we will," he added in a practised tone of certainty. "Back to the money motive. An intriguing avenue of investigation and makes at least as much sense as a lovers quarrel gone wrong. Would you not agree, Commissar Sholtz?'

"I wouldn't know," Sholtz snapped. "As I said, this is the first that I've heard of any financial improprieties or theft." He shifted uncomfortably in his chair, his fingers toying nervously with a pen. "Where did these … allegations of corruption come from, if I may ask?"

Perfect, thought Krypniuk. Inadvertently, Sholtz had provided the segue he wanted to put an added dollop of fear into the commissar of Procurement and Labour, whether he proved to be guilty or not. "The OGPU, actually. They too have taken an interest in this criminal investigation."

Again, to his credit, Sholtz remained impassive, his expression unchanged, although, Krypniuk noticed, he stopped twirling his pen, setting it down and clasping his hands together on top of the desk as if to control any shaking. After a pause he said, "I assure you that neither I nor my office know of any financial irregularities."

"Yet, you mentioned that the departments work together. You even have a key to the late commissar's office."

"Yes. I explained that."

Lubick flipped a couple of pages in his notebook and read aloud, "Commissar Gromeko and I have intertwined responsibilities that involved building projects, contracts, and the like. Quote, unquote. That is what you said."

"Yes, but if there were any shady deals, I certainly was not aware of it. We worked together of necessity to enhance the city's housing projects. These are badly needed. As you know, there's a housing crisis looming, and more and more are coming in from the countryside."

"Hmm …yes. How many contracts have you and Commissar Gromeko jointly worked on?"

"I'd have to look that up. Maybe half a dozen."

"Well, I'd have them on hand when the OGPU come asking." Krypniuk produced a patently insincere smile while Lubick sat back in his seat and snapped his notebook closed.

***

For almost an hour after Krypniuk and his pencil-pushing partner left, Sholtz remained rooted to his chair. His mind was like a scratched record stuck on one refrain: *What to do? What to do?* Now, he'd be looking over his shoulder not only for the Kyiv police but also for the more ominous OGPU.

He cursed his judgement, or at least the unforeseen consequences of scheming with Gromeko. The late commissar had a smooth, well-oiled brain; between the inflated contracts, building permit bribes, and suppliers who provided construction materials (of dubious quality from black market sources, if the truth be known), they had done extremely well, developing a network of apparatchiks and political fixers who kept their "business" away from "official" (those who were not on the take) purview. Had to give Gromeko credit; he was a master of fudging the accounts. And therein lay the rub. Gromeko was ripping off not only the "official" state but their "business" as well to the tune of thousands of rubles. In essence, the commissar of Commerce and Industry was making side deals and overcooking the already overcooked books. Sholtz had discovered the game within the game Gromeko was playing when one of the new contractors complained about the extra licencing and servicing costs he was obliged to pay. With the help of a trusted accountant in his own department, it didn't take long to figure out the extent to which Gromeko was double-dipping the "business," never mind the "official" state! Moreover, he did it in such a way that if he were ever discovered, Sholtz and a whole cadre of others would be implicated! *No wonder he was so smug when confronted*, Sholtz surmised in retrospect.

For Sholtz, it was time to have it out with Gromeko. The *I know what you have been up to* and *we need to meet* message was duly delivered and a meeting arranged — in his mistress's apartment as it turned out. Sholtz had no intention of resorting to violence; the business was too lucrative, and surely Gromeko would relent, see the error of his ways, and make suitable restitution to him and possibly others who were bound to figure out Gromeko's creative bookkeeping. He brought his Nagant along (acquired in the service of the Red Army) only to convince his double-dealing comrade to take their discussion seriously.

The dumbass had laughed at him, told him to be happy with his share of the "take," and let him run the "business." In fact, Gromeko had implied that if Sholtz didn't leave it alone, there might be unfortunate repercussions for him! After the threat, Sholtz lost his focus; things got out of hand, a struggle ensued, and, well, he shot the bastard. In his heart of hearts, he wasn't sorry, but there were consequences he was just now beginning to realize. First, Gromeko's death had quickly dried up the network of contractors, suppliers, middlemen, and apparatchik enablers, as it became riskier to pilfer the state's resources given the severe penalties. As a result, they suddenly went dark, shutting down their particular activities. Which, secondly, left Sholtz holding the bag if the full extent of the "business" ever came out. *All the rats will scurry into their sewers, leaving the big rat exposed.* He laughed bitterly. In fact, he could be a dead man walking, targeted not only by the official state but also his clandestine business partners.

What to do indeed. The biggest loose end was Katya Kharsova. He had toyed with the idea that if he could talk to her before the authorities did, an arrangement could perhaps be made. However, he dismissed the idea; rapprochement was not possible. He simply couldn't take the chance. She was a witness, someone who could seal his fate. He needed to deal with her permanently, which meant finding her before Krypniuk or the OGPU. His only advantage was that he was willing to offer a large sum of money for information on her whereabouts and ultimate elimination.

CHAPTER ELEVEN

Bila Sich

As the days turned into weeks, Belynski became increasingly frantic. The persuasion campaigns were not working; villagers were not joining the collective farms. This despite the brigades sent through the countryside. They knocked on doors, harangued, cajoled, pleaded, and ultimately threatened. Still, they were falling behind. Even the compulsory meetings had become as tiresome to the presenters as to the brooding audience. More to the point, he was receiving nasty epistles from Fedryk demanding results. Why was he not attaining his targets? Why was he not chasing down the kulaks? Why was he not fulfilling the plan in general?

Meanwhile, he learned from numerous snitches about secret gatherings and potential organized resistance. He was a patient man, a diplomat at heart, but this could not be tolerated much longer. More than one informant mentioned two names, according to Prasha, who was in charge of information collection: Lev Devchenko, who had some elevated standing (apparently) in the community, although he held no formal position in the village; and the newcomer from Kyiv who had a local connection, including 7.5 hectares of land. Significantly, Belynski recalled from his conversation on the church grounds, Pylyp was Devchenko's brother-in-law.

Still, of the two, Belynski found Pylyp the more interesting and the one he decided to concentrate on for the time being. He was, after all, an agronomist from the Kyiv Agricultural Institute, and if he could be co-opted to the idea of joining the kolkhoz, he would bring a good number of these stubborn, wayward peasant farmers with him.

He'd start with a conversation, offering a carrot or two, and if that didn't work, he'd progressively squeeze him. Bottom line: Pylyp needed to sign his land over to the state.

Related to Belynski's focus on the agronomist was his fiancée, Oxana Gerkil. He couldn't get her out of his mind, not only because he was smitten (if he were honest), but also he was positive he'd seen her somewhere before in a setting far from the grubbiness of Bila Sich. But where?

Probably should stop drinking, he admonished himself. *It hurts the brain.* He had always been overindulgent; however, since his arrival at the village, he'd succumbed to nightly drinking bouts. It helped him with insomnia, he told himself, but in truth it continued to escalate unabated, in part from the stress of putting up with Fedryk — an absolute idiot — and the growing knowledge that the goals to be achieved were unachievable in any sane way and that disaster was sure to follow for everyone, him included.

Night after night, Belynski had drunk himself into a stupor. He was in a morose state with no way out, at least no way to advance upward, stuck in a place that was sucking his soul into a black morass while his immediate superior was writing poison-pen dispatches about his incompetence. If he didn't make some bold moves to improve his situation, he was doomed. As it was, he existed on a knife's edge, a precipice, with Fedryk eager to shove him over when the right moment appeared. He was the chosen scapegoat who would be made to fall on his sword when the reckoning came, as it surely would.

"Comrade Prasha," he called one night, finally finding resolve through the fog of vodka.

His secretary appeared at the door to his quarters, originally the deported local merchant's accounting room. "Come in, Ivan." He beckoned him toward his desk littered with useless reports and statistics that lied, as far as he was concerned. True, he had begun his drinking ritual: however, he was still clear-headed enough. Putting down the report he had been perusing, he addressed his chief of staff: "I'd like to invite that agronomist I asked you to look into, Oleksander Pylyp, for a chat."

"He's what he says he is—" Prasha started to remind Belynski but was cut off.

"Yes, yes, no doubt," he blurted with a trace of slurred annoyance in his tone. "I'd like to invite him," he repeated, "to a meeting at the party office. And," he raised his right index finger to make his point, "be polite; I don't want a couple of militiamen manhandling and marching him over. Not yet, anyway…"

***

"Glad you could come," said Belynski, directing Oleksander to a seat in the Soviet council chambers, which in former times was the old municipal village office. In either case, it was a drab place, with a low ceiling and poor lighting, not enhanced by the heavy blue paint on the walls. A large scarred wooden desk and a couple of chairs in front constituted the furniture. A filing cabinet against the wall directly behind the desk was all that suggested organized functionality. The actual walls were bleak, with whatever former pictures and artwork removed. There wasn't even a rendering of Lenin or Stalin hanging, which Oleksander believed were almost obligatory in Soviet offices.

Actually, didn't have a choice, did I? thought Oleksander.

Belynski's representative, a diminutive officious fellow with a notebook, had banged on his door and hand-delivered the invitation with two OGPU goons at his side. "I'm presuming I haven't been summoned for a social call?" he asked wryly.

Belynski smiled, appreciating Oleksander's levity. "No, but I can offer you a drink." He noticed the agronomist eyeing the bottle of vodka and glass on the desk amid scattered papers.

"Er … no, thank you."

"Suit yourself." Belynski shifted in his chair and focused on Oleksander with renewed interest.

From Oleksander's perspective, if Belynski had been drinking (and there was gossip about his drunkenness in the village), he was holding his alcohol well. Glazed eyes, slurred words, and lopsided facial expressions often gave away the intoxicated, but none of these signs were evident, despite the half-empty vodka bottle on the desk.

"You know," Belynski continued after a pause, "you're here because I've realized that success or failure in this village depends on people like you. I mean that sincerely. My job here is to persuade, convince the farmers and indeed the village of something that goes against their grain, something that they just don't want to do. Now, I can force them, but in a way that defeats the goal. Angry people do not make for successful, productive outcomes. Admittedly, we were a bit high-handed when we first arrived — deposing the village priest and other locals; however, that was not my decision, just so you know, but Commissar Fedryk's—"

"What happened to Father Parayma?"

"To be honest, I rightly don't know. Fedryk had him whisked away."

Oleksander sighed inwardly; this was not what he wanted to hear. But to the matter at hand. *Will I too be whisked away?* He had been anticipating some sort of confrontation ever since their encounter outside the church. "What do you want of me?"

"Ah ... down to business, is it?" Belynski seemed to gather himself, laying his hands on the desk and leaning forward. "Very simple. I want you to join the kolkhoz and convince your farming and village friends to follow you. Convince them that it is their best course of action and that their future prosperity as a collective community will be assured. The kolkhoz could use an agronomist like you. There would be considerations ... rewards."

"I see... You want me to approve of what is being done here and elsewhere throughout the countryside, even if I think it's wrong?"

"Whether it's right or wrong is not the issue here — only your compliance."

"And if I don't?"

Belynski shook his head as if in sad reflection. "The consequences will be dire for you, your relatives, your fiancée, and, ironically enough, for me if I don't deliver on what I'm tasked to do... By the way, how is Oxana enjoying her visit here?"

The sudden change of topic threw Oleksander off kilter for a moment. "Oxana is fine," was all he could manage.

"You met her in Kyiv, I take it?"

"Yes."

Belynski nodded as if remembering a pleasant experience. "Love the city. Civilized, you know. I suppose it's all that history and culture." As he spoke, he pulled out a pipe and pouch from the desk drawer, opened the pouch, and took out small pinches of tobacco, stuffing and tamping each firmly into the bowl. With a practised hand, he produced a match from the same drawer, striking it against the roughened edge of the drawer and lighting in one motion. "An old comrade once said to me that a woman is just a woman, but a pipe is a good smoke. Not sure that I believe that. What do you think?"

"I don't smoke."

"Ah ... a man with few vices. Refuses a drink and doesn't smoke... Very well. I've met your fiancée somewhere before. Been racking my brain where... Must have been Kyiv, don't you think?"

"I–I wouldn't know."

"Ach, no matter." Belynski took a couple more pulls on the pipe, allowing the curling, blue-tinged cloud to dissipate before returning to the business at hand. "Soon, you will be summoned to our court and records office, where you will be asked to sign a document that releases your landholdings to the Bila Sich Kolkhoz. Ultimately, that is your and the villagers' only choice. So, think very carefully about the consequences. In the meantime, spread the word — voluntary sign-up is the least painful choice. I will see you in the people's court soon. I'm sure that given the circumstances you'll make the right decision. Give my regards to Oxana and thank her again for me."

***

"Belynski is putting the pressure on." Oleksander told Katya that night. "He's feeling it from those above him so..." he spread his hands, "I had hoped it wouldn't have come to such a direct confrontation."

"What will you do?"

"Remain firm in my resolve. There's not much choice in the matter."

"But won't they arrest you — deport you?" Katya said anxiously. They were in his home, drinking tea after supper, Oleksander keeping his tone casual as he answered her questions.

"We're not there yet," he assured her. "I still have to appear before the local Soviet council court or whatever Belynski calls it."

"When is that?"

"I don't know."

"Surely, you won't be deported?" she repeated her concern.

"We must be prepared," he said stoically. "I'll go talk to Lev, tell him what happened. You are in danger as well. He again said he recognized you but couldn't recall where. Do you remember encountering him before — at the commissariat in Kyiv, perhaps?"

Katya frowned, thinking. She had attended meetings and a number of receptions with Kreil Gromeko, who liked to show her off; so it was possible that if Belynski travelled in those circles, he might have seen them together. But she simply could not be sure. He certainly scrutinized her in the churchyard to the point of lechery, but she was accustomed to such attention. "No, not that I can recall. I'd remember if I had actually spoken to him, I think."

"Anyway, just to be prepared, we must make a contingency plan for what may happen." Oleksander rose from his chair and snatched up his worn satchel from beneath the bench along the wall. Unstrapping it and reaching in, he produced a silver key with a square head. "To my apartment. It's still paid up to the end of March. Take it. If it becomes necessary, you can go there. You and I have no connection in Kyiv, and I have some funds hidden in the place... Of course, you'll have to avoid your former colleagues; however, it may be safer for you in Kyiv than here..." He trailed off.

"I'm not going anywhere," she said firmly.

"You may have little choice. For now, it's just a contingency plan which," he continued, thinking aloud, "if it comes about, will depend on Lev finding a way to get you out of Bila Sich and to the Korsun Railway Station."

***

"So, Comrade Pylyp, why have you not yet joined the kolkhoz?"

Oleksander stood before the so-called Soviet court with Makar Belynski presiding. The chairman of the Soviet local council sat behind a long wooden table, shuffling some papers before him. A young man, probably a university student or Komsomol recruit, sat beside him, pen and ledger in hand, no doubt the note keeper and recorder.

Oleksander remained mute. *Control yourself and think*, he told himself. Whatever else, he knew that he wasn't going to sign. It was his land bequeathed to him by his father as part of his inheritance, and although he was not exactly a farmer, this was his village, where generations of Pylyps had lived, worked, and died. He wasn't going to give up his birthright to the state and allow his land and house to be appropriated.

"Well? Say something." Belynski leaned forward, elbows on the table. "Do you need a militiaman to loosen your tongue along with your teeth?" He gave a small chortle at his witticism.

This was a different Belynski, somehow transformed from the last time Oleksander saw him a few days ago. He had become the stern judge, the communist autocrat, more vulgar in language and actions. The eyes were glazed and the speech slightly slurred. *Alcohol.*

"I need more time," Oleksander said quietly, straightening his lean posture a little. A note of defiance crept into his voice. He had hoped to avoid being summoned before this hastily set-up court — at least for a little while longer — but such was not the case, and now he had to make the best of it. Katya had wanted to come with him, but he said no; best he appear alone. There was always a chance, he reminded her, that someone might still recognize her or that Belynski suddenly remembered.

"More time? Only enemies of the people are opposed to collectivization."

"I didn't say I was opposed. I just need more time."

"Why is that? What could possibly be your objections?"

"This is a voluntary process, is it not?" His tone was sharp, clear.

The question caught Belynski off guard. *Cheeky bastard!* Belynski shifted in his seat and said, "I have a pen and the documents. I suggest that you be a good volunteer and sign your name."

"As I said," Oleksander insisted, "I need more time to think about it."

Belynski sat back and pursed his lips. He could just declare him a kurkul, and that would be that. Of course, that could invite more resistance, defiance, and even rebellion. And the directives did strongly encourage these wayward peasants to join of their own volition, even if the definition of what that entailed had been stretched. It was somehow important to maintain the illusion of choice.

"Very well, Comrade Pylyp," Belynski stated in a formal voice, "today I feel … benevolent. Like a shepherd coaxing a straying lamb, a little patience is allowed — just a little. It is evident you need more persuasion, so you will meet with some of my comrades tonight who will have some questions for you. Tonight, nine o'clock at the grist mill. This is not an optional meeting subject to negotiations."

CHAPTER TWELVE

Bila Sich

It was a crisp late February evening with the snow deep but light. The grist mill, which Oleksander thought a strange place for a meeting, was almost three kilometres from his house. Regardless, he knew he had to show up.

"Do you have to go?" Katya had asked earlier that evening.

"Yes, I must go," he informed her. "It cannot be avoided. I can't say no, not without further peril and with what's going on in the village…" What choice did he have?

So, he trudged along the snow-covered paths, bundled against the cold to keep this dubious appointment. Otherwise, he was sure that Belynski with some militiamen in tow would appear at his door in the dead of the night.

With only the wintry light of the moon as his guide, he arrived at the mill, a towering structure with indistinct edges against the brooding sky of varying illumination dependent on the ever-moving cloud cover. To Oleksander, it was like an eerie impressionistic landscape painted in broad brushstrokes. As he approached, he was greeted by a surly militiaman, no doubt on duty.

"I have a meeting—"

"Wait here," he ordered before Oleksander could finish. He turned and disappeared inside.

About fifteen minutes later, he returned. "They will see you now."

Oleksander followed the bulky man through the mill entrance into a small makeshift room to the right. The functional mill lay well beyond. A crude wooden table and two seated men occupied the room, with dim kerosene lamps judiciously placed near them. Oleksander didn't know either. *Must be members of the propaganda brigade,* he assumed, possibly brought in from a neighbouring village. He glanced around into the pale hues of poor light around him but saw no one else waiting. *Not particularly encouraging...* For some moments he stood silent, appreciating the warmth, before one of the two men deigned to raise his head from some document in front of him, glaring intently with rheumy eyes and a puckered frown. It was an older, pugilistic face, as sour as bad kvass. The other was a bit younger, with pince-nez resting precariously on the bridge of his nose. Oleksander didn't distinguish much of his facial features because he was still looking down, sorting out some papers, most of his balding head reflecting the dancing shadows the lamps cast. He proved to be the one in charge.

"Citizen Pylyp, is it?" he finally spoke in a reedy voice, looking up. He had a pointed chin and a sharp, narrow nose on a narrow face.

"Yes."

"I trust you have had time to reconsider?"

Oleksander remained silent. He didn't know what to expect. Perhaps a discussion of the kolkhoz — what it could provide? Maybe some option ... choices. Not "have you reconsidered?"

"Well? Have you changed your mind?" the man persisted. "You can join the collective tonight."

"As I told Chairman Belynski, I need time to think on it."

Before Oleksander explained any further, Comrade Pince-Nez, as Oleksander labelled him, held up his hand. "And so you shall." He nodded. As if by some telepathic understanding, the militiaman standing at the back stepped forward. "Please take Comrade Pylyp to our waiting room, where he can think!"

"Yes, Comrade."

Before Oleksander could marshal further protest, he was escorted out of the room. Once outside, he was marched across the road to the sound of boots crunching to a shed. "In here," the militiaman ordered.

"But it's a tool shed!"

"No, it's the official waiting room." There was a sardonic tone to his voice. He opened the door. "Don't worry, they'll give you another opportunity to reconsider."

With that, the chunky militiaman opened the door. Nothing but darkness inside as Oleksander was gestured in and stumbled over some object directly ahead on the floor. At that moment, the door slammed shut and he heard a latch click into place. "You will be called when they are ready for you," the muffled voice declared. "Try not to freeze." This was followed by what Oleksander thought was a chortle.

"So, this is their form of persuasion. I guess they hope I'll cool off," he said to himself wryly. "Well, we'll see." He knew this would not be a pleasant experience, but he refused to be cowed — not yet. "I'll survive," he assured himself as he stomped his feet and beat his arms against the sides of his coat.

In just over an hour or so, Oleksander heard the latch and the shed door open. A new guard, shorter but portlier, gestured him out. "They will see you now," he said simply.

Stiff, with his cold toes burning and his breath escaping in curling puffs into the night air, he followed his keeper across the road, wondering if there were more scattered sheds at the mill that served as waiting rooms. He wouldn't doubt that.

Comrade Pince-Nez sat in the spot Oleksander had last seen him, but his companion had evidently been replaced by a younger apparatchik who stared at him as if entranced.

"So, Comrade Oleksander, I trust you have had sufficient time to reflect?"

Oleksander said nothing for a few seconds, then, "I will need more time to consider this." He could have said more — in protest or just as a political statement — but decided it didn't matter. He had said his piece, and they could do what they willed.

Comrade Pince-Nez sighed. "Chairman Belynski told me you were a hard case. Well, no matter..." He laid down his pen and glared at Pylyp. "You know what," he picked up his discarded pen and glanced at the man beside him. "Take note," he said, "Oleksander needs another appointment." Turning more directly to the agronomist, he said, "I summon you to another meeting tomorrow night — same time. Enjoy your walk home."

***

Makar Belynski was well into his nightly drinking binge when he decided to visit Pylyp's home. He hadn't intended to, but it became too irresistible. Pylyp was out on his second visit to the grist mill, leaving the enticing Oxana home and presumably alone. He had become obsessed with her; it was driving him crazy that he couldn't remember where he'd seen her before. Besides, he rationalized, the house and property's true value needed to be officially assessed. One never knew what wealth lay hidden in modest abodes. Thus, at a relatively late hour, he summoned Prasha to arrange a trip as expeditiously as he could. It took an hour before a sleigh and two members of the local Soviet council arrived to take him to his destination. It was not a long ride, and within a half hour they pulled up to the little house. One sat in the sleigh in charge of the horse while the other accompanied him to the dwelling. A dim light shone through the window, attesting that someone was inside. Belynski pounded on the door. "Open up!" he shouted.

"Who is it? What do you want?" a female voice replied through the door.

"Open up in the name of the people," Belynski ordered, his words slurred. The extra couple of vodka shots to warm him for the brisk evening ride were taking effect, augmenting his earlier intake. "Open up or we will break it down. Not to open is to defy the people's representative — enough reason to get you shot!"

There was silence on the other side of the door. Belynski tried a more conciliatory tack. "However, there is no need to go there. Help us and we will help you."

A moment later Katya (a.k.a. Oxana) opened the door. Belynski burst in, followed more timidly by a fur-capped comrade who stood silently at a distance while Belynski strolled about the modest living quarters, taking in the table, chairs, hearth, and numerous other chattels before settling his eyes on Katya. *Where, oh where, have I seen your face?*

"I know you from somewhere, I'm sure of it?" He tried to remain the composed gentleman, but it was difficult in his condition not to leer like a drunken sod. He sensed he was losing control.

"I don't think so… What is it that you and … your friend want?" She stole a glance at the other man, who seemed to have slouched away into a corner. His body language suggested that he was ill at ease and did not wish to be there.

"Hmm…" His eyes were still casting about, deciding how to answer. "I didn't notice in the darkness and the snow. Does this house have a tin roof?"

Katya looked at him puzzled. "I–I don't know… Why?"

"Ah … not everyone can afford a tin roof," he replied, smiling. "A sign of wealth. And how many hectares does your fiancé own?" He asked the question, although he already knew. It gave him time to engage, study her.

"I'm not sure," Katya replied honestly.

"And there is the matter of horses and a cow — certainly pigs and chickens…"

"We don't have any animals."

"Ah, but Comrade Pylyp's brother-in-law has. Neither Comrade Devchenko nor Comrade Pylyp have fulfilled grain quotas from last fall, according to the Grain Procurement Committee."

"I don't know anything about that. Take it up with them."

"It will be taken up soon enough, as part of kolkhoz affairs. Ah, well…" He let the matter drop.

"What is your business here? What do you want?" Katya repeated with an edge of both defiance and fear.

Belynski suddenly wasn't sure what he really wanted. He felt both woozy from the booze, and angry. Ever since he had been demoted to his position, he felt that he was losing his grip, that Fedryk pulled all the strings, and that the locals didn't take him seriously. They seemed to snicker whenever he turned his head. Why was that? He was the party's representative in this jurisdiction and needed to be taken seriously. "I'm ... me!" he blurted out, thumping is chest. "*I'm* the business here. Do you understand?"

He grabbed Katya's wrists and drew her closer. "I'm in charge of the Soviet council. I have authority over the village and everyone else." He then was compelled, for reasons he later could not quite articulate, to take out his symbol of authority, the Nagant revolver tucked into the holster under his coat. She moved away as he waved the gun around, glaring at her. He swayed noticeably, feeling a stream of bile coming up. He forced it down.

"Chairman Belynski," his comrade in the corner said tensely with a tremor in his tone, "our official business?"

"Right, yes." He tucked his gun away and refocused. "Tell Comrade Pylyp to sign — to join the collective farm, if he knows what's good for him ... and you. Kurkuls have no rights, you know." He gave the room one more cursory sweep. "Tell him he can prevent much lamenting and weeping... He knows what to do."

Having said his piece, Belynski gestured to the other man. "Time to go... Give him the message," he emphasized to Katya on his way out.

***

Once in the sleigh and with the brace of the cold air, Belynski felt a tinge of remorse, chastening himself for being undisciplined and crude. He shouldn't have gone there when he was under the influence and not sufficiently clear-headed. He sensed he'd slipped when the generally silent Comrade Yarko stepped forward with alarm in his eyes, nervous and unsure of what his boss with the gun might do. Was this a warning? Would the subordinates revolt if he crossed *their* line? Certainly, he had to be sober and more decisive, exercising authority in a controlled yet firm manner.

Time to reassert his authority before things got out of hand. His two companions needed to know that he meant business. He ordered the sleigh to stop at Fedor Arken's cottage on their way back to the village. The old widower had been thumbing his nose at the Soviet council ever since it replaced the village council (which he also had no use for, apparently), ignoring all summons and swearing at the propaganda brigades sent his way. Belynski hadn't gotten around to dealing with him yet, although he, like so many others, was on the list. He was going to rectify this oversight and make a statement not only to Arken but also to the two reluctant companions out with him tonight.

The old man hadn't joined the kolkhoz but sat alone in his cottage. Belynski knew this, having been told that after his wife's death, his daughter and son had moved on to one of the big cities to try their luck at urban living. Not that he could blame them… "Let's pay Comrade Arken a visit," he declared. "We'll deliver a friendly reminder that he has been delinquent at attending meetings."

"How do we know that?" asked Shusky, the sleigh driver, pulling lightly on the reins of the horse, whose heavy breathing and accompanying bells disturbed the stillness of the night air. Yarko, meanwhile, said nothing but sat bundled like a lump beside Shusky.

"Have you seen him at any meetings?" asked Belynski.

"No, but—"

"Then, there you are!" Belynski smiled. The liquor was wearing thin in the winter bite, and he felt he could think more clearly. Neither Yarko nor Shusky were apparatchik material, at least when it came to moving up the party ranks, but still, they had to be shown authority. Besides, the party council employed enough informants to keep tabs on the village and surrounding farming population that Belynski knew Arken had not attended any meetings, and he too had not met the previous year's grain quota. He was a delinquent, and a collection was overdue.

They stopped the sleigh in front of a dimly lit little home almost invisible from the road, the snow piled on along a singular path in. As before, Shusky stayed with the horse. Belynski, with Yarko in tow, walked down the path to the frost-encrusted wooden front door, their boots crushing snow crystals. Belynski pounded hard on the door with a fur-lined gloved fist. "Fedor Arken, open up. Order of the local Soviet council."

Arken was in his sixties, a small, wrinkled fellow who eyed his guests with disdain. He had no use for Bolsheviks, having survived

Lenin's collectivization attempt in the early twenties, and here they were back again. He especially didn't like Belynski. He was the worst because, as Arken saw it, he was the "local" politico, even though he wasn't local, having come from the north somewhere. He considered Belynski and his ilk bullies, pilferers, possibly even worse, with the morals of a ferret.

As if to demonstrate the point, Belynski, in no mood to practise guest protocols, dispensed with formalities, shoved the old man aside, and ordered Yarko to search the house.

"For what?" Yarko asked.

"For anything of value. Comrade Citizen Arken here has shirked his duty; he is in tax arrears, has contributed nothing, in fact, and certainly has not joined the kolkhoz. Reparations are now due."

"You've come here to steal from me?" Arken spat out the words before catching his breath. "And here I thought it was too cold for maggots and thieving weevils to be out."

Belynski shoved Arken again, much harder this time. The old man stumbled and fell. Belynski could not resist a quick kick with his boot into the man's midsection. Not too hard, but enough to set the tone. "Where is it? I know you have stashed your money somewhere here. I'll have Comrade Yarko rip the place apart starting with the walls... Ah, wait, what do we have here?" He noticed a lumpy sock wrapped around Arken's ankle as he lay wheezing.

"Here, hold him down," Belynski ordered Yarko, who, after a brief hesitation, grabbed the man's arms and forced him to sit up. Resistance was minimal. "Sit still, and don't kick, or you'll feel real pain," Belynski warned as he got a hold of the thin, blue-veined leg. He straightened it out and unwound the knot of the bulging sock just above the ankle.

It revealed a reasonably thick stack of curled rubles. He'd sort it out later with whatever compensation Yarko and Shusky thought reasonable. "This," he waved the stash of rubles in the air, "is your fine for failing to comply with party directives."

"As if any of it will find its way to the Soviet council," muttered Arken, resigned to his loss.

Belynski ignored him. "Consider yourself fortunate that I don't haul you in as a kurkul. I hear that there is a shortage of workers to dig the White Sea–Baltic Canal. Not that you would last long."

After a further cursory search just in case there were other treasures to be found, Belynski and Yarko left, with the former well satisfied that the night was not a total waste. Not only had he reaffirmed his authority, but he had also provided a small profit for himself and his two officials.

Belynski knew that Arken would remain stubborn and noncompliant. However, that was not going to be tolerated much longer. Collectivization had to proceed much quicker. The directives had become more insistent each day, and the pressure was on to get it done. If he and Fedryk couldn't do it, then the party would send strangers speaking Russian. These would be especially assigned individuals the party hierarchy depended on to bring the required result, regardless of the methods or cost.

For Belynski, it was perform or perish. There was a possibility that if he failed, he also would be digging the White Sea–Baltic ditch that he had mentioned. He had to achieve results. These individualized approaches, mind games, and endless meetings built up the necessary preconditions, but it took time, and as Pylyp had shown, there was resistance. More meaningful levels of fear and intimidation were required. The time was coming for a show of force.

***

For three consecutive nights, Oleksander made the long walk to the grist mill, where he refused to join the kolkhoz, repeating in each instance that he needed more time. Each time, this was followed by a march to the waiting room, which seemed to grow longer and longer. On the third night, Comrade Pince-Nez became totally exasperated and confided in a plaintive manner that he was just doing his job, and that he and his assistant — the ruddy-faced young man shifted uncomfortably as he spoke — were obliged to report on a weekly basis to his superior how many he'd convinced to join the collective farm. "There is a competition to collectivize," he said somewhat apologetically, "and if I fail in my assigned quota, there will be consequences for me. But I assure you, I will pass along to you and your family more dire consequences before it comes to that. So, this game must end now. Neither of us can be coy about this. There is really nothing to think about. Am I being blunt enough for you, Comrade Oleksander Pylyp?"

"Yes."

"And?"

"I am not ready to sign."

"I am disappointed. This was your last chance. Chairman Belynski and the local Soviet council will decide your fate. In the end, militiamen will show up at your door, and matters will take their course. Do you really want that to happen?"

Pylyp reiterated that he would not sign, and he had nothing further to say. Making his way back home, he knew that he had crossed the Rubicon and sealed his fate and probably that of those around him.

CHAPTER THIRTEEN

Kyiv

Emil Krypniuk had been in his office just long enough to brew a pot of tea when his phone rang.

"Yes."

"Captain Krypniuk?"

"Yes." It was the same voice he had heard the night he was informed that he'd be visiting Commissar Pavlick. Krypniuk had hoped that by some miracle, the local OGPU boss had forgotten about him. No such luck.

"Commissar Pavlick wishes to speak to you." When there was no response, the voice continued, "He would like a report."

Krypniuk sighed inwardly. He was dreading this because, in fact, he had little to report. "I could quickly update the commissar over the phone—"

"If it's not too inconvenient, the commissar would like it to be in person. A car can be sent in twenty minutes — say, the front doors of the police station?" *Of course it can!* Krypniuk mused, thoroughly chagrined.

"Fine." He chose not to argue. What was the point? Pavlick was flexing his authority, and it was too early in whatever game was being played to push back. Still quite annoying, as he could have easily told Pavlick over the phone that he had nothing of substance to share about Commissar Gromeko's demise. And yet, forty-five minutes later he was sitting in the same uncomfortable chair as before. This morning it was doubly so because of an old tailbone injury that this particular chair seemed to delight in aggravating.

Dutifully, Krypniuk recited his department's activities to date, noting that Katya Kharsova's photo had been distributed widely in the city and in the countryside as far south as her hometown, and that chairmen of all the local Soviet councils had received notices that she was wanted for questioning in the death of Kreil Gromeko, commissar of Commerce and Industry, Kyiv. She was to be detained so that arrangements could be made to interview her, and, if necessary, transport her back to Kyiv. "I'm confident that she is no longer in the city," Krypniuk added as an obvious afterthought.

"And you've heard nothing of her whereabouts at all?"

"Not as yet, Commissar. Of course, we've followed other avenues of inquiry — interviewed Commissar Sholtz and others in the commissariat who knew and worked with Commissar Gromeko." Krypniuk judiciously omitted telling Pavlick about the pressure he and Lubick had put on Sholtz, invoking the OGPU in the process.

"And?"

"They were helpful for background information but nothing concrete to date. We also went to the commissar's home just outside the city, on the road to the airport."

"How is Madame Gromekovna dealing with the tragedy?" Pavlick's voice was wooden, as if he couldn't give a toss about how she felt but went through with the gesture of sympathy.

"She seemed … composed," Krypniuk said, weighing his words, "almost detached… She explained that while they shared the same home, they had separate quarters. As she put it, they were 'estranged.'"

"I see… I suppose having a mistress on the side doesn't endear one in a relationship." Pavlick almost chortled but caught himself.

"If I may be so forward…" Krypniuk cleared his throat. "When I asked if I could see the commissar's living quarters. Madame Gromekovna informed me that it had already been searched by the OGPU. Am I to infer that there is a parallel investigation occurring?"

Pavlick took a moment to answer. "You and your department are doing the homicide portion. We have an obligation to investigate improper business practices — fraud, bribes, the theft of state property that spills over into political and state affairs."

"I understand … but just to clarify … what if our two investigations intersect?" *Which they surely must!* "We'd need to compare notes, share information."

"Ah, that's why you are reporting directly to me… From what you've said so far, it seems that your case revolves around Katya Kharsova, wouldn't you agree?"

"Finding her is imperative; however, at this point she is only a person of interest, possibly a witness. Once we find and question her—"

"Just find her. We'll do the interrogation and decide whether she's guilty or not."

Krypniuk stiffened in his chair and winced as his tailbone protested; he had to make a point of principle. "If we are going to solve the *murder* portion of this case, I need to speak with Madame Kharsova frankly and unfettered."

Pavlick blinked rapidly twice, his ears reddening, consternation clouding his face. "Careful, Comrade Captain, do not step out of *your* bounds. You're allowed to continue with this investigation as a courtesy extended to your head of police by me. As such, you need to be prudent!"

And there it was. At the very least, Krypniuk and his team were being used as extra hands to help the OGPU in the case. Moreover, at any moment the Kyiv Police Criminal Investigation Department could be removed from the case, deemed irrelevant, redundant, or worse — made scapegoats. He and the department were handy to have around to blame for whatever reason(s) Pavlick decided the situation warranted. Krypniuk suspected that very few (including Pavlick) cared that Gromeko was shot dead. It was who was involved, how high up did it go, how much money was taken, and who stood to gain or lose. Details he was not privy to, nor, if the truth be known, would he want to be for his own sake and his family's. This was an unsolvable case. It was time to be contrite. "Yes, Commissar Pavlick." *Bite your tongue and say no more.*

The fat man behind the desk grunted then sighed. "It would have been more convenient for both of us if Commissar Gromeko fell out of a window. Then, the cause of death would be obvious — and you wouldn't be looking into a homicide. Still, I need to know who and why. Find Gromeko's secretary!"

***

"Yes, yes, I know," said Vasar Sholtz, keeping his voice level. He was seated at his desk, quite anxious in his own right given the two ongoing investigations into Gromeko's death, when his second, secure phone rang. He knew who it was and that this individual needed the kind of reassurance he himself was struggling with. "It's bad for business and no, we and our assets are well protected... No paper trail, although it appears that both the Kyiv Police and the OGPU are snooping around... I agree, the probe into Commissar Gromeko's death — yes, I know he was a great friend and colleague... Yes, it will entail his financial affairs, but we are safe. Nothing can come to light."

Sholtz gritted his teeth; he could only hope this was true. "A Captain Krypniuk — heard of him? ... Yes, he needs to be derailed, redirected, along with the OGPU, which has greater resources, I should think... That would be good — if you can... No. No, I don't for sure, but all indications are it's his secretary, his mistress.... Sex, money, or both. Who knows? ... No, disappeared... Proof of guilt, right? ... Katya Kharsova... Yes, potentially; she may know something if Gromeko talked too much; she was his personal secretary, after all, with access to the files... I know, but if they find her, they'll squeeze her, and I don't want to take the chance. Better she not talk either to Krypniuk or OGPU agents."

Sholtz took a sip of his tea while the man at the other end of the line listed his concerns at length. "Haven't yet as far as I know... They're still trying to locate her... Agreed, we must find her before Krypniuk or the OGPU... Actually, that information and her photo have been sent out to all local Soviet council chairmen throughout the oblast... Yes, that would be helpful; she must be hiding somewhere... Yes, this is a setback, but we can quickly recover — business as usual, depending on who replaces Commissar Gromeko... Yes, I know you're not in charge; still, you can influence the people who are." *Some flattery never hurts*, thought Sholtz. "Right, good day."

Sholtz put the receiver down and shook his head. Another nervous collaborator, city facilitator/fixer who, in fact, had smoothed the path to his and Gromeko's many lucrative building contracts, from the unending construction of Kyiv's new railway station (three years and still counting) to massive apartment projects with inferior materials and inflated costs. Even with large sums siphoned off for the endless payoffs and other forms of palm greasing, there was still a most handsome profit to be made. It was rumoured that the clandestine funds went up the political hierarchy, possibly as high as Pavel Postyshev. Sholtz didn't know but wouldn't challenge the notion. If this fellow ever discovered that it was Sholtz who shot the manipulative cheat, he would die forthwith and probably in a most unpleasant way. *Ah, Vasar, what a* dummkopf *you are making all this trouble for yourself. Even if Gromeko deserved it!* It was imperative that he get to Katya Kharsova before anyone else did.

CHAPTER FOURTEEN

Bila Sich

"The pressure is increasing by the day," whispered Lev, glancing about nervously.

"Don't I know it," replied Oleksander, his head on a swivel, mimicking Lev. They were in the Dnipro Tavern, having a beer away from the handful of other muziks doing the same. It was difficult to know who was friend or foe; outsiders were easy to spot, but not so local informers. So they sat huddled in the corner and kept their voices low. "Three summons in three nights — to the grist mill each time. The question is always the same: are you ready to join? No ... well, cool off in our waiting room, and in a couple of hours we'll ask again." Oleksander snorted in derision.

"I just received my summons today, nailed to my door. Nina is anxious, worried about Misha. What happens if we don't comply?"

"I wish I had an answer... Katya ... excuse me, Oxana, got a visit from Belynski when I was out at the mill."

"And?" Lev pulled his chair closer.

"The usual shit. Threatened her — enemy of the state and deportation if I didn't join his precious kolkhoz."

"Sleazy bastard. Did we ever figure out where he's from? I know Vlas heard some rumours he mentioned a while ago..."

"Kyiv, I think," said Oleksander, trying to remember his conversation with Belynski. He implied it but did not explicitly state it. "Not sure ... or who he was or what he did, for that matter... Certainly fancies himself more important than a low-level, pencil-pushing party clerk. Which begs the question: who did he piss off to get appointed here?"

"What d'you mean?"

"No offence, Lev, but we're not exactly an envious place to be, particularly for an urbanite like Belynski."

"Oh, it's not that bad here — your hometown, and all."

"Just making a point, nothing more. He doesn't want to be here. It's a demotion, one of thousands of self-inflated bureaucrats the party needs to organize and run villages and the countryside."

"Right … and how is any of this going to help us? Sounds like he's got incentive to get on with it, sooner rather than later. Stalin's little helper!" Lev became more animated.

"Better keep a lid on it," advised Oleksander, casting a surreptitious eye about to see if curious heads had suddenly arisen. "The beer may have ears, and you don't want the wrong people to hear you."

"So, what's our next move?" Lev said quietly. "Honestly, I don't know what to do."

"I have no answers. For my part, I will continue to resist. Fatalistic, perhaps, but still a plan. Really, though, I cannot advise you and others on what to do now. The situation seems to be coming to some climax, and it doesn't bode well for the citizens of Bila Sich."

Lev stared into his beer. "Wonderful choice. Comply, lose our land; don't and be branded a kurkul, kicked out of our home, ostracized, our neighbours too fearful to help and then … disappear if we're lucky. Life on the kolkhoz will not be wonderful, but still, we'd be alive. I have to think of Nina and Misha."

"I understand completely. And time seems to be running out. But I will hang on until spring and seeding. I can only hope that it's a bluff and that crops need to be put in the ground by people who know what they're doing… Our new kolkhoz masters don't. They'll probably continue with speeches, and we'll see more young pioneers, Komsomol volunteer brigades. End up freezing our toes in waiting rooms, but it's still persuasion. "

"Until Belynski and OGPU goons show up at the door and wave a gun in our faces and tell us to get out," said Lev.

"There is truth to that," Oleksander acknowledged grimly.

"It's all very laughable, if it were not so insane and serious," said Lev with a bitter smile. "A horde of strangers suddenly appear, enlist a few local politicos, and declare the Communist Party — or rather Comrade Stalin — wants to make you happy. And how do you become happy, other than drinking a lot of vodka? Join the collective, give up everything you own, including your independence and dignity. That's what this is about. And, if you don't," Lev drank the last of his beer, "if you don't join — well, we know what happens..." He trailed off.

"No more perogies on Sunday for sure." Oleksander smiled.

"The point is I don't know how long I can hang on and tempt fate. Nina is really worried."

"I know. You must do what you believe is best. As I said, I'll try to resist at least till spring in the delirious hope that a miracle will occur; that perhaps circumstances will change; that the great vozhd will reconsider; that God will intervene; or that a selective plague will wipe out Belynski and his communist friends."

***

Strangely enough, both Oleksander and Lev and most of the village folk managed to avoid joining the kolkhoz. No one was more surprised than Makar Belynski. He convinced himself finally that it was either him or them; that his own survival rested on his attaining the collectivization quota as per party directives; that there was no recourse but to crack down on Oleksander, Lev, and the rest of these intractable peasant farmers. Then, abruptly, Fedryk's frenzied dispatches to "get this job done" ceased. The confusion was palpable until *revised directives* came down from none other than Stalin himself!

Apparently, Stalin had heard of the coercive methods used to implement collectivization. The whole campaign, he insisted, had been misinterpreted and too vigorously applied. This became all too evident when Comrade Stalin himself published an article, "Dizzy from Success," in *Pravda*.

"Comrades, comrades," he beseeched the local party apparatchiks. "You have been too zealous... Collectivization is not to be compulsory and forced but implemented with persuasion! The kulaks are not to be eliminated as a social class but reformed, reeducated, and integrated..." It seemed that the local and district officials had perpetrated a jest, a bad joke in the Ukrainian Soviet Republic and other borderlands. Further, that the politburo could not be held responsible for party directives being distorted. "Stop the compulsion, stop the seizure of farmers' dwellings and domestic animals, and be more careful of labelling the mass of peasants kulaks."* So wrote Stalin.

What the fuck! thought Belynski. No wonder Fedryk had suddenly gone silent. Pandora's box had just been opened. Everyone was trying to figure out what this meant. More to the point, what officials were going to be held accountable? Was Fedryk in trouble, or was he? *Any shortcomings or blame for overt actions in Bila Sich will be laid at my feet,* Belynski realized sourly deep into his third nightcap.

As predicted, a Pandora's box indeed had been opened albeit a crack ... but a significant crack. Within a few days, Belynski was reading reports of angry peasant mobs attacking village Soviet councils, sending frightened local party officials packing. Kolkhozes were also targeted; again, those in charge prudently disappeared, allowing owners to reclaim their equipment and animals that had been confiscated. One kolkhoz hosted the "great repossession," where every last horse, cow, wagon, and farming tool disappeared. Apparently, the militiamen on guard were overpowered, their weapons seized. They were bound and left in a barn.

In at least one village in Poltava Oblast, Belynski noted that more direct action was taken against the local authorities. Telephone lines were cut from the village to the nearest train station, and a number of buildings appropriated by party officials were burned to the ground. There was no official report on how many casualties, and Belynski

---

* As quoted in Robert Conquest, *The Harvest of Sorrow* (Edmonton: University of Alberta Press, 1986), 160.

assumed that most simply fled. A footnote added that one party official was found in a ditch, beaten to death, but it had more to do with unsolicited advances on someone else's wife than party directives per se. *Thank God I'm spared that here*, he mused, thinking of his entanglements with at least one married woman in Kyiv.

Belynski realized that he was fortunate in that, unlike many other villages scattered throughout the countryside, Bila Sich remained relatively calm. In part it was because it was behind in the collectivization process; except for the initial dispossessions of personal dwellings and the disappearance of Father Parayma (not his doing), he had moved with deliberate pace, allowing for at least the illusion of choice. Villagers were annoyed, perhaps very angry, but they still had their land, homes, and belongings, by and large. Moreover, the village was well fortified with militiamen. Thus, while taking flak from Fedryk, he was saved facing any serious revolt or confrontation. Still, he ordered Prasha to double the guards around key party buildings and the kolkhoz. "And oh," as an afterthought, he remembered, "did we ever do anything about that woman's cow ... the one that disrupted the meeting. I've forgotten her name?"

"It was Markov or Markovski, something like that... I don't know what happened, but I'll check with the kolkhoz manager," Prasha said, notebook in one hand, scratching his ear with the other.

"Good idea. If he has her cow, make sure it's given back, and if the cow has disappeared, impress on him that he should find one!"

After Prasha left, Belynski poured himself another splash of vodka, briefly lamenting his brutish behaviour toward Oxana but particularly toward the old hermit that one night when he lost control. He was drunk. *Still, no excuse for kicking the sod while he was down...* Of greater concern, he had still to hear from Fedryk. It was now well into April and no word — most unusual.

***

It came to Belynski in one gigantic rush, pieces of a puzzle. Not exactly how they fit, but the tapestry of intersecting lines. Perhaps, if his brain wasn't so sodden with alcohol, he could see at least the edges clearer, but no matter, the general landscape was evident enough. The question was how could he exploit it to his advantage? The pieces presented themselves in three distinct information packages.

First, a copy of the Kyiv version of *Pravda* finally arrived, and while carelessly flipping through its propaganda drivel disguised as journalism, he read a short article about the death of Commissar Gromeko on page three. The story was vague, very incomplete, with no definitive statement of how he died, but with a hint of foul play involved. *The commissar of Commerce and Industry was found deceased in his apartment. The investigation is ongoing.* That was the extent of the actual reporting. The rest of the column highlighted Gromeko's career and his "hard work" and "dedication" to party and state. Belynski had met Gromeko a number of times — nothing particularly "dedicated" or "honourable" about him, but Belynski remembered a reception at Minsky Palace where he was in the company of an arrestingly beautiful woman. That was it! That striking female looked a lot like Oxana, except that wasn't her name.

Second, that very same day, he received an odd dispatch with a photo, a poster, really, probably sent to all local Soviet councils. A certain Katya Kharsova, featured in the photo, was a person of interest in the death of Commissar Kreil Gromeko. If he had any information as to the whereabouts of Miss Kharsova, he was to contact Captain Emil Krypniuk of the Kyiv Police Criminal Investigation Department. Again, a double-take. Katya bore an undeniable resemblance to Oxana Gerkil. Even in a drunken stupor, he beheld the same woman.

Third was a dispatch from Fedryk; it contained no mention of Stalin's article or a clarification of collectivization procedure moving forward. Instead, it contained the exact same poster that had been distributed by this Captain Krypniuk of the Kyiv Police. Fedryk's attached note was short and to the point: *This person they're seeking looks like that woman that stepped forward to comfort the hag at our meeting, does she not?*

Well, what the hell, thought Belynski, *the little toad did notice then.* The fact was that they had both seen Katya, a.k.a. Oxana, from their perch on stage when the "missing cow" lady protested. They just didn't recognize her as such, in his case, even after he'd seen her with Gromeko previously. But then why would they?

So, the question arose. What was this all about? In all probability, Fedryk's interest was piqued, and he was just passing information. He'd have to think about this, interrogate Oxana — Katya — and maybe Oleksander... Meanwhile, he'd write back, tell Fedryk no, not the lady in question, the vague resemblance notwithstanding! There had to be a way to leverage this to his advantage; he just had to know what he was leveraging and against whom.

***

The abrupt policy change from the top seemed to totally disrupt the equilibrium of the local Soviet councils and paralyze further action. This proved true in Bila Sich no less so than the other, more volatile regions affected. Belynski waited in vain for Fedryk to issue further directives. Meanwhile, the stream of summons ceased, a hiatus appeared in the endless compulsory meetings scheduled, and village inhabitants were generally left alone.

"Can this be really true..." Vlas Chorney sat down, making himself comfortable, joining Lev and Oleksander in their favourite (and the only) drinking establishment in Bila Sich. It was allowed to function, they speculated, because it was popular with the militiamen, who thankfully generally kept to themselves. "...that they've stopped?"

"For now," Lev affirmed tentatively. "Been quiet lately."

"It's definitely a reprieve of some sort," Oleksander agreed. "Obviously, the politburo — Stalin — got cold feet. I doubt that any further collectivization plans will come, not if they want undisrupted planting and harvesting... We're probably good until late fall."

"So, was it really a misunderstanding?" asked Vlas.

"Oh, I doubt that," replied Lev. "More like a miscalculation… How do we take advantage, though?"

"I'm not sure that we can," argued Oleksander. "Any overt action to actually take over the kolkhoz or kick these interlopers out will lead to confrontation. They'll come down on us. They'll bring even more troops because it will be seen as a direct challenge to party and state — a declaration of war." Oleksander stared into his beer. "Best we go about our business as always, speaking of which," he downed the last of the bitter brew. "I should get going … been spending too much time sitting with you guys drinking lately."

As he rose from the table and waved at Denys, the stout pub-house owner, it hit him that he should be making other plans. There was no future for him in Bila Sich. *Time to go back to Kyiv and see if I still have a job and apartment!*

CHAPTER FIFTEEN

Bila Sich

Katya received a note, discreetly delivered by the ubiquitous Ivan Prasha, Belynski's assistant/manservant (she wasn't sure exactly what). He seemed a shadow who appeared at will, this time while she was in the state store buying household supplies. "Chairman Belynski wanted me to give you this," he said quietly as she stood before a bin of sad-looking potatoes. He had come up beside her, surreptitiously dropped the envelope in her shopping bag, and just as quickly withdrew. It contained a short, ominous message:

I should like to discuss an urgent matter with you privately. Looking forward to seeing you, Oxana, or should I say Katya Kharsova — 5:00 p.m. today, my residence — Makar Belynski.

He knew! But how? She quickly left the shop, her head pounding, ears ringing. Her pace increased in time with her panic, her thoughts askew, losing focus. By the time she reached home, though, she got a hold of herself. She consciously slowed her pulse, took a few deep breaths, and rationally assessed her situation. The fact that Oleksander was out today with Lev and others to discuss village affairs was significant; more likely than not, that was the reason Belynski picked the time and date. It was an open secret that the village was rife with spies who watched and reported. The question was: what did Belynski want, or was it over and he was savouring his role, perhaps reward, in delivering her to the authorities and/or Commissar Sholtz? The only other consideration was whether she should tell Oleksander, the man who had saved her initially, no questions asked, or was it better to remain silent, not implicate him at all, not put him in further jeopardy than he was already.

The fact was that she had not been entirely honest with Oleksander and his Bila Sich community. True, she told him that she was witness to a crime and had run away, fearful for her life; however, she told her story vaguely in the context of being in the wrong place at the wrong time. Omitted were pertinent details like the shooting took place in her apartment; that the victim was not only her boss but that she was also his mistress; and that the authorities (as well as Commissar Sholtz) were looking for her. She had been fortunate that Oleksander had a certain charming gentlemanly naïveté (unusual in Slavic men, she believed) that did not allow him to press too hard on the issue and respected her privacy in terms of what and when she wanted to divulge.

An honourable and quite sweet man, she decided, who had given her safe haven. As a result, she had been content to play the traditional role inside his home and within the village. What choice did she have, really? The first time they had slept together was intimate but restrained. It had been a particularly cold night and, of course, he had gallantly given her the bed closest to the hearth. She invited him to her bed, saying she didn't want to be responsible for him freezing during the night. They stripped to their undergarments and huddled together under the heavy blanket, neither pushing the intimacy further, as if it were forbidden fruit. Indeed, she became a bit impatient at his deliberate, ploughman's pace. In due course, his hands found the various parts of her body, as hers did his, they kissed and finally let basic instincts take over.

But then, this was not a novel activity for her. She left her village at the age of fourteen, glad to get away from her dour, drunken father and his cowering, hapless wife (actually, she liked her mother, who was just … overwhelmed. And she vowed not to be). There were three siblings, two brothers and a sister, all younger, when she left. They too evidently had scattered with the death of their father (knifed in some brawl, she'd heard years later from her mother). The debt-ridden patch of dirt and the cottage on it could barely support her mother, who relied on Katya's monthly stipends when she finally got a decent job in Kyiv to support the Kharsova clan. *Till a while ago.* She was headed to Shervobne and her mother when fate took a decided turn on the train. *The family is on its own now...*

No illusions. Katya was accustomed to the rougher side of life, including the mean side streets and hovels of Kyiv. She had held a variety of jobs, including a short period of prostitution for Madame Bovarsky, who took her off the streets and provided a room and food. The old baba-madame was generally kind (could have been much worse) until shut down by the police. There were supposed to be no "street walkers" in a socialist state. From there, Katya worked in a small shop making birch-bark shoes. She wanted, needed, to elevate herself above the level of her circumstances, and to do so, she realized, required an improvement not only in her language and communication but also in other practical skills such as typing and office management. This was the key to finding suitable employment. She saved, went to night school, and acquired what she had to acquire. However, it was her intelligence, efficiency, and above all, innate beauty that got her noticed in the halls of power. Once arrived, she quickly discovered how to keep her bread buttered.

Kreil Gromeko was an arrogant man, quite unpredictable, and completely stupid when he was drunk, but he was also good to her, providing a lifestyle that was well beyond her humble background and circumstances. She thought that at the right time she'd find a way to leave him, or maybe he'd become tired of her; she never imaged such an unexpected and abrupt ending.

Meanwhile, she learned things and began to systematically put together a portfolio of some of Kyiv's most powerful (if not well-known) apparatchiks, carefully duplicating files that would advance her career (or possibly get her killed). After all, men talked much more to their mistresses than to their wives. They unburdened their souls, believing that their spouses just didn't understand. But she did, taking notes and mimeographing documents. She had them hidden in a relatively safe place, she hoped. The problem now was twofold: getting access and, even if she did, trusting someone enough to utilize her "trove" in a way that was beneficial to her — if that was even possible.

It was simply unfortunate happenstance that she was there at the exact time her boss was murdered. Of course, it wouldn't have helped much to come later and discover his body — except that Sholtz wouldn't be looking for her. And now, Makar Belynski was added to the list of impending threats. She found him a bit like her former boss. He had a certain sense of decorum and integrity, as demonstrated by how he handled that distressed woman — while sober. When he visited her the night Oleksander was sent off to the grist mill, he was drunk and, like Gromeko, got ugly. She had considered not telling Oleksander about the incident — it was what it was — but then he might hear of it from someone else. She didn't know what he would do or could do, but it was best to make it sound as innocuous as possible and let it pass.

About Oleksander... It was taking a while for her to digest, comprehend, her feelings for him. After all, who would offer his apartment key in Kyiv in such good faith? It was a chivalrous gesture that might be taken up, she realized, if she needed to make a quick exit. Without a doubt, she was warming up to him, a decent man who perhaps was too decent for his own good and hers...

***

"Ah, you came." Belynski smiled, taking her coat and ushering her into a large parlour. It looked a bit neglected and smelled earthy, with lingering notes of stale pipe tobacco. Katya couldn't be sure whether it was Belynski's doing or just part of the original odour of the merchant's home that he had confiscated and proclaimed socialist property. There was a modest fireplace peacefully burning, an ornate wooden chest close by. At the far wall was a large, cluttered desk, perhaps the merchant's accounting area, now scattered with piles of documents. Katya presumed that was where Belynski worked and drank during the evenings. He directed her to a dated brocade sofa near the middle of the room, no doubt another item that came with the house. She sat and straightened her modest linen blouse and skirt ever so slightly. She had deliberately downplayed her appearance with unadorned attire and her hair pulled back beneath a colourful scarf. A comedown from the haute couture days in Kyiv with Gromeko.

"Sherry?" Belynski offered before turning to a side table in the corner of the room and pouring two glasses from a crystal decanter. He extended the glass to her, and she accepted with a moment's hesitation. He sat in a high armchair opposite from her at a respectable distance.

Might as well get to the point, Katya thought. "You have me at a disadvantage. What is it that you want?"

Belynski sat back and appraised her. "First, I want to apologize for my behaviour at your home. It was ... uncalled for."

She nodded and took a sip of the very sweet sherry.

"Rest assured," he continued, "that my behaviour here will be proper to a fault ... but yes, it is true I have some questions and would appreciate answers." Rather delicately, he placed his glass on a small table beside his chair, rose, straightened his loose-fitting tunic, walked over to his messy desk, and picked up a red folder. He came back, took out a poster from the folder, and handed it to her. It had her photo and particulars from Captain Krypniuk and the Kyiv Police regarding their interest in her. She felt herself paling but kept her composure as she read.

"See my problem... You are Katya Kharsova, correct?" he asked in a casual voice.

"Yes." There was no point in lying.

"And Oxana Gerkil is an alias, I take it."

"Yes, I didn't want the authorities to find me."

"Why would they be so interested in finding you?"

"I am a witness to a crime."

"You mean Commissar Kreil Gromeko's death?"

"Yes; he was shot. I saw the shooter."

"Do the police know this?"

"No, I've spoken to no one... The shooter saw me. That's why I ran... Why I'm here and changed my name."

"So, the person who did the deed wants to locate you, but why are the police so keenly interested?" He raised his sherry glass and leaned forward, studying her closely. He guessed the answer but wanted her to say it.

"I was Commissar Gromeko's personal secretary, and the event took place in my apartment. They would need to speak to me." It was a matter-of-fact reply. She was trying to get a measure of Belynski and what he wanted.

"Naturally, you are afraid of the perpetrator locating you, but why not talk to the police?"

"I don't know who I could trust if I stepped forward — including the police." She glanced at the poster.

"I can certainly understand that. I take it you don't know Captain Krypniuk, head of the Criminal Investigation Department?"

"No ... just read his name now."

"But as Commissar Gromeko's personal secretary, you would have met many prominent people?"

"Captain Krypniuk was not one among them, if that's what you mean," she said flatly.

"How about Commissar Fedryk? Was he part of Gromeko's acquaintances?"

Katya frowned; the question surprised her. "Not that I recall. I saw him but, as you know, it was here — at the meeting."

"Never met him in Kyiv then, perhaps in Commissar Gromeko's office or at a function?"

"Not that I recall," she reiterated. "Why do you ask?"

Why indeed, wondered Belynski. *Covering my ass in case it was more than just a routine matter to him...* "Oh, nothing of note." He waved a dismissive hand. "Just a thought..." He trailed off, changing tack. "Have you discussed Commissar Gromeko's death with anyone?"

"No."

"Not even your fiancé?"

"No."

Belynski straightened in his chair. "Is Oleksander your fiancé, or is that a ruse like your alias?"

Katya too straightened and did not answer immediately. She wasn't prepared to discuss the matter. "That's our business," she asserted with a touch of defiance.

"As you wish, but tell me this: how much does Oleksander know?"

"No more than what I just told you." *Maybe less*, she thought. "That's all I'm prepared to say."

"Fair enough." Belynski paused and took another sip of sherry. "Enlighten me, just so I am clear. You do not know the individual who killed Commissar Gromeko?"

Again, Katya hesitated, not sure how much she should divulge, and decided that a blunt "no" would be a reasonable lie.

Belynski frowned. "So, no idea of who or the motive, personal ... business ... political?"

"None."

He nodded and abruptly asked an unrelated question. "Do you wish to remain in this village?"

She half shrugged. "I didn't have much choice in the matter."

"But you'd like to be elsewhere — Kyiv?" he insisted. "As a matter of preference?"

"I made my home there — yes."

"Well, so do I," Belynski said, regarding her intensely. "Alas." He sighed. "We've both been exiled albeit for different reasons."

"Well, Chairman Belynski," Katya said formally with a touch of exasperation, "you've uncovered who I am and my situation, so what is it that you want, other than summoning the militiamen to arrest me?"

"That would be an option," Belynski conceded, "and probably the correct one, but no; you can continue to be Oxana Gerkil..." he raised a finger, "under certain conditions — actually, one: as my personal secretary. Your secret will be safe, and who knows," he gave her a crooked smile, "you may even return to Kyiv someday."

Katya stared at him stunned. "I don't understand... You are wanting me to move in here — with you?"

"A stark way of putting it, but yes. Officially, you'd be in charge of the household in general and other duties similar to the ones you performed for Commissar Gromeko."

"What about your present secretary?" she said with a hard edge. "Wouldn't he be put out?"

"Oh, Ivan." Belynski waved his hand dismissively. "He came with my appointment. He'll be fine. There's enough to do for the both of you." He rose from his chair and made his way to the side table. "More sherry?"

She shook her head.

"Think I'll refill with something a little stronger," he said, pouring himself a generous shot of vodka. "Listen," he continued earnestly, "instead of turning you in, I'm offering you a reasonably comfortable home and indeed employment. And at some risk, I might add, if the wrong people found out. You are a fugitive, a wanted woman I should turn over to the police or Commissar Fedryk, who, it seems, for reasons I cannot fathom, has taken a special interest in your apprehension. I'm giving you a way out."

You are saying I should become your mistress, she thought grimly. "To be clear, I'd have to move out of my present location into this house?"

"That would be the arrangement," Belynski confirmed.

"In exchange for not revealing my true identity and arresting me?"

"Yes."

"And what about Oleksander?"

Belynski returned to his seat, raised his glass, and took a swallow. "What about him? You're not really his fiancée, are you? But never mind... I have no interest in him, or his brother- in-law, for that matter, if that's what you're worried about. Accept my offer and their lives will not be disrupted while our arrangement remains in place. This is not a permanent situation, after all; as I said, I plan to get back to Kyiv, and no doubt so will you — when circumstances become more favourable."

***

Oleksander was becoming restless. His visit home had stretched into months, and he'd done all that he could to protect his property. The immediate danger seemed to have passed, and he certainly had no desire to reclaim his land or to farm. He was more than satisfied with the arrangement he had with Lev.

Of course, there was still the unresolved situation surrounding Katya. Here a maelstrom of conflicting thoughts bruised his brain. He realized that she hadn't confided in him, or at least had not told him the whole story, and he hadn't pressed her. Why hadn't he pressed her? He couldn't quite put his finger on it. *Maybe I'm a coward — don't want to know the truth*, he thought. But what was the truth? As painful as it may be to her and ultimately to him, he needed to talk to her honestly. How much danger was she in? What were her plans? Could she … would she go back to Kyiv? And more to the point, with him?

Undeniably, he had developed feelings for her. In fact, he was quite smitten from the moment she appeared in front of him on the train. And they had set up a household with a comfortable relationship, including those intimate moments when desire and instinct seemed to overtake both of them. Still, imagined or not, he felt a touch of reticence in their interactions. Was she genuinely interested in him, or in a most fundamental way was it for her a case of necessity followed by convenience? Yes, it was time to seriously talk forthrightly, since his place was in Kyiv and she too would have to move on, with him if possible, or separately…

Now, he sat at his kitchen table, grim-faced and jaw tight as Katya explained her work at the commissariat, her relationship with Gromeko, and the situation she found herself in. She refrained, however, from telling him who she saw in the apartment. It seemed that it was safer not to divulge that information to those around her. Fortunately, he did not press the point. Belynski's proposition stung.

"You simply can't let Belynski take advantage of you. Get away… Go to Kyiv — to my apartment, while I figure this out."

She shook her head. *There really is nothing to figure out!* "I need permission to leave the village now. Besides, there would be repercussions for you and Lev if I suddenly vanished!"

"I had been thinking of returning to Kyiv lately and taking you with me. I meant to talk to you about it." His voice was distant; his eyes fixed on hers.

At that moment, Katya knew she would have gone and let their relationship play out. It wasn't love and passion on first encounter (it rarely was), but he was definitely growing on her. "I would have gone, but you know I can't now… Still, you could go."

"Not without you! There has to be a way… Surely the police—"

"Will either charge me with the killing or hand me over to the man who did it!" she finished.

"Perhaps if I talked to Belynski myself—"

"And say what?" She placed her hand over his. "At least he promised to leave you, Lev, and his family in peace."

"Not sure I can trust him," Oleksander responded, indignant and despondent at the same time.

"I … we have no choice at the moment, but I know we'll come out of this together." She didn't know why she said that — except it was affirmative and offered *hope.*

CHAPTER SIXTEEN

Bila Sich

Katya knew that moving to Belynski's home was equivalent to sleeping with the enemy as far as most villagers were concerned. And indeed it was, but it was also a matter of survival; the alternative would have been much worse, certainly for her, and no doubt for Oleksander, and possibly his immediate relatives and friends. Even to the whole of Bila Sich; she had no way of assessing Belynski's true character.

Still, this did not diminish the village gossip, sideways glances, and avoidance of her when, on the rare occasion, she went out and about in the village. Although never outright confronted — fear of consequences, no doubt — there was a sense, an aura of general maliciousness swirling about her when she ventured to the government store or elsewhere. She was a traitor, and a whore at that.

As it turned out through the spring, summer, and fall, while she adjusted to her duties as chairman Belynski's "personal assistant" and live-in domestic, the village returned to a shaky status quo with no further displacement of kulaks or seizures of properties. Some sort of uneasy equilibrium had been granted, and the village and farmers went on with their business of ploughing, sowing, and harvesting of their crops. For his part, Lev could hardly believe it, but Oleksander had been right. Passive resistance had won back their independence — or at least brought about a favourable stalemate. Poor Oleksander. A cruel twist it was, thought Lev, to have Katya suddenly become Belynski's mistress. "She had no choice," he told Nina, who shook her head sadly, understanding and yet resentful. At whom, Lev was not sure. A month after Katya left, a rather morose Oleksander left too, back to Kyiv. Fortunately, his job was still available, as was his apartment. There really wasn't much for him to do, Lev supposed, unless he wanted to become one of them again and work the land.

Surprisingly, from the first day, Belynski was quite accommodating and decent to Oxana. He even tried to restrain his drinking, and when he did imbibe too much, unlike Gromeko, she noted, he did not engage in abusive behaviour but generally became philosophical, rambling on about life's misadventures in a maudlin fashion, with the emphasis on his particular woes. She was required to listen until he stumbled away to his room to sleep it off.

Sex, of course, was a given part of her duties, but even that wasn't a boorish affair. He was polite, practised, and considerate, treating her with a certain appreciative reserve, like a fine bottle of wine. Despite her abhorrence of the situation she found herself in and her preparedness to loathe him, it was difficult to sustain. There was an element of decency that shone through — not always, but enough.

The first time, she lay inert, awaiting his advances but not sure what to expect. Initially, he proved quite tepid and gentle, touching her cheek, stroking her hair, breathing in her scent, slowly emptying the space between them, his lips brushing her neck. He smelled of alcohol and tobacco, a faint musky odour, but not unpleasant.

Unlike some past encounters and what she expected given his actions at Oleksander's house, she steeled herself to endure. But such wasn't the case. He was more retrospective, probing and teasing, layering in sensation. His hands moved down her belly and lower still. She responded almost by rote. Oleksander too had some of these qualities, but not as skilfully honed. It was not that she was comparing, making a judgement; Belynski had, after all, put her in a compromised position. And she much preferred to be with Oleksander for his intrinsic integrity, if nothing else, which Belynski clearly lacked. Further, there was, she suspected, a latent cruelty and ruthlessness to the village chairman that she had yet to fully witness. Still, for now, Belynski seemed to satisfy his needs, and that was the only practical way of viewing it, she thought.

They established an unspoken routine. She kept house, would occasionally type correspondence, and filed. Once a week, normally Thursday night, he endeavoured to be reasonably sober, and they'd have their intimate encounter. Afterward little was said; she rose from his bed, put on her clothes, and quietly made her way to the door. Her room was on the second floor.

"I'll see you tomorrow," he'd often say, also getting out of bed and reaching for his pipe on the night dresser. He'd exhale a measured breath, strike a match, stoke, and draw on the stem — contentment. She nodded and closed the door. An understanding had been reached, rules of engagement, so to speak, and a pattern developed, a quid pro quo that defined her precarious situation.

***

Ivan Ivanovich Prasha, Belynski's official assistant/secretary, was less than pleased with his boss's new "acquisition," as he put it to one of his comrades in Dnipro Tavern. Rumours spread quickly, it seemed. Not only was she diminishing his status and undermining socialist morality on a daily basis, but it was also driving him crazy.

Prasha believed himself to be a true revolutionary, dedicated and uncompromised, doing his part for party and state. He had been a young pioneer, had gone through the required Komsomol programs, and had never wavered. He served his superiors impassively and loyally, but he was being tested now. He let it build stoically for a couple of months, but when it became clear that she was to be a permanent fixture (and thorn in his side), he could stand it no longer. It took the proportions of a primeval outburst one night after Belynski had drunk himself into a stupor and collapsed onto his bed. "You know Ivan that I appreciate your diligence," Belynski said, slurring his words while looking up at the little man, "but the house is getting crowded for you, is it not"?

"I'm not sure what you mean?" he replied, not liking the implication.

"Well, look, it's getting awkward. Perhaps it's time to find new accommodations. You know with Katya and me... You'd want your privacy."

You mean you and your concubine want more privacy, Prasha thought. For the first time, he realized that he was on tenuous ground, perhaps expendable, and he bristled at the thought. Was his place being usurped and he being eased out without thought for his position or his wants?

"I'll think about it," he muttered to his comatose boss as he left the room.

"You're undermining me," he sputtered at Oxana as she emerged from her room at one end of the second floor, making her way to the bathroom located halfway down the corridor. Prasha's room was at the opposite end with another bedroom (used mostly for storage) and toilet/bath in between. Katya had insisted on her own bedroom, and Belynski acquiesced, leaving his bedroom near the large study on the main floor. "I don't want to negotiate those stairs," he told Prasha. "Especially when I'm corked!" he added with a smile. So, Katya shared the upper floor with Prasha, including the toilet/bath facilities.

"Undermining you?" *I hardly talk to you*, she thought, wondering why this sudden outburst.

"I see you together using your enticements to no good end—"

"Spying, were you?" she retorted sharply. "A peeping pervert, are you?" She was well on her way to despising this little man who always seemed to be lurking and leering about.

"You're a tramp, a prostitute," he enunciated through his yellow, gritted teeth, his eyes widening behind undersized, round spectacles. "A blight on the socialist state!" he hissed.

"Comrade Prasha," she said formally, "I see you have a problem with me. I'm here not of my own volition, as you well know, and whatever issues you have with me you should take up with Comrade Belynski." *You're probably jealous and want to get into my bed*, she thought disdainfully.

Prasha grabbed her arm, his anger barely contained. She stared into his bulging, unblinking eyes, felt a tremor of fear, and collected herself. Slowly and deliberately, she said, "Be careful, Comrade, you don't want to create a serious problem for yourself."

Prasha hesitated, then relaxed his wiry grip, stepped back, composed himself, and marched down the corridor to his quarters. Katya realized that she had made an implacable enemy, which would not bode well for her.

***

Ivan Alexandrovich Prasha chided himself immediately after his confrontation with Oxana. He had lost control, and that wasn't what he had in mind. In fact, he understood her situation brought about by his boss and bore no particular malice for her. He presumed that Belynski threatened her, her agronomist partner, and by extension their other relatives/friends if she did not comply. Still, he could not let this slide to a point where he might be shunted to some barracks like a grubby militiaman — not at this stage of his life. He had come from nothing, a street waif in Kharkov, whose parents had died in the tsarist war, to a faithful party functionary. Street survival, cold, unforgiving orphanages, and finally party youth camps and Komsomol schooling had prepared him for a different course, and he had charted it with care. He kept in the shadows, the efficient assistant, a faithful, servant of the party taking his duties seriously, making sure that those honoured with leadership positions had the best assistance possible in doing their jobs. He organized, facilitated, provided information, and generally could be counted on for advice, whoever was his superior. It had held him in good stead. Belynski was the third administrator he had been assigned to; one moved up the apparatchik ladder, the other had disappeared. If the truth be known, he had no quarrel with Belynski, who had appreciated his qualities of efficiency and due diligence, until now.

What Prasha couldn't quite articulate even to himself without sounding overly bourgeois was that Oxana was an alluring distraction not only for Belynski but also for himself. Somehow, she had intruded and corrupted both his working and private world. His room was above Belynski's, and he could not only feel the vibrations but occasionally hear the moans of their lovemaking. It was a reminder of his own monkish existence and encouraged the siren call of carnal lust to which he was not immune.

Two days after his confrontation with Oxana, providence provided him an opportunity to reassert his control. It was a typical Wednesday. As the day wore on, Belynski began his drinking ritual in earnest. By late evening, Oxana had long retired, and Belynski staggered from his workroom/study to his bedroom. This night, he needed help and called Prasha, who was about to go upstairs to his chambers. "Give me a hand," Belynski slurred, giving him a lopsided smile. "Just to the bed… Want to collapse on something soft…"

As Prasha steered him through the doorway onto his bed, they both stumbled, hitting the night dresser and spilling the glass of water sitting on top. Belynski rolled onto the bed, dead to the world, while his assistant looked around for a cloth to wipe up the water on the dresser and floor. He opened the top drawer and found a thin file underneath a linen facecloth. Curious, he opened the folder, and there staring at him was a poster with Oxana Gerkil's photograph, except the name beneath was that of Katya Karina Kharsova. She was identified as a person that a certain Captain Krypniuk of the Kyiv Police Criminal Investigation Department was searching for in connection to a homicide in the city. Attached to the poster was another one the same with a note from Commissar Fedryk to contact him if Belynski had any information. Normally, he would have been privy to such correspondence, but for obvious reasons his boss had not shared this.

Prasha's first thought was that he should contact this Captain Krypniuk and/or Commissar Fedryk, who, he surmised, was just passing along the information, and get rid of this troublesome female. *Problem solved*, he reasoned, but then such things were never straightforward and quite often didn't get resolved in the way intended. It was best to leave the commissar out, for it would get Belynski into trouble, which served him right, but it could put Prasha directly in the path of Belynski's wrath. Going over the head of your superior was never a good idea. He was no less vulnerable than his boss.

After much second and third sober thought, Prasha decided on a more personal tack. He had leverage; why not use it? Perhaps now he could convince Oxana/Katya to whisper nice things about him to Belynski while expanding her household duties to include him. A discreet arrangement — perhaps Wednesday nights, when Belynski usually descended into the depths of his vodka bottle.

***

One morning, a week later, as Katya was preparing breakfast, Prasha walked in. Noting that Belynski was still to emerge from his bedroom, he casually stated he'd like to speak to her privately. "This is not a request, Oxana … or should I say, Katya," he whispered, adding tetchily, "I should turn you in."

Her whole body stiffened as she turned to face him. "Later, we'll talk." He smiled and walked out of the kitchen, leaving Katya trembling and aghast. *The sleazy little wart found out!* How hardly mattered. The fact was he knew that she was a fugitive that police (not to mention Sholtz) were looking for. What did he want for not reporting her? *Not hard to guess*, she mused bitterly.

And, as it turned out, she was correct. "First, your continued secret depends on my continued duties and residence in this house. I trust you can dissuade any thoughts that Comrade Belynski may have to the contrary. Secondly, well… Wednesdays would be most opportune," he suggested with a slight tremor in his voice. "Comrade Belynski is usually indisposed."

Prasha had caught up with her later that day as she emerged from her room. He did have a habit of appearing — from nowhere, it seemed. She did not argue, did not threaten to tell Belynski (what good would that do if Prasha informed the police?) or react in any demonstrative way. She nodded and pushed past him.

It took her a very short time to decide. She had to leave Belynski and Bila Sich as soon as possible. Staying would result in no good outcome. It was becoming too complicated, with no good ending in sight. She'd go back to Kyiv and get in touch with Oleksander (she still had a key to his apartment). Risky as it might be, in the short term there was no other reasonable option.

Leaving was surprisingly easy. Wednesday proved the perfect getaway day. A couple of days before, she acquired blank internal travel forms from Belynski's desk, part of the necessary documentation to leave the village. She filled them out and forged Belynski's signature. She knew that there was a daily truck run to the Korsun Railway Station to pick up passengers (usually party types) and supplies. She was well known as "the chairman's woman," and no one, least of all the sentry at the road checkpoint, would question her right to travel, but documentation was insurance. And indeed, the young militiaman barely looked at her papers when the vehicle halted at the check spot. The two other passengers' travel permits received more thorough scrutiny.

The timing was pure happenstance. Belynski and Prasha were out together on official business at the kolkhoz and MTS. They would return late with Belynski, no doubt, on his way to being sauced, since these occasions entailed consumption of alcohol at every opportunity. Prasha would not come to her room before ten at the earliest — that was the arrangement — to make sure Belynski was "tucked away" for the night. As she got on the Kyiv-bound train, she indulged in a smile. *The little wart will be disappointed.*

CHAPTER SEVENTEEN

Kyiv

Captain Emil Kryniuk was fast approaching a dead end in the Gromeko case. No hard leads had been forthcoming, and to date, Katya Kharsova was nowhere to be found, this despite her photo being circulated far and wide. The only additional information they had garnered served as background to her life in Kyiv before employment at the commissariat. And it scarcely amounted to a page.

A search of their own files revealed her name on a list taken from a raid on Madame Bovarsky's premises. Kharsova had apparently lived there along with other female migrants from the countryside. She was detained but never arrested as part of a prostitution ring that Madame Bovarsky allegedly ran. Of course, in due course, Bovarsky's ramshackle two-storey house was confiscated by the city and divided into apartments, the former tenants disappearing into Kyiv's growing underclass. Madame Bovarsky too had vanished, leaving no forwarding address. Lubick asked if they should try to track her down; Krypniuk thought about it and decided not. It would have been a waste of manpower, for almost certainly they would not find her, and even if they did, any information obtained would range from extremely nebulous to useless.

Besides, he knew that Kharsova had moved on, first enrolling part-time at Red Star Secretarial School and into the commissariat immediately after completing her studies. These facts were readily established from her employment record. Forthwith, in short order, she had her own apartment kept by Commissar Gromeko (albeit under an alias), which was quite remarkable, even if she had both beauty and brains.

So, what happened to her? Krypniuk wondered as time went on. *Did she kill Gromeko in some sort of lover's spat — self-defence, perhaps? If so, where did she obtain the gun?* Certainly, as far as they could determine, it wasn't Gromeko's; he didn't own one. *Or is she simply a witness on the run? Moreover, was she resourceful enough to have survived, or is she dead and buried somewhere?* Questions upon questions for which he had no answers.

Luckily, Krypniuk had received no further summons from Commissar Pavlick. Either the OGPU Kyivan chief had forgotten about him (highly unlikely), or it was just a matter of time. The lack of progress on this case would no doubt be seen as a sign of incompetence on his part and that of his department — in fact, the police in general. They were all feeling the muscle of the OGPU's heavy-handed bureaucracy in its attempt to subsume and ultimately control all policing functions. The walls were closing in; that, however, he'd leave to his superiors to sort out. At that moment he was still in charge of the case — nominally, at least.

Meanwhile, his and his officers' attention was diverted into the increasingly unstable and volatile city population as displaced and desperate newcomers flooded in from the chaotic countryside, seeking relief and refuge from Moscow's first five-year plan to industrialize. Large movements of displaced people into the city created havoc, opportunity for ill gain, and common crime, all part, it seemed, of Comrade Stalin's goal of creating a proletarian society.

***

Vasar Sholtz too was worried that Katya Kharsova was nowhere to be found. For him, she was the witness who could not only ruin his career but also put him in front of a firing squad, or worse, if certain individuals knew he was responsible for the elimination of Gromeko. After all, the man had greased many palms, some very high-ranking. While he fervently hoped that Kharsova had fallen into some deep sinkhole in the countryside, never to come out, his thinking over the months had evolved. Of course, he could simply deny, and it would be his word against hers, and who would believe her? More to the point, from his limited encounters at the commissariat, he thought her a rational woman who could see profit in reaching a mutual understanding. But he'd have to find her and convince her to keep her mouth shut! *Stay disappeared and you will be rewarded* was the message he wanted to convey. It all depended on her disposition, if he could actually meet her and relay it. *Too risky*, he decided, albeit with some remorse. There was only one solution that would appease his colleagues.

What if she knew about Gromeko's, and by extension, their operations and various embezzlement schemes that involved the "who's who" of Kyiv and the surrounding oblast? Thousands of rubles had gone missing in dubious contracts and hollow/fabricated projects that would not pass scrutiny if an investigation were ordered; incriminating documents were signed and duplicated; and Katya potentially had intimate access to all, to the man, his work, and their secrets. She might know little or enough to unravel all their schemes and seal their fates.

"We are not safe as long as she's out there somewhere," Sholtz was told emphatically by his associates. "No chances. Whatever she knows, whomever she might have talked to, we need to know about and contain. This cannot spread outside our circle. She must be dealt with — permanently."

Sholtz reluctantly agreed. And he had resources at his disposal, much of it readily provided by these nervous associates who could tap into an army of informers. It was a lucrative business with so many enemies of the state lurking about! If Katya Kharsova were in Kyiv, she would eventually be found. Once that occurred, it was a matter of obtaining an address and hiring a professional to do the rest.

Of course, these same associates did not know that he had, in an unadulterated moment of madness, shot the commissar of Commerce and Industry. And that, under any circumstance, could not come out! No, she had to be silenced. Regardless of what she knew about the inner workings of Gromeko's department, she was a witness, the only person who could place him in the apartment.

Whether she was believed or not hardly mattered. Once that came out, suspicions would arise that could not be tolerated.

Yet time had elapsed. There were no reports of her in Kyiv, or anywhere else, for that matter. Sholtz felt more relaxed, more confident that she might never surface.

***

Since his return to Kyiv, Oleksander Pylyp had experienced bouts of melancholy, which occasionally spilled over into anger. Of course, the situation was impossible for Katya; he understood that. Although Lev and Nina knew at least some of her story and plight and were sympathetic, the villagers didn't, and she became the gossip of choice — a wicked Baba Yaga who turned her back on them and sold out to the hated Bolsheviks!

Lev offered to "set things straight," as he put it, with the help of Tomash Chozh and others, by paying Belynski an unexpected visit, but that would have been a disaster with severe retaliation, as was the case with other communities that had decided to take retribution against the party overseers. "No, under no circumstances," Oleksander exclaimed emphatically, solemnly shaking his head. "We've maintained our collective discipline despite the pressures exerted and have survived largely intact. We cannot now engage in violence, which will surely provoke a military response for which we are no match." He had to accept that Katya had done what she had to do for her own welfare but also for that of the village.

At least, that was what he chose to believe. He hoped that it was temporary, that perhaps Belynski would be reappointed, that circumstances would change for Katya, and that she would find her way back to him. He was the eternal optimist and took her at her word that she wanted to come back.

Meanwhile, he laboured alongside Lev, Nina, Misha, and their neighbours, Vlas and Tomash, preparing the fields for planting. However, as the summer drew to a close, decisions had to be made; he couldn't extend his leave from Kyiv Agricultural Institute any longer, not if he wanted to retain both his job and his apartment. He received an ultimatum of sorts from the research department, declaring that as much as his contribution was valued, he needed to return immediately or not come at all. Thus, by the end of July he was back in Kyiv, in his old laboratory with his colleagues and in his small apartment less than a ten-minute walk from the Agricultural Institute. Life marched on!

But it didn't really, both personally and at the institute. He was suddenly lonely and increasingly despondent, realizing that optimism could take one only so far. This was compounded by his work environment. His agronomist experiments designed to test Trofim Lysenko's theories that eschewed or at least greatly modified natural selection and Mendelian genetics were not going well; he had been obtaining negative results before his hiatus from the laboratory, and now there was no doubt. The samples did not flourish as predicted, but in fact did not survive. The conclusion: Lysenko's hypotheses were incorrect! If implemented, they would do more harm than good.

Before he began writing his report, he spoke to his mentor and immediate supervisor, Maxim Robanov. He found him at his scarred desk in his tiny office, looking every bit an academic, complete with unruly puffs of white hair, flushed face, and silver-rimmed spectacles that seemed to narrow his eyes and lengthen his nose. He had on a laboratory coat with buttons that did not seem to line up with the holes. Oleksander wanted his opinion on the discouraging (to say the least) results. Before he was able to get too far into a recitation of his findings, Robanov brushed a hand through his unruly hair and suggested they take a walk. As he closed his office door, he whispered, "Not a word about disappointing results. You can't say that. And you most certainly cannot write that — not if you want to keep your position here and possibly your freedom!"

Oleksander gave him a look of alarm. "I can't fudge the data."

Robanov took Oleksander's elbow and directed him down the corridor. It was dimly lit, and no one was lingering. "It pains me to say this, but we are no longer scientists but propagandists. We are required to report that these tests ... experiments — yours included — were a resounding success. The seeds thrived, and the glorious state will soon have the ability to double, perhaps triple our crop yields."

"But that's—" Oleksander started to protest.

"Absolute rubbish," Robanov countered, lowering his voice. "I've known this for a long time."

"So, all this work is meaningless?"

Robanov did not answer his question directly. "No doubt you've noticed a few new faces since coming back?"

Oleksander nodded.

"Replacements for ones that have gone — on involuntary sabbaticals." He smiled grimly with a touch of irony. "Why? They were obtaining the wrong results. The *replacements*," he repeated with harsh sarcasm, "run around in white smocks, but they wouldn't know what constitutes scientific research if they tripped over it. They're political attachés, state spies keeping a vigilant eye on us, reporting to their local party masters. We're the intelligentsia, potential saboteurs who would undermine socialist progress. This is especially true if you are Ukrainian. So, if you don't want to be another involuntary sabbatical statistic, you need to lie — write a glowing report and destroy any evidence to the contrary. A purge began while you were away. I fear it's only going to get worse. Not all of us may survive."

"What happens if they proceed on the basis of these reports based on erroneous data? It'll be a disaster."

"And we'll be blamed."

CHAPTER EIGHTEEN

Bila Sich

At first, Belynski was puzzled, not quite believing that Oxana (he maintained her alias cover) had disappeared. "What do you mean she's gone?" he shouted when Prasha reported that his special assistant was nowhere to be found. "Perhaps something has happened to her," he said and then ordered Prasha to organize a search of the village. Later, when it was confirmed that Oxana Gerkil had left of her own accord, Belynski raged and drank, vowing revenge on her and on the village. Prasha stood stoically by, saying little. He hadn't gotten what he wanted, but good riddance, the harlot was gone!

For his part, rather than to pursue her and bring her back — no doubt she was in Kyiv with her "agronomist" fiancé — Belynski swallowed the bitter fact (with extra shots of vodka) and grimly got on with the business at hand. Not that he really had a choice. It would not do to have it come out that he had knowingly harboured a fugitive wanted by the Kyiv Police. Fedryk would probably have him shot! "Forget that Oxana was ever here," he instructed Prasha. "Too many questions will be asked. I can count on your discretion."

"Always, Comrade Belynski."

There needed to be punitive repercussions for the community, he decided, just to make a point, but before he could bring any demonstrative actions to bear, larger events overtook him and the community. As December and the end of 1930 approached, new directives were issued: collectivization was now to proceed by whatever means necessary. There had been no misunderstanding after all, and the campaign to place farmers onto the kolkhoz had not been misinterpreted or too zealously applied. The uneasy village calm was about to burst; the truce was over, and the fiction of voluntarism was eschewed for forced conscription. Party directives issued from Moscow declared collectivization needed to be completed by the end of 1931 using any means necessary.

It was with some trepidation that Belynski received a dispatch informing him that Comrade Fedryk, commissar of the Oblast Party Regional Council, was coming to visit, bringing a large entourage with him. This was in preparation for a large district plenum to be held with the oblast's who's who. *But why in such an insignificant village as Bila Sich?* Belynski wondered. True, the process of voluntary collectivization had slowed to a trickle, but policy had changed; the writing was on the wall, and he would ramp up the campaign to force the farmers onto the state kolkhoz, including clamping down on the kulaks.

***

Anton Fedryk opened the meeting flanked by important regional personages, including the commissar of the MTS and the commissar of the oblast OGPU. They were in the village church now dedicated entirely to state/party functions. Commissar Fedryk sat on a raised platform behind the same confiscated desk and chair as he did when he was presiding the last time. A striking red-star banner below a large portrait of Stalin where the altar used to be remained as the backdrop. It was officious indeed with the vozhd looking sternly on local Soviet Council Chairman Belynski and his councillors seated below. On his right were the high-ranking guests brought in for the meeting. Slivka, Fedryk's personal assistant, sat nearest to Fedryk, pen in hand, ready to take notes as the recording secretary. Prasha, his counterpart, sat, impassive, with the local village officials. The glow of scattered kerosene lamps gave Fedryk's narrow face a sinister tinge.

"The kolkhoz is everything, the collective is everything, the individual is nothing," he stated dramatically. "But here we are, Comrade Belynski." He shook his head. "This area has fallen further and further behind in those joining the collective. Why is that?"

"I—" Belynski began and abruptly stopped, realizing that it was a rhetorical question.

"I will tell you why." Fedryk stared at him, his lips curled in a cruel smile. "This village, this area, is in the grip of undesirable elements. You have failed to root them out — these enemies of the people. So … why is that?" Fedryk had a nasal voice that increased in pitch as he warmed up to his subject matter. His dark hawk eyes peered down at Belynski as if he were a scurrying mole. The local Soviet council chairperson looked away eventually, inspecting the wet patches of melting snow brought in on his boots. *How did this happen?* He suddenly found himself in the same position — or worse — as the countless farmers he summarily berated and passed judgement on in the local court.

"Again, I say the kolkhoz is everything, individuals are nothing. It should have been clear that there was no alternative but to join — joyfully and without reservation. Why is there resistance? That is the question I must ponder … *we* must ponder…" He cast his eyes on his colleagues to the right of him. "And there can be only one conclusion: that you are incompetent, lazy, and/or a saboteur deliberately not fulfilling collectivization goals in your district. The party punishes those who wilfully harm the party and the people."

"I do not wish to—" Belynski began pleading in a voice that sounded strangely like other voices he had heard before him and had dismissed with scorn. He abruptly stopped; he wasn't allowed to talk unless he wanted to confess.

"For not being diligent in your duties, for allowing, perhaps encouraging vandalism at the kolkhoz; and for…" Fedryk paused, looking down at his notes, "failure to reach your quota, you and some of your comrades will be detained and dealt with."

***

The sudden removal of Belynski spread like a prairie fire through the village. And for a couple of weeks it seemed that time had stopped. Certainly, it disrupted the equilibrium of the local party council while a new chairperson arrived, along with mostly strangers from the regional party organization, to take over. It would take the local Soviet council a little time to sort themselves out before turning their full attention to the village.

"It's been quiet lately," Vlas Chorney noted as he and Lev sat at the Dnipro Tavern.

"No bosses, no orders, and there's no one authorized to carry them out." Lev shrugged and took a gulp of his brew.

"What happened to Belynski?" Vlas asked.

"According to what I heard, he's now kaput — disappeared, along with at least four other members of the local Soviet council, including Martov and Sobil.

"Good riddance."

"I heard that practically the whole council was whisked away into the night. Gone." Lev waved his hand in dismissal.

"Hopefully, the collectivization campaign is gone with them. I'd drink to that!" Vlas raised his glass.

"I don't think that's why Belynski has been removed. In fact, I heard quite the opposite," said Lev. "Our reprieve may be coming to an end."

***

The new chairman who replaced Belynski bore a famous name, Tolstoy, except it was Dimitri and not Leo, and he had no familial or otherwise connection with the famous writer. He quickly distinguished himself as being even less likeable than Belynski. Even Ivan Prasha, who, oddly enough, stayed on as his assistant (for the sake of continuity, according to Fedryk, although Prasha thought it was because they couldn't find anyone else, given the purges that the party was conducting) had, in short order, reservations about his new boss. There was a fog of darkness that did not bode well.

Physically, Tolstoy was short, stocky, and carried a large bald head and pear-shaped face accented by pronounced jowls. *You were picked on and beaten as a kid,* thought Prasha after his first meeting.

Having a bad childhood and youth was one thing and could be forgiven, but Prasha could not shake the feeling that Tolstoy was not a particularly astute or strategic administrator. *Dumb as a plough*, he concluded, which would surely put the village, the kolkhoz, and the surrounding countryside into chaos and potential ruin.

True, Prasha had lingering resentment of Belynski and wasn't overwrought when his boss was taken away (overjoyed, in fact, that he wasn't removed as well by association, like most of the council), but still, comparatively speaking, as far as bosses were concerned, Tolstoy was a notch or two below. Under his direction, Bila Sich was not going to be absorbed into a functioning, prosperous kolkhoz as per the plan, but emptied of people, either gone to prison or displaced to the growing gulags.

Confirmation came less than a week after he was installed chairman of the local Soviet council. The vehicle was the *kolkhosp* court, where one by one, wayward peasant farmers were required to appear for any infraction against the state or disputes with their neighbours. Tolstoy proved a zealous judge, berating all who came before him and handing out outrageous punishments for trivial activity. As the official recorder at these court proceedings, Prasha could only cringe; some of it was quite laughable, if it were not so deadly.

As the acting court clerk, he witnessed and recorded all manner of cases brought before Tolstoy, from low-level crime (usually reported by state-sponsored spies), including personal insults, fights, theft, and failure to pay taxes, to crimes of a political nature, like accusations of being a kulak, resisting collectivization by various means, and/or spreading propaganda/untruths against the state. No matter the nature of alleged crimes, Tolstoy's sentences (invariably, anyone who appeared before his court was judged guilty) were harsh, ranging from deportation to "corrective labour" camps deep in the northern wastelands of Siberia, to imprisonment and death. The local population was debilitated by Tolstoy's unrelenting parade of inane and cruel court judgements.

The tone for crime and punishment was set with Tolstoy's very first case. "You are charged with agitation against the Soviet regime.

Attempting to undermine the authority of the party and government officials," he thundered from his judicial platform in the church.

"I was drunk," answered the accused, cap in hand, "and talked too much."

"So, it was just drunken loose talk?"

"*Tak.*" The man nodded.

"So, you didn't mean it?"

"I can't remember what I said," the nervous man answered.

"You were derogatory to the state — libellous, in fact — and critical of what the peoples' store provides."

"Oh that." The accused brightened for a moment. "Well, your comradeship, drunk or not, the shelves were empty, no kerosene, matches, salt … nothing. Anybody could see that, and what I said was not a lie—"

"Silence," Tolstoy roared, his jowls shaking, cheeks turning red. Prasha thought that Tolstoy was going to soil his socialist pants but stifled the thought. "You were overheard denouncing the state."

"No! Never. I was buying herring… I was told there was plenty of it … told there was a sale."

"You're a counterrevolutionary," Tolstoy spat out.

"Trying to buy herring is not counterrevolutionary," protested the beleaguered fellow. "I admit I talked too much and sang a couple of dirty, but not *anticommunist*," he emphasized, "songs."

"Think you're smart, do you?"

"I just want to go home."

Tolstoy ignored the man. "You're an ignorant *zhlob* (boor), and you will have an opportunity to reflect upon your state of affairs on a long, long train ride. Take him away," he ordered the stationed militiamen.

As Prasha recorded Simon Budka's fate, he wondered what would happen to his wife and five kids — the kolkhoz or a train ride as well. He sighed. For the sake of bookkeeping, that would have to be clarified.

CHAPTER NINETEEN

Kyiv

Katya had no difficulty either on the train or in Kyiv once she arrived. There were no menacing policemen or other sinister characters waiting, no one that recognized her or paid any attention. The only disconcerting item she encountered was staring at her on a poster in Kyiv's central station. Thank God there weren't any posters (that she saw) at the Korsun station. There, she might have been recognized! Staring at the poster before quickly moving on, for the second time she wondered who this Captain Krypniuk was and if he could be trusted not to simply put her away for murder, or worse, turn her over to Sholtz. There was nothing in her experience either growing up as a child in her native village or, indeed, in her brief *work* for Madame Bovarsky that would lead to trust or at least the possibility of a fair hearing from the police. Quite the opposite, she thought.

Nervous and feeling an empty desperation, with her worldly possessions in a small suitcase, she exited Central Station as quickly as she could, hopping a tram to the Agricultural Institute. Oleksander had mentioned when he gave her his city address that it was within a short walking distance of his place of work. She had no trouble finding the street or the building, a four-storey stone and concrete structure that blended baroque architecture, with minute pediments over the corners, and a central loggia, into an austere Soviet cube. Oleksander resided in apartment 302.

Katya fingered the key he had given her apprehensively, wondering what kind of reception she'd receive as she trudged up the dim and sour-smelling stairs to the third floor. Thankfully, she saw no one. Stopping at his door and taking a breath, she thought of what Belynski had said in a reflective moment. "Women, my weakness… Be mindful of them in your life, particularly the beautiful ones — like you. They can cause mayhem." Was she about to cause more mayhem in Oleksander's life?

Shaking the thought away, she knocked and waited. There was no response. Hoping that this was the right place, that Oleksander hadn't moved (they hadn't spoken or otherwise communicated with each other in over two months), she inserted the key and heard a reassuring click. She expelled a sigh of relief.

The apartment was pleasant enough, she decided, essentially two rooms split between a tiny kitchen/eating and living area and a bedroom adjacent to a bathroom/toilet. A grade or two below the apartment Gromeko had provided for her but a notch above the standard available. Looking around, she noted it was tidy, well kept, like his cottage. Certainly, he was neat, if nothing else. Moreover, she recognized some of his shirts hanging from a wooden bar inside the door of the bedroom. She proceeded to drop her suitcase beside one of the two chairs on either side of the modest kitchen table and stepped toward the cupboards over the cooking area. Bread, tea, and whatever else he had to eat was her main immediate occupation; she was starving and suddenly also very weary. It was good to indulge in food and sleep, a reward for reaching sanctuary — at least for the time being.

***

Her sleep fell away abruptly, and she sat up from the faded sofa the instant she heard the key inserted and the door opening. Oleksander came in and took off his winter coat and boots, hanging the former on a hook beside the entrance, before noticing that he had a visitor. Any trepidation Katya harboured about her reception was laid to rest the instant Oleksander saw her.

"Katya?"

The moment of shock and surprise transformed into an exclamatory "Katya!" He embraced her as she arose from the sofa.

"Oleksander... I'm glad I found you." She hugged him tightly, feeling relief mixed with reassurance. It mattered that he was there more than she could have imagined.

Gripping her by the shoulders, he stared directly into her eyes, suddenly fearful. "Has something happened? Is ... everyone all right?"

"Yes ... everyone is fine (*although I haven't seen Lev and Nina in over a month*). "It has more to do with my personal circumstances." She trembled and paused to collect her thoughts.

"As long as you are okay." He brought her closer to him, wrapping his arms around her once again.

"I'm fine. A little overwhelmed. But so happy I got here."

"Well," he smiled and put a finger to her lips, "you can tell me all about it, but first, what can I get you? You look exhausted."

"I was tired and hungry... I raided your cupboards and made use of your sofa. Feeling much better now."

Oleksander nodded. "Haven't got much food in here. I'll go out to the market. Pick up some things ... cook a proper meal."

"I helped myself to your bread, jam, and eggs, so I'm good. Could handle another cup of tea, though."

"Coming up." He disengaged himself from her and set about pouring water into a white porcelain kettle chipped in many places and heating it on the tiny stove. "Don't have a samovar or milk, I'm afraid," he said. "If I knew you'd be coming..." He smiled and gestured around the room. "This is it."

"How have you been since you got back?" she asked in turn, noting that he seemed to have lost weight. "Adjusted to work and life in the city once again?"

He shrugged. "I missed Lev and Nina and friends in the village... I missed you too," he stressed, "but life continues. I have much the same job I had before." He paused. "However, I'm not the point of discussion at the moment. I'm more interested in learning what happened to you — your unexpected but totally welcome visit," he hastily added. "I've gotten no news from Bila Sich. I can't imagine that Belynski let you go?"

"The village is much the same as you left it a couple of months ago. All is well with Lev, Nina, and Misha," she reassured him, coming closer and sitting on one of the kitchen table chairs. "And you're right, Belynski didn't just let me go. I ran away."

She proceeded to tell him about Ivan Prasha and his discovery of her true identity and the potential consequences. "I made a decision, because it would have created an impossible situation if I had stayed. Maybe I was too distraught, not thinking clearly. I hope my actions won't result in harsh repercussions on the village — not Lev, Nina, and Misha..." She trailed off.

Oleksander listened intently, pulling up a chair across from the small table. "Your situation from the beginning has been ... impossible." He reached out and placed his hand on hers. "You did the right thing. You would have been betrayed — inevitably."

"But what am I to do now? Belynski knows about us. He will find us. Set the police on you here."

Oleksander thought about that. "I don't think so — not yet. He withheld information that would not sit well with the authorities. On the other hand, Prasha might, out of spite if nothing else. We'll deal with this, find a safe place for you. But for now, we have a little time still to work this out. So, relax and get some more rest. I'll go out later to purchase some produce, and I need to talk to someone who may be able to help. We can make plans, figure this out over a meal and a bottle of wine. I'm overjoyed that you came." He smiled.

They made love that night, not so much enwrapped in the lust of sex as just being together in each other's arms. Passion aside, Katya felt safe again, an aspect that had eluded her stay with Belynski, no matter how hard he tried.

***

Oleksander's thoughts were mixed. He *was* overjoyed that Katya had come, notwithstanding the potential risks to Lev, Nina, and Misha. There certainly would be reprisals. Not too severe. He could only hope. However, there was also the question of what now? Katya couldn't stay in his flat for too long; indeed, someone, either Belynski/Prasha, Krypniuk/the police, and/or the killer of Gromeko (she still hadn't told him who she saw) were figuring it out and closing in. Added to this was the situation at the Agricultural Institute. Working there was becoming unbearable. Some sort of purge had begun, and he was sure to be on the list. Professor Robanov's words were coming to fruition. The administration, now dominated by new personnel, wanted his research notes, his reports, and were asking uncomfortable questions not only of him but of the whole research team. "There are political overseers everywhere," pronounced Robanov. "Our days are numbered, I fear. They'll be coming for us soon."

The next morning, Oleksander got up very early, prepared to go to work. He told Katya to stay in the apartment until he came home. When she protested that that would make for a long day, he relented. "It's probably safe to go for a short walk, but bundle up, keep your face covered, and your head down. Don't want someone to recognize you."

"Do you have to go today?" she asked with some trepidation.

"Be patient. I do need to show up at the institute. It'd be suspicious if I didn't. When I return, we'll discuss our next actions. I've been speaking to someone who might be in a position to help both of us out. This apartment will not be safe before too long, since I am probably on a list of 'undesirables' as well." He went on to briefly explain. "Dr. Robanov thinks his and my time are almost up."

"And who would help us?" she asked, trying to absorb what this meant for both of their situations.

"My neighbour across the hall. You'll meet him later tonight."

"How ... how can he help?" she asked, frowning.

"I'll explain later. I do have to go."

***

Oleksander referred to Anton Rubiniuk, a sixty-two-year-old widower who lived on his own across the hall in an identical apartment as Oleksander's. "More than meets the eye," Oleksander explained to Katya later that day. "A Cossack capitalist at one time.

Entrepreneur who imported and exported certain goods until the communists decided to take over. At least that's what he tells me, and I have had no reason to doubt him."

"What kind of goods?"

"The kind we probably don't want to know about." Oleksander smiled. "He never specified about his products. Chances are they weren't totally legal."

"So, how did you get to know him?"

"Met him in the building about a month ago. He invited me to play chess. So, I did. We play at least three times a week. Not a grand master but extremely good. I rarely beat him. But that's not the point. While we played, he talked mostly — lonely, I think — about how the Bolsheviks ruined everything, that 'Old Russia,' even under the most stupid tsar, was better than the Bolsheviks and their 'monkey men.' I never asked why he called them that. Told me that he still had connections. You asked me earlier how he can help?" He shrugged. "We'll see after our visit. I do believe he was in the smuggling business."

"What does he do now?"

"Lives quietly on a pension and other dividends, I suspect."

"I still don't understand."

"I don't quite myself. I mentioned my increasingly tenuous position at the institute and that I would of necessity have to move — disappear. I had no idea where to or how. He indicated that he might be in a position to help." Oleksander shrugged. "My options — *our* options are limited, so…" He trailed off.

"And he can do that?"

"Honestly, I have no idea or what he may demand in return for his services."

"Can you trust him?"

"No guarantees, but I have no reason not to, given his criticism of the regime. The way he talks, it's a miracle he hasn't been denounced and hauled away. Of course, he keeps to himself. More importantly, he trusts me enough not to report him, so…" Oleksander shrugged again. "Besides, at this point, we might not have much of a choice." He smiled. "Shall we go, say hello? He's expecting us…"

Rubiniuk greeted them with a toothy grin, crinkled cheeks, and unreserved enthusiasm that was uncommon among older Soviet citizens who, with justification, tended to be dour and suspicious. A stooped figure with a pronounced limp, his eyes took full measure of them before lingering on Katya. He possessed a full head of hair, curly, unruly, accented by a protruding forehead and square face. These features were somewhat softened by a small, straight nose and a yellowing Saint Nicholaya moustache that overflowed his upper lip.

"*Proshe, proshe,*" ("Please, please"), he said, ushering them in and taking a quick survey of the hall before closing the door.

He pointed to the ornate brocade sofa with a fading sunflower pattern quilt draped in the middle. On one side was a small table with a chessboard and pieces set, ready to play; on the other was a lone standing lamp with a yellowing shade. "Make yourselves comfortable," he said while moving to the tiny kitchen, where he had a large plate of thickly cut black bread, pickled herring, head cheese, blini, and what appeared to be some sort of delicacy. "It's real caviar," he proclaimed when they turned their attention to the table. "My son continues the business — unofficially, of course." He chuckled.

"The import/export business," whispered Oleksander, seeing Katya's puzzled look.

"Let's have a drink and a bite to eat, shall we? I have some kvass or *medo vukha,* Georgian mead wine, if you prefer." He addressed Katya. "Aside from Oleksander, I don't have many visitors, so the fare is limited, or should I say, customized." He laughed. "No not many visitors at all, especially such beautiful ones." He bowed his head to Katya.

"Thank you. Most kind," she said, adding, "kvass will be fine."

"Not at all, not at all. Please..." He gestured to the table.

Once the glass of kvass and two generous vodka shots had been poured, the standard "*nazdrovia*" ("to your health") salute given and the drinks downed (the vodka in one swift action), the meal began. Rubiniuk spread a generous layer of caviar over the coarse grain bread. "So," he began, turning to Katya, "Oleksander briefly mentioned that there may be difficult times ahead not only for him but also for you?"

Katya glanced at Oleksander, wondering how much he had told him of her situation.

"Do not worry; whatever it is, you and your secrets are safe," Rubiniuk reassured her.

"As I mentioned," Oleksander interjected, "Katya too may need a safe place to hide."

"I see." He nodded and poured more generous splashes into the two empty vodka glasses. Katya had taken only a sip or two of her kvass. "You want to disappear. Why is that? Who is after you? Oleksander was not overly informative." His attention was now squarely focused on her.

Katya glanced at Oleksander, who nodded. "I was a witness to a shooting here in Kyiv. The shooter saw me, knows me. He is a powerful man with connections. The police are also looking for me. They've posted pictures of me around the city. I'm probably their main suspect."

"Ah, a powerful man with connections," Anton repeated. "Who might that be?"

"I cannot tell you. It's best not to know. I don't want to compromise anyone — put them in danger." This was really a feeble excuse; the fact was that as a last resort, the documentation she had stashed if she indeed needed it was still there, and identifying Sholtz gave her leverage. She hoped it wouldn't come to that.

"Hmm…" Anton was not convinced but let it go. "Very well then."

"If I thought I could trust the local police, I would gladly give an interview. Tell them what I saw. But I don't want to be arrested for murder or have my head served on a platter to the perpetrator. And as I said, my photo is circulating about the city and countryside at the moment."

"A problem indeed," agreed Anton.

"Can you help?" asked Oleksander, leaning over the table.

"The question is: can my son help? He's in charge of the business now."

"Whatever price…"

The older man waved his hand dismissively, downed his refurbished drink, smacked his lips, and placing the glass on the table with a thud, declared, "I believe he can. It will take a few days to get a hold of him and make arrangements…"

***

While "arrangements" were being made (neither he nor Katya quite knew what that entailed, since Anton Rubiniuk remained enigmatic to the core, including about his son and "the business"), Oleksander kept up appearances at the Agricultural Institute, his anxiety increasing every day. Two days after their evening meeting with Anton, Oleksander's fears spiked when on his arrival at work that morning he saw two men in Professor Robanov's office going through his desk and files. They were haphazardly throwing his papers/reports into a wooden box. The professor was nowhere to be seen, and he dared not stop and ask questions. These men wore leather coats and grim expressions. Certainly not fellow researchers.

For the rest of the day, Oleksander went through the motions of peering into a microscope, observing seedlings, and making notes in the laboratory that were pointless; the hypotheses were utterly disproven. Except that the state could not allow that to be revealed. He constantly looked over his shoulder, believing that this was his last day of work, perhaps freedom. He was also certain that he wouldn't see his mentor again.

It was with extreme relief that he was able to leave the institute and hurriedly walk home. He didn't think he was followed, but the proverbial walls were closing in.

"There isn't much time left before they come for me," he informed Katya bluntly. "Either here or at the institute. I'm sure they've arrested Professor Robanov, saw them searching his office—"

"Who?" Katya asked.

"OGPU types, undoubtedly. Which means that I will need to expedite things with Anton."

"Well, my suitcase is packed. I guess you should pack too."

"Hopefully, Anton has come up with new accommodations. This may be the last night here for us. I do not plan to go to the laboratory tomorrow."

Prophetic words, as it turned out. OGPU agents came that night. Fortunately, Oleksander spotted the ominous black sedan rolling up to the curb just as they were about to climb into bed. Two heavily bundled figures exited from the back seat, and he knew instinctively that time had just run out.

"Quick, Katya, take your bag and leave. Bang on Anton's door. He'll let you in. They're coming!"

"What about you?" she asked urgently, scrambling to dress and pick up her scattered chattels.

"You go now! If they don't find me here, they will search every apartment in the building. I'll be all right. I'll get word to Anton when I can, if I can. Now hurry. They'll be up here any moment."

There was no time to argue or reason. Katya grabbed her suitcase, gave him a quick kiss, and fled across the hall, frantically banging on Anton's door. She heard the slow shuffle, the unhinging of a latch, and finally, interminably, the opening of the door. She had just made it in when thunderous footsteps intruded, making their way up the stairway. Anton and Katya remained frozen behind the door. There was a pause, then heavy pounding on the door opposite. After a moment it opened, there were loud but indistinct voices, and the door slammed shut.

Anton motioned to Katya. "Go to the bedroom ... crawl under the bed. In case they decide to visit Oleksander's neighbours."

The whole affair lasted about thirty minutes. They tossed Oleksander's apartment, looking for God knows what. Certainly, he didn't know, and then he was led away. Neither spoke much; that wasn't their job. Later, the interrogator would do the questioning.

Anton and Katya watched through the dark bedroom window as the two gorillas stuffed Oleksander into the back seat of the car before squeezing in on either side, and the driver sped them away.

"At least they didn't throw him out the window," Anton stated grimly.

"What will happen to Oleksander?" Katya asked anxiously.

"Nothing good," replied Rubiniuk. They sat at the small kitchen table in gloomy silence for a few moments, her host working on his fourth or fifth shot of vodka. After a while, he sighed heavily and shook his head "I fear I've lost a good chess opponent… There is nothing we can do for him now."

"Will they come back — to the apartment, I mean?"

"Probably not, at least not tonight." He shrugged. "They got what they came for. It will take them some time to get him down to Volodymyrska Street and the OGPU headquarters, to process him and arrange his accommodations." Rubiniuk gave a knowing chortle. "These goons may have to hang around for the interrogation. Besides, it's a cold night; they likely want to go home and/or get drunk somewhere. They'd figure there'll be time enough tomorrow to search the apartment more thoroughly and confiscate whatever they deem valuable."

"So, it's safe to go to the apartment tonight?" she asked.

"I suppose … if you have a key."

"I do, and there are some items I'd like to retrieve — like my coat…"

***

Katya decided to spend the night in Oleksander's apartment. Although feeling weary and alone, she was not sure that she could trust this old man she had just so recently met.

There were things in the apartment she needed. Most importantly, she knew that Oleksander kept a stash of "emergency rubles" in the sugar container. He had mentioned it the night before. "Not much, but in case you need it and I'm not here," he said, smiling.

"Well … you're not here," she whispered to herself as she pocketed enough rubles to sustain her for a week — if she was frugal.

Meanwhile, she thought again about the old man across the hall; she really didn't know what, if anything, he could arrange. And he certainly wasn't living high at a corrupt commissar's level, no matter where he obtained the caviar or the business he and/or his son were apparently in. Perhaps it'd be better to walk out into the street and disappear. But where would she go? Her only true connection in the city had been Gromeko and the commissariat. She had shunned her past with Madame Bovarsky, who was probably long gone anyway. Her only ace card was what she knew and what she had witnessed and the documents she had compiled that would expose high-ranking individuals in the commissariat and city, including Vasar Sholtz. Of course, it was also a doubled-edged sword that could just as likely get her killed.

The problem remained. She had no access to the place she had stored them, nor were her chances of survival that good even if she could. She needed allies who couldn't be bribed or betray her to save their own skins or that of their relatives. She sighed, sinking into the well-worn sofa. There seemed no way out, and now with Oleksander gone, no one she could trust.

The question came down to casting her fate to whatever decisions she made: disappearing into the bowels of Kyiv's broad proletariat with the few rubles in her pocket or throwing her lot in with Rubiniuk, who said he had connections and could help both her and Oleksander. *Too late for Oleksander now...* She'd decide in the morning.

CHAPTER TWENTY

Bila Sich

"It's a damn crime... Murder is what it is," declared Vlas Chorney, stepping inside Lev's stable/shed. The winter sunlight that streamed through the open door and window was weak and pale, surrounded by dark patches of gloom that threatened to engulf them both.

Lev turned from sorting piles of hay for the milk cows and rested his pitchfork against a beam support pillar. "Good to see you too, Vlas. You're speaking of Fedor Arken, I take it?"

"So, you've heard?"

"Yes, bad news travels fast."

Vlas seemed angry and at the same time deflated. "It was one thing for Belynski to beat him and take a few coins, it's another simply to blow him up!"

"What happened, exactly?" asked Lev gesturing, toward the open door, wanting some fresh air. "The story I heard was that he protested and was shot."

Vlas preceded Lev outside. "No, not shot. The old man was blown up! The requisition committee or whatever they call themselves came by to confiscate his possessions and probably to kick him out of his home. He scared them off by firing a shotgun into the air. Of course, the militiamen were called, surrounded the house, and when he didn't give up — kaboom!" Lev waved his hands toward the heavens. "They threw a grenade in through the window. The poor sod, didn't stand a chance." Vlas paused, and giving Arken his due, added, "At least he died resisting, with his boots on."

Lev pursed his lips and stroked his beard. "A hero — symbolically, perhaps. Still, resisting makes him no less dead! That's why I can't be a hero, and Vlas," Lev looked directly to the other man's eyes, "neither can you." He then turned his gaze to the village a distance down the road. "We have families. We need to survive if they are to survive." He paused and directed his attention back to Vlas. "I've been summoned to the kolkhosp court. I either join the kolkhoz or … you know the alternative."

Vlas nodded and changed the subject "Have you heard from Oleksander?"

Lev shook his head. "I wrote a while ago but have received no response. Perhaps the letter hasn't gotten through."

"Censored, you mean?"

Lev shrugged. "Wouldn't doubt it."

Vlas frowned and returned to the previous discussion. "The news about Arken is not the primary reason I came here. I too have been summoned to Tolstoy's court."

"When?"

"Tomorrow."

"I'll probably see you there then."

"I came for advice on what to do."

"And I've given it," said Lev quietly. "Join. There is no other choice if you don't want to ride the kurkul train to nowhere. I hear that the OGPU is looking for brigades to construct the White Sea-Baltic Canal"

Vlas Chorney did not argue. "Looks like we'll both be signing our birthright away."

"True," Lev responded solemnly. "If you fight, you die. If you run away or are taken away, your land can't come with you. This narrows your perspectives and the choices before you."

***

Tomash Chozh had a similar problem. The requisition committee, complete with an armed escort, had arrived at his home and informed him that his taxes were in arrears. They threatened to seize his property there and then, but he had one last chance before the kolkhosp court to avoid disaster.

Standing before Tolstoy's pinched face, flanked by other stone-faced and silent individuals, he could only think that thank God his beloved Sofia wasn't there to see this injustice. Everything they had worked for was about to become state property. She had died a couple years before the Bolsheviks arrived in Bila Sich and started causing trouble. Complications during birth. The midwife could save neither the mother nor the baby. *God takes what he wills, and without pain there is no life.*

Thereafter, grief distanced Tomash from God. From a gentle giant he became, on occasion, a belligerent beast to be given a wide berth. His animus was particularly reserved for the Bolshevik leaders and the army of young recruits they had hired to invade the village and harass the inhabitants into joining the kolkhoz. The man seated judging him epitomized everything he hated about these malevolent locusts sent to scourge the rural communities.

"I'm not signing anything," he declared, his fists clenched tightly, barely restraining himself from lunging forward and putting his hands around the weasel's flabby neck.

Tolstoy looked up from the document he had before him. "So be it. Suit yourself. You're obviously a traitorous kulak and will be treated as such." He nodded to Prasha, sitting on his left, who dutifully made a note. "Get him out of here."

Two militiamen stepped forward and grabbed his arm on either side. When Tomash briskly shook them off while staring at Tolstoy with undisguised malice, the men drew their weapons.

"Shoot him if he resists," Tolstoy ordered.

Tomash raised his hands and was marched out of the court. Head slightly bowed and seemingly resigned to his fate, he was escorted to a large waiting sleigh with a team of impatient horses. Ten or so prisoners (kulaks one and all, Tomash surmised) were already squeezed onto the sleigh.

Tomash knew it was stupid, but something inside burst. Less than a kilometre down the hard, snow-packed road, he jumped out of the sleigh and ran for it across the field. It took a moment for the accompanying militiamen to react. Finally, registering that a prisoner was escaping, the captain of the troops barked an order, and two guards on horseback were dispatched to bring him back.

"He went that way!" The older, stouter guard pointed toward a hill with a cluster of trees now bare of their foliage. He and the younger, more agile man had dismounted and led their animals atop the semi-frozen snow. It was too risky for the horses lest they hit a hole or otherwise injure themselves in the pursuit. They didn't want to be accused of carelessness, or worse, sabotaging military equipment. The times were precarious, and one never knew the future.

"He can't get far," said the older guard, stopping, hands on hips, catching his breath. The cold, pristine air he sucked in was searing his throat like a sharp shot of cheap vodka without the acrid smell.

"Give up," the other man shouted. "You have no chance of getting away."

Silence.

"Don't be stupid," the young guard persisted. "We promise not to shoot!"

"Says who?" the older guard wheezed. The other ignored him.

"Don't make us have to find you. You wouldn't walk out then."

Still silence.

"Shit," hissed the older guard, evidently catching his breath and straightening up. "We can't stay here the whole day waiting for the fucker."

The other held up his hand. "One last chance before we go and get you."

Chozh, who had crawled behind an old birch stump, knew he was in trouble and would soon be exposed. It was a foolish, compulsive thing to do, tumbling out of the sleigh like that, and he couldn't quite explain why he did it, but here he was. Should he surrender and risk being summarily executed or make a run and no doubt be shot? These really weren't promising choices to weigh if he wished to live. Still, he'd bet on the former sooner than the latter.

"Okay. Okay. Don't shoot. I surrender."

"Show yourself, hands up," ordered the younger guard, focusing on the copse of trees.

Chozh slowly rose from his cover and stepped out from the stump. *Will they shoot me or will they not?* He had no idea. *Please God spare me for now!*

His wish was granted, although the older guard took aim and was ready to pull the trigger. The taller, younger, and possibly brighter guard put his gloved hand over the barrel. "If you shoot him, we'll have to drag him to your horse, hoist him up, and then onto the sleigh. Do you want to do that?"

The older guard paused and reflected, then thought better of pulling the trigger. "You're right… Besides, I don't want any blood on my coat."

Instead, they frog-marched Chozh to the horses a few metres down the hill, tied a rope to his hands clasped in front of him, got on their mounts, and gingerly made their way to the sleigh. Chozh managed to stumble along without falling, but as he climbed back into the waiting sleigh, he was forcefully shoved by a rifle butt strategically aimed into the small of his back. This sent him sprawling into the knees and arms of other prisoners.

"Next time you need a piss, ask first!" the old guard sneered.

***

As Tolstoy became more and more agitated under pressure to fulfill party quotas both in terms of collectivization and grain quotas, conviction rates mounted, along with the severity of the sentences.

After brief appearances before the court, many stalwart farmers and villagers whose roots ran generations in Bila Sich found themselves slated for dispossession and deportation. Most were accused and found guilty of theft and/or destruction of socialist property, which meant they had offered some form of resistance against those officials who seized what was rightly their property. Tolstoy interpreted such resistance as kulak attacks on the people's representatives, technically punishable by death but most often commuted for a long train ride to a penal colony in Siberia. As he told an increasingly apprehensive Prasha, "An example has to be set for everyone to see, otherwise these peasants will run amok, have their way, and the party and state plans will fail. We cannot allow them to do that, not here in this miserable village or throughout the oblast as a whole. They have been convicted before the kolkhosp court, have they not?"

"Yes," Prasha dutifully affirmed. *Of course, you convicted them.*

"Then what's the problem? Socialist justice has been done, and the transportation has finally arrived."

And that was precisely the problem as far as Prasha was concerned. It was most unsettling and potentially a recipe for disaster to have hordes of villagers/farmers and their wives and kids herded into the town square awaiting transport to arrive, in this case a lorry and a number of sleighs, to haul them away.

Yet that was exactly what Tolstoy ordered. So, there they were, crowded into the square across from the former church/courthouse with OGPU soldiers on the perimeter. They stood huddled and shivering in the cold mid-February sun. The wind was blowing from the east, promising more snow. The immediate destination was the Korsun Railway Station.

Trouble should have been anticipated, Prasha thought, especially when husbands could not join their wives and children but were arbitrarily, indiscriminately divided into groups for transport, with no regard for family ties and clans. They knew or had a pretty good idea where they were going but assumed that they would do so with family. It was at least a twofold process: pack them into the lorries/sleighs for transport to the railway station where a "special" line of boxcars awaited them. Fifty or so to a car was the standard capacity before the sliding door was then abruptly closed and the long ride north would commence.

The trouble this day began from a single incident. A husband found himself separated from his wife and three children, who were in another group farther down the square. If they were not united, then they would travel on different sleighs, and it was feared they would end up travelling in a different boxcar — if not an entirely different train! He wanted his family with him. And after frantically gesturing to them and the guards, trying to make his case, he broke ranks with his group and started walking across the square to where his family was sequestered. Tolstoy, who wanted to be front and centre in the activities, ordered the distraught muzik to stop or suffer the consequences. He took out from the inside of his thick coat the ubiquitous revolver that high officials seemed fond of brandishing and made his way down the steps of the former church. Prasha hung back, thinking, *Don't do something stupid*, as Tolstoy moved forward and pointed the gun at the distraught fellow.

"I said stop! Go back to your place!" Tolstoy ordered in a scratchy, high-pitched voice.

Events thereafter became a blur as the man ignored the order and ran toward the group with his family. Tolstoy's gun fired, and the man dropped; there was a collective gasp from those in the square, and the crowd seemed to surge forward toward Tolstoy and his assistant, who still stood on the church steps, stunned, prisoners' lists slipping from his hand. There was a moment where all were paralyzed, unnerved by what occurred. Still staring at his smoking gun as if in disbelief that he had actually pulled the trigger, Tolstoy started to back away toward the church. A number of individuals rushed forward, not to attack the perpetrator but to aid the fallen man. This, however, had the effect of setting the OGPU soldiers into action. A panicked command was given to fire.

A few more men and women went down, creating an equal measure of chaos and rage. For a few moments, the authorities lost control and a couple of hastily assembled cordon lines were breached as people ran for their lives. Tolstoy quickly retreated into the church/kolkhosp court, with Prasha and a couple of other officials following suit.

Heavier military weaponry strategically placed near the church-cum-courthouse was quickly repositioned and the order given. A few prolonged bursts of machine-gun fire echoed in the clear air, after which bodies spewed randomly throughout the square like fallen chess pieces. The snow blotched with oozing red. The Bila Sich Massacre, as it was locally labelled, was quashed, and in due course enough sleighs arrived to load the survivors and ship them off. There was a train schedule to keep, after all. The sleighs were reinforced with additional armed OGPU horsemen, just in case.

***

For most of his adult life, Ivan Prasha had survived as a petty official willing to do what was necessary to retain and advance (if possible) his standing. And he'd done some unsavoury things at the behest of his superiors, from cheerfully signing death warrants for "enemies of the state" to soliciting bribes, currying favours, and turning a blind eye to all manner of misdeeds. He promoted himself as a very useful tool who efficiently arranged events and carried out orders. When Oxana/Katya presented a threat to him (which he surmised she surely did), he had sought to neutralize her while taking advantage; she would have provided a pleasant diversion from his mundane duties if it had worked out. Still, she had left, and he retained his position even after Belynski's demise. While not insensitive to her circumstances, he didn't have any lingering guilt or anxiety because of his actions. Whether in regard to Oxana/Katya, his role in seizing peasant lands and chattels for the kolkhoz, or deporting kurkuls to the depths of Siberia — it all constituted part of his job. His future, he had long surmised, depended on how ruthless he could be.

However, to actually see these people pointlessly shot was not only a little disturbing but also disruptive to the success of the collectivization programme in Bila Sich. It was totally unnecessary. Certainly, it made the populace angry, unruly, and unpredictable. He couldn't accept that what had happened was unavoidable. No, it was Tolstoy who, in fact, had precipitated the massacre.

Prasha grew increasingly uneasy, not only about those in the village community who'd love to slit their collective throats, but also about his superiors, Tolstoy in particular, who would, if necessary, cover his own ass. Prasha had no doubt that if party officials decided that what occurred in the square was "counterproductive" to achieving the required goals for the kolkhoz, it would be he and select local council members who would fall on Bolshevik swords.

CHAPTER TWENTY-ONE

Kyiv

Oleksander found himself in the bowels of OGPU headquarters, hustled down a set of stairs to a dark chamber that smelled of urine and human feces. Not his cell but a holding pen — he hoped. His escorts said nothing, nor did he encourage them to. There was no point. They were just following orders. He had no doubt that they were inside the imposing structure that housed the centre of the Ukraine's "political police"; quite possibly he was under 33 Volodymyrska Street, where, in due course, he imagined his fate would be decided.

It was suddenly very cold, almost as bad as the waiting room at the grist mill. The dampness made it worse, however. Even with his winter coat, which he thankfully had managed to shrug into before they marched him away from the apartment, he began to shiver. There were no discernable objects in the room they had shoved him into before closing the door. The only light came from the corridor through a small square opening dissected into two by a vertical steel bar strategically placed at eye level on the door. As his eyes adjusted, he saw that indeed no bed, no chair — in fact, no amenities whatsoever appeared except for a lone bucket in the far corner. Surely, these weren't his living quarters?

He couldn't say how many hours he remained in this guest room, alternately pacing to keep warm and resting against a corner wall, but he tried to treat it as a reprieve from the unpleasantness that was to come. Eventually, two different guards showed up at his door. One stepped forward, blocking the light. "Get back," he ordered, after which

Oleksander heard the release of the lock as a key was turned and the door squeaked open. "Come with us," the guard continued gruffly.

Oleksander was marched down the corridor and up a set of stairs, where he was escorted down another hall. At the end, they came to a door with a discreet plaque: *Boris Pavlick, Commissar, Office of Special Investigations.* The lead guard gave a polite, formal knock and heard a definitive "enter." Oleksander was ushered into a warm, brightly lit room dominated by an enormous desk, behind which sat a very large — to the point of overflowing opulence — bald man wearing a strained khaki uniform with epaulettes that indicated high, but from Oleksander's perspective, indeterminate rank. The wall beyond was adorned with the increasingly familiar red Soviet flag and two portraits: a smiling Stalin on the right and another on the left that Oleksander recognized as the bearded Felix Dzerzhinsky, first head of CHEKA. *Seems fitting*, he thought. The two guards guided him to a solitary chair in front of the desk and promptly stepped back a few feet almost in unison, positioning themselves on either side of the guest.

"Your name?" asked the man behind the desk, setting down his pen and looking up from whatever he was writing.

"Oleksander Pylyp."

"You are a researcher at Kyiv Agricultural Institute?"

"Yes."

"For how long?"

"Three years — a little over ... since I came to the institute."

"You, of course, know Maxim Robanov?"

"Yes, he is head of the genetic research department."

"Your superior?"

"Yes."

"How long have you known him?"

"Ever since I came to the institute — about three years," Oleksander repeated. He didn't mention that he had also been a student in a number of Professor Robanov's classes.

The man, Commissar Pavlick, Oleksander assumed, since he had not introduced himself, nodded and shifted his weight with a grunt. "The nature of your research?"

"I'm an agronomist experimenting on plant genetics." He was about to further explain his work of verifying Trofim Lysenko's unorthodox theories regarding germination and enhanced crop growth but decided the less said, the better. Robanov had warned him, but he didn't know where this was going.

Pavlick pursed his lips. "Would you say the experiments you do at the institute are valuable?"

"Yes — crucial, in fact." Oleksander's response was enthusiastic. "How else can we test the hypothesis for implementation?"

"Even if it's falsified?"

"Falsified?"

"Of course!" Pavlick leaned forward, the chair groaning in protest. "And you know this perfectly well, Comrade Pylyp. We have irrefutable proof!"

Oleksander did not know how to answer other than a flat denial, which he knew was not the answer sought. He remained silent.

Pavlick continued, "The question emerges, are you part of the traitors, saboteurs who conspired with Robanov to discredit the Soviet state's eminent scientist and undermine his important project destined to feed the proletariat — or were you duped?"

"What?" Oleksander was incredulous. "I — we are dedicated researchers who seek to discover the truth based on scientific verification—"

Pavlick slapped the palms of his hands on the desk. "Enough! Documents have been seized that clearly show that Robanov and your colleagues have destroyed relevant results and produced false reports that impute the whole scientific community. No doubt, they were working at the behest of foreign, capitalistic powers and agitators to undermine the confidence in our agrarian sector and deprive farmers of planting and harvesting bountiful grain crops."

Oleksander had never heard of such utter nonsense. "You mean our Lysenko experiments? I assure you that such was not the case at—"

"Are you part of this nefarious conspiracy?" Pavlick interrupted. "That is the only question you need to answer."

"What conspiracy? There is no—"

Again, Pavlick cut Oleksander off, glancing at some papers in front of him. "I see you've been away from the institute for a while... Leave of absence?"

"Yes ... true." Oleksander was caught off guard by this new line of questioning.

"You own land in a village." Pavlick squinted at the piece of paper before him, his stubby forefinger running down the page. "Bila Sich, is it?"

"Yes."

"And you took this leave for what purpose?"

"I had some personal business to attend to."

"Comrade Pylyp. Are you not a kurkul engaged in sowing dissension in the countryside to further unrest against collectivization and the five-year plan?"

"No. I—"

"Well..." Pavlick looked up from the document with a satisfied smile. "Now you have a chance to prove your innocence and demonstrate your loyalty to the state." From beneath the pile, Pavlick produced a single sheet of paper. "I have here a statement outlining Robanov's crimes against the people. It confirms Robanov's treachery, his false research results, and his intentions to subvert Comrade Lysenko's esteemed work. It is your duty to sign it."

"I know nothing of this document." Oleksander felt weak-kneed. He was being trapped and pressured into denouncing his boss.

"Most of your ... colleagues signed," Pavlick stated as he shoved the document toward Oleksander.

Oleksander stared at the two paragraphs presented for his signature. Essentially, Robanov was accused of being a foreign agent paid by nefarious enemies of the state to discredit Lysenko and Soviet scientific achievements.

"You were duped, misled — here's your chance to acknowledge this fact and denounce the man who deceived not only you but many others working under him. I'd advise you to take it!"

The only thing Oleksander could think was: *Is this my moment of self-worth? Will I denounce, slander my mentor to save myself or refuse to be party to an outrageous lie?* Perhaps he could stall, prevaricate in the hopes of ... what? "I would need time to review and think—"

Pavlick laughed. "This isn't up for discussion, thinking, or sorting out." He placed a pen on the statement Oleksander was required to sign. "Your time has run out."

"And if I do sign?"

"We will reconsider your part in this traitorous act." Pavlick smiled smugly.

"I see..."

***

"These are dangerous, difficult times at the moment," averred Anton Rubiniuk, slurping his tea while regarding Katya with a mixture of concern and curiosity. "I've got word from Lushka, my son, and he needs more time to make arrangements for your new living quarters away from prying eyes. It seems you are anxiously sought after, and not only by the police. Of course, you'll stay here in the meantime."

"Why are you doing this, really?" Katya asked. After spending a restless night in Oleksander's apartment, terrified that the OGPU agents or whoever they were might return, she had decided that her chances on the streets of Kyiv were not great and that she needed to trust someone. It might as well be Anton. Still, she was not completely sure.

"Ah ... good question, and you are correct to be skeptical..." He thought for a moment. "Because I like Oleksander, even though his chess game could use improvement, and I believe I like you too! Besides, you are in trouble, need help, and I can do so." He shrugged. "Lushka has seen your face on posters around Kyiv. You are famous!" He gave a small chortle. "Anyway, Lushka is intrigued. However, you must have a new identity, a new name."

"I already have an alias — Oxana Gerkil — along with identity papers."

"Is it a safe one to use, not known to the authorities?"

Katya wasn't sure. She had forged the document while in Belynski's employ, but he wasn't in any position to reveal this information, given his complicity. "No reason not to — at least in Kyiv."

"Good, very good. It makes things easier."

"Do you know where I'll go?" Katya asked, reaching for a piece of dark bread and breaking it in two. Suddenly hungry, she spread some sort of indeterminate jelly on each piece.

"I don't know exactly, but I can give the general location. You'll be in Kyiv, if that's what you are worried about." He cleared his throat. "As you probably know, Berestove Mountain provides not only a magnificent view of the Dnipro River but also contains a huge network of caves."

"You mean the Pechersk Lavra?" Katya knew that the Kyivan Monastery of Caves went back hundreds of years, with hundreds of kilometres of catacombs on numerous levels famously inhabited over the centuries by orthodox monks. Just about every inhabitant of Kyiv at one time or other passed by the great main landmark, Church of Elevation of the Cross.

"Not quite, but the same idea," affirmed Rubiniuk. "One can hide anything or anyone in there, from smuggled caviar," he smiled, "to beautiful women!"

"So, why have you not moved? You'd be closer to your son, I presume?"

"That I could, and God knows this apartment has its issues." As if to the point, he slowly rose from the kitchen table and retrieved a woollen sweater from the tiny closest to the right of the entrance door. "The heating seems to be on the blink again... Nevertheless, I like it here. Lived here with Marta practically all my married life until — well, she's passed on." With his right hand, he made the sign of the cross. "Such is life." He sighed. "But no, I'm too old and settled to move; Lushka has quit trying."

"I'm sorry about your wife."

Rubiniuk waved Katya's comment away. "Over five years ago now. I am fine. Natural, inevitable in the course of life. We had many good years."

They sat silent for a moment, each submerged in their own thoughts. Katya broke the silence. "Do you think they'll let Oleksander go?"

"As I said before — and I don't mean to be unkind — but truthfully, no. The Bolsheviks, their political police, and their tactics are worse than the tsar's Okhrana. We can only hope that he'll survive. His fate is uncertain, as is ours. If by some miracle he reappears or I know what's become of him, I'll get word to you. That is if I'm still around, but never mind that; for the next while you will remain my guest. The bedroom is yours. I think it not wise to return to Oleksander's apartment for the night. You've taken out what you want?"

"Yes, but I couldn't take your bed," Katya began to argue.

He would hear none of it. "I'll be comfortable on this old sofa — no argument! Besides, this is the most useful I've been in a long time. Also, the most excitement I've experienced in many years. By the way, do you play chess.?"

"No." She shook her head.

"Pity, but no problem. I'll teach you."

***

Police work, like most activities in life, had its surprises, thought Emil Krypniuk as he settled into his chair and stared at the stack of miscellaneous files on his desk. And this one was indeed unexpected. The Gromeko case had gone nowhere — all the leads had dried up, dead ends abounded; then, quite inexplicably, there was a break, a way forward in an investigation. *Will wonders never cease?* He shook his head. The information he had received came about in a capricious and random fashion. Gromeko's/Kharsova's apartment had remained unoccupied for weeks first, because it was the scene of a murder, which proved too macabre for many potential occupants, and second, because it had suffered water damage when the heating pipes burst.

One of the workers came upon a sag in the ceiling inside the small clothes closet. A couple of tiles were loose, dangling, in fact. He gave them a tug and out fell an oilskin sack with a leather satchel filled with red file folders containing what looked like stacks of official papers. Since his reading skills were quite poor and nothing good could come out of knowing anyway, the prudent course, he decided, was to pass the bundle along to the project foreman, Vlady Kroopsk, and make it his problem. Still, the leather satchel would prove useful, so why not keep the satchel, dump the papers into the sack, and present it to the savvy old boss of the repair crew? It would, he reasoned, put him in good stead as an honest workman.

Upon receiving the bag and its contents, Kroopsk, scowled, scratched his head, and decided he too wanted nothing to do with what appeared to be nefarious state business. There had been a shooting in the place, after all; best let the police handle it. He promptly found the poster of the person who presumably committed the crime still tacked inside the front door of the apartment building and took note of the name and number of the policeman in charge. Later that day, he had phoned from a public kiosk, asking if Captain Krypniuk was available and was fortunate enough to get the head of the Criminal Investigation Department on the line. Giving his name, who and where he was, the foreman told Krypniuk of the discovery of some official documents that had literally fallen out of the ceiling. And would he like to have them?

Krypniuk informed the foreman that he would be right over and to keep them secure. "It's best that we keep this between ourselves," he said solemnly. His words had an implied warning that was taken to heart.

"I understand," said the foreman.

After Krypniuk took possession of the documents, however, he did not go back to the station but rather to his home. Too many eyes and ears at the station were curious about his business. It was an intuitive, back-of-the-neck feeling that over the years he had come to trust. These papers were best read privately in his favourite chair over a beer. Ivanka understood that he took work home occasionally (more often, it seemed, these days) and she wouldn't mind his neglect; his son, Yuri, wouldn't notice, too preoccupied with his studies and usually out and about after supper with his school friends.

Usually, Lubick would drive when they were on official business, but since Krypniuk couldn't locate his sergeant, he took the tram instead (he never trusted his own driving), and now with the sack tucked securely under his arm, he rode it to his apartment, where he surprised Ivanka with a midday hello and quickly tucked the trove of documents into the bedroom drawer before going back to the police station. Once ensconced in his office, he decided not to tell anyone of his acquisition until he had thoroughly gone through the material. Patience came at a premium for the rest of the day as he worked through the usual pile of cases, most petty and routine, and gave out assignments to those most worthy of investigation. He could hardly wait to get home.

For two nights, Krypniuk meticulously sifted through the mimeographed letters and contracts, making detailed notes as he read. What he discovered was revealing and totally dumbfounding in its depth and scope.

It appeared that three-quarters of the appointed commissars and high-ranking apparatchiks were lining their pockets; bribes, blackmail, kickbacks, illegal contracts, illicit deals, and partnerships seem to be the normal of "socialist" business. Of course, he had suspected that such was the case, given the nature of Bolshevik rule, but the prevalence, extent, and more to the point, individuals listed in explicit criminal activity took him aback. Gromeko and/or Kharsova were privy to deadly documents that had at the very least made many important people nervous. Was that why Gromeko was killed? Yet there was no evidence that the apartment had been searched or indeed ransacked in any way. If someone were looking for the documents, surely they wouldn't have left the place so neat and tidy? According to the foreman, the documents were hidden inside the ceiling tiles. Was that Kharsova's doing? Was that why she was so difficult to find? Or dead! Krypniuk sighed. Without evidence to the contrary, he had to assume that she was out there, alive and hiding.

But a more immediate problem loomed. What to do with this information, particularly the lists of payoffs, bribes, and quid quo pro deals, everything from clandestine contracts to nepotistic hiring practices/promotions, to under-the-table payments for alleged services rendered — or not. What made his next move difficult was there was only one person in the Criminal Investigation Department he could trust.

Next day, Krypniuk sat stoically at his desk, waiting for Sergeant Nickolay Lubick to make his appearance. He rose, grabbed his heavy coat, and stepped into the hallway, intercepting the shorter, stockier policeman as soon as he walked through the main door. Lubick stopped and studied his boss's face as if to say, *what's up?*

"Saving you the trouble of taking your coat off, *Sergeant Comrade*," the code words they used when in need of a private conservation. Lubick nodded and immediately walked out again.

Once out in the street, Krypniuk got to the point. "I have quite unexpectedly come across interesting documents that most certainly have a bearing on the Gromeko case. I need to warn you, however, that they contain highly volatile material that like excessive vodka and tobacco may not be good for your health." Krypniuk paused, his breath floating in the crisp winter air. "So, do you want to know?"

Lubick gave his boss a wounded look. "You know the answer."

"I do, but I had to ask. For the moment no one else can know."

Krypniuk proceeded to relate that there had been a cache of documents hidden in the apartment and how these documents came into his possession.

"Fortunate that he gave them to you and not simply disposed of them."

"Yes, most fortunate … if we survive!" Krypniuk stated flatly. "I want you to read them… You are a better notetaker than me. Come by the apartment after work. Take them home for a couple of days. We'll compare notes."

"You mean find the likely suspect on a who's who criminal list?"

"They're all criminals, but at least one is a killer," Krypniuk replied. "Of course, at this point I would be foolish to turn the documents over either to the chief or our OGPU friend."

Lubick had no objection. Both knew their careers, possibly their lives, depended on their discretion. "So, what is our next move?"

"After you read them, we compare notes and go from there. Hopefully, a course of action will present itself. One thing is for certain: whether Kharsova shot Gromeko or not, she's in grave danger. We need to find her before it's too late!"

"If she's alive."

"If she's alive," Krypniuk agreed.

CHAPTER TWENTY-TWO

Bila Sich

Lev Devchenko and Vlas Chorney joined the kolkhoz with the knowledge that this was their only choice if they and their families were to survive. Refusal would result either in deportation to a labour camp or being shot as a kurkul. As it turned out, the Devchenkos fared better than Chorney, his wife Iona, and their three offspring. Although Lev gave up his home and livestock, he was allowed to "appropriate" Oleksander's smaller cottage on the edge of the village. He really didn't know why. Perhaps no party official wanted such a modest home, and even with steady deportation that decimated the more than three hundred families that constituted Bila Sich, the kolkhoz was hard pressed to accommodate all those displaced and forced to join. Regardless, it was more comfortable than the hastily erected barracks that the Chorney clan had to share with other families, including the communal dining and toilet facilities. He learned of his friend's fate third hand, since the Chorneys were relocated on the opposite side of the village. He missed their frequent get-togethers, which now proved more difficult.

Lev was more fortunate in another way, which he scarcely realized at the time. It just so happened that he had quarantined one of his two milking cows in Oleksander's shed adjacent to the cottage. The Holstein was always a bit underweight and had gotten sick, and it appeared to be from more than just eating too many apples in the orchard, Lev figured. He didn't want to risk some sort of contamination of his other milking cow and thus "stowed" her away at Oleksander's. Having taken his best milking cow, the requisition committee did not bother or forgot to search his brother-in-law's place. If Lucia could be nourished back to health and remain undetected, he, Nina, and their son could survive what food deprivations the winter would bring. For Lev, it was worth the risk, especially when rumours began circulating of food shortages and potential starvation in the countryside.

***

It soon became apparent that the Bila Sich kolkhoz was never going to reach its quotas (they were totally unrealistic anyway), and that, in fact, the collective farm would have trouble producing enough surplus for its own members. The reasons became very clear, at least to Vlas Chorney. The people running the kolkhoz, from the chairman to the foreman to the party clerks and accountants — had no agricultural experience. Most were outsiders, city dwellers who spoke Russian for the most part and knew nothing about what seeds to plant, when to plant and harvest or, for that matter, how to store the grain.

"They're only good at parading around like peacocks, looking stupid and haranguing those who actually know something about farming," Vlas complained to his fellow kolkhoznik.

"I don't doubt that," replied Sergi in a low whisper through the side of his mouth as they walked toward a sleigh that would take them to a woodlot as part of a firewood-cutting brigade. "I heard that this collective can't pay its taxes and has no resources to rent the MTS tractors."

"That's a laugh. From what I see, most of the tractors are broken; no one around with the tools to fix them. The chairman is now looking for wreckers and saboteurs to blame." Vlas chortled sarcastically.

"Not surprised. Someone has to be blamed," Sergi said as they approached a forlorn horse attached to a sleigh with two other kolkhoz "volunteers."

"Well, if our dear idiot chairman is not careful, he'll still end up taking the blame, if not for incompetence — which he richly deserves — then for not stopping the so-called saboteurs. Isn't that the way it works?"

Sergi shrugged, pulling on his wiry beard. "I'm out of clues."

To be sure, a consummate critic of authorities at the best of times, Vlas was angry and resentful. He and Iona had lived in a modest enough but comfortable house with a kitchen and proper furnishings, icons covering whitewashed walls and a wide wooden bench that served as a warm bed over the oven during cold winter nights. Now they were crowded with others in a single room, sleeping in wretched cots, with a communal toilet at the end of a dingy hall. Instead of reasonable heating, the flooring allowed freezing drafts of air that penetrated not only from the thinly insulated walls but also from beneath.

It was only Iona who kept him in check, on a survival course. "I know it's hard; I know it's unfair," she consoled him, "but we do have a roof over our and the children's heads and food to eat."

"So far," Vlas grumbled as they sat in their small, partitioned space while the children slept. "I'm beginning to see lots of ragged folks wandering along the roads and in fields — and it's not only the vagrant class. People are hungry. You can see it in their faces, their eyes. It will get worse. The harvest was poor, and there'll be little left after the state takes its portion."

"I suppose we must have a little faith that we'll be provided for," Iona whispered as they got ready for bed.

Vlas nodded, but his "faith" was shattered. The kolkhoz could not repay its loans, or the taxes imposed (he wasn't sure which, or was it both!), could not meet impossible grain requirements, and had no resources to rent tractors — fixed or not! Starvation on the kolkhoz was a real possibility. This grand, state-operated farm — the one they were beseeched, cajoled, and ultimately forced to join — could simply stop functioning because people with no food and no future ceased to work. What irony to a key institution of the new socialist order. And what a hiccup in the five-year plan.

***

While better off than Vlas, Lev too had his issues. In his case, it was the kolkhoz manager, Dmytro Maserkin, in charge of "cultivation."

The two men took an instant dislike to each other, particularly after Lev took exception to some of Maserkin's seeding orders that he knew were both wasteful and inefficient.

"You're a troublemaker. Do you know that?" Maserkin sneered one day as Lev came in from the field. "Think you know everything — like a kulak!"

I know more about farming than you ever will, Lev thought, trying not to rise to the bait. "No… It's that I have had some experience running a farm, and perhaps you haven't as much… Just trying to be helpful."

Maserkin's eyes narrowed. "Be careful what you say, or there will be consequences." Maserkin's voice rose to a notable pitch, so much so that others nearby shovelling manure into a wagon in the main barn paused and noticed before deciding not to.

Lev said nothing while Maserkin badgered on. "You're the problem. Think I didn't notice your carelessness with the plough?" he declared, his voice edgy. "You damaged it."

"No, it was barely useable to begin with," Lev replied quietly before being cut off.

"And the horse under your care has a sprained tendon. Is that more carelessness or sabotage? You did it on purpose, didn't you? You're a kulak, aren't you? How much land did you own — ten, fifteen hectares, two, three horses, milk cows, pigs, chickens?"

There it was: the accusation. "Does it matter how much I had? The collective has it now." *Or most of it.*

"I should report you as a kulak saboteur undermining the kolkhoz!"

Lev remained silent. He didn't know how seriously he needed to take Maserkin's threats; he tended to be bombastic and full of himself in general, but Lev needed to be careful. *Hopefully, he'll skewer himself in time through his incompetence, if nothing else!*

***

After the Bila Sich Massacre, Tolstoy became increasingly paranoid and cruel; or so it seemed to his personal assistant. Prasha, on the other hand, grew more pensive, reflective, and alarmed. He did not know much about the nasty little man except that he came from the Donetsk region, that he had a wife somewhere from there who, if the rumours were to be believed, had left him, and that he was not highly regarded by anyone who knew him. Why Fedryk had appointed him as Belynski's replacement was beyond Prasha's comprehension. Perhaps the appointment was a form of punishment, and the commissar of the Oblast Party Regional Council had no choice but to pick him.

It hardly mattered now, as far as Prasha was concerned. In Bila Sich, the building of prosperous socialism was in disarray, the promise of the revolution betrayed. The kolkhoz was failing and failing badly. The kolkhosp courts had weeded out every conceivable malcontent/kulak, and those who remained "joined" the collective farm. And yet it solved nothing. In fact, the kolkhoz became the problem. Certainly, there was no way it could meet the objectives set for it. He saw the figures and the required grain quotas. (*Even Tolstoy can see that!* he hoped). The harvest had been low, and the reasons were not hard to ascertain, from poor management and inexperienced cadres to a resentful workforce who had little stake in the land that once was theirs. How could it be otherwise for those who had witnessed their friends die or be vanquished and their community crushed? And with no hope of life improving, what remained was despair.

But that wasn't the worst of it. Prasha worried that there might be a food shortage for the collective, never mind the general countryside. Stocks were thinning, since everything the farm produced was shipped out, even the seed grains, with no provision for incoming rations. He noted clear signs of food distress already, and if no aid came, the winter of '32/'33 would indeed be hard — devastating, in fact. Surely, in the interest of the party and state, Fedryk and his superiors — if not Tolstoy — would take appropriate measures.

And yet as the weeks went by and the food situation got worse, no relief came. Quite the opposite.

CHAPTER TWENTY-THREE

Kyiv

After his meeting with Pavlick, Oleksander was taken back to the holding room. *Maybe this is my cell after all,* he thought. If so, it would have been nice to provide a cot and blanket! He had no idea what they'd do to him after he refused to sign the document denouncing Professor Robanov; he expected the worst. His other thought was for Katya; he hoped that his recently acquired friend across the hall was true to his word and could get her to a safe location — if there was such a place.

Oleksander spent three days in his tiny hovel, anticipating that he'd be marched out and either shot or interrogated again more strenuously. When not pacing along the walls, inspecting every crack and rough edge in the brick and stone, he walked diagonally from one corner to another just for variety, until finally exhausted. Then he'd curl up on the floor and sleep. At least it wasn't as cold and damp as it could have been (no water dripping from the ceiling or frost collecting on the walls). And they allowed him to retain his coat.

Left to his own amusements during these long, tedious hours, Oleksander's fear grew palpable; he envisioned OGPU thugs appearing at any moment to beat a signature out of him. Yet the anticipated visits never came. He was disturbed but twice a day: once for his rations, a stale piece of bread and a cup of brackish water, and an hour later when the same surly guard came to reclaim the tin plate and cup. Conversation was limited to one question: "Ready to sign?"

"No, I cannot," Oleksander replied, each time receiving only a nod and a disinterested shrug.

"Could you empty my bucket?" Oleksander asked on the third day. "It's getting rather full."

"It's emptied once every five days," came the perfunctory answer. There the exchange ended.

However, toward the end of the day, the guard and his cohort came back, and he was allowed out of his cell. "Come with us," he ordered (Oleksander nicknamed him Comrade Surly, which seemed to suit) "You're going for a ride," he added, smiling. *Surly, with a sense of humour!* That, however, was the extent of his remarks. Pavlick, Oleksander presumed, had tired of trying to persuade some insignificant junior researcher and decided to send him into exile.

He was escorted out into the chilly evening air and stuffed into a running car. It turned off at the end of Volodymyrska Street and proceeded to weave its way north, outside the city to a low, whitewashed building with tracks alongside, on which sat a long line of boxcars, lorries, and milling people segregated into groups, with militiamen on the perimeter keeping a watchful eye. Farther up the tracks Oleksander spotted a locomotive silhouetted against the night sky. It was pointing north, belching smoke and fumes in rhythmic patterns.

Oleksander was marched to a cordoned-off area, beyond which "Comrade Surly" pointed and declared that he proceed to where a large group of shivering people stood. With that, Comrade Surly turned and was gone. A militiaman suddenly appeared at his side, giving him a shove in the right direction. Oleksander joined the motley mass just in time to witness the boxcar doors slide open and the prisoners (there was no other word for it, he decided) herded in. All was dark except for the intermittent shafts of moonlight intermixed with kerosene lamps on the platform peeking through the rough wooden planks of the boxcars. He was shoved forward and sought to find a free space. It was going to be a tight ride, he realized, feeling his way along the side to a corner. He'd need to rest and get his wits together.

***

Oleksander awakened after a restless sleep of troubling dreams that seemed to feature Katya, Lev, and Professor Robanov in some undetermined agony with a fat man (Pavlick?) pulling levers. The train was moving, its undercarriage swaying to a steady rhythm accompanied by periodic jolts, clicks, and clangs. There was a crush of people in the darkness around him, some sprawled on the straw that layered the floor, others sitting clutching sacks or battered suitcases, no doubt containing their worldly possessions. It was a sea of jiggling humanity gone strangely inert and silent as the kilometres rolled by. His attention was drawn to a huddled figure to his right shrouded in a heavy coat with a woollen toque pulled low over his head. The light was too weak to make a distinct identity, but he thought he recognized the voice declaring in a low, sardonic tone, "Being an enemy of the state is killing me. Haven't had a drink or a smoke in two months." Who, if anyone in particular, he spoke to, Oleksander couldn't be sure, but to his ears it was fitting, albeit sad irony, because the man within arm's length was the same who had made his life miserable.

"Belynski!" he spat.

Makar Belynski turned, blinked, hesitated momentarily, puzzled, then focused. "Comrade Pylyp — the agronomist."

"Belynski," Oleksander repeated, slightly more affably. "It is you!"

"I guess I should've sent you on this trip earlier — would have saved me some embarrassment."

"Well, I'm pleasantly surprised that you can join me now," Oleksander said, matching the forced levity of the former chairman.

"It came suddenly ... and, I see, is popular. Standing room only if more join us. We might have to sit and sleep in shifts," Belynski propped himself up with a grunt, "otherwise we might get trampled."

"You best find another spot for the remainder of this journey," Oleksander stated flatly with malice, all levity suddenly gone.

"Ah, a warning not to trust you in these close quarters... What, a knife jammed below the ribs while sleeping?"

"A tempting consideration, but my reduced circumstances have stripped me of such a convenient weapon. However, there are many who would not take kindly to find among them a Bolshevik bureaucratic who put them here. I repeat, you should make your way to the other end of this carriage."

The train began to slow down as the conversation took a menacing tone, finally grinding to a faltering stop after a couple of abrupt jolts that almost sent them into each other. Before Belynski could respond, the door slid open, allowing a blast of frigid air into the car. A large OGPU militiaman with a cherubic face banged on the door with a club, and satisfied he had everyone's attention, addressed the fifty or so men and women, a number with small, clinging children.

His remarks were short and to the point. The toilet was located in the middle of the car. That meant, Oleksander knew, that a bucket had been provided. The prisoners were instructed to pick someone among them to periodically distribute in an orderly fashion the rations of water and food that would consist of a loaf of bread for every four persons, more or less, and a herring.

"You're the man for the job," Oleksander suggested to Belynski with a sneer. "Organize us for survival — be in authority again, eh."

If anyone died, they were told perfunctorily, the corpse should be placed in front of the car doors for removal at the next stop. With that, the OGPU official concluded his speech, the door was abruptly closed and locked, and they were again left to carry on in the cold, increasingly rank, and dark compartment.

"So, where were we before this interlude?" Belynski asked rhetorically as the train once again began its jerky movement.

"I was about to tell you about your despicable abuse of authority, your lack of morals, integrity, honour, and a dozen other human traits you lack," Oleksander spat out, not caring who around him heard. It came out as an outraged stream of words, tight but barely controlled.

Belynski took a half step back to the wall as Oleksander moved into whatever little personal space existed but otherwise remained calm. "I did what I did as chairman, believing it was necessary for the new order and the greater good."

"And look where it got you!"

"On a train ride with you! Tell me, which of those human qualities you mentioned I lack caught up with you?" The men stared fiercely at each other, almost nose to nose. Even in the confined quarters, people edged away, not wanting to get involved.

The question gave Oleksander pause. "I refused to denounce a colleague."

"Ah, loyalty and integrity with a dash of courage. Irony goes both ways."

Oleksander had no real response but a blunt observation. "There is no justice. But at least I'm true to myself and my principles."

Belynski raised his hands in surrender. "I cannot argue. I betrayed mine long ago. Weak character perhaps — unrestrained to temptation — both drink and women. My only defence—"

"You have no defence," Oleksander snapped.

"As a summation then of my actions… I took outrageous advantage but did not mistreat your fiancée." Finally, they truly got to the issue between them. "How is Oxana?" Belynski asked, his voice softening. "I presume she found you in Kyiv."

"She did," Oleksander replied tersely.

"Well… I'm glad she did. And for the record, I'm thankful that it wasn't me who put you on the train."

"Small comfort. It was the people you represent."

"Not anymore… Look, I'm much too sober, dried out, and as a result quite miserable, if that makes you feel better. So … can we come to an understanding? It'll be a long, cold journey to where we're going. If we can't cooperate, will you at least try not to kill me? There is no place for either of us to go…"

***

Once the train crossed a bridge over the wide expanse of the Dnipro River, it travelled northwest into the Sumy region and beyond. Lights were seen through the cracks between the planks, but no one could say for certain which town or city they had gone through. There were infrequent stops for supplies and at least at one stop — someone thought they read a sign saying Alexandrov — everyone was ordered out while "volunteers" were made to sweep out the stale straw, matted, muddied, and soaked with urine and feces, and spread a fresh layer. Thereafter, the locomotive picked up the pace and the air felt more frigid. They were moving into the frontier zone, which as the crow flies would eventually get them to Archangelsk on the White Sea.

People cried, cursed, and died; many became sullen and silent, resigned to accepting whatever awaited them. Yet a community was forming; individuals had organized themselves into standing and sitting groups so that more room to rest and sleep could be gained, as well as corridors created for quicker mobility should the need arise. Belynski indeed took it upon himself the task of distributing food as equitably as possible and of identifying and disposing of the dead when the train made its designated stops. Others, including Oleksander, agreed to look after the bucket and replace soiled straw with new. Oleksander and Belynski kept their truce. His animosity toward the former Bila Sich Soviet council chairman could wait, thought Oleksander, given their circumstances.

After two weeks of relentless travel, the train came to a final screeching halt. The eerie silence and stillness were unsettling, as was the realization that they had arrived at their final destination. As the tall tin-and-wood door slid open, the occupants struggled to shield their eyes from the sharp light of the cold winter sun reflecting on the snow. This time the guards did not pass out the usual rations but ordered everyone off. Oleksander was one of the last off; he lost track of Belynski, who moved forward in anticipation of receiving food supplies for distribution. As he stepped on to Mother Earth for the first time in some while, Oleksander noticed that the emerging inhabitants of a half dozen boxcars were being lined up along the railway tracks. End of the line? No more track? He didn't know. His squinted vision took in a sparse landscape beyond — no road, no buildings, no humans, just the barren snowy expanse broken by the odd stubble of weeds and shrubs sticking through. Still, in the far distance there appeared a fairly thick growth of evergreens.

"This way," ordered the guard, who then turned and started to march away from the tracks and toward the stand of evergreens. Columns of weary, undernourished prisoners began to walk. Oleksander briefly spotted Belynski falling into line some distance ahead, which was fine with him. Belynski was no longer a person to bring to account but more an object of curiosity and ultimately dismissal. What would have been the point of ... revenge?

It was a difficult trudge through the deep snow for people weakened by hunger and atrophied by captivity. No sleighs awaited them, or even a cleared path. By the time they reached their destination, a number of individuals had simply expired. Those who could not manage were left behind. Oleksander tried to help an older, exhausted man dressed in a patchy coat who collapsed in front of him but was harshly ordered to keep going or be shot.

Well over an hour later, they reached their goal. All that anyone could see were a number of small huts scattered in an opening. These, they were informed, were mostly for the guards. Their homes were only partially built. Eventually, they would be completed once the new arrivals were processed and divided into labour groups. The younger and more vigorous men would be segregated into work gangs to cut and haul wood in sufficient quantity. Another, less vigorous group would, under supervision, complete construction and build a fence around the camp, as if there were a place of sanctuary to escape to. And finally, older, more infirm men, along with the women and their children, would perform all the other necessary domestic tasks that came along. To Oleksander it seemed impossibly daunting.

Temporary shelters had been erected, but first — warmth. A group was organized to collect wood to light campfires before nightfall. It would take a good while to sort everyone out administratively, so huddling around a series of large campfires seemed prudent, especially since, Oleksander noted, other than militiamen, they had yet to see or receive directions from the local party official in charge.

CHAPTER TWENTY-FOUR

Bila Sich

Boris Nikolayevich Sholakov and Magda Berenzina were young activists paid by the party to do important work, which they took seriously. Like so many other villages, Bila Sich had fallen behind in achieving their grain quotas. Apparently, kulaks were still around and had infiltrated the kolkhoz. Magda and Boris were part of a young team sent to reinvigorate the community for a renewed procurement campaign.

Alas, they encountered a hungry, undernourished population who were less and less able to function, let alone collect and deliver the assigned amount of grain to the state. It had been a frustrating day with a lethargic, sullen group of kolkhoz workers simply staring at them with hollow eyes and gauntly drawn faces making a mockery of their arguments, their slogans, their exhortations. All rallying cries fell flat with hardly an acknowledgement. If they listened, they didn't hear or care.

On the way back to their quarters from the "old church meeting centre," as the locals called it, Boris, much to the chagrin of Magda, his "partner," let his frustrations be known, inexplicably pushing aside an older man walking from the opposite direction along the narrow footpath. "Watch where you're going. And why aren't you in the field over there," he pointed to an open pasture, "making yourself useful?"

The man stumbled, held tight to whatever he had in his coat pockets, and kept walking.

"Fucking kulak."

"Boris! Why are you so mean? He was minding his own business — gave us plenty of room," Magda admonished.

"I'm just tired of these people … their insolence, their resentment of our efforts, of us. And besides, he's definitely a kulak."

"How do you know?"

"Well, he didn't appear to be starving, did he? Seemed healthy, nourished. Doesn't that arouse your suspicion?"

Magda gave him a startled look. "That's your criteria? He doesn't have swollen legs?"

"All I'm saying is that he looks too well fed. Like others in this miserable settlement, he's hiding food and not doing his job — not diligently enough."

"And you were, what — going to confront him?"

"No… I really don't know."

"He didn't look like a rich man, a kulak to me," she observed, still trying to digest what her colleague (and lover) had said.

Boris squinted into the afternoon sun as the man hurriedly continued on without a backward glance. Indifference? Disrespect? The man didn't give a fig? He just looked like a kulak. Boris couldn't quite put his finger on it, but he was irritated. "Look, we have a job to do. The people here are even less engaged than in the last pathetic village we visited," he retorted with a tinge of anger mixed with frustration. That was it. Their proselytizing had no discernable impact thus far. "We will not be well thought of if we don't produce results. You know that."

'I know but," she sighed, "maybe there is no more to give. This village, the kolkhoz seems depleted and suffering."

"Don't get soft. The revolution demands that we be diligent. No good will come of pitying them. They're hoarders, and it's our responsibility to—"

"I know what our responsibility is," Magda cut him off, raising her voice, not willing to have his diatribe continue, "but because they have been able to sustain themselves — at least so far — doesn't mean that we take everything they have. There'll be no harvest if you remove what they have left. The state needs someone left here, and as in the other villages to plant, nurture, and bring in the crops."

"That's what collective farms are for — plenty of workers there."

"Are there really?" Magda's dark eyes bore into him. "These people today on the kolkhoz looked almost as underfed as those we see in the countryside."

"What are you trying to say?"

Magda hesitated, formulating her thoughts. "I'm not sure really … but at times, it seems that we are the exploiters here. We eat — maybe not as much as we like, but we eat. Kolkhoz workers eat too but less. The others," she shrugged, "if they are hoarding all that food, where is it?"

"Kulaks are clever. They sabotage the Soviet supply and hide their own," Boris said adamantly.

"How do they do that? The grain storage depots are guarded. No one can get near them. Exactly where do they hide their illegal grain, potatoes, beetroots, or whatever they've grown?"

"You're starting to sound less dedicated to our mission," Boris stated in a disquieting tone.

"It's not that… It's just — we're not blind, are we? I've seen very hungry children recently, the mothers pleading, the men afraid, defiant, and hateful. They look at us with feral eyes, like we're the vermin." She shook her head, suddenly remembering one particular episode. She and Boris had been part of the Komsomol brigades who were sent out searching for contraband. Their requisition captain, a Red Army veteran with a pronounced limp and ill disposition, burst into a tiny cottage where an emaciated man and wife with two shrivelled children huddled in the corner. They certainly weren't receiving their monthly rations — eighteen kilograms of meal, two kilograms of meat, and one kilogram of fat, as promised to collectivized farmers. Magda was shocked at what she saw.

"Take it all," the man croaked, his voice cracking. "Whatever you want — take it away. There might still be some borscht in the pot. Maybe a beet or two, a rusted head of cabbage, half eaten pumpkin… I'm not sure. Wait! Perhaps you want my coat or shoes — they might be of use to some dear Soviet comrades."

Muttering some words about "kulak insolence" that Magda didn't quite catch, their leader (she couldn't remember his name) waved his pistol around and ordered a search of the property. They left empty-handed; there was nothing to be had. Magda left grateful that at least the family hadn't been kicked out of their home. It seemed a small mercy.

Boris frowned and shook his head. "Look, Magda, don't be difficult. Now's not the time for either of us. We have to stay strong and not prostrate ourselves to debilitating pity. What we are engaged in is historical necessity — a revolutionary crucible. Procuring grain for the socialist fatherland, for the five-year plan, is paramount if our destiny is to be fulfilled."

"So, the end justifies the means?" She had heard this all before in Komsomol lectures.

"Yes, I believe that! Remember the ultimate goal is universal triumph of communism. And for that, everything is permissible."

"Everything — including the starving of people—"

"You don't see it, do you?" he cut her off. "All those who are opposed to us, who are obstinate, who have hindered the plan, who stand in the way, must be dealt with mercilessly. We are at war."

"And at what terrible cost, to ourselves, our humanity."

"You are being intellectually squeamish. Don't be in the fog of stupid liberalism, which doesn't allow you to see the forest for the trees. Total collectivization is our goal here. That's why we must scour the countryside. The grain is hidden somewhere."

"That's why we empty whatever remains of poor and old folks' storage chests and destroy their ovens?"

"Don't be melodramatic. It needs to be done to accomplish the great and necessary transformation of the countryside. These peasants will be better off for our actions someday."

"Really?"

Boris ignored the evident sarcasm and her troublesome doubts. "Yes, their distress and suffering are of their own making due to their own ignorance, their susceptibility to the banishments of the class enemy." He waved his hands around as if the class enemy surrounded them.

"So, it's okay to hear whimpering children, mothers with extended bellies and vacant eyes, quivering hands out, begging? And what about the corpses in ragged coats and cheap felt boots patched multiple times, scattered willy-nilly in the fields, abandoned huts on roadways and under bridges. I've seen them; you've seen them. Can we just ignore it?"

"Look Magda, I agree. It's not okay — just necessary. Terrible, yes, but a historical necessity. You can't lose your faith in our mission. You need to believe or…" He let the thought dissipate.

"You're saying that even as you see those barely walking, skeleton humans with swollen legs — you … we still should demand our pound of flesh to fulfill a quota — the party's bureaucratic plan?"

"Magda," Boris replied in a tone designed to chide and warn.

"Do you not worry that these horrors are not accidental, that they have less to do with historical necessity than execution by hunger?"

"What are you suggesting?" Boris lowered his voice and glanced around, although they were alone on the path with no one in sight.

"This just isn't happening as a response to some organized resistance; it's planned by the highest authorities. And we are as much their cannon fodder as the so-called kulaks."

"What nonsense."

"Listen, Boris Nikolayevich, we could be the instruments of bad deeds. If the plan falters, if they fail, if it all goes wrong, we will be blamed along with our committees and local authorities. The blood and shame will be placed on our hands. The finger will be pointed at us — naïve idealistic students — for *our* excesses. You can see that, can't you?" There was a sudden desperation in her voice.

"Don't talk that way. Please, Magda, for both our sakes, you must develop an inner resistance to what you see and think. There is the higher purpose. Believe, otherwise, you will go mad."

"So, we should silence our conscience? See reality differently, that black is really white and—"

"No, no!" Boris held up his hands. "We must realize that there is a socialist reality that needs to play out, and sentimentality has no useful place here. And please, please, be careful talking about this in front of others who may not be so tolerant or understanding."

***

"I bumped into a couple of Komsomol agitators along the path," Vlas explained to his wife after he came back from his clandestine visit to their cramped quarters. "The man, a student maybe —certainly an outsider — was rude and arrogant."

"I hope there was no trouble?" Iona asked as she worked on mending a pair of boy's trousers.

"I didn't stop to chat. I couldn't afford to break these," Vlas mused, pulling out two small jars of milk, one from each side pocket of his coats. Direct from Lev's wonder cow!" He beamed.

"Thank God… Lucia is still producing."

"That she is. She's recovered her health, as far as Lev can tell. The big problem is to keep her hidden. So far, so good. It'll be tougher when winter comes. Lev's started putting away hay and corn, but he must be careful. The kolkhoz foreman has got it out for him, and there are eyes and spies everywhere."

"Well, thank him and Nina for this." She took the precious jars of milk and slid them in the corner of a small shelf, pulling a linen curtain across. "The rations have become so meagre here, and the kids will appreciate a little extra." She glanced over to the opposite end of the room, where their three young boys, four, six, and eight, were settling down for the night on a large mattress. Space had become a premium for those displaced from their homes.

"Lev said they'll save dairy products for us for next time. It's just that we have to be careful meeting, since our paths don't normally cross. We'll find a way, though." Vlas lowered his voice lest someone heard through the thin wall. "We're working on a plan to save some extra provisions to get through the winter, just in case."

"Do you think that's wise? If you are caught—"

"We are being starved. Our boys won't have enough to eat. The crops in the field will be taken by the state, every bit of it that's salvageable." He knew that a great deal would be lost in the cutting, collection, and storage process given the kolkhoz's lack of functioning tractors and its inefficiencies. "What we have here is general malpractice with idiots in charge of the farm," he had told Sergi, his fellow mate on the farm's many work groups.

"They can't just withhold food from us?" Iona persisted, lines of worry crossing her forehead.

"Why not? Towers are being erected at various points around the wheat and cornfields, potato patches, and other edible crops. Why do you think that is? There can be only one reason: to keep *us* out! I heard that new laws are being written: steal from the fields and face extreme consequences."

"Surely, they wouldn't—" Iona began.

"Yes, they would," Vlas declared, anticipating her words. "Shoot on site is the directive. That's what I've heard."

"But if you and Lev plan to hide food and get caught?" she whispered in horror.

"We'll be shot!" Vlas answered cheerfully. "Don't worry. We wouldn't get caught."

"How do you know?"

"Well, little chance of getting caught," he amended. "Listen, it's either this or starve. I'm convinced of this. Little by little, we'll put aside potatoes, corn, beets — whatever is available into burlap sacks — enough for both families to share."

"But where will you hide these sacks? They're very good at searching and finding even the cleverest hiding spots."

"Lev has it worked out. He found a perfect hollow in which to dig winter storage caves that no procurement unit or OGPU henchman will locate."

Iona regarded him skeptically. "Can you be sure?'

"Absolutely! It's under their noses on the kolkhoz property, bordering the edge of the woods. The procurement brigades are good at ripping apart floorboards, destroying chimneys and ovens, digging holes in gardens, or looking under wood piles, but they don't have the imagination or inclination to snoop on the state's own property."

"You hope! Doing this is a huge risk…" She trailed off, shaking her head.

"Whatever the risks, it's necessary," he repeated. "I fear that the winter of '32 will be bleak — very bleak, from what I see. So yes, I must do this if our family is to survive."

***

Dimitri Tolstoy was both cruel and ignorant in most regards. Prasha now added lacking insight — *clueless* — to the list. "I have just been informed of a new campaign," Tolstoy announced, waving a letter at his personal secretary. He had a puzzled expression, as if he didn't know quite what to make of it. Prasha noticed that his right eye twitch had gotten worse over the last couple of months. The man was showing signs of stress. Ever since the Bila Sich Massacre, he had shrunk within himself. Nightmares had become common; Prasha heard the shouts in his upstairs room coming directly from Tolstoy's sleeping quarters below.

They were in Belynski's old office with the diminutive chairman of the local Soviet council sitting behind a large, paper-strewn desk. Prasha remained standing in front with his notebook in hand. Events had overtaken Tolstoy and the Soviet council, spiralling out of control, it seemed to him, on a course of their own. Prasha almost felt sorry for his boss; he did not see the looming catastrophe, let alone have the talent or resolve to address it. From Prasha's perspective, Bila Sich was doomed as a village, as a kolkhoz, as a community. The signs were everywhere.

Although it was officially denied, there now was famine spreading, not only in the immediate countryside but throughout the entire oblast and beyond. Bodies were starting to appear like mushrooms after heavy rains beside well-trod paths and roadways; emancipated souls, some with growing bellies, peered like ephemeral ghosts out of dark doorways, as did listless men with swelling legs too weak to work the fields. Then there was the steady exodus of raggedly clothed men, women, and children deciding that salvation might be found elsewhere, beyond the village, in the towns and cities. Most did not arrive at their destination, whether a railway station or directly to a larger urban centre, ending their existence in a ditch, under a shrub or tree. Others were duly apprehended by the militiamen because they weren't legally allowed to leave their village or kolkhoz. Orders were issued to return them to their residence or place of origin. If that could not be established or conveniently arranged, mobile units simply deposited these "waifs" in remote areas. Better they die in a field or forest unnoticed by anyone than have them in cities, creating anxieties about food supplies and numerous other disagreeable issues — mothers with dying babies begging in the streets, corpse-strewn alleys, and the removal of them.

"Commissar Fedryk has just informed me of this new campaign," Tolstoy continued, interrupting Prasha's brooding thoughts. "Direct from Postyshev, no doubt. And you know who he gets his orders from."

Prasha did — the great vozhd himself. But it was Pavel Postyshev who was earning the title of "Tsar of Starvation" among the dying and those apparatchiks who bore witness firsthand.

"What do you make of this directive?" Tolstoy handed the document to his secretary, whose eyebrows raised as he read. It confirmed his worse fear, the one threshold that undermined his whole belief in the socialist experiment.

"I–I rightly don't know." But he did. Only if famine was part of official policy did this new directive make sense. But why practise the mass death of the very people needed to fulfill the quotas critical to the five-year plan?

"Hmm…" Tolstoy's right eye twitched rapidly, his lips curled in a distasteful moue. "I suppose that you will have to organize the shooting parties."

"How to explain this to the locals?" Prasha pondered.

"We don't…" Tolstoy leaned back wearily in his chair, "just follow orders."

"It says here," Prasha scrutinized the document one more time, "that the state will pay for the delivery of these hides, but since the villagers have been relieved of their firearms, then presumably only the militiamen will do the hunting… Do they receive extra compensation for their effort? It's not clear here."

"That'll have to sort it out. This campaign is to get underway quickly, though."

"I'll talk to the militia captain."

"Oh, one more item I also forgot. According to the kolkhoz manager, horses are disappearing."

"How many are missing?"

"At least five to date. Stealing from the kolkhoz cooperative is a grave offence. These animals are key to the collective farm's success. Have the militiamen do a thorough household-to-household search. Those responsible must be severely punished!"

"I shall see to it," Prasha said perfunctorily.

"We need those horses back!"

If they haven't been eaten, thought Prasha.

***

Lev read the notice on the former church door. As of September 1, 1932, it stated that the government was paying for the delivery of cat and dog hides. They had become, it seemed, a "valuable commodity."

"What are they talking about, a valuable commodity?" Georgi Molotavich snorted as he read over Lev's shoulder. The fellow kolkhoznik's voice rose heatedly. "Why shoot pets? How did their hides suddenly become valuable?"

"I suspect they're not," Lev replied in a low, disgusted voice. "There is a darker purpose at work here." He did not elaborate; Molotavich would figure it out soon enough.

"Says they can be delivered to particular locations... Carts will come by, and they will be piled into them and taken away — doesn't say where and why dog and cat pelts have value."

Lev said nothing. This was a senseless order for a senseless slaughter that served but one purpose: to preempt the inevitability of starvation when it truly set in.

Three days later, four men arrived, each sporting a shotgun and revolver. Although they were dressed in loose peasant shirts and trousers, they had a military bearing, as was borne out in their ruthless efficiency. They systematically divided the village up into quadrants, and all that could be heard were volleys of shotguns for the next couple of days. It was assumed that they hunted feral cats and dogs, but the distinction became moot once the shooting started. Meanwhile, the pile of cat and dog carcasses grew with each dumped off in the village square. A couple of militiamen stood guard.

"They're being guarded?" Molotavich remarked in surprise as he and Lev made their way to the kolkhoz fields.

"And it's not because of the pelts," said Lev. "I suspect they have orders to shoot anyone attempting to get fresh cat or dog meat."

"But they can't just leave them in the square to rot. It'll smell up their own headquarters."

A week passed before Molotavich's observation was proven correct. The carcasses were not skinned, as per the directives, but just left to rot on the ground, scrupulously guarded until Tolstoy decreed that anyone from the village who wanted what was left could simply haul it away. Of course, the meat was rancid. Nevertheless, the starving arrived anyway, dragging away what they could.

With the cat and dog cull over, a couple of weeks later, Tolstoy received another dispatch. A new campaign was about to begin. He couldn't believe the directives. Even he, who followed his instructions to the letter, found this one disturbing.

Prasha needed to arrange another hunt. This time, however, there would be no announcement pinned to the local Soviet headquarters door. Militiamen would be out shooting again — nightingales, Ukraine's national bird, for those who deemed to notice. Legend was that misfortune would fall on any household where the bird died. It seemed that the legend was to be realized on a grand scale.

CHAPTER TWENTY-FIVE

Kyiv

As one week turned into another, Katya was increasingly anxious and frustrated. She was stuck, at a dead end, no closer to finding a way out to her own safe space than when she ran across the hall the night they came for Oleksander. As far as she could tell, Anton Rubiniuk was sincere and seriously trying, but as he apologetically kept reiterating, the situation was becoming more complex. Then, one day, he hobbled back to his apartment from one of his rare sojourns and declared, "Lushka wants to meet you, but not here in the apartment. He'll explain…"

Katya was relieved; at least she'd get to meet Anton's mysterious son. She just wanted to escape her circumstances. To be sure, she was grateful; Rubiniuk had not only harboured her but also treated her like a daughter. Nevertheless, the situation in the apartment was stifling. She feared going out and being spotted on the street. Logically, little chance perhaps, but the mind plays tricks! The posters were probably still out there, and neither the police nor Sholtz had stopped looking for her — of that she was certain. Finally, however, she forced herself out for brief periods mostly to do their shopping. Rubiniuk was slow and had difficulty walking too far, and they needed food and supplies from the local Torgin government store. Fortunately, Rubiniuk always managed to have the necessary rubles for whatever purchases were required. Lushka, she suspected, contributed to his father's meagre monthly stipend, and she had almost exhausted Oleksander's emergency fund.

Thus, she'd shrug into one of Anton's oversized coats, put on his boots — the toes stuffed with bits of newspaper to give a tighter fit —

tied a babushka scarf over her hair and wrapped a scarf around her neck, half concealing her face. It was a nervous but at the same time liberating trek to the to the local state co–op store. She usually went out between two and three in the afternoon for supplies, since the store hours were restricted. And no wonder; outside, there was always a group of badly clothed, clearly undernourished men, women, and children, their hands out, hoping for whatever could be spared from those coming out. Katya could do no nothing but turn a blind eye and hurry away from the misery she witnessed.

***

They met at the Kyiv Agricultural Institute library, a few blocks from the apartment. Lushka was in the reading room, away from the main collection, just as Anton said he'd be, sitting on a well-worn sofa chair, reading or at least pretending to read a copy of *Ukrainska Pravda*. He was as Anton described him, lanky in a physical way, with broad shoulders. His charcoal-grey eyes immediately lightened when he looked up and saw her. A young version of his dad, she decided, as he gestured to the sofa. He quickly scanned the room while running a hand through a dark, curly mop of hair, worry lines fanning from the corners of his smile. A few years older than herself, she guessed, but that remained indeterminate. He could have been a twenty-nine-year-old with worldly wear or a well-preserved forty-year-old. She had no clue.

"Pleased to meet you," he said, tilting his head, his eyes appraising, searching for a focal point. "My father has spoken at length about you, and from what he said, I thought I'd better meet you."

"I'm pleased to meet you as well. I hope I haven't irritated him too much during my stay."

"Oh no, not at all. On the contrary. He is glad for your company and fears that he is the tiresome one." Folding his newspaper and setting it aside, he indicated that she should sit in the matching chair beside him. "His only complaint to date is that your chess game still needs much improvement. His expert instruction notwithstanding." He cleared his throat and once again scouted the room. There were only a half dozen or so others scattered about, reading or writing various epistles/notes at small tables, all well out of audio range. "He said you worked for the city commissar of what was it?"

"Commerce and Industry."

"Yes, before your ... troubles, said that you are a skilled secretary with a good head on your shoulders, and, I might add, a pretty one." His smile grew wider. "Should I believe that?"

"No reason not to, from my perspective," she responded with a small smile of her own.

"The fact is," he continued, turning fully toward her, "we can help each other. I need someone with your skills for my business, and you need employment and a good place to hide until your troubles are over."

"What happened to your last secretary?"

"Didn't have one — this is my father's suggestion. Thinks I need one to keep better track of inventory."

"What business are you in?" Katya had never received a straight answer from Anton.

Lushka was no less ambiguous and cryptic. "Imports and exports — mostly import."

"Of what?" She was genuinely curious.

"A variety of goods. Anything that might sell, from religious icons to luxury items ... perfumes from Europe, French cognac, fancy footwear and clothes, and other practical necessities. At the moment it's food — fresh, canned, jarred, or dried, it doesn't matter. These imports usually find their way down the Dnipro on barges to our warehouses. The business is built on a network based on trust and, of course, funds exchanging hands. Of late, the local police and the OGPU have cracked down on our formerly secure shipping routes — patrols on the river, militiamen raiding warehouses, probing into our labyrinth of caves — hoping to get lucky.

"There are spies everywhere, reporting not only to state officials but also to others ... anyone who pays to know. And right now, the

OGPU, in particular, are extremely vigilant. At the moment they're searching for 'tainted food,' which officially cannot be allowed into the hands of citizens because of safety concerns." He laughed quietly. "Imagine that!"

"I see…" Katya said, thinking, *Where does this leave me?*

"All bogus, of course," Lushka continued, "but never mind… What it means is at the moment our network is being watched while the authorities at various levels argue about what to do. Don't worry — I took evasive precautions getting here and avoided a couple of military types who were following. They were … diverted elsewhere. We are safe." He gave her a reassuring smile. "That is why I didn't want to meet at my father's apartment, just in case."

Katya frowned. "Surely, the OGPU would know where your father lives?" Then a horrible thought sprang to mind. *If they come for Anton, they will also find me!*

"Good point," Lushka agreed, "if they knew we were father and son. Permit me to introduce myself officially: Lushka Dub at your service." He gave her a little bow, as if tipping his cap. Like Oxana Gerkil, I too have a second name and identity. Pop tells me you even have the proper papers for yours. How resourceful! He also told me about Oleksander, by the way, and for that I am sorry. So is Pop; he really liked him."

Katya nodded, momentarily picturing Oleksander and wondering where he was, if still alive, before returning to her present situation. "Have you been compromised, do you think?" she asked because that was always foremost on Gromeko's mind, a worry he carried constantly.

"Ah, a good, practical question. One never knows, but I think not, otherwise," he shrugged, "I would not be here. No, it's more a question of who or what group of government apparatchiki get to share in the business. For now, it is more difficult to operate the business as usual while this is being sorted out, and hence the precautions in case of a harsh, ill-tempered decision. That is why you have not been relocated — not just yet. As much as I would appreciate your services, we both need to be patient. It will straighten itself out."

One way or another, she thought, but asked instead, "How long, do you think, before, as you say, it will straighten itself out and the situation improves?"

"Soon — very soon. I don't know at the moment who is friend or foe. Arrangements are being made through a third party."

Katya did not reply. She could appreciate the byzantine world of Soviet politics and hierarchy. Kreil Gromeko was always talking about who to trust enough so that the proper palms could be greased. And even at that, trust could sometimes be derailed, as in the case of her boss and Sholtz.

As if on cue, Lushka elaborated, "We've had a small problem, some random raids on our trading routes, not sanctioned officially as far as I heard, but to make a point. Protection doesn't come cheap... But enough of all that. Issues will be resolved in a week or so. I'll expedite your relocation thereafter, even though my father will miss your company."

"Where will I be going?"

"Ah, that's a surprise."

∗∗∗

By early fall of '32, Kyiv's city life was changing dramatically as a result of the crop crisis in the countryside. The capital was deluged with an influx of malnourished and starving peasant farmers believing that their best prospects of obtaining daily bread were in the urban centres. Some arrived on trains, managing to hitch a ride (by nefarious means usually); most, however, arrived on foot. In either case, they materialized by the hundreds as grey, ragged lumps of hungry humans, the vast majority with nothing but the clothes on their backs and a thin thread of hope.

They need not have bothered. There was no food to be had; what awaited them was total destitution and death, unless they were the very few who possessed something of value — a family heirloom, piece of jewellery, gold ring, leather goods, fine boots, perhaps a hand-stitched fancy shirt — items that could be bartered for bread, a few potatoes, and other edible roots.

Yagii Urchyn was a street waif turned petty criminal in adulthood whose speciality was pickpocketing and keeping his ear to the ground in case there was a score to be made. Over the years he had survived by innate cunning, street intelligence, and snitching for anyone who would pay for his information, from individuals to organizations who were in search of someone or something. Throughout the summer and fall of '32, surviving in the city had become harder, and he pivoted to whatever scheme/activity could sustain him for another day. He was prepared to do what he needed to do to eat, have a drink, and pay the rent for his room in the Kurenivka ghetto. It was truly a hovel in back of a dilapidated single-storey building, but it was his home and better than sleeping in the streets with the starving.

Recently, he had discovered a new source of income, albeit involving a little more physical work than he was accustomed to. Dubbing himself the "grave hunter," he began hanging around cemeteries, scouting for freshly dug graves and funeral processions, noting who went where. He revisited the plots after hours armed with a shovel (stolen from a cemetery tool shed) and lantern to perform "resurrections," as he called them in rare moments of levity. Invariably, bodies had valuable items attached that could be liberated. *The dead really don't need worldly goods, do they?* he told himself.

Sometimes, the resurrection was a bust, not even a good suit for his troubles, but at other times the corpse could have a wedding ring, a pocket watch, and one always checked the mouth for gold teeth! The best part, though, was that the items procured were readily accepted by the state co-op stores, no questions asked where they were exchanged for more immediate necessities: booze, bags of flour, sundry supplies, et cetera.

Yagii had heard rumours that these stores not only encouraged but organized squads of "grave hunters." That's what Eugene Yarchuk, the "street man" and the closest he had to a friend (he'd known him since they ran together in a juvenile gang) told him, anyway. "Organized hooliganism unofficially sponsored by the state!"

he declared. "Be careful, loners aren't welcome. You could end up sharing the grave with the deceased! Besides, it's too much work for one person."

Yagii was a loner; that was how he survived the underbelly of Kyiv, trusting no one (with the exception perhaps of Yarchuk). For his entire life — all twenty-six years of it — he had considered himself an independent sort of fellow. Not that it mattered much in this instant; it was getting on to late fall, and the ground would become too hard to excavate with a simple shovel. Best to move on to something else.

Through the ever-buzzing underground news pipeline, he heard that the city dump might be the place to pick up valuables, if he could find a way to the outskirts of Kyiv. He finally had the opportunity when he hitched a ride on a cart pulled by a donkey. He had been walking along the "Dog Path," a good route for a spot of pickpocketing, when near the Monastery of Caves he spotted the old man, the donkey, and the empty two-wheeled cart. The fellow didn't mind the company, although he said very little, and as they slowly rolled by a fringe of land touching the boundary of the city, he pointed to what appeared to be slag heaps strewn at irregular intervals across a desolate field. "Your stop," he declared. "God knows what you'll find. Not much here but … garbage."

The man with the donkey was right. It was a wasted trip, he soon realized. Scavenging the landscape were indeterminate groups of people, probably peasant farmers run away from collective farms, all destitute and literally on their last legs. They weren't looking for treasures or durable goods to sell or barter but food. A half-eaten cabbage head could let one survive another day, after all. And important party apparatchiks ate well; what they threw out ended in the dump. It didn't matter what it was — apple core, stripped corn cob, fruit peels — it constituted survival cuisine.

Moreover, Yagii hadn't fully appreciated that dump hunting was more dangerous than grave hunting, potential organized competition notwithstanding. Militiamen showed up on a regular basis to round up the "dump diners."

"You better find a hiding spot," he was told by a bent, grizzled man in a torn, mud-caked army coat. "A truck is coming."

"Damn," Yagii muttered, running for a patch of low land and dropping to the ground behind some bushes and discarded objects rusted beyond recognition. He later learned that anyone caught on the site was loaded into the back of the truck and driven farther from the city limits to a remote area and simply dumped off. Chances of survival were thus drastically diminished for people who had already exhausted their physical, and in many ways, their mental reserves.

With this dump option explored and found wanting, Yagii decided to concentrate on petty theft and snooping. Yarchuk was connected, Yagii knew, to high-placed individuals who offered rewards for information that often circulated on the street level. In fact, Yarchuk had a list of pay-for-information items that someone with good observational skills and ears to the ground would potentially find quite lucrative. Intelligence gathering was not new to Yagii; he had practised it over the years as a street person. Keeping his eyes open and ears attuned was crucial to survival. This meant noticing posters, remembering the faces and names on those posters or discarded newspapers. They were more often than not fugitives or individuals on the run who didn't want to be found but were worth a bounty to those who were looking for them.

In the Soviet state, keeping a low profile while on high alert had become second nature, a national pastime. Some snitched for the state and/or police (the distinction was at times hard to fathom); others, more selective or too afraid, did business in the private sphere, retained as part of a network by anonymous persons who paid what the market could bear for information, usually for the location/addresses of those who had gone missing and/or into hiding. Yarchuk was a low-rung player in a hierarchal chain. He needed a great many eyes and ears on the street like his friend. Yagii was readily co-opted, but Yarchuk stressed that the information provided better be accurate and timely.

"We are on the alert for one person in particular at the moment," Yarchuk explained, handing Yagii a folded broadsheet. "Be on the lookout for her. Chances are probably small to slim, but there's a substantial reward to be shared for the right information as to her whereabouts."

"How much?" Yagii asked. They were sitting in a dark corner of a greasy canteen almost hidden in an alley off Besarabsky Street. Beer and bowls of pea soup with a piece of herring on the plate had been set in front of them. It was an indulgence.

"Enough," Yarchuk said, giving Yagii a wry grin through yellowed teeth. His face was at such an angle as to accent its gaunt length and inherently villainous nose that protruded to a curved point.

"What would be my share of ... enough?"

"It's a sixty/forty split always. I have the connections — you don't."

Yagii shrugged; no use arguing. Ever since their street gang days, Eugene had always emerged as the middleman, the broker, the indispensable enabler. And here he was setting the rules again. "I'll keep my eyes open," Yagii said, tucking the poster into his coat pocket.

***

Three weeks later, Yagii saw her, or at least he thought he did. Despite wearing an oversized coat, a kerchief/scarf over her hair, and a shawl wrapped about her face, it was Katya Kharsova, the woman on the poster. He was almost sure of it. She had come out of the Torgin shop with a shopping bag in her hand. He was about to go in, having managed to lift a money purse from an unsuspecting *panyi* standing in line at a bakery. His vodka bottle could wait, he decided as he made a discreet about-face and followed her, a tasty piece, judging from her poster photo. Where was she going, to a tram stop, or perhaps she lived nearby? That indeed would be a bonus, he thought. He didn't have long to wait for his answer; twenty minutes later, she turned right down a walkway and up four steps into a three-storey apartment building with a pretentious triangular façade. He kept his head down, walking steadily by as she glanced about before opening the heavy front door and going in.

He quickly reversed course and rushed up the walk and front steps. He was afraid that the door would lock on him, but he needn't have worried. There was no lock. He swung it open gingerly and cautiously stepped inside. He didn't want to be spotted and be tossed out as a vagrant or hooligan (it had happened to him before), but there was no one there. He heard her going up the dingy stairs, the door squeaking on the second floor. Taking two steps at a time, he made it just in time. The floors had three apartments on each side. She stopped at the middle one on the left side, putting her bag down and fishing out a key from her coat. She then took off her scarf and unwound the shawl, and Yagii was now certain that this was Katya Kharsova, the woman in the poster. He knew where she lived, an address that promised a handsome payday once he got a hold of Yarchuk.

It took a couple of days of leaving word here and there in the usual places before Yagii managed to connect with his elusive friend. A meeting was arranged in the same hole-in-the-wall canteen as they had met before.

"They could at least have an accordion player to lighten the mood and deaden the sound around here," Yarchuk remarked, noting that there were a few people huddled, most in an unsavoury silence, in scattered parts of the room. Yagii had told him about his chance sighting. Finally, Eugene's eyes focused completely on Yagii. "Are you sure it's her? If not ... if such a mistake were made, either with the identity or the location, it would be bad — for both of us."

"I'm sure," Yagii said confidently, hoping that it was true.

"Okay, then!" Yarchuk said brightly. "Meet me here tomorrow. I'll have the money. Once you give me the address, I'll give you your share."

Next day, Yagii received a fistful of rubles, his forty-percent share, which he deemed was fair enough. It was, after all, dumb luck that he had spotted and recognized her. He hadn't done all that much except follow her and get the info. They parted happy and on amicable terms, each looking forward to the next time they could do business.

***

However, before Yagii could fully enjoy his newfound wealth, proportionally divided and hidden in the pair of socks he wore, an unrelated incident landed him in a local police station. It was his fault; he just couldn't resist. Normally, he was an excellent pickpocketer with dextrous, light fingers and a well-developed smooth snatch technique. On this occasion, he got careless (maybe one vodka shot too many), and on the busy Bessarabska Market Square got his fingers stuck trying to liberate a citizen's pocket watch. The bonehead had left the chain dangling from the side pocket of his coat. It should have been an easy lift-and-snatch. In his haste to do exactly that, he inadvertently hit the man with his elbow in the face and slipped when he went down. The blow not only felled the fellow but also took Yagii with him. In fact, he landed on top, his fingers cruelly bent, still firmly entangled and clutching the watch, now in the lining of the coat.

Before he could extricate himself from the situation, strong, rough hands grabbed him, lifted him into midair, it seemed, flipped him onto his stomach, and forcefully pushed his face into the cobblestone. His arms were yanked behind him in brutal, painful fashion.

"All right, all right!" he screamed.

But it wasn't all right. The man he tried to rob had received a nasty bump to the back of his head and was carted away for medical attention. Meanwhile, he found himself unceremoniously thrown into a vehicle and driven to the local police station. It was just his bad luck that two "gendarmes" (as one of his street cronies called them, for unspecified reasons) were close by when he had his slip-up. What made it worse, he soon discovered, was that his mark was a high-ranking Bolshevik bureaucrat with ties to the mayor. This was serious; he needed to think and quickly. In between a split lip and bloodied nose, he crocked out a name: "Captain Krypniuk."

That brought a flicker of recognition, and the two policemen who had hauled him in and were about to interrogate him Soviet -style in the small windowless room looked at each other. The usual procedure would include a beating, a confession, a damp and cold cell, while the procurator's office dealt with the case.

"What about the Comrade Captain detective?" asked the larger, meaner one who had manhandled him, probably breaking his nose, mashing him into the cobblestones.

"I need to see him."

"How do you know him?" asked the smaller policeman with the wooden face and the small but alert eyes, assessing him.

"His name is on a poster — for that fugitive, Katya Kharsova."

"So?" The smarter, less violent policemen was skeptical.

"I have information … important information, but I will only speak to him."

After silent exchanges between the policemen, they left the room, leaving him sitting at a small table, his nose periodically dripping blood onto his clothes and the tabletop.

It took almost two hours before Krypniuk was contacted at the central station and asked whether he had any interest in talking to an apprehended petty thief who said he had information on a Katya Kharsova. If he didn't, they would process him for attempted theft, assault, and criminal hooliganism.

Captain Krypniuk indicated that he would speak to the prisoner. His voice was calm and measured; he didn't want to arouse any speculation about the particular case referred to or that he (never mind the OGPU) was personally very interested.

"Well … he's at the police station on Tarasivska Street," the coarse voice at the other end of the telephone line informed him. "Ask for Chief Kovich."

"Keep him there. I'll be over as quickly as possible."

Immediately after setting his phone down, Krypniuk walked over to where Lubick sat in the large main room known as "the pitch," consisting of a number of desks scattered seemingly in random fashion, where investigators did their work. There were few about. Lubick sat forlornly staring at a stack of papers on his heavily used and abused desk.

"Time to take a ride," Krypniuk announced, stopping at the sergeant's desk. On the way out, in a quiet voice, he elaborated, "We may have gotten a break in the Gromeko case."

The drive to Tarasivska Street took only twenty minutes with Lubick wheeling the black sedan into a slot in front of the two-storey grey stone edifice that served as a police station. They both had visited before. However, neither knew the station chief.

Nestor Kovich greeted them at the front door before gesturing them to his office, a tiny cubicle set off in a corner away from the normal traffic and activity. His creased, narrow face looked the worse for wear with bleak grey eyes and sagging jowls contrasted by a skinny neck peeking out from the askew tunic. Approaching about sixty years of age, Krypniuk judged as the chief ran a liver-spotted hand through thinning hair and gestured to the only two chairs in the room besides the one behind his desk, which looked like it had been there since the building opened.

"Yagii Urchyn is a common criminal," he said by way of introduction, dropping into his chair with a grunt. "We've encountered him before, mostly a nuisance until this assault. Anyway, he mentioned your name, Captain, and said he has information you want. No doubt, he wants something in return... Whatever he says, though, is hardly trustworthy. He's a liar..."

Krypniuk sat silently waiting. Kovich had something on his mind. "You can, of course, talk to him here or...," there was a brief pause, "if you wish take him with you, charge him at your place, and do what you will after. I'll provide the incident report but," he gave them both a knowing look, "I'd like to avoid any more paperwork. We are overworked and understaffed here. So, you're welcome to take him and, of course, assume responsibility. As I say, I'm undermanned at the moment, the facility is overcrowded with assorted hooligans — mostly drunkards — and the paperwork has become ... burdensome."

Krypniuk listened, nodded, indicating he understood perfectly, and readily agreed. In a practical way, it made sense; Kovich would get the case off his books because of exigent circumstances. The central station had taken over. He could wash his hands of it. The influx of so many desperate people into the city had resulted in an uptake of petty (mostly) crime and increased the added chore of clearing the streets of corpses. Dead bodies didn't mean a crime was committed, but in his district, they were beginning to accumulate, and it was incumbent on him to redeploy some of his men for ... removals.

"Just remember," Kovich reminded Krypniuk and Lubick as they stood to go and take custody of Urchyn from his holding cell, "he assaulted someone important. There could be repercussions, depending on how badly he was hurt."

Once outside, Lubick quickly ushered Urchyn into the back seat of their sedan with Krypniuk sidling in beside him from the other side. The man was diminutive in stature, no more than a couple of inches over five feet at best, Krypniuk figured, thin, wiry, with a crumpled face that seemed to resemble a prune. He gave Yagii a handkerchief. "Wipe your nose."

"And don't get blood on the seat," Lubick warned, turning his neck toward the back before starting the vehicle and pulling away.

They drove at a leisurely pace, taking a circuitous route to the main station. Lubick appeared content to sightsee as early evening settled on the city.

Krypniuk spoke after a few minutes of silence. "You have information about Katya Kharsova, yes?"

"Yes," spat Yagii, dabbing his lower lip that, like his nose, had bled. "I know where to find her."

"You have an address — here in Kyiv?"

Yagii nodded. "But I want a deal. I didn't mean to hurt the man... I do not want to go to prison."

"You stole from him," Krypniuk pointed out.

"I attempted to," Yagii corrected.

"A moot distinction. Even if I overlook such grievous behaviour, you assaulted the man."

"It was an accident. I fell on him when my fingers got stuck ... in his coat."

Krypniuk sat quietly for a moment. Lubick pulled the car over into a side street and let it idle while he too stoically observed the feebly lit view. Both policemen could have been pondering what to do next or discerning the meaning of the universe in the dark patches of night that surrounded them. Finally, Krypniuk spoke. "There has to be a price paid for your actions, but I can minimize the punishment, perhaps even keep you out of prison. That, however, would depend on three factors: that the man you … fell on, is not badly injured; that he can be persuaded not to press charges; and, most importantly, that your information on Katya Kharsova is both accurate and pertinent."

"You can't just let me go?" This sounded like a pathetic plea even to Yagii, which elicited a hearty laugh from Lubick.

"Not possible," said Krypniuk. "You have been caught red-handed, I take it. You have as much as confessed. You were transferred over to us in good faith (although Krypniuk was not as sure about that), and we are responsible for you. How would it look if we simply let you go or you somehow escaped?"

"Don't think about it," Lubick chirped in.

"No, some form of punishment must be meted out if justice is to prevail," Krypniuk continued. "However, as I said, I can minimize the form and length of your sentence. You asked to speak to me, so speak! Tell me what you know. You won't get a better deal."

Yagii sat still and collected his thoughts before turning his head to the policeman. "You'll help me for sure?" His voice quivered; he had played his best hand, and now he had to trust Krypniuk at his word.

"*Tak*," Krypniuk affirmed with a nod.

Yagii Urchyn then told his story, albeit slightly fudged. He explained how he happened to see the poster on a tram kiosk and how by pure chance he recognized Kharsova and followed her to where she lived.

"And that's where?" Lubick interjected, pulling out his notebook.

Yagii gave them the apartment building address and her second-floor location. He didn't have an apartment number.

"Tell me, Yagii, if I can call you that… You're not or have ever been a police snitch?"

"Of course not!" Yagii replied indignantly.

"So, why? Why would you follow Kharsova, whom you recognized from the poster? What was in it for you?"

"I–I…"

"It certainly wasn't out of any civic duty, since you and the police don't get along. You see, I have to ask myself this question because your actions didn't make sense. What am I missing?"

"I–I don't know."

"Yes, you do. So, back up and tell us again. This time don't lie, or our deal is off." Krypniuk gave Yagii his patented hawk-eye look. "Who else is looking for her?"

Yagii's pale face pinched and shrivelled further. "Please, I don't want to get anyone in trouble."

"Give me a name!" Krypniuk demanded.

"If I do, please don't tell that I ratted him out. I think he just passes the information along." Yagii explained his business arrangement with Yarchuk, who had provided him the poster. "The rest of what I told you is true. I did see her by chance coming out of the Torgin shop, and I followed her to the address I gave you."

"And, of course, you gave Yarchuk the address?" Krypniuk asked as Lubick furiously wrote in his notebook.

"Yes. It was a simple business arrangement."

"So, you got paid?"

"Yes. I spent it all, though," Yagii quickly added.

"How long ago was this … that you gave Yarchuk Kharsova's address?"

Yagii screwed up his eyes thinking. "A couple of days ago, maybe."

"Think, Yagii, think," Krypniuk admonished. "This is important."

"No more than two days ago — not quite, even."

"Hmm, we might not be too late," Krypniuk muttered more to himself than anyone else.

"We're taking you to the station now, where you will be processed and held. I'd advise you to under no circumstances mention Katya Kharsova or that you spoke to me. It may be the difference between surviving your incarceration time or being found dead. Understood?"

Yagii nodded vigorously.

Lubick pulled away from the curb with speed. The pair of detectives had no time to lose.

***

Initially, Vasar Sholtz had hoped to avoid what was to transpire. He would have liked to talk to Katya and offer her a substantial bribe for her to keep her mouth shut and disappear. *But it's too late now.* He sighed. The City Commissar of Procurement and Labour didn't know whether she'd revealed what see saw (*what exactly did she see?*), but the only way out was that she ceased talking altogether.

His associates, worried that the woman knew too much about Gromeko's, and, concomitantly, their affairs, gave Sholtz a number and a name — Petrov — as soon as word from the street came that she had been found. Sholtz, of course, had even a stronger personal motive. If she blabbed to the wrong comrades, it would be he who would need to run and hide.

"Petrov will take care of the package," he was told. All he needed to do was call the number that would be provided on a secure line and say Petrov, her name, and the address. Petrov would do the rest. Sholtz didn't know how Katya was found or by whom, only that she was. As if to confirm, Petrov's number, along with the instructions, were also delivered by special post to his office anonymously. He wasn't surprised, though, since he had reached out for a fixer/enforcer. It was assumed that as Commissar Gromeko's friend and colleague, he'd want to personally make the arrangements.

Sholtz poured himself a stiff cognac, took a good gulp, and made the call, scrupulously following the instructions. "Petrov."

"*Da.*"

"Katya Kharsova, 331 Kyrylivka Street, second floor, middle apartment, left side."

"*Da.*"

The line went dead.

Sholtz sat back in his office chair. He might still put all of this behind him. He might survive his one rash action unscathed, even live longer and prosper. The last few months had taken their toll; his anxiety had increased threefold, as had his drinking and paranoia (he often stared at his office door, waiting for it to burst open and OGPU men rushing in and taking him away). Other aspects of his life had lately taken a downward turn as well — his health and sex life. In both cases, he just didn't feel himself. His wife didn't care, but his mistress noticed.

CHAPTER TWENTY-SIX

Moscow

Ivanko Targanovich, Pavel Postyshev's special envoy, was led to Stalin's Kremlin office after submitting to a thorough search by Nikolai Vlasik, the general secretary's personal bodyguard. The great vozhd stood beside his large, ornate wooden desk with a green felt top. Understandably, Targanovich was both apprehensive and awed, having heard about the man and viewed his portraits in every building in the country, it seemed. Strangely enough, the figure in front of him dressed in a plain white open-collared field shirt that came down loosely to his khaki trousers, hiding a protruding but diminutive form, was not particularly impressive. His hair was whiter and thinner than his public photos, the face seemed sunken and pockmarked, the cheeks pale, the eyes hard, small lumps of black coal (or was it his imagination?), the nose not as prominent as he thought, scarred with deep pores and concentric veins. A supercilious smile lay frozen on his lips, overlapped by his moustache.

Stalin raised an eyebrow and invited him to speak, delivering his message from the man in charge of the Ukrainian Soviet Socialist State. "There is a problem throughout the republic," Targanovich said nervously.

"Oh?" Stalin's smile disappeared. "And what might that be?"

"It appears that peasants are dying in large numbers. If the reports are to be believed, there is a famine in our breadbasket. It seems quite serious — widespread malnutrition and dystrophy."

"Did you get this diagnosis from Dr. Dystrophy?" Stalin snarled, waving his hands in dismissal. He moved around the desk to his seat, sat down, and picked up a pipe that had lain on a pile of papers. He banged it vigorously on a large glass ashtray filled with cigarette butts as well as pipe crud and ashes, found his well-worn leather tobacco pouch, and began the process of filling his pipe. "I really don't want to hear any more fantasies about dead bodies on the roads, babies with swollen bellies, and mothers begging in the streets. Already heard it! The kulak hoards the grain, and I get the blame — is that it?"

Targanovich's posture involuntarily stiffened, and he swallowed hard. "No — I understand. It's just that the dispatches call for relief supplies — urgently." He cringed inwardly; he was only the messenger. Why should he be the one to feel the wrath of the little tyrant? "The request was that relief shipments would—"

"Why should relief supplies be sent," Stalin cut him off, "when none are needed? These are Trotskyite rumours."

"I—"

"Spreading Western propaganda that we can't feed our own. It's a big lie, you know." Stalin tamped down the tobacco into his pipe with his middle finger, dug out a box of matches from a pullout drawer, and violently scraped a stout matchstick across the coarse side of the box. The match burst into flames, and he brought it down over the bowl, sucking furiously, creating a blueish hue of smoke that encircled him before extinguishing the match with a practised flick of the wrist and depositing the charred stubble in the ashtray. "Even Nadezhda heard it," he continued in an agitated tone, "at some fucking course she was taking at the university. Some subversive students filled her head with these vile rumours. She chastised me for it. I said no, not possible, but she wouldn't believe me. Imagine! My wife wouldn't believe me." He shook his head. "Well, I set her straight and have summoned Karl Pauker to set those students straight, to set the whole class straight, to set the whole university straight..." Stalin trailed off.

Stone-faced, at rigid attention, Targanovich could only imagine how Pauker, another of the general secretary's zealous bodyguards, would go about setting the students, or anyone for that matter, straight.

"The peasants are holding out," Stalin continued. "That's what peasants do. They refuse to reap the harvest. They're the ones who are trying to starve us out with their bony hands of famine — choke the Soviet government, choke me! So, why not turn the tables, turn their bony fingers inward on themselves. Tell Pavel to collect the grain; stop the kulak sabotage. There is plenty of food, and we will find it in whatever crevices and pits they hid it. We will get the grain and whatever else they have taken and hidden."

Targanovich nodded and winced at the same time, then cleared his throat. "There is one more matter in this regard that has been deemed even more..." he didn't know quite how to put it, "under wraps — in a separate, more confidential report." He fiddled with his attaché case latch before it sprang open. Awkwardly, with a slight tremble in his fingers, he pulled out a red file folder with large black letters *SECRET by order of the OGPU.*

"More from Pavel?"

"From reports to him by the Office of Special Investigations in Ukraine..." Targanovich cleared his throat. "It refers to numerous instances of cannibalism."

"Cannibalism?" Stalin gave the young man a look of genuine surprise.

"Apparently, the OGPU in Ukraine is worried that it may get out as common knowledge."

"Who is eating whom?"

"Some particulars are in here, sir." Targanovich took three steps forward and laid the file on Stalin's desk before taking exactly three steps back.

Stalin eyed it distastefully. "Give me a quick summary," he ordered.

"Random, isolated cases, for the most part, of people dying and being consumed, sometimes by family members. A bit of madness, no doubt. But there are more calculated killings — hunters. Reports of children gone missing. Worse, there is evidence that it is organized, corpses cut up, pickled, and blended with other meats and then sold."

"Kulak cuisine." Stalin almost smiled. He liked to be witty. He puffed a little harder on the pipe. But true enough; this was a sensitive matter that had to be treated with care lest it leaked out. "How widespread is this activity?"

"Hard to say. The OGPU have taken steps to handle all such cases and have not let them go before the local kolkhosp courts. But..." Targanovich paused and again cleared his throat, "cannibalism is not covered in the criminal code, so—"

"You mean we can't eat each other?"

Targanovich kept silent, at a loss at how to respond. Stalin pursed his lips before taking another pull of the pipe as if it were a sobering soother. "It is not a matter for the courts, quite right. It's a matter for the security people, and we do not need to worry about the criminal code..." He put his pipe down into the ashtray and gave the matter more thought. "How much is known about this group of 'capitalists' who are pickling and distributing humans for consumption?"

"It operates out of Poltava district from a number of clandestine locations."

"Well, we can't have that, can we? It will give the Trotskyites a propaganda windfall if it got out, won't it? Added to the stories of millions of swollen bellies, dead old men and women in patched rags on the sides of roads, skeletons in the middle of the streets — now I hear all of the cows, horses, pigs, and children snatched up and gone. Not by a massive plague and they didn't emigrate. Oh no; they are being made lunch of. Pickled herring with little fingers, is that it?"

Stalin's semi-coherent rant did not encourage a response. Targanovich gave a nod but remained tight-lipped. Nor did the general secretary expect an answer. He realized that this needed to be addressed with urgency and the perpetrators punished. Most certainly, all such reports were to be suppressed. He finally picked up the file and advised Targanovich that the words *famine* and *cannibalism* were not to be mentioned. What was heard or might have been witnessed and reported constituted kulak/Trotskyite/Western propaganda. "The OGPU needs to ensure that mouths are kept shut about this," he ordered Postyshev's envoy.

After Targanovich was sent on his way, Stalin perused the report which contained a number of unsavoury cases of familial cannibalism, a couple of murder cases where children were stalked and killed for feed, and finally a brief note about this apparently growing network of commercialized cannibalism. What gave him pause, however, was that these pickled barrels of human remains were potentially attaining wide distribution — the "product" getting into the urban areas, not only in Ukraine but also in Soviet Russia. Indeed, the capital! What really got his attention and ultimately an uneasy outrage was that one of the photographed barrels apprehended by security agents had peculiar markings etched into the side, double hammers over a scythe, which on analysis contained the tainted meat. Stalin would check, but he thought that similar barrels had been delivered to his dacha where just the night before he and his politburo cronies had wined and dined!

***

Bila Sich

Ivan Prasha saw all the signs by early spring of 1932. After the crops and livestock were confiscated and/or slaughtered, after the grain was piled and guarded in warehouses, after access to food was systematically denied, came an inevitable chain of events. Cats and dogs disappeared, followed by rodents, grubs, and earthworms. The land progressively became denuded of vegetation, from dandelions and willow root to bluebells and nettle; any plant above or below the soil became part of the survivalists' recipe. Mixed with ground-up leather and tree bark, it formed a pasty but passable stew to stave off hunger. When even those were gone; when not a bird flew or a leaf rustled; when the landscape became cold, barren, and hard; when the snow finally fell and settled, then death and despair truly arrived. Prasha tried to warn his boss about the consequences. To no avail. Instead of taking measures to ameliorate the situation, save the village and kolkhoz, Tolstoy did the opposite: he embraced the horror that was to come. In fact, it seemed to rejuvenate him, providing a renewed sense of purpose.

"They're kulaks, after all," the chairman of the local Soviet council told him. "They brought this upon themselves. Should've handed over the grain long ago. The directive is to fill the quotas. If these aren't filled, guess who will be blamed and made to suffer a most severe socialist justice? Whatever problems are occurring in the village and at the kolkhoz, the kulaks are behind it, and it's for the manager to sort out."

Prasha tried to point out the obvious. "But these quotas cannot be filled, and people need to eat. Surely, the worker's state cannot possibly be happy to see its people starve. I thought we were supposed to organize and improve the peasantry, not kill it!"

"You can't make a proletarian omelette without cracking the kulak egg."

"There are rumours — horrible rumours," Prasha was compelled to report. "Children are disappearing... People are descending into madness and anarchy... There are two cases of cannibalism..."

"I received a confidential memorandum from Commissar Fedryk on that very topic. The ... rumours are being looked into by the Office of Special Investigations, and all cases referring to such activity will be passed on to it. We need not concern ourselves here. I follow orders. And if it's a case of eat or be eaten, well, that's the way kulaks are!" Tolstoy smiled as if he had just delivered a clever joke. "However, there is to be no more reporting or talk of cannibalism to me or anyone else."

As the winter wore on into the depths of January and February of the new year, Tolstoy's position hardened. He relished enforcing strict laws that forbade what he called the "stalking" of socialist crop fields for leftovers: an ear of corn, a missed potato or discarded beet were now precious state property. The towers that guarded these fields were reinforced, and the "shoot on sight" decree from the party hierarchy of anyone caught in possession of an unlawfully obtained edible was enforced. Prasha was chagrined; it seemed that Tolstoy had lost whatever constituted his sense of humanity, and morality had become inconvenient. *He's descending into a dark, even depraved place.*

Prasha didn't know what he could do about it. He was still party faithful, desperately wanting to believe that he and his fellow Bolsheviks were agents of improvement for the workers and peasants. Certainly not the instruments of wilfully killing them. As it stood, he had a job to do — the job assigned to him by the party to which he owed his existence. And he was determined to do it, just not at the expense of losing his own humanity.

Tolstoy and Prasha let winter surround them in relative isolation. Except for a couple more distant regional meetings, they stayed close to home, organizing the biweekly Bila Sich Soviet council meetings in the party headquarters, meeting the odd official, receiving and responding to various state directives. Prasha, after brief thoughts of a rendezvous/dalliance with Oxana/Katya, alas unrequited, remained a solitary figure, retiring to his room upstairs every night relatively early, where he recopied his notes and often read before bed. There was little else to do since a cook/charwoman came in on a daily basis to perform the basic household functions from food preparation (food supplies were not a problem, with deliveries once a week) to cleaning and laundry. She usually left after dinner washing-up.

Tolstoy did have a more active social life. Thankfully, for the most part, he kept it outside his bedroom, disappearing once a week in the company of a bodyguard for parts unknown. Every so often, when presumably he didn't wish to go out, a female companion would come in. As with Belynski and Oxana, he'd hear the muffled groans from below, but they were usually of short duration, and whoever visited Tolstoy was gone shortly thereafter. Prasha surmised this by the creaking of feet on the floor, sometimes the rustle of clothing hastily put on, and the firm closing of the door. It instilled a certain restlessness within him, but it passed quickly. He even wondered if all the effort Tolstoy went to with his clandestine trysts and drop-in guests was worth the bother.

Meanwhile, with the first signs of warming weather and melting snow, the silent and stoic land began releasing its storage; bodies appeared. They were scattered everywhere and stank in overpowering envelopes of air, assaulting the nostrils and penetrating every pore of those nearby still living. Rats, hunted to extinction, some thought, suddenly made a comeback, along with other, lesser rodents that couldn't resist the odour of dead flesh. Those that had not been killed for food took their revenge. Once attacked by humans, they now attacked back. Their demise had been badly exaggerated, thought Prasha as he organized "volunteers" for corpse removals. If possible, they would be identified and stricken off the village lists; otherwise, they would be hauled away to large pits for mass burials. *Where were they hiding?* A rat on a stick over an open flame was as good as a pig on a spit to a starving human. Enough harvested could have fed a whole village.

With spring on the horizon, Prasha hoped that the worst would be over and that the party and, by extension, Tolstoy would relent. The village, the kolkhoz — what was left of it — needed a reprieve, an injection of humanity in the form of food aid. Yet here he was beside Tolstoy, a couple of armed men, and half a dozen others at the entrance to a desolate homestead bereft of any promise of hidden bounty. For some macabre reason, as far as Prasha was concerned, Tolstoy insisted on taking him along with one of the Bread Procurement Brigades that were still diligently searching cottages and properties for the fabled caches of grain. "I feel like some fresh air and exercise," he chirped, "and what better activity than with the Procurement Brigade, checking in on Bila Sich citizens. We have a number of new Komsomol recruits that we should welcome as well…"

A tall, gaunt man dressed in loose clothes (rag clumps and patches to the more focused observer) but otherwise physically in good shape appeared at the cottage door as the brigade approached. There were seven in all: Tolstoy, Prasha, two militiamen, and three young volunteers. The man before them, Prasha presumed, was one Fedor Rostynovich; he consulted his notebook just to make sure. To Prasha's eye, Rostynovich defied logic, which made him uneasy. Despite apparently having nothing — confirmed by a Procurement Brigade search in December of his home and property — he was alive and well. Why was that?

He had none of the classic symptoms. No sagging, grey-yellowish skin, thin and translucent over the bones of what Prasha could see. His face was firm, not rubbery in texture; the neck was not depressed as if the shoulders were struggling under the weight. He held his head high, aloft. It was hard to tell given the thick trousers he was wearing, but the legs did not appear to be swollen. Certainly, he was far from the less fortunate ones in their last stages with bloating faces, ballooning legs and stomachs. The only tell-tale sign that something was not quite right was his stillness, rigid posture, and hollow stare.

Prasha was wary of coming too close. Irrationally, perhaps, he feared that the man might lose control, turn on them, and become a wild beast. Of course, they had the two militiamen at the ready. Yet he was serene as they got closer, too calm, thought Prasha, as if he was going to welcome them with bread and salt!

Tolstoy did not seem to perceive any of this. "You appear in fine fettle, Comrade..." Tolstoy glanced at Prasha's notebook, "Rostynovich. Why is that?"

Prasha frowned. This was a clear acknowledgement that people were starving and surprise that some hadn't.

The man remained silent. Tolstoy's sadistic smile hovering, challenging. He wanted to put pressure on Rostynovich — crack him. Obviously, he was hoarding grain. He was too well fed and healthy not to be. "A new seed collection campaign is underway. Spring will come soon enough. So, where is it? Where is the seed needed for this spring's sowing?"

Rostynovich took a small step forward, negated by Tolstoy stepping back in turn, but said nothing. The two militiamen barely twitched. Their rifles remained slung over their shoulders.

"Very well, then," Tolstoy continued, "it's time to search again." He ordered the three volunteers, two males and one female, huddled together at the back to spread out and "This time," he raised his voice, "do a thorough job!" He nodded to the two guards to escort Rostynovich inside. He and his secretary would follow.

They had barely crossed the threshold when one of the searchers gave a startled shout. "Over here!"

Tolstoy with his entourage in tow marched across a path to a shed, behind which was a woodpile. Human remains — bone, mostly — were clearly visible from under the pile. The only reason it was spotted was because animals had dragged pieces out from underneath.

While the others stood in horror, Tolstoy seemed to relish the find, almost pleased with himself. "So, Comrade Rostynovich," Tolstoy intoned gleefully, "no grain but plenty of meat. Who are they? Your wife? Your children? In-laws? Or did you go hunting?"

Rostynovich again did not answer. He stood calmly beside the two guards while the others collected themselves.

Tolstoy shook his head and smirked. "Why didn't you just hang yourself? It would have been the proper thing to do. This," he waved his hands around, "I cannot explain and really don't want to report. It's so uncivilized! It's best to shoot you."

Rostynovich smiled and spoke for the first time in a rich, civilized baritone. "The *proper* thing to do would have been to give people food... But you are right. I should have and would have shot myself, but your lot confiscated everyone's guns. As for being disgusting well ... no more than your ilk's actions. What would you do? A starving man does not sniff his meal. I ran out of potatoes and your precious grain months ago. They died; I didn't. I got over the queasiness of it all."

"I should shoot you," Tolstoy stated vehemently.

"By all means, if you have room in that cart over there for another corpse." Rostynovich stared beyond Tolstoy's left shoulder to the road where a wagon and a horse with a load of piled bodies was mired in snow and mud.

Prasha looked over. It was the corpse collectors making their rounds. He had organized them like a cleaning crew to scour the roads and ditches for bodies and knock on doors to see if anyone was left alive or politely ask, "Do you have any today?"

Tolstoy turned to Rostynovich. "You're mad!"

"You may well be right — but no madder than you or the others in charge."

"Take him away," Tolstoy ordered. He decided not to shoot him after all. A report to the OGPU would have to be filed.

***

Lev Devchenko and Vlas Chorney, along with their families, were among the fortunate to have survived the winter of '32/'33. In large part, it was because of Lucia, the runted milking cow that Lev managed to keep under wraps, and the hidden caches of food both men contributed to. The Procurement Brigades in their periodic sweeps found neither.

Under their noses, Vlas thought. Like squirrels, they buried bags of potatoes and grain in a number of choice locations in adjoining woods on kolkhoz property proper instead of their former land that the Procurement Brigades tended to focus their searches on. True, in winter the bags were harder to dig out, but like the squirrels, they knew exactly where to dig. Of course, precautions were taken. Retrieval could be undertaken only in the dead of night. Cooking and eating could be risked only at night too with no moon, lest the smoke attract unwanted visitors, including starving collective farm workers, given the dire circumstances.

For Lev, the most serious and pressing problem remained: the kolkhoz manager, Dmytro Maserkin. Ever watchful and critical, he was becoming suspicious of how well Lev and his family seemed to be surviving. The personal animosity, evident from the first day of Lev's arrival on the collective, escalated through the fall and winter, particularly as Maserkin and the kolkhoz he ran were stripped of the harvest by government quotas and thus faced starvation like the rest of the countryside. Yet, as he cleaned out the stall and gave Lucia fresh hay, Lev was feeling relatively secure and lucky given the tragedy unfolding in Bila Sich. His big worry at that moment was whether he had enough hay to get Lucia through the latter part of winter.

He heard the shed door opening. "Ah, Vlas," he said, looking up from his work, "you're here early." He expected his friend later on to obtain his milk quota and plan their next night excursion.

"Drop the pitchfork and move away from the cow!" It was the harsh but excited voice of Dmytro Maserkin, his archnemesis (as he had jokingly called him at one point). Suddenly, he was no joke. "I knew it! I knew it! You're a hoarding kulak!

Lev rested his implement against the shed wall and moved out from the stall to confront the kolkhoz manager. He had never liked the man and tried to avoid him whenever he could. Lev mentally kicked himself for not being more vigilant. He heard the talk of Maserkin's increasingly erratic behaviour and paranoid actions. It seemed that everybody was out to get him — the kulaks, the kolkhoz workers, the Bolsheviks. No one was quite sure. Even Maserkin's wife came under suspicion, living under duress and fearful for herself and their two children when he succumbed to his weekly drinking sprees. It was common knowledge; certainly, Nina heard the gossip.

And here he was, dishevelled, angry, and definitely out for blood. In the feeble light, Lev could see that Maserkin had produced his treasured revolver (which he carried and on occasion exposed as a symbol of authority on the kolkhoz); it was pointed at him.

"I should shoot you!" He spat out the words with the spittle highlighted like dust in the slivers of daylight left seeping through the small window and ajar door behind Maserkin.

"Just take the cow," Lev said as calmly as he could. "That's what you're here for."

"I'll shoot you and then take the cow!" he jeered. "Perfectly within my rights. I caught a saboteur, a hoarder, a filthy kulak with state — kolkhoz property. Standing directive is to shoot on sight!"

Lev's mouth went dry. This was for real. In all probability, he was about to die.

"Listen… Dmytro… We've had our difference, but—"

"Shut up!" the agitated man screamed. "I caught you. I'm going to do my duty."

With the revolver firmly gripped in his extended hand, Maserkin took a step forward as Lev backed up against a corral post. He could dive behind the cow, but as crazy as it seemed, his first thought was that he did not want a stray bullet hitting the animal. She was too valuable.

Suddenly, light flooded in. Startled, Maserkin turned his head to see what or who had caused it. Before he could properly assess and react, he was hit on the side of the head with a heavy object. He went down as if dropped down a chute, the revolver skittering away under a pile of straw.

Vlas stood stunned, a mallet in his right hand now dropped to his side. It took a moment for both men to recover as they stared at the crumbled form with a thick red pool of blood congealing around his head, the hair matted and the army cap askew.

"I–I thought he was going to shoot you," said Vlas, still rooted to his spot.

"He was. You saved my life. I…"

There was a moan from Maserkin, who evidently wasn't dead. Lev moved swiftly, stepping around the prone figure, grabbing the mallet from Vlas's hand, and in one fluid motion he brought it down on the manager's head a second time.

"There," Lev exhaled, "I don't want you to take full responsibility for this. We are in this together."

Vlas stared for a moment longer before weaning himself off the shock. "So, what do we do now?"

"Get rid of him, but the question is how without arousing suspicion and investigation. You didn't see anyone else out there?" Lev asked, his voice spiking with anxiety.

"No."

"Good. The bastard came alone. Must have followed me. He was losing it at the kolkhoz, and from day one we didn't get along."

"We could haul him out to the bush and drop a thick tree branch over his head. It'll be chalked up as an accident, maybe."

Lev thought about that and decided that it was too risky. A patrolling militiaman or nosy kolkhozian might see and report. Moreover, it would be no small feat to get the body into the collective farm's bush. "Hmm… We need to think about this carefully. First, let's wrap him up and drag him out of here behind the shed. We'll lay him out against the wall, cover him with snow, and place wood overtop. His body will stay fresh for a while… Give us time to figure this out."

"Okay." Vlas nodded. "That can be done."

"Actually, the more I think about it, the more I'm convinced of what to do. I've been asked to 'volunteer' as a corpse collector. I think I most definitely will, as my civic duty. In due course, I'll stop here and together, since you too will volunteer and be on duty with me, we'll take him away along with a pile of others to a mass grave, an anonymous, unidentified body."

"I've never killed anyone before, not even in the war," Vlas said numbly as if what occurred had just dawned on his conscience.

"Actually, I probably killed him, or at least finished him off. Don't feel bad about it. Even his wife wanted to be rid of him…"

CHAPTER TWENTY-SEVEN

Kyiv

Arkady (Petrov) Olinsky considered himself a professional fixer. Physically unassuming, stocky with a slight paunch, but thick-limbed with muscle subsuming the softer flabby bits, he nevertheless had an admirable track record of serving his clients, those who had much to lose if he failed. Officially, his day job was security at Khreshchatyk Hotel, arguably Kyiv's most prestigious in the heart of the city. Outwardly, his job was routine and unexciting, consisting of keeping unwanted individuals from entering, spying and reporting on foreign visitors (as a matter of course), dealing with drunk comrades fighting and/or destroying hotel property, and occasionally investigating theft (usually petty) from guest rooms. However, inside the fancy cast-iron fence and within the confines of this pseudo-Gothic, three-storey structure arrived important party members and high-ranking apparatchiks who had "business" problems to sort and scores to settle. And that was where he proved useful. Unofficially, certain individuals discreetly called on him from time to time to take care of problematic people. The service ranged from simple but direct warnings to elimination. From his days in the Red Army, he had acquired the skills to kill without malice. If an execution bothered him afterward, it was lessened greatly, if not alleviated, by the handsome stipend received. This would be his third "elimination."

He had all he needed: the building address and the location of the apartment. Leaving nothing to chance and to reassure himself that there would be no obvious surprises, he made a scouting trip, discovering that building access was laughably easy and would not hinder his entry or exit. His cap pulled down low, covering his balding spot and curly black hair, he even took a stroll through the third-floor hallway. All the doors were the same faded green, revealing shoddy workmanship and flimsy locks that could be picked in seconds. There was no one about, so he briefly stopped in front of apartment 302, the middle one on the left side. This was going to be child's play. He decided to return late the following evening. He hoped that his target, the female wanted in the Gromeko murder, lived alone (there was no time to watch and ascertain who went in and out). It would be regrettable if that were not the case; there could be no witnesses.

How to do it? Noiselessly would be best, although he doubted anyone in the building would venture out from their apartment to investigate, even if they heard a loud gunshot. He'd take along his treasured Luger, a model 1900 Parabellum, liberated from a German soldier on the Eastern Front over a decade ago, just in case she wasn't alone or there were other complications. Otherwise, he'd employ his *Nahkampfmesser* trench knife, designed for close-quarters fighting, taken from the same hapless German soldier he had stumbled over in the water and mud. The knife, with its short, sturdy blade and heavy metal handle, was superior to what the Red Army soldier had, as was the *Deutsche Waffen- und Munitionsfabriken* Luger, a notch above in materials and precision compared to the Nagant. A quick thrust or two while she lay asleep and it would be over in a moment — a quick in and out.

***

There was nobody about outside or inside the building. But at 2:00 a.m., why would there be, Petrov thought as he made his way up the stairs to the third floor. After a quick glance up and down the hall, he arrived at his destination. Old building, old lock. As he surmised, the door unlocked in seconds when he inserted his "special" tool, making short work of the mechanism inside. He slowly opened the door, stepped inside, and gently closed it. A squeak, not too loud (he hoped) and a click were unavoidable. He stopped and listened, letting his eyes adjust to the darkness. Fortunately, it was absolute; a pool of pale moonlight leaked through a window and partially closed door leading to the bedroom.

Taking a couple of settling breaths, Petrov psyched himself into kill mode and made his way gingerly, lest he bump into an object in the dark or the floor creaked, to the partially ajar bedroom door. He viewed the lump form on the bed and slowly drew out his combat knife from its leather sheath in his right pocket; the left contained the Luger. His mind focused: *Do it and get out. Receive the remainder of the promised payment and be happy!*

He realized that something wasn't quite right even as he raised his knife and brought it down. The sleeping form didn't look human, even in the limited light.

Then he heard the metallic click of a revolver trigger hammer. "Drop the knife! Turn around."

Fuck!

Petrov spun around and saw the shadow of a man in the doorway. He took a step, debating whether to charge or throw the knife when the gun flashed into a loud explosion.

Lubick turned the light on, and with his revolver smoking and still pointed at the crumbled man beside the bed, walked over and kicked the knife out of reach. Krypniuk came out of the closet. "Good thing you're a good shot; I was behind him."

They had discussed earlier how best to capture the assassin. After some debate, it was decided to do so in the apartment rather than in the hall or outside, where there were more avenues of escape and potentially bystanders who could be in harm's way. Admittedly, at that hour it was unlikely, but then it wasn't known when (and if) the assassin was going to strike. Then there were the tenants; most knew better than to open their doors when some sort of trouble brewed on the other side, but one never knew, and there was also the risk of stray bullets if it came down to a gunfight. Placing themselves inside the apartment was perhaps a bit more dangerous, depending on the assassin's weapon of choice, but Krypniuk's main concern was comfort. He did not relish spending hours waiting in the bedroom, only to quietly and rapidly get himself ensconced into the closet when the apartment door opened. He assumed the same for Lubick, who took the living room and emerged from behind the sofa.

"I would not have shot you," Lubick said confidently.

"Good to know... I'll check for other weapons," Krypniuk informed his sergeant, stepping closer to the prone man and bending down carefully to avoid getting any blood on himself. *Ivanka would not be happy if she had to wash it out!* "Ah..." He pulled out a German Luger from the assassin's left coat pocket and set it on the small night table beside the bed.

Standing up, Krypniuk addressed the man, who moaned, clutched his side, and was starting to breathe erratically in shallow breaths. "No doubt you have realized that you have been shot. Quite a serious wound that, if not treated promptly, will result in your death. I'm Captain Krypniuk of the Kyiv Police Criminal Investigation Department, and I can get you to the hospital not far from here. However, I should like you to tell me who sent you here ... along with a few other details — like your name."

"If I talk, I am dead," Petrov whispered and grimaced.

"Perhaps," said Krypniuk, "but if you stay silent, you'll be equally dead — in a much shorter timeframe. The question is: do you want to live long enough to get to the hospital or not? Of course, I and the good sergeant here will do all we can to protect you."

At that moment, there was a pounding on the door before it abruptly swung open and a breathless young policeman came rushing in. Lubick stopped him. "All is in hand, Jacob. Stand outside the door, make sure no one gets too close, friendly or not."

"Yes, sir."

"Well," Krypniuk turned to the would-be assassin curled on the floor. "You are leaking quite badly; so, which is it, death here and rather quickly or the hope of surviving?"

***

Eight hours earlier, Krypniuk and Lubick had visited apartment 302. An old man leaning on a cane opened the door and appeared confused when they showed their credentials and inquired about a Katya Kharsova, who, according to credible information, was staying there. Lubick then pulled out a photo, the same as was on the poster. "Her. This person." He brought the photo closer to the man's face.

"Sorry, I know no such person."

"I hope you are telling us the truth, Citizen Rubiniuk," said Krypniuk, frowning. He had the city records pulled and knew that Anton Rubiniuk had lived there for many, many years, in fact. Was Yagii's information wrong? Was the street urchin simply bullshitting his way out of a tough predicament? His gut told him no. "There are people looking for her — bad people who believe she resides at this address. They will not be polite when they come looking for her. If a mistake has been made and they don't have the right address, you are still in danger. I suggest that you gather what you need and leave the apartment now."

"Where would I go?"

"No place to go? A relative or close friend perhaps — just for a couple of days."

Rubiniuk shook his head. The irony was that while he had no intention of leaving his apartment, his son, perhaps intrigued by his guest, had expedited matters. A tucked-away apartment not far from the caves and his place of business had been secured, and she should pack and be ready to move in two days. Of course, he couldn't tell the insistent policeman that. He simply nodded gravely and hoped they'd go away. In the meanwhile, he prayed that they wouldn't decide to search the apartment; Katya was in the bedroom, no doubt quietly listening at the door.

"I think we better come in," Krypniuk declared, not waiting for an answer, but stepped through with his sergeant in tow, deftly avoiding the protruding walking stick the old man had been leaning on.

"I..." Clearly annoyed, Rubiniuk could do no other but follow them in.

"May we sit down and have a chat?" Krypniuk asked politely.

230 Holodomor: A Crime Novel

"Yes, yes, of course." In unison, they moved to the chairs at the kitchen table.

Rubiniuk hooked his cane on the seat back and sat; Krypniuk occupied the chair opposite, while Lubick remained standing unobtrusively, fading into the background. Rubiniuk recovered some composure and goodwill (he hoped) by offering them a drink.

"No, thank you," demurred Krypniuk. "We are on business. Now, Citizen Rubiniuk, I must be clear about two things. First, you must leave this apartment. This is not optional. Your life will be in peril if you do not. Hopefully, it will be only for a short time. But you cannot stay here. Secondly, you must be absolutely truthful. So, I ask again, is the woman in the photo shown to you staying here or has she ever stayed here previously?"

"I—" Rubiniuk stopped himself, removing his hands from the table to his lap to keep them from shaking.

"Citizen Rubiniuk," interjected Lubick, "how do you explain this?" He had picked up a handbag beside the sofa that clearly belonged to a female, pulling out a scarf.

"I think we better search your apartment," Krypniuk announced.

"That won't be necessary." The bedroom door had swung open, and Katya came out.

Rubiniuk turned to Katya and said, "Sorry."

"Nothing to be sorry for," she said with a small smile. "Looks like my time is up."

"Ah, Miss Kharsova. So nice to finally meet you," Krypniuk said, rising from his chair, giving her a slight bow. Even a thinner, more haggard Katya Karina Kharsova captured his attention. "I have many questions for you; however, as I explained to Citizen Rubiniuk, it would be better that I ask them elsewhere. You are in danger."

"Are you taking us to the police station?" There was resignation with a hint of defiance in her voice.

"No, that would create … complications. Your trip will be a short one, across the hall, in fact. We have ascertained that the apartment is currently unoccupied. So please, take what you need — clothing and other things. We may not have much time."

Oleksander Pylyp's former apartment had been pretty well stripped bare, Katya noted when she and Anton entered. Except for a couple of chairs, the kitchen table, and the old sofa, very little remained. The cupboards were open and empty, discarded clothing was unceremoniously dumped in a pile beside the closet wall, muddy boot imprints glazed the floor, and the air had a sour, musty smell intermixed with strong tobacco odours.

For a fleeting moment, Katya thought of Oleksander and shuddered at his probable fate. The tall, gaunt policeman brought her out of her melancholic reverie, directing her to the sofa.

Rubiniuk once again hooked his cane on the back of the kitchen chair and dropped heavily onto the seat. Lubick leaned against the tiny kitchen sink, his pen and notebook out and poised. A young policeman stood at the door. (He had been vetted and selected by Lubick to ensure as far as possible that he would be discreet and no information of this operation leaked out). Krypniuk wanted at least one other backup on hand, since he had no idea of how many and in what form the assassination would come — if Yagii's information was reliable.

For now, he needed to interrogate Katya and get some proper answers, keenly aware that if he simply arrested her and brought her to the station, she would be quickly whisked away by the OGPU and in all probability never be seen again.

She seemed to anticipate his dilemma. "Are you going to take me … us," she glanced at Anton, "in?"

Krypniuk folded himself on to the sofa beside her (no place else to sit, and his left leg was throbbing, as it always did when the weather was about to change), creating a modest but non-threatening space between them. "Ah … that is both a question and a conundrum."

She put her hands together in her lap into the folds of her brightly patterned peasant skirt. "You know that I will not fare well in custody?"

Krypniuk nodded. "I will consider this seriously."

Although she had no reason to, Katya believed him and felt reasonably assured that he would seriously think about the implications. There was something upright and honest about the man that she had not seen in those in authority for a long time. Still, the question remained: could she trust him? But then, what choice did she have? If only Lushka had come by a day earlier; she would have disappeared. On the other hand, if Sholtz was coming for her and found out where she stayed, Anton too was in danger.

"I need to know," Krypniuk continued, "first, did you kill Commissar Gromeko?"

"No!"

"Good." That seemed shocked and emphatic enough, thought Krypniuk. "But you did witness the shooting?"

"No. I heard who it was. I recognized the voice. I was outside the apartment door about to enter when I heard them argue and the gunshot."

Krypniuk nodded while Lubick wrote furiously. Even Rubiniuk suddenly perked up. "What did you do after hearing the shot?"

"I ran. I think he saw me from the window because he came looking for me. I had to disappear."

"And quite effectively and for some time," Krypniuk remarked, impressed. "I should like to know the details... For now, though, please tell me, whose voice did you recognize in the apartment?"

"I wish to barter. That information for our freedom," Katya said with a determined edge and a glance at Anton.

"You can barter — yes, and as I mentioned I will consider your ... predicament. However, I wish for the moment to separate the two. Can you trust me enough to do that?"

Katya took another look at Anton, as if trying to ascertain what he thought. He remained stoic. It was like playing a game of chance. He couldn't advise her as to the odds or what she should do.

"I don't know you well enough to answer such a question."

"True," Krypniuk conceded, "nevertheless, what are your alternatives?"

At this point, she revealed her last remaining ace, she hoped. "I have hidden some important documents that will be very useful in your investigation."

Krypniuk nodded and then promptly totally deflated her. "You are referring to those documents in the closet of your, or was it Commissar Gromeko's apartment? I agree; they are very useful. Certainly made for some interesting reading. I presume you put them there?"

Katya's eyes widened and her lips thinned. "Yes, I put them there — for insurance and protection. Stupid me. They would not have saved me, would they? Besides, once gone, out of the apartment, I had no way to retrieve them."

"They might have if delivered into the right hands," Krypniuk stated cryptically. "They are less relevant for our purposes now, however. So, to the matter at hand. You know who shot Commissar Gromeko. Please tell me."

"Does it really matter?" she asked. "The powerful in this city and the new socialist state protect themselves and each other if necessary for mutual benefit."

"Oh, but yes, it matters," Krypniuk retorted, his voice slightly elevated. "I'm a criminal case detective, and homicide qualifies. I intend to close this case with the guilty party identified and exposed." *If perhaps not brought to justice,* he added silently. "That is my primary concern."

Katya sighed. "I will tell you then with the fervent hope that after, you let me — us — go. I'll disappear again…"

Later, while they were setting the trap in Rubiniuk's apartment for a visit from the assassin in all probability that night, Lubick said, "You were right. Had him pegged all the way."

"Not all the way. But yes, those documents we read shed light and underlined the motive. As old as can be: a fight over the spoils illegally obtained to begin with."

"How are you going to play this?" Lubick asked as he peeled back the bedcover and spread a pile of clothing longitudinally with a pillow at the top end and in the middle. "There, that should do it."

"You're talking about Pavlick, our local OGPU commissar?"

"*Tak.*"

"It will be a bit tricky, and I'm not sure how strong a hand I have or if he'd let it go. I think it was the right thing to do. I hope I haven't gotten you into serious trouble. I'll know soon enough, I suppose."

"Don't worry on my account. I think you made the right decision… Think he'll come?"

"Oh, he or they will come. The question is when."

"Soon, I hope. Can't keep Katya and Rubiniuk cooped up with Jacob in the other apartment for too long."

"I agree."

CHAPTER TWENTY-EIGHT

Bila Sich

Dimitri Tolstoy was in a good mood. Olga had come to visit and put on her burlesque show with total Moulin Rouge decadence. Although he had never heard of Moulin Rouge, she assured him that it was a real gentleman's club in Paris, where the women were bold ("you know, oh la la" she puckered) and that very important men like himself could have fun and slum it. He laughed liking the idea; Olga was pretty bold, and as for slumming, well, why not, although to be perfectly honest, Olga wasn't exactly a Georgia peach. A bit older and stouter than he would have liked, but then he wasn't the epitome of a Cossack either, he rationalized, slapping his paunch.

They had their rendezvous (the word sounded sexy and exotic when she said it), and he was spent. He paid her extra for the extra because she came to him, instead of him going out as he most often did. Olga resided at the edge of Bila Sich in the confiscated home of a well-known merchant long since disappeared. She and four other ladies had set up their business on a discreet and temporary basis, although everyone in the village knew about it. There was no such thing as prostitution in the new Soviet socialist utopia, but allowances were made; Bila Sich was a frontier town, and those who came to do the party's work needed their recreational diversions and rewards. Too bad his earnest secretary was such a stickler or prude, Tolstoy amended in his thoughts. Ivan Prasha frowned on such "noncommunist" activities, and so blatantly displayed.

"Sure, sure," Tolstoy agreed, "Lenin would roll over in his grave if he weren't on display." He chuckled at his own joke and encouraged the sombre little man to loosen up, indulge in life a little. Prasha was unmoved, but nevertheless, Tolstoy appreciated that he removed himself discreetly, retiring early on such nights when the chairman of the local Soviet council decided to entertain.

Tolstoy nudged Olga, taking away his hand that had draped over her ample breasts (she was a bit heftier in bed than she appeared in her black negligee, but then, no doubt, he had been distracted). Now … not so much; he was tired and simply wanted to send her on her way and go to sleep.

"Time to get your butt out of here," he cajoled, nudging a little harder.

"All right, all right." She moved to her side of the bed and put her feet on the parquet floor. "Sure, you don't want me to straighten your uncle one more time? Once I put my clothes on, the session is over."

"I'm good… I'll get Ilya to give you a ride home." Tolstoy always had the militiaman on duty to protect him and take Olga home when he'd had her over. That was part of the deal, to be picked up and brought back when she left the "women's quarters," as it was unofficially called. The last few times it had been Ilya who did the honours.

Probably serviced him as well, Tolstoy thought as he rose from the bed, shrugged his night robe on, and went to fetch the young guard somewhere outside, probably near the burning barrel, keeping warm if not making his periodic perimeter sweeps — not that there was anyone out there to worry about. Olga struggled into her increasingly strained bra. Bent over extravagantly like a Moulin Rouge cancan girl, picking up her underwear and other scattered pieces of clothing.

Cinching the sash on his robe, Tolstoy opened the front door to a blast of cold westerly air and spotted Ilya just a few feet away, coming around the corner of the building. "She's ready," he shouted. "I'll send her out in a moment!"

Ten minutes later, Olga was finally dressed and out the door. With a sigh of relief, he closed it and made his way back to the bedroom adjacent to the study. The fire was burning low, so he put another log on, and to warm his innards poured himself a double shot of vodka from a half-full bottle on the night table. Olga preferred wine, red, which gave him a headache. Vodka was always a good chaser...

Tolstoy was about to take off his robe and slide into bed when he heard a creak and the front door swung open. He thought he'd locked it. *What now? Had Olga forgotten or lost her knickers or something?*

His thoughts were rudely interrupted when a large, linear shadow filled the doorframe. The light from the kerosene lamp in the foyer was weak, and it took a moment for Tolstoy's brain to check in. *An intruder? Certainly not a militiaman...* He tightened the sash around the robe and made his way to the office and his desk where in the upper right-side drawer resided his trusty Nagant, the symbol of his authority.

However, he was too late. As he pulled on the drawer knob, strong, wiry fingers gripped his hand, digging in, exerting pressure like a mule sinking its teeth into the neck of a wolf. The force was overwhelming, and he was pulled away and slammed into his heavy wooden chair that with a loud scrape flew back against the wall.

Staring, leering at him, was a tall, angular, emaciated, savage-looking man in a Soviet army cap and a dirty, ragged coat that had seen better days. His eyes were feral, focused, and menacing. Tolstoy vaguely recognized him but couldn't place the context or when. "Prasha," he screamed, although it sounded more like a squeak. Surely, his secretary would have heard the chair hitting the wall and vibrating throughout the structure.

"You better shut up!" the man said in a low, nasty voice. "Or I'll snap your neck like a chicken. Understand?"

Tolstoy's pulse raced as he struggled to calm down.

"Do you understand?" the man repeated.

The chairman nodded. "Yes."

"Now, let's see what is in the drawer..." The man pulled hard, and the drawer rolled out to its farthest point, almost dislodging from the desk completely. "A gun, of course! You killed Simon Panki in the church courtyard. That was after you declared me a kulak and sent me away."

"That was a mistake!" Tolstoy protested.

"Simon is still dead and his family ... gone! But never mind... As you can see, I'm back, and I'm going to right the wrong here — a promise I made to myself." The man curled his lips into a visceral, cruel smile that made Tolstoy shrink in his chair. "I suppose you don't remember me, given that you sent so many others on their way. Yes, I was sentenced to exile in some labour camp about four thousand kilometres from my home for reasons that now elude me. As you can appreciate, it has taken some time to return. And I am grateful you're still here so that I can properly repay you."

"Who are you?" Tolstoy managed to sputter, his eyes watering from the violent shove he had received.

"Tomash, Tomash Chozh — the kulak, one of many you merrily sent to Siberia." As he spoke, Chozh tucked the gun into his coat pocket and patted it. "For safekeeping."

"Chozh..." Tolstoy articulated the name, recalling that he had seen him before, no doubt in his court, but none of the details. "How did you get back?"

"A profound question!" Chozh straightened from his hunched posture. "No easy feat. Let's say a careless guard who wanted to take my boots. I, on the other hand, wanted his coat and rifle!" Chozh chortled. "Of course, it wouldn't have been a fair exchange, since he had no intention of giving me his coat, let alone the rifle. Stupid man; I got his coat and rifle, and he found himself dead under the train in my coat. Alas, when the train moved, well ... he became another hapless and unrecognizable kulak who fell under a locomotive. But as you can see, even a good government-issue coat can be worn out quickly. So, I became a guard, travelled north and then back south, eventually to Kyiv and Korsun station, where I disappeared to become Tomash Chozh instead of Ihor Luka, the guard who tried to steal my boots. He should have been more careful and brought along some friends, but then they would have wanted the boots he was about to steal. They are fine boots!"

Tolstoy could not help but glance down at Chozh's boots. Even scuffed and dirty, it was obvious that they were made by a craftsman using fine leather. Although tempted, he didn't ask Chozh where he got them in the first place.

"I was fortunate, very fortunate. No one looked too closely or asked questions. By the way, there is an abundance of food in Russia. It's just when you cross the border into Ukraine that the land becomes barren and there is nothing to eat. I see this is equally true in Bila Sich. You are in charge, so you are responsible."

"But I can get you food, here in the pantry — it just got stocked the other day!" Tolstoy babbled hopefully.

Chozh gave a sad smile. "I'm sure there is, and you'd wine and dine me, but it is not necessary, nor will it save you."

Tolstoy's eyes widened in fear. "Please, can we discuss this? I am willing to do what you want. Name your price."

Chozh waved his right hand dismissively. "I know, I know, you'd do anything to save yourself. But have you stopped and thought whether you are worth saving?"

"I— "

Chozh grabbed the chair by the arms and leaned down as Tolstoy shrank against the seatback. "At this moment your body is worth more as fresh meat than as a breathing, miserable human."

"That's ... that's monstrous," Tolstoy managed to say, alarm rising in his voice.

"Is it?" Chozh stepped back as if in contemplation. "What's unthinkable is what has occurred here and throughout the countryside. People are mad with starvation, and anything edible means survival; it means life, no matter how distasteful. It is no more distasteful socially or otherwise to have those you are deliberately starving to turn around and eat you. Wouldn't you agree? And true, it is monstrous, but here we are."

"I wasn't deliberately starving the village," Tolstoy pleaded, finding his voice. "I was just following directives for the grain quotas. Had I known—"

"But you did!" shouted Chozh, which made Tolstoy seem to shrivel further. "How could you not? Take the pile of rotting grain sitting at the end of the road; yes, I saw it on my way here — dumped on the ground with a tarpaulin thrown over top and guards stationed around it. You ordered the guards to protect it, did you not? You were protecting the grain from whom? Certainly, not from the army of rodents that have infested it. From the starving, then. Why was it not distributed before it went bad? The militiamen are guarding a rotting pile at this moment from those who would gladly devour the inedible!"

"I…" Tolstoy licked his lips. "I had my orders."

"Yes, you had your orders," Chozh said sarcastically. "I suppose that applies to the cat and dog hunt. For their pelts, was it? Oh, yes, I heard about that the moment I arrived. You never did collect those pelts. Why was that? Leaving the whole pile of rot and stink in the village square — explain that?"

"I–I can't." Tolstoy's voice was subdued, almost a whisper. "I simply followed orders."

"Workers from the collective farm, I'm also told, can no longer enter Soviet shops. Why is that?"

"Because they didn't fulfill their required quotas of grain," Tolstoy answered in a small, sullen voice.

"So, that means that no one from the village and the kolkhoz can buy food or supplies?"

Tolstoy remained silent.

"Except, of course, you and your party comrades. Not only are you well fed, you invited me to check out your cupboards — ample, no doubt — bread, eggs, milk, and maybe even meat? Other niceties of life as well, I imagine, lots of kerosene, sugar, salt, and soap. I could use a bath, as you probably have noticed."

Chozh abruptly stopped his diatribe and stepped back, giving Tolstoy some space. He continued, "Oh, don't worry about what I said earlier. No one is going to eat you. I was joking! Besides, you are too rancid to eat. So, that is the good news. The bad is that I am going to kill you. I wasn't sure how — with my bare hands, probably. Now, I have a better idea." He pulled the revolver out from his coat pocket. "Much more efficient, don't you think?"

With every last ounce of strength, the chairman of the local Soviet council lashed out with his right foot aimed at Chozh's genitals, followed by an attempt to heave himself out of the chair. Unfortunately for him, it had little impact; neither the element of surprise nor the damage inflicted. The wild kick missed.

For his effort, Tolstoy was hit on top of the head with the butt end of the gun and rudely shoved into the chair again. This time, Chozh took no chances; he stuffed the weapon back into his pocket and grabbed the black telephone on the desk, another symbol of authority, yanked at the long cord that snaked to the wall, and in furious fashion wrapped the cord around the chair with Tolstoy securely enmeshed. The telephone, still attached, hung precariously at the side while the receiver with its own cord banged off the scuffed parquet floor.

"As I was saying," Chozh resumed in a reasonable tone, "you are going to die. You simply have to. A promise I made to myself. Still ... I am a fair man, and your revolver has given me the perfect opportunity to show my fairness! By giving you a chance. You probably don't know this, but after you sentenced me to exile, I tried to escape — yes, not far from the village. Of course, I was caught. Well, I did not go unpunished. Later, while we waited for the cattle car going north, a couple of the guards took me aside and played a little game. They called it 'Russian roulette,' based on a short story that one of them said they read or heard." As he talked, Chozh took the revolver out of his pocket again and examined it, popping out the cylinder. "Seven rounds per chamber. You have only six bullets; an empty chamber. Did you know that? Maybe you forgot to replace the bullet after shooting Simon? But never mind..."

Tolstoy was dazed by the blow to his head, but it had drawn no blood, and in short order he was alert again, giving a tentative wiggle and pull on the cord strung around him and the chair.

"Relax," Chozh continued, "you're not going anywhere. As I said, they played this Russian roulette game. There was one bullet in the chamber of the revolver, almost the same as this one — a Nagant, is it? Anyway, that's what they said, and one guard, an ugly, fat fellow, spun the cylinder, pointed the gun at my forehead, and pulled the trigger. He spun, pointed, and pulled the trigger two more times. What were the chances... I heard a click and not a bang three times. Believe that or not,

I'm not a ghost come back to torment you. Yes, three clicks and no bang," Chozh repeated, shaking his head. "The fat fellow was so disgusted that he pulled the trigger a fourth time close to my right ear. It hasn't stopped ringing since! But I got my prize — to continue my long trip to Siberia! So ... what I'm saying is that as a sporting man, I'll give you the same chance and play the same game of Russian roulette with you. As you can see," he popped open the cylinder of the revolver again and took out five bullets, "there, only one remains. I will pull the trigger three times — assuming you survive that long — with spins in between. Your odds are the same as mine. Do you feel lucky? Let's play."

"No... Please!"

Chozh put the barrel of the gun to Tolstoy's temple and pulled the trigger.

Click.

Tolstoy shuddered while his bladder released, soaking his pants and the seat with what earlier in the evening had been good wine and passable vodka.

"You are lucky. Shall we try again? Technically, you communists don't believe in God, but it never hurts to pray — just in case. I'll give you a moment."

"Please, *Tovarish*, I'm truly sorry!"

Chozh paid him no heed and spun the cylinder again, put the barrel up to Tolstoy's temple, and pulled the trigger.

Click.

"You've survived two rounds of Russian roulette! Quite remarkable," Chozh enthused as he spun the cylinder a third time.

"Someone will find me," Tolstoy screamed, violently jostling, trying to loosen the cord, spittle coming from his mouth. "The militia will find you. Prasha! Prasha! Help me!"

"Your Prasha obviously is nowhere to be found, whoever he may be. I saw the guard escort your lady friend away. Nobody will venture out at night. So..."

"Please, *Tovarish*, I beg you." Tolstoy started to cry.

"If it is to be, try to die with dignity," Chozh admonished. "Don't shout or whimper; don't curse or cry. Be silent and accept what is happening. Have some pride as a human being. Chin up. Be brave. Odds are that the third time — well, you know…"

He brought the barrel to Tolstoy's temple one more time and pulled the trigger.

***

Ivan Prasha heard the loud bang and realized that whatever was going on downstairs, it had probably concluded, and not in a good way. He had been awake for quite a while ever since a muffled disturbance interrupted his sleep. At first, he thought it was Tolstoy getting on with the "bordello lady" who had started to come on a more regular basis (much to his chagrin, Tolstoy was getting too lazy to leave the house, he presumed), but then he remembered that she had gone, Tolstoy summoning the guard and the front door closing. This was something else. This was an intruder!

When the chairman called out his name in panic, Prasha first froze, collected himself, got out of bed, put his trousers on, and was about to investigate when he thought better of it. Instead, he sat down on the chair beside his night table and waited, hoping that whoever was down there would not come up. He really had no place to go, no obvious escape route or place to hide.

After the big bang, Prasha heard footsteps that came to the stairs, stopped, and then receded into the kitchen area, he wasn't sure. He dared not move lest the floor creak or his motion give his presence away in some form. He wasn't afraid, exactly; nor did he wish to confront whoever it was — especially if they had a pistol. Thus, long after the outer door closed, Prasha stayed glued in his chair.

Finally, he decided that he'd have to go down and investigate. There was, after all, no way of ignoring or getting around it. With great trepidation, he slowly came down the stairs and rounded the corner leading into Tolstoy's office. The chairman of the local Soviet council was slumped in Belynski's favourite chair, blood oozing from the side of his head. He was tied down, or he would no doubt have slid to the floor. On closer inspection, it was the telephone's cord with

the instrument still dangling on the side that held him in place. *Well,
he did piss off a lot of people*, Prasha supposed.

The problem now was what to do? How to explain this? The
charwoman didn't arrive until 7:00 a.m. to provide breakfast and
other duties as required. He still had a couple of hours to work out a
plan of action. And he definitely needed one. He couldn't just leave
the scene, a messy crime scene, as is. Too many questions would be
asked. *Where were you? Didn't you hear anything? Did he call out? Did
you come down to help?* Most importantly, *did* you *do it?* No, it just
wouldn't do to let the OGPU come to the wrong conclusion. Thus,
the option to do nothing was dismissed.

Of course, there was always the other way out, one he had
contemplated since the Rostynovich incident, where instead of
finding a secret cache of grain, the procurement committee had found
human remains. He felt disoriented and disconnected. *Was this what
the socialist ideal had come to?* He tried to brush aside such harsh
thoughts. Still, he kept having these ghastly dreams: pale, bloated
faces, vaguely recognizable as those that had appeared before him in
the court, who pointed bony fingers at him, fluid oozing out of cracks
in their skin followed by the armies of lice coming out of eye sockets,
ears, and mouths, marching down to other warmer regions. Seeing
Tolstoy's revolver conveniently laid on the desktop, he thought how
easy it would be to walk away with it in hand into the woods or along
the bank of the stream and shoot himself — get it over with.

He had actually taken walks earlier in the fall to find the most
suitable spot. Oddly enough, no place seemed right; not the water's
edge, denuded of animal life, from which even frogs and crustaceans
had disappeared; nor the woods, increasingly barren not only of
berries and mushrooms but any vegetation. Worst of all, there were
no birds of any kind — no crows, magpies, and certainly no
nightingales. They were gone, leaving only silence. It seemed
unnatural to shoot oneself where nature became indifferent and
turned a blind eye. He couldn't explain it, really. Besides, and this was
the essential point, he was too much of a coward to take his own life,
to get it over with.

That left him with the third and most viable option, since removing Tolstoy's body was out of the question. Suicide. *Yes! The man committed suicide.* Life and its responsibilities got too much, and he became unhinged, snapped. This scenario required some staging, however.

As unpleasant as it was, Prasha carefully worked his way around the body, unwound the cord, put the telephone in its accustomed place, and stretched the cord to the wall. That it had been ripped out from its socket was obvious but good drama. Maybe the chairman had received a devastating phone call, expressed his frustration and /or anger, and ultimately taken the revolver out of the drawer, put it to his head, and pulled the trigger. How fortunate that the killer had left the gun on the desk, and it was a matter of carefully placing the weapon into Tolstoy's right hand, circling his stiffening fingers around the handle and trigger mechanism and letting the hand hang down. Prasha was grateful that the body did not slide to the floor after all when released from its restraints. Finally, he had enough wits about him to notice and gather up the loose bullets on the desk. They would have represented an anomaly, which would have led to questions and conjecture.

It took almost an hour to set the suicide scene to his satisfaction. A little before seven, Prasha met the charwoman at the door to inform her that something terrible had happened and her services would not be required for the day. After, he went to the chief of the guards and informed him of the tragic event.

Commissar Fedryk was informed, and an investigation was initiated. In the meantime, Prasha was to carry on his duties as usual until there was a new appointee. Whoever it was couldn't be as incompetent and stupid as Tolstoy — he hoped. And speaking of hope, as the days went by and spring finally arrived, Prasha came to believe that maybe the socialist experiment could still be salvaged. There were signs that at last relief supplies might be forthcoming to the areas most severely stricken by this "natural disaster." Surely, Bila Sich would qualify.

CHAPTER TWENTY-NINE

Kyiv

"I have completed my investigation," Krypniuk announced blandly, staring at some point beyond Pavlick's left shoulder. He was sitting stiffly on the same uncomfortable wooden chair as before, appearing professional and composed. He hoped he had calculated correctly; this fat man in front of him was manipulative, shrewd, and above all, nasty. Krypniuk had to present a solution that allowed for mutual self-preservation.

"Yes?" Pavlick put his pen down and regarded the policeman with guarded intensity. This news was unexpected, a potentially complicating development. "You have a suspect?"

"Commissar Gromeko's killer has been identified. However, as per your instructions, I'll leave the arrest to the OGPU."

Pavlick leaned forward, his eyes narrowed, the brow wrinkled, his face darkened into distrust, suspicion. "You have finally caught up with the woman then, this," he glanced down at the document that lay before him, "Katya Kharsova?"

"Yes and no," Krypniuk replied cryptically.

The lines across Pavlick's forehead deepened as his wary face turned into a scowl. "Captain, I don't like riddles. Careful what game you play."

"Sorry, I did not mean to be flippant or confusing. To clarify, Katya Kharsova was found thanks to a tip from one of our citizen informers who saw the posters we distributed. Last evening, my sergeant and I went to the apartment where she was believed to reside.

Indeed, she was there, and I had the opportunity to interrogate her at length before an unfortunate incident took place."

"Unfortunate incident?"

"Yes. An intruder tried to kill her."

"What? Who? Revenge for what she did?"

"No." Krypniuk noted that Pavlick was genuinely surprised at the news.

"You better explain."

"As I said, we visited her last night, verified who she was, and I proceeded to interview her; she was cooperative but fearful for her safety, and understandably so, given what occurred. As she turned to go to her bedroom, collect her coat, and other items before accompanying us to the station for a formal statement, a man managed to unlock the door and enter the apartment. No doubt, he expected to find Miss Kharsova alone and not confronted by two policemen. "

"And you are sure he was there to harm her? Not a friend or lover with the key to the apartment?"

"Absolutely. He was brandishing a knife and was in possession of a handgun — a German Luger, in fact."

"I see," said Pavlick, clearly puzzled, his suspicion unabated by what the head of Kyiv's Criminal Investigation Department was spinning.

"A nasty confrontation ensued, with Sergeant Lubick having to discharge his weapon or face serious injury or death. However, in the confusion and struggle, Kharsova rushed out of the apartment, no doubt fearful for her life, and again has disappeared."

"You did not pursue her?"

"We had our hands full with the would-be assassin."

"Is he in custody?"

"In the hospital. Sergeant Lubick's discharged bullet hit him; otherwise, the sergeant and/or I might have been the casualties. It is a serious wound, so it will be a while before we can interrogate him further — if he wakes up."

"You spoke to him?"

"Yes, he was — informative."

There was a long pause while Pavlick digested what Krypniuk had presented. The captain could almost envision the commissar's greasy brain furiously spinning trying to sort out what this meant. Krypniuk had been very loose with his version of events — deliberately so.

"Let's back up for a moment to your interrogation of the commissar's secretary/mistress before this man broke in... Did she shoot the commissar?"

"No, however, she was a witness. She knows who did." That wasn't exactly the truth, since she hadn't seen Sholtz pull the trigger, but it was more than enough that she heard and recognized the voice of the commissar of Procurement and Labour, as far as Krypniuk was concerned.

"Who?" Pavlick asked in a flat voice, as if dreading the answer.

"Commissar Vasar Sholtz."

"What? And you believe her?" Pavlick's eyes grew wide, pinching back the folds of his flushing cheeks. It appeared that the Kyiv OGPU boss was taken aback.

For Krypniuk, this was a good sign that perhaps he was not involved, not part of some conspiracy among local oligarchs to rid one of their own. "Yes, I do, especially since there is corroborating testimony."

"Corroborating testimony? I don't follow."

"The assassin himself — his name, by the way, is Arkady Olinsky, employed as chief of security by our famous Khreshchatyk Hotel." Pavlick was now stone-faced, listening intently. Krypniuk continued, "As I mentioned, we spoke to him before the ambulance came. He confirmed that he was hired by Sholtz to silence Kharsova."

"Is that all he said?"

"That is all I could ask before he lost consciousness." Krypniuk was not about to announce the other high-ranking names that had spilled out of Olinsky's mouth. At least, Pavlick's name wasn't mentioned, but Krypniuk wanted to keep him guessing.

"Why would Commissar Sholtz shoot his colleague at the commissariat?"

"This I do not know. Could have been personal or business… If you wish my investigative unit to pursue further, we will do so. However, I was led to believe that the OGPU would make the arrest."

"Quite right," Pavlick said perfunctorily. He gave nothing away, but Krypniuk knew that the local OGPU commissar had a stake in the outcome of the investigation. Pavlick's name had appeared on what he labelled his "ceiling file." He was included in Gromeko's pay-off list. Krypniuk just didn't know how deep the graft went or how close of an associate he was. No doubt, he was corrupt, but he seemed genuinely surprised by Gromeko's murder, and more to the point, that Sholtz had committed it. If that were the case, then other powerful city oligarchs would be equally surprised and chagrined to discover that it wasn't the mistress but one from their inner circle who had pulled the trigger. Regardless, it wouldn't have stopped them from trying to silence her for what she potentially knew and the documents she had access to. Guilty or not, Kharsova was perceived as a direct threat and needed to be eliminated. What occurred at the apartment was a sanctioned hit, of that Krypniuk was sure, although it appeared that Pavlick was out of the loop. If he were making the right assumptions, then both Olinsky (if indeed he recovered) and Sholtz were too much of a liability and thus expendable.

The next course of action was up to Pavlick. Krypniuk knew he was still in peril, and possibly his sergeant as well if Pavlick thought that they had uncovered too much. *That certainly would be the case if he knew about the ceiling files*, thought Krypniuk. It was a calculated risk and the only way he could see of removing Kharsova from an untimely end and sidestepping his own untenable situation. Loose ends would be tied up; he could only hope that it did not include him, his family, and his colleague. Undoubtedly, Pavlick had brought Krypniuk and the Criminal Investigation Department in because he wanted to be at arm's length while controlling events. That Kharsova was identified as a person of interest made her the ideal scapegoat. In the end, she would be blamed and neutralized, but Krypniuk had now changed the narrative and perhaps the game.

"So. This is the extent of your investigation to date?" Pavlick asked, picking up the pen from his desk and rolling it in his fingers.

"Yes."

"You have nothing further to add?"

"No. This is what my report will conclude."

"Vasar Sholtz is responsible for Kreil Gromeko's death?"

"Yes. As to his motive — that has to be answered by Sholtz himself."

"And no other names, possible accomplices provided by Olinsky or Kharsova?"

"No," Krypniuk lied, "none were mentioned."

"You realize that this may be an extremely sensitive case," Pavlick lowered his voice as if delivering a confidential aside, "that needs to be completed with extreme caution and care?"

"Yes." *Oligarchs killing each other is indeed serious.* "That is why I am happy to leave the arrest and prosecution of Commissar Sholtz to you and the OGPU."

"What about Miss Kharsova?"

"Gone and no longer relevant to the case."

"Are you sure? She will not reappear at an inopportune time?"

"She will not. There would be no point to do so for anyone — certainly not for her."

Pavlick twisted in his chair, which squeaked in protest. After a long silence, he said, "I will hold you responsible if she does."

"Yes, of course." Krypniuk gave a slight bow of acknowledgement.

"Good. I think we understand each other."

***

"Olinsky died. I just got the word. Never regained consciousness," Krypniuk informed his sergeant. "And before you ask... I do not know whether it was as a result of his wound or other interventions." They were in Ivan's Hideaway, an unassuming drinking establishment not far from the central police station, where individuals could sit in dark corners and tell stories that they didn't want others to hear.

Lubick took a long, slow sip of his bitter. "Totally expected," he said. "He couldn't be saved or rehabilitated, given the circumstances."

"True…"

"And what about Kharsova and her *dedushka*? Pavlick wasn't suspicious about her escape?"

"I didn't mention the old man in the apartment, but yes, he was unconvinced. However, I reassured him that she has disappeared and would not reappear. Let us hope that this is true. If not … we're both in trouble."

"That was quite a gamble agreeing to let her go."

Krypniuk stared into his glass of beer. "If I didn't, she would not have survived."

"Well, I hope she appreciates your soft heart!" Lubick smiled.

"Oh, I'm sure she does. And I don't think we need to worry about Katya Kharsova suddenly reemerging. She's proven that she can stay hidden … most resourceful."

"And the file?"

"Ah, yes, the file… Our last, rather desperate piece of insurance should it come to that. It is in a safe place."

"But we are safe?"

Krypniuk shrugged. One could never know in the system and times they lived in. "Here's hoping that Pavlick will let sleeping dogs lie and that it's not in his best interest to pursue us."

***

Vasar Sholtz had a bad feeling, one that originated in the pit of his stomach and worked its way up, leaving the taste of bile in his mouth. He should have heard by now; the problem should have been taken care of. And yet nothing. When he could stand the wait no longer, he made a couple of phone calls on his secure line to those who had put him in touch with Petrov. No one was picking up! This definitely wasn't good.

With anxiety building as the day wore on, he decided that his office was becoming too claustrophobic. He needed to get out for a while. He didn't dare go home; he and his wife barely tolerated each other, but for various reasons (convenience mostly) hadn't gotten around to going their separate ways. Besides, if the "fixer" had truly screwed up and he was exposed, the office and his home would be the first place they would visit. He wasn't even sure who they were, exactly — the police? the OGPU? or another fixer employed by fellow oligarchs he did business with?

Like Gromeko, Sholtz had an apartment nestled away in a stucco-brick six-storey building about a half hour's car drive from the commissariat. There he would stay when he didn't feel like going home and would entertain his lady friends on occasion, including one longtime mistress. He decided to go there now; he needed to think. At this point, he had no concrete information, He'd make some more phone calls and, if necessary, start making the appropriate arrangements in terms of his assets and departure from Kyiv and the country, if it came to that. He had hidden an emergency stash of rubles in the apartment, as well as some valuables he could stuff in a suitcase, just in case.

After informing his secretary that he was not to be disturbed, he took the back way out of the building instead of calling for his driver. Emerging onto a narrow alley, he pulled his hat farther down, pulled up the heavy coat collar, hunched his shoulders, and walked as briskly as he dared without actually running to the nearest tram kiosk. It didn't appear that anyone was following. *Calm down*, he chided himself. *Get a hold of yourself. You're overreacting... Fucking Gromeko.* If he hadn't been such a greedy bastard and hadn't provoked him, laughed at him — *too late now.*

It was a good fifty-minute ride to the tram stop closest to his apartment building, followed by a ten-minute walk. As he stepped off the tram, he took special care to observe who stepped off after. He was gratified to see only an old babushka and a couple of younger women who started off in the opposite direction from him. Kyiv was in the midst of very bad times with food rationing and the occasional inert body lying in an alley, not yet whisked away. Fortunately, in this section of the city, a sense of normality prevailed with people going about their business, including the old lady and two female students, perhaps. No matter — that he wasn't followed was all that counted.

The particular apartment building was modest on the outside, mostly brick with a hint of Baroque masonry around the doors and windows. It was well kept, catering to prosperous Soviet officials/apparatchiks of rank who could afford to live there. Sholtz had his two-bedroom apartment on the top floor. After a canvass of the front doors and the street, noting no suspicious persons or parked black cars, he hurried up the steps and waited impatiently for what to him was the overly creaky and slow elevator to arrive. (It was the one feature of the building that needed an update.) Not until he was inside his apartment with the door locked did he breathe a sigh of relief.

It was probably safe enough to spend one night, at least, he decided. Meanwhile, he'd make more phone calls to those who owed him favours. He needed to know what was going on. Pouring himself a generous splash of vodka, he started to go down the list of names he had brought with him from the office. No one answered, or the receiver was picked up and quickly put down the moment he identified himself. *Not good.* Finally, after several calls with no results, he got hold of Georgi, a large contractor who owed him a huge favour.

"Georgi, it's Vasar. I—"

"Get out of town. You're finished. And don't call me again."

This was followed by an abrupt click. *Confirmation!* Sholtz sat stunned on the bed. He had to act, get out of the city, find a hiding spot. He rose from the bed, stepped over to a modest closet, and from the back yanked out a medium-sized suitcase. After plopping it on the bed, he shoved the heavy bureau to one side and pried out the vent. In behind was a small iron box with a combination lock securely attached to wooden studs that supported the wall. Sholtz dropped to one knee and spun the numbers that would open his secret safe. It was time to get his emergency stash of rubles and the pieces of valuable jewellery and stick them into the suitcase, along with a couple of shirts and other apparel. Further, he realized that it probably was not a good idea to stay the night in the apartment after all. It was too easily compromised.

Gulping the last of his drink, he finished his packing and snapped the suitcase clasp shut. He'd find an obscure, out-of-the-way hotel to spend the night. He was about to depart when a loud pounding erupted on his door. *Too late. Fuck. Double fuck.* Sholtz wished he'd kept the Nagant after shooting Gromeko instead of throwing it into the Dnipro River. Not that it would help him much with whoever was on the other side of the door.

"Open up, Commissar Sholtz. We know you are in there. If you do not, we'll have to break it down. It's over; you will surrender."

Sholtz supposed that this was true. However, maybe he could buy his way out of this. Not likely, he realized. They were hardcore, and what could he offer them that they couldn't just take? He really had no choice but to open the door. "All right," he shouted. "I will unlock the door. Please identify yourselves."

"You know who we are. It's getting late. Let's get this business over with."

Sholtz shuddered. There wasn't much chance of talking and/or bribing his way out of this. The die had been cast. Petrov must have screwed up royally, leaving him as the fall guy. He had been encouraged to eliminate Kharsova not because they assumed she was guilty but because she potentially knew too much. Of course, he needed little encouragement; if his colleagues got wind of the fact that he had killed Gromeko, his fate would be sealed as surely as hers.

"Last chance!" came the voice. "We will not be polite."

Sholtz unlocked the door and stepped back. Two men in thick coats came in, the larger one quickly shoving him against the wall face first while he efficiently frisked him. "No weapon," he announced curtly to the other smaller man. Sholtz recognized him as an OGPU colonel. This was serious; experienced muscle had been deployed. He should have known that the apartment would be watched. *Stupid.* It was undoubtedly an open secret that he had kept it for his rendezvous...

The smaller man closed and locked the door. "Commissar, I am afraid we have bad news." The larger man spun Sholtz around to face the colonel. "We are here to help you with your apparent suicide."

Sholtz's mouth went dry. He began to speak, but the man raised his hand. "You only have two choices. You can be found on your couch or bed, if you prefer, with a self-inflicted bullet hole in your head. Or have a fall off your balcony," the colonel cast his eyes beyond the kitchen area to the glass door, "assuming the door isn't frozen shut. Personally, I hope that you choose the latter; anonymous handguns are a pain to acquire…"

CHAPTER THIRTY

Kyiv, 1955

The tall, frail man with the stooped posture made his way into the huge building, walking slowly up the stairs with a distinct limp. In his right hand he clutched his internal passport, which allowed him to be in the city, along with a folded piece of paper that might, moreover, allow him to live here again. He looked around bewildered, seemingly lost in the huge entrance and foyer of this new monolith of Soviet architecture as part of the reconstruction project after the devastation of the city during the Nazi occupation. The edifice housed the Central Committee of the Communist Party of Ukraine as well as Ukraine Republic's Council of People's Commissars.

Stopping to reorient himself, he observed that the bulk of equally uncertain visitors were moving down the long corridor to a large archway to the right. He shuffled along with the flow rounding the corner and finding long queues of citizens with the correct credentials (he had no doubt, since one had to present them just to step through the doors) for an opportunity to petition local government bureaucrats for the scarce available apartments in the Soviet Union's third largest city. He finally found the proper line and patiently inched his way until it was his turn to face an anonymous, low-level apparatchik behind the glass partition.

Not long ago, he had been in the Norilsk Corrective Labour Camp in one of the remotest regions of the USSR. Just surviving years of hard labour and the brutal Norilsk winters was a worthy feat; however, it had taken its toll. His face, now at least shaven, still had an unhealthy greyish tinge; his cough spat up blood; his body, as evidenced by clothing that hung loosely like a garment on a scarecrow, had endured years of malnourishment; and most importantly, his feet hurt at times and at other times felt numb, although he had acquired good boots since his return (which was particularly important when prisoners had to make do with rags and/or ill-fitting footwear from the dead or dying). Boots were a black-market commodity worth killing for. Not that he would have, and if he did, it wouldn't have mattered that much. The larger problem was insufficient rations and almost nonexistent medical care. *I'm dying — probably of lung disease*, he thought without rancour as he moved closer to the head of the line. Many of those around him didn't look much better, he concluded.

He had been at the Norilsk gulag almost since the beginning. Along with hundreds of others, he was part of the construction crew of the Norilsk Mining and Metallurgical Plant. He grew with the settlement, and it left an indelible and enduring mark on him. It wasn't only the unrelenting cold and deprivation that formed or scarred, depending on how he felt some days, his perspective; the land itself — an endless grey canvas of stunted, snarled shrubs — estranged the mind and distorted reality in the long polar light of winter. The mind played tricks with everyone and everything existing on the cusp as ethereal shadows.

During his time in Norilsk, he had witnessed men become crazed, animalistic, letting their humanity recede into the darkness. He fought hard to hang on, not to shun his human self, to put under lock his cruder, more basic instincts. Unbridled nature, he believed, could not be allowed to fill the breach of acquired civility. Yet monsters plagued him, monsters arising from the frozen permafrost reaching through from the polar darkness and whispering destructive thoughts throughout the noxious layers of the sulphur-tainted arctic air.

It took two decades to develop his progressive stoop and almost as long to quell, if not totally, control, his apprehension of these nebulous shadows. He had fought them off and slowly became more at peace with himself. His reward, it seemed, was "rehabilitation." Indeed, that's what brought him back to Kyiv. Stalin was dead: long live the rehabilitation of those who had been vanquished. Why or how he was chosen from lists of thousands, he had no idea, but it had brought him here and out of the wilderness with a last chance to live.

He expected to encounter a stone-faced bureaucrat or a hardened militiaman whom he had encountered for so many years in similar positions. Thus, he was surprised and slightly taken aback when he spied a female at the kiosk, her head down, making a notation after speaking to the sad little man a couple of individuals still ahead of him. He noted her tightly swept-back dark hair streaked with strands of grey tied in back with a scarlet ribbon. Of what he could see, she wore a khaki blouse, complete with a red tie. Formal, but striking and familiar, he thought, straining to see clearly. (His eyesight had become demonstratively worse, and he had lost his eyeglasses years ago). As he finally made it to the front of the queue, she stamped a document with the office seal and set it aside.

"Next," she announced automatically before looking up. Her eyes caught his simultaneously, creating a silent gasp, neither trusting who they were seeing before them.

"Katya?" His voice was hesitant, faltering. "Is that you?"

There was a pause that spanned a long abyss before she spoke. "Oxana. I'm Oxana..." She pointed to her name neatly printed on a small card in the corner of the kiosk. "You must have mistaken me for someone else."

The man stared at her confused. "Oleksander... Don't you remember?"

"I'm sorry ... Oleksander, I don't think we've met. Please state the nature of your request."

He frowned, totally at a loss. "The years, I'm afraid, have not been kind to me." There was a tremor in his voice. "And forgive me if I've mistaken you for someone else, but you are as lovely as ever." He gave her a small, wan smile. She was older, yes, but Oleksander knew for certain he had found Katya. Age could not eradicate her mane of dark hair, large, liquid eyes, perfectly level cheekbones, the shape of her lips and chin, and the way she held her head poised on her long neck.

"Your documents, please," she said curtly without returning his gaze after the initial shock.

He passed his internal passport and the letter through the slot in the glass. She quickly scanned both and wrote a note. "Your documents appear to be in order. You will have to come back next week while your petition for an apartment is considered."

Totally flummoxed, Oleksander blinked and stayed rooted to his spot, not sure what that meant. She shoved the note that she quickly scribbled, along with his passport, back through the slot and pointed to it. Oleksander read it through rheumy eyes: *I will meet you in the corridor outside this room in about one hour. Please wait.*

Oleksander looked at her and nodded; she acknowledged with a slight, almost imperceptible tilt of her head. "Next," she announced crisply.

"We can't talk here," she said quietly to Oleksander once she emerged into the corridor. As instructed, he stood stoically with many others in the hallway against the wall opposite the entrance. Waiting was, after all, a national pastime. It didn't seem to matter for what. "There's a canteen, Pytor's, not far from here. Turn right through the front door, walk straight down to it. I'll meet you in twenty-five to thirty minutes." With that, she walked away and disappeared into a myriad of enquiring souls crowding the hallway.

***

"I'm sorry for — well, one never knows who may be listening. I was shocked to see you. I… I still don't quite believe it. I thought that you were gone forever when they took you away."

"So did I," he said. They were sitting in a quiet corner in Pytor's Place, each drinking tea with a plate of blini rolls between them.

"It's been a long time," she acknowledged, "a couple of lifetimes ago." She produced her old infectious smile that had remained in his memory despite the years.

"I heard that much has happened while I was gone — famine, chaos, and, of course, war and destruction. Kyiv, I read, did not fare well under the Nazis… Of course, I wasn't here."

"Where were you?" she asked, her hands around the teacup, giving him intense scrutiny. "I thought that they had locked you up in Lukyanivska Prison or worse."

"I'm not sure that it is worse, but I was given a one-way ticket to Siberia. The journey ended at the Norilsk gulag. Lots to do there, from building a metallurgical plant to mining for nickel, copper, and palladium, all of which took on enhanced importance to Mother Russia during the war." Oleksander spoke through pinched lips. "Dismal place, really, but I got used to it; it was home until last year, when I received permission to leave, to travel back here."

"I–I never imagined seeing you again."

"Nor I you…"

They began to speak at once but stopped abruptly, filled in by an awkward silence. Each had many questions and much to say but not necessarily the wherewithal of how much to tell and if it mattered now. Certainly, curiosity had to be satisfied, if nothing else. Somehow, both were alive. Everything else was detail. Still, important detail…

Oleksander cleared his throat and brought the napkin to his mouth, emitting a muted cough before continuing. "I've been gone — what is it? Over twenty years, and here I am, rehabilitated, apparently. I hardly know how to act." He gave her another wan smile.

She took a sip of her tea before setting it side. Oleksander did not look well. "You need to get that cough looked at."

"I will."

She gave him a skeptical look but did not press. She needed to fill in the void for him as clinically and efficiently as she could so that he would understand. "I haven't been Katya for a very long time."

"Yes, I understand, Oxana," he began.

"But not the Oxana you think. You may remember Gerkil, but it's Oxana Dub. I married Anton's son, although he did not use his father's surname." She sighed. "It is complicated, and he was in a complicated business."

Oleksander frowned. "Anton — Anton Rubiniuk, my old neighbour from across the hall?"

"Yes…. He died about fifteen years ago now. Nothing sinister, though," Katya quickly added. "His heart gave way. He moved from the apartment after his son, Lushka — my husband to be — arranged for a safer place for both of us to live. We had been compromised, or at least I had, and needed to move. Like his father, Lushka was a good man."

"Was?"

"Died during the war. Here in Kyiv, a huge explosion involving a number of buildings on Khreshchatyk Street. It was the beginning of the Nazi occupation in September '41. The NKVD detonated the bombs to kill the entering Germans, but it also killed city inhabitants. Lushka had a business meeting in one of the offices. Wrong place at the wrong time…"

"Sorry."

Katya shrugged and lowered her voice. "Lushka lived on the edge between legal and illegal. His politics were fluid. He did business with both the Soviets and the Germans. Why not, he told me. Stalin had no trouble signing a nonaggression pact with Hitler in '39. Anyway, that is what happened."

Oleksander nodded. Most certainly, the Nazis were seen as liberators of Ukraine for a brief time, until they weren't. Berlin and the Kremlin were about equal when it came to brutality and extermination. Totally understandable from his point of view, given his experience in the Norilsk gulag. He abruptly changed the subject. "So … children?"

"Yes." Katya brightened. "Yuri, now nineteen, and Yulia. Both doing well, Yuri in university and Yulia about to graduate from school."

"And you have a responsible position in the local government."

"Life goes on."

"Obviously, the problem was left behind you. Otherwise, you would not have your job."

"Yes, but it is not that simple. The problem, as you say, or the man who created the problem for me, is dead. Nevertheless, I can never be Katya Kharsova. That is impossible."

Katya's statement was both emphatic and cryptic. Oleksander waited, but it soon became clear that was all she had to say about the subject. She never did reveal to him who the man was, and it would remain so. "Fair enough, you have established yourself as Oxana Dub and wish to remain so. If I may ask, for my own enlightenment, how did you end up at what I presume is the Housing Commissariat?" Indeed, it was hard for him to understand how from a wanted fugitive she could transfer herself into a state employee.

"I was extremely lucky. The war took its toll with the destruction of Kyiv before the Nazis left. I was hired in the Procurator's Office initially and became secretary to the Reconstruction, Restoration, and Reintegration Committee. Last couple of years, I've moved up to my current status as resettlement officer helping returning veterans, those who were evacuated before the Nazi arrival and others…"

"Like me, the rehabilitated former prisoners."

"Yes. There are numerous categories. As a result of the war and occupation, the city was levelled and only now is recovering, Of course, with Stalin dead and the power struggle still continuing, who knows what new directives will come from Moscow? I hope it's Khrushchev who comes out victorious. He was born in Ukraine, you know, and was the first secretary of the Ukrainian Party after liberation in '44. He at least knows what needs to be done." She stopped abruptly, suddenly conscious that she sounded too political, like a party cadre part of the governing structure. She quickly changed the focus. "Enough about me. I want to hear more about you … your life and plans?"

"Me? Well not that much to tell in the end, really. When they took me away that night, I was interrogated by the OGPU, and when I refused to denounce my boss at the institute — remember I told you about Professor Robanov," he waited for her nod of acknowledgement, "was shipped off on the cattle car express to Siberia."

"How awful!"

"By the way, on the train I met our nemesis in Bila Sich, none other than Makar Belynski!"

"Oh?" was all Katya said, raising a curious eyebrow.

"A bit of irony there. He fell out of favour. I suppose it's karma, God's will perhaps… We spoke and actually got along to a point; then, we had to given the circumstances…" Oleksander grimaced and coughed into the napkin clutched in his right hand. It shook noticeably as he brought it up to his mouth. He eyed his tea but left it stranded beside the one remaining blini. "Anyway, I lost touch with him early in the gulag days. Don't know what happened to him. He too could have been rehabilitated and is looking for housing in Kyiv!"

Oleksander thought that the mention of Belynski would elicit a more forceful response — indignation, anger, even an expression of forbearance — but there was nothing. Initial curiosity turned into total indifference. She made no comment, changing the subject instead. "Have you heard from your sister and Lev?

"Ah, yes…" Oleksander began with renewed vigour. "In fact, that was the first place I visited after my release. Lev is still with us, over seventy now and slowed down, almost in as bad shape as me." Oleksander let out a small chuckle. "He and Nina, who is as active as ever, continue to live in my old house. They've expanded it, and life isn't so bad. Bila Sich, like Kyiv, was pretty well decimated and is only now returning to its former self. I could have stayed with them if I wished, become part of the kolkhoz. It didn't seem right. I want to be back in Kyiv, and I do have a job — library assistant, scientific section, at my old institute, so…"

"What about some of the others, Lev's neighbours?"

"Vlas and Iona too have survived those hunger years. They are on the kolkhoz. According to Lev, at least one or maybe two of the offspring have fled to the city and secured jobs. So, all is well… Oh, not quite," Oleksander amended. "When the Nazis came, they kidnapped people to work behind the lines in Germany. '*Ostarbeiter*,' they called them, according to Lev — 'eastern workers.' They hauled away many fourteen-year-olds and over from the village and countryside. Misha was taken."

"Oh, no!"

"Yes… In this case, though, it was not as bad as what one might imagine with slave labourers. Lev and Nina eventually received news that after the war, Misha found himself in a displaced persons camp somewhere in northern Germany. Anyway, he's just made it to Britain and hopes eventually to get to Canada and start a new life. He also met a girl, so…"

Katya nodded, then surprised him with another question. "How about you? Did you meet someone in your Siberian exile?"

Oleksander straightened in his chair, and his eyes brightened.

"If I'm prying…" Katya hesitated, "it's okay. You can tell only if you want to."

"The answer is yes — Marta. We had a few good years that produced a son, Andriy. Marta died a few years back. Life is hard in Norilsk. Andriy is about your son's age He's got a job in the metallurgical company, a bureaucrat's job, fortunately," he smiled, "and a girlfriend. They are happy at the moment, more so since he occupies my apartment now. He has no desire to come to Kyiv or anywhere else. Not in the short term, anyway. Norilsk is the only home he's ever known. Maybe he'll visit or I'll visit him."

"I see," said Katya, sensing the underlying sadness and hidden nuance in the story.

"Marta and I weren't married," Oleksander added casually as if it somehow made a difference.

A liaison of convenience in a hostile environment, or love? Katya wondered but decided not to pry further.

"Andriy may visit someday," Oleksander repeated as if trying to convince himself. "Who knows, he and Zoya may want to move to a larger centre where it's less harsh. But then, that could be anywhere in the Soviet Union! Such is life…" He sighed.

"Well … you're back home, where you belong."

"Yes … yes, I am."

They looked at each other introspectively across the table before shaking off the notion of what might have been. It was what it was. *God wills what he does*, sprang into Oleksander's head, followed by the more prosaic *fate does not ask*, and finally the peasant's pragmatic creed: *without pain there is no life.* Whatever love he had felt for her — and it had grown stronger with distance and time — she probably did not reciprocate. Not to his level. He once hoped it would be a process of growing together. Now, he was too broken to try.

It was almost a relief when she informed him, "I have a partner; he works in the same building in the Procurator's Office. We have been together for over five years."

"I see..." And he truly did; since their first meeting on the train, he'd always known that Katya was a pragmatist who would do whatever she needed to survive. It was an ingrained self-preservation instinct that allowed her not only to survive but also, evidently, to thrive. It had held her in good stead, and he couldn't begrudge that.

There was a pause; suddenly, it seemed that they were running out of things to say. Details of their lives were not necessary now that each had received the general outlines.

"Come back to my kiosk tomorrow afternoon. I should be able to secure you an apartment close to the institute."

"Thank you."

"Well... I must go. I will look for you tomorrow... You have a place to stay meanwhile?"

"Yes, I'm at a hostel with some lads. It's working out fine." All was true to a point; he had spent the last couple of nights since arriving from Bila Sich in a large boarding room with cooking at one end and sleeping bunks at the other. It was dark, smokey, with unsavoury smells, inhabited by desperate men (and possibly women; he wasn't sure) who had no other place to go and no means to get there. That he hadn't been robbed was a minor miracle.

Katya's question, Oleksander sensed, was perfunctory, being polite, he guessed, and that was quite acceptable. As she rose to leave, he felt sad but at peace with himself. It wasn't tragic, after all, just melancholy. Most importantly, he had seen her again and now knew of her fate. Perhaps, he thought with a smile on his face as he got up from the small table, that was why he had convinced himself to come back: to see her alive and well. It didn't need to be requited.

Oleksander would see her one more time tomorrow and be done, satisfied that this was as good as it could be. He doubted that they would cross paths again.

ACKNOWLEDGEMENTS

First and foremost, I am grateful to my wife, Diane, who encouraged, critically read and cheerfully put up with my writing hibernations. Second, to my wonderful daughters, Alisha and Halyna, who too initially vetted the manuscript and provided insightful critiques.

I also thank Allister Thompson and Vilma Vitols for the careful edits and proofreading. A huge kudo to Melissa Novak for a great cover illustration and Jonathan Relph for the cover design. Finally, my appreciation to Cheryl Hawley and Greg Ioannou of Iguana Books for their support.

Any errors of commission and/or omission are entirely mine.

www.ingramcontent.com/pod-product-compliance
Lightning Source LLC
Chambersburg PA
CBHW022350020726
47500CB00002B/207

9 781771 807487